CW00521878

A Beginner's Guide To Saying I Do

JENNIFER JOYCE

For my wonderful girls, Rianne and Isobel

ABOUT THE AUTHOR

Jennifer Joyce is a writer of romantic comedies. She's been scribbling down bits of stories for as long as she can remember, graduating from a pen to a typewriter and then an electronic typewriter. And she felt like the bee's knees typing on THAT. She now writes her books on a laptop (which has a proper delete button and everything).

Jennifer lives in Oldham, Greater Manchester with her daughters, Rianne and Isobel, plus their Jack Russell Luna.

Find out more about Jennifer and her books or subscribe to her newsletter at jenniferjoycewrites.co.uk. You can also find her on social media:

Twitter/Instagram: @writer_jenn

Facebook: facebook.com/jenniferjoycewrites

.

ALSO BY JENNIFER JOYCE

The 12 Christmases of You & Me
The Accidental Life Swap
The Single Mums' Picnic Club
The Wedding That Changed Everything
The Little Bed & Breakfast by the Sea
The Little Teashop of Broken Hearts
The Wedding Date
The Mince Pie Mix-Up
Everything Changes But You
A Beginner's Guide To Salad
A Beginner's Guide To Christmas
(short story)

ONE

Ruth

A hush suddenly descended on the room as the string quartet began to play from the corner of the room that had been beautifully swathed with fairy lights, their music a soft, entrancing lullaby that soothed the restless guests. The congregation's breathing mellowed and shoulders softened until the moment the heavy doors swung open to reveal the bride and her delighted father. A collective gasp swallowed the gentle music as the guests turned, en masse, for a first look. A tingle wormed its way up my spine as I looked around the vast room – or, rather, the Great Hall. I couldn't believe how stunning it all was. The ivory and gold colour scheme was elegant, but the twinkling fairy lights threaded along the rows of chairs added a whimsical, fairy tale quality. Every detail was perfect, from the oversized vases of lilies perched high on golden plinths at the end of each row of seats, to the archway of creamy roses, lilies and yet more fairy lights where the vows were soon to be exchanged. A lot of planning had gone into this wedding and it had certainly

1

paid off. It was stunning. I couldn't have dreamed of a more romantic setting.

'Doesn't she look beautiful?'

'Wow. Just wow.'

'This must have cost a *fortune*.'

I could hear the murmur of voices around me, and I had to agree with them all. It was, without a doubt, the most magnificent wedding known to man (or woman), and no expense had been spared to create this lavish setting. The morning had begun with a champagne welcome in the library of Durban Castle – yes, an actual, real-life castle – before the guests moved into the Great Hall for the ceremony. Afterwards, we would enjoy a sumptuous five-course meal in the drawing room, followed by drinks in the wine cellar before we moved back into the Great Hall to continue the festivities until late. I was exhausted just thinking about the long day that lay ahead, but I wouldn't have missed out on any of it.

Jared turned to face me and it hit me all over again how very lucky I was to be with him. I'd been beginning to think I would never find a man I wanted to spend the rest of my life with (I was struggling to find a bloke I wanted to spend an entire evening with, if I'm being completely honest here), and I'd had a string of hopeless relationships with hopeless men, but then along came Jared, who was sweet and kind and funny. And *gorgeous*. What more could a girl ask for?

'Are you okay?' Jared's skin had taken on a greenish hue, so I reached for his hand and gave it a reassuring squeeze. The day seemed to be taking its toll on him, and we hadn't even reached the most important part yet.

Jared swallowed. Hard. 'I love you, you know.'

'I do know.' It was strange, but true. Jared Williams loved me. Jared Williams, who could have any woman he chose, loved me, Ruth Lynch. Now, I don't want to put a downer on this lavish wedding, but I was no supermodel. I wasn't even a run-of-the-mill model. I'd spent my childhood bearing the brunt of jokes about being fat, and my confidence had been chipped away at so severely and frequently that I never expected to find myself with a man like Jared. A man who was so fit he looked good sweating (which was handy, as he was one of those weird types who enjoyed spending time at the gym) and who could cause a roomful of knickers to drop with one dashing smile (something he thankfully didn't put into practice). If I'd have known it was possible to bag a Jared, I wouldn't have wasted so much time with the losers I'd settled for before. Losers who thought farting to the tune of *The Simpsons* was hilarious, or thought showering more than once a week was wasting water. Losers who thought being vaguely pleasant to their girlfriend was optional.

But all that was behind me. I had a Jared now and I wasn't letting go of him.

'I love you too.' And I did. I honestly and truly did.

Butterflies took flight in my stomach as Jared leaned towards me, pressing his lips against mine. Kissing Jared was still a novelty, even though we'd been together for two glorious years.

'It'll be you two next, eh?' A head popped up from the row behind us, grinning as she gave an elaborate wink. I vaguely recognised her from previous family functions, but I couldn't give her a name or a place on my family tree.

'You never know,' I replied, because I didn't know what else to say. I could hardly reveal that I longed to marry the man sitting beside me, that it made me feel sick with envy that my twenty-two-year-old cousin was getting married before me. I mean, come on! *Twenty-two*. That's practically a foetus! What right did she have to be tying herself to the man of her dreams so soon? Although, come to think of it, the groom was hardly dream man material. From what I could gather, Rory spent the majority of his waking hours glued to his office chair, and any free time was taken up with playing golf. But he was apparently loaded. Like, proper minted. So I could sort of see the attraction, if that's the kind of marriage you're after. And Trina hadn't had much in the way of guidance when it came to love and relationships. Her mother, my aunt Gloria, had married for money when she was eighteen and was now on her fifth divorce, with each ex-husband being richer than the last.

'Have you popped the question yet?' Our unnamed spectator waggled a gnarled hand at Jared, where her own wedding band lay shining against her dull skin.

'Not yet.' Poor Jared turned a shade greener as he tugged at his collar, loosening his tie ever so slightly. If he carried on like this, my plus one would morph into Kermit the frog.

'Betty, will you be quiet?' Our spectator – who we now had a name for, even if I still had no idea who she actually was – was on the receiving end of a deathly glare from her neighbour. Betty sank back into her seat and mimed zipping her lips, while winking at me. I shifted in my seat so I was facing the bride and groom once more. Trina really did look beautiful as she stood facing her soon-to-be husband, a look of pure serenity on her face. Her voice was clear, so sure of the man standing beside her and the life they would lead that there wasn't a hint of nerves or uncertainty.

'I, foetus, take thee, Rory, to be my husband, to have and to hold from this day forward, for better for worse, for richer but not poorer.'

Okay, she didn't actually say that, but it really wasn't on that a young girl, barely out of school, was getting married while I was almost thirty and had never even sniffed a proposal. But still, I was happy with the life I had, which I hadn't always been able to say. I had Jared, a man who loved and respected me and had yet to question what the hell he was doing with a woman like me. I had to be grateful for *that,* at the very least.

Durban Castle was a truly beautiful setting, with its vast rooms, ornate staircases and extensive gardens. And believe me, the gardens *were* extensive. We traipsed every last sodding acre of them in the bid for the perfect photo. It was quite fun posing for the photos at first, as I could pretend I was on a shoot for *Vogue* or *Cosmopolitan.* Until the photographer shattered my illusions and asked 'the chubby one' to move over as I was overshadowing the bridesmaids. I wouldn't mind, but he was no Adonis himself, the cheeky git. Jared was fuming, but I managed to calm him down before he garrotted the man with his own camera strap. The 'photo shoot' lost its shine from that point, and only grew worse as we moved from one location to the next, my feet aching more with every minute that passed. The drinks in the wine cellar couldn't come quickly enough.

Eventually, after what felt like hours, the photo session was over and we were permitted to hobble into the drawing room. The large room was swathed with golden ribbons which swept majestically from the ceiling, twined around stone pillars, and were tied to the backs of chairs. The head table was framed by more oversized vases of lilies, while smaller versions created the centrepieces for the remaining tables. The tables were set beautifully, with tiny ivory boxes labelled with each guest's name creating the place settings. Inside each box was a miniature golden macaron nestled on a bed of ivory tissue paper. Taking a look at the other boxes, I saw that I would be sitting next to my mum and somebody named Aidan, who I had never met. I hoped he wasn't a posh relative of Rory's. I'd be self-conscious enough slurping my soup without being judged by a member of the social elite.

'You'll never guess what he's bloody gone and done

now.' Mum plonked herself down on her chair and glared at my dad, who was sitting opposite us, merrily chatting away to Great Uncle Gerald. Her face was pinched as she drove unsavoury thoughts towards her husband.

Was it too late to switch seats?

'He's bought a caravan.'

A caravan? *Noooooo!* I was about to gasp over-dramatically, but by the look on Mum's face, she wouldn't have appreciated my sarcasm.

'What's wrong with a caravan? You can go away any time you want to now.'

It sounded lovely, actually. Perhaps Jared and I could borrow it. I had fond memories of staying in some ancient relative's caravan in Blackpool during the school holidays, snuggled up inside as it pissed it down outside, all hopes of hitting the beach dashed as the drops of rain snaked down the windowpanes. Yes, I'd hated it at the time, but memories were funny little beasts and suddenly I longed to hear the rain pounding on the tin roof while I gazed out of the rain-spattered window (and not glared miserably out of it as I had back then, obviously).

'Oh no. He hasn't bought it for holidays.' Mum gave a humourless laugh. 'Holidays are what normal people do with caravans, but when has your father ever been normal? Tell her what you're doing with that blasted caravan, Louie.'

I cringed as she shouted across the table, causing a barrage of curious glances from the other guests. Dad opened his mouth to speak, but Mum got in there first. 'He's turning it into a gym. A gym!' Mum gave a hoot. 'When has your father ever set foot in a *gym?*'

'I've never had access to one, have I?' Dad called across the table, but he may as well not have spoken as far as Mum was concerned.

'It isn't enough that he turned the loft into a home cinema that nobody ever uses, or the garden shed into a

6

sauna. No, he has to buy a rusting old caravan and turn it into a gym.' She said the word 'gym' like it was a disease, which I totally got. I couldn't stand the places either. 'I blame that George whatshisface. The one off the telly with the tiny spaces.'

'George Clarke,' Dad piped up. 'And it's amazing spaces, not tiny.'

'In fact, no.' Mum, ignoring Dad, swivelled in her chair so she was facing me. 'I blame *you*. You were into all that fitness stuff not so long ago. He must have got a taste of it from you.'

'Hey, don't blame me.' I held up my hands in surrender. 'I'm hardly an advertisement for healthy living.' In fact, I'd already scoffed my golden macaron – which was delicious, by the way – as a pre-appetiser. 'Anyway, you might like it if you gave it a chance. You hated the thought of Dad turning the shed into a sauna, but you love it now.'

Mum gave a slight one-shouldered shrug. 'It's strangely invigorating.'

'See? You might like working out too.'

Mum's eyes narrowed. 'Why? Have I put on weight? Because Aunty Pat said I was looking a bit chunky last week.'

Next time Dad could fight his own battles. This was too much like hard work for my liking.

'No, Mum, you haven't put on weight. I'm trying to be positive.'

'And I'm trying to be realistic. Do you think I'm getting bingo wings?' Mum lifted her arms and flapped them up and down. I decided the best course of action was to turn away and pretend she wasn't there.

TWO

Trina

Her cheeks were beginning to ache but, camera or no camera, Trina couldn't wipe the grin from her face. This had to be a dream, surely. Was it really possible that she was now Mrs Hamilton-Wraith, wife of Rory, one of the most incredible men she had ever met? Rory was handsome, with wavy auburn hair and intense brown eyes framed by dark brows and never-ending eyelashes. He was always immaculately dressed and today – obviously – was no exception. His suit had been beautifully tailored and fitted his lean body like a second skin.

Trina couldn't believe her luck.

'All done, guys.' The photographer unhooked the camera from around his neck and started to pack up his equipment as Trina and Rory's guests breathed a collective sigh of relief, wandering back towards the castle and the five-course dinner that awaited them.

Trina held back, grasping hold of Rory's hand. 'I can't believe we're married. Can you?'

Rory gave her hand a squeeze, squashing the unfamiliar

gold band into her fingers in a pleasant sort of way. 'I'm the luckiest man alive.' Rory stooped to place a whispery kiss on her forehead.

'No, I'm the lucky one.'

Trina had known Rory Hamilton-Wraith forever. Their fathers were members of the same golf club so their paths had often crossed at functions. But it had been during last year's annual dinner dance that they'd really hit it off. Meeting Rory had come at the exact time she'd needed a confidence boost. She'd been feeling low and had been contemplating sneaking off home when Rory had appeared and lifted her mood. They'd started chatting over something inconsequential, but by the end of the night they were inseparable. Sort of. Rory was very dedicated to his work, which Trina most admired about him. After his dashing good looks, of course.

'We're both lucky.' Rory grinned at his new wife before his attention was snapped away by the feathery blue head-dress of Winnie Hamilton-Wraith wafting by. 'Mother! What did you think of ...' Rory's voice trailed away as he scurried after his mother, leaving Trina standing by herself, a serene smile still plastered over her face.

She'd done it. She'd actually married Rory, and she was so glad she hadn't allowed the nerves she'd awoken with that morning to push her into a decision she would regret. Marriage was a huge, scary step but she'd taken it and she couldn't be happier.

'Hey, you.' Trina's best friend appeared by her side, giving her a friendly nudge. 'How does it feel to be married?'

Trina gave a fluttery sigh. 'Amazing, Aidan. It feels utterly amazing.' She reached up to touch her intricate up-do. 'How's my hair? I was a bit worried when it started to get breezy.'

Aidan peered at her head. 'There are a few loose

strands but nothing to worry about. I can fix it easily.'

'Do we have time?' Most of the guests had arrived back at the castle by now and would be expecting to eat the sumptuous meal they'd been promised. On the other hand, Trina didn't want to ruin the day by showing up with hideous hair. Aidan had spent the morning creating the perfect do and she wanted to show off her friend's magnificent handiwork.

'You're the bride! It's your day. You have time to do whatever you want to. Come on. My kit's up in my room. It won't take long.' Aidan took Trina's hand and led her through the ornate doors of the castle. Their footsteps echoed on the beautiful stone floor of the entrance hall, but came to a stop as Rory's sister loomed in front of them. Carrington Hamilton-Wraith was rake-thin and not very tall, but still she posed a threat as she blocked Trina and Aidan's path, rather like a yapping Chihuahua guarding its territory.

'Cheating on Rory already?' Carrington was two years younger than Rory but was fiercely protective of her older brother. She'd never liked Trina, and looked suspicious of her whenever they met. 'That was much quicker than even I anticipated, so bravo on that score. But on your wedding day? Before we've even dined? How tacky!'

'I'm not cheating on Rory,' Trina told her new sister-in-law, but she dropped Aidan's hand anyway. 'Don't be so ridiculous.'

'So you're hopping upstairs with this rather dishy man because ...' Carrington gave Aidan an appreciative once-over. Aidan scrubbed up well in his tailored suit and fit in with Rory's uber-rich relatives, but underneath lurked the real Aidan: the edgier version with a plethora of tattoos. His entire left arm was covered in designs, while a dragon lay across his shoulder blades, its tail winding down Aidan's right arm to the elbow crease. Carrington always seemed to date super-rich pretty boys whose idea of body art was buying overpriced paintings of naked women to hang in their vast halls, so she'd be in for a surprise if she managed to shed Aidan of his suit.

Trina placed a territorial hand on Aidan's arm. Her new sister-in-law could play her games with somebody else. 'We're going up to my suite so Aidan can fix my hair.'

Carrington gave a horse-like snort. 'You'd better think of something better than that to tell my brother.'

'It's the truth. Aidan is my hair stylist.'

Carrington narrowed her eyes. 'Your hair stylist?'

Aidan thrust his hand towards Carrington. 'Aidan Scott. Pleased to meet you. Can I give you my card?' Aidan reached into his jacket pocket and pulled out a creamy business card embossed with gold lettering. Carrington plucked the card from his fingers. The sneer she'd been wearing since she'd set eyes on the pair dropped.

'You work at Salvi Fiore?'

'He's one of their top stylists.' Trina grabbed Aidan's hand and tugged him towards the staircase. 'And right now he needs to fix my hair before my guests starve.'

'How do I look?' Trina, perching on the stool in front of the dressing table in the enormous bridal suite, twisted her head this way and that to get a good look at her hair in the mirror. Aidan had pinned up the loose wisps and given her hair another blast of spray to hold it in place.

'You look gorgeous, Trina. You always do.'

'Thank you.' Trina leaped from the stool, planting a kiss on her friend's cheek. 'She fancied you, you know.'

Aidan started to pack up his kit. 'Who?'

'Carrington.'

Aidan looked up from his leather case with a snort. 'Not my type.'

'That won't stop Carrington. She's very determined. Although she *did* try to talk Rory out of marrying me and that didn't work.' Trina giggled. She still couldn't believe she was actually married! 'Come on, let's get back to the others. They'll all be waiting.'

'Don't you want to stay for a minute? To get your breath back?' Aidan picked up the flute of champagne he'd poured for Trina before tackling her hair. 'At least finish your drink. Nobody will mind waiting another minute or two.'

Trina relented. She could use a minute to get her bearings, actually. The day had been a bit of a whirlwind, starting at the crack of dawn when Winnie and Troy, the drill-sergeant-like wedding planner, had charged into her room and started barking orders. Before she knew it, she was being swept down the aisle by her father to take her vows. That short walk was the longest time she'd spent with her father in years and she'd wanted it to last a bit longer, to really appreciate his hand on hers as she linked her arm through his, clinging on as tightly as she could. Her father hadn't featured much in Trina's life since he and her mother divorced (and he hadn't featured much before that, to be frank), preferring his string of lady friends to his offspring. For the few seconds it took them to reach Rory and the registrar, Trina had felt like the centre of his world and she wanted to cherish that feeling as she knew it was highly unlikely to occur again.

'I still can't believe it's actually happened.' Trina settled on the edge of the bed, being careful not to crumple her dress. 'I can't believe I'm married – and to Rory!'

Aidan perched on the stool Trina had vacated. 'Are you happy?'

'Over the moon!' To demonstrate, Trina's mouth stretched into a wide grin. 'I feel like it's all a dream and I'm going to wake up alone. It isn't a dream, is it?'

'No, it isn't a dream. It's very real.'

'I hope so.' Trina drained her glass of champagne. 'We really should be getting back downstairs. Rory will be sending out a search party.'

Aidan rose from his stool and held out a hand for Trina to take, helping her up from the bed and guiding her back downstairs to the drawing room, which was dressed beautifully in gold and cream. Troy, despite his fearsome manner and foul temper, had done a stunning job in planning the wedding. Perhaps he'd been right when he'd talked Trina out of the silver and pink theme she'd set her heart on.

'We've seated you next to my cousin, Ruth.' Trina pointed Aidan in the direction of the table. 'Don't worry, she's lovely. We were really close when I was younger. She was like a sister to me.' More so than Tori, her actual sister. Ruth was older than Trina but, instead of seeing her as an annoying baby cousin, she'd taken her under her wing and heaped attention on her, which Trina had lapped up. She'd been devastated when she'd been sent away to school just before her eighth birthday, because it meant she would hardly see her beloved cousin.

'We'll catch up later, yeah?' Aidan checked before he made his way over.

'Of course.' Trina pushed herself up on her tiptoes to kiss Aidan's cheek. 'I need at least one dance with my best man.'

While Aidan threaded his way towards his table, Trina searched the room for her new husband. Rather than waiting impatiently at the head table, Rory was chatting in a corner with his sister.

'Ah, here she is.' Carrington examined Trina's hair and was disappointed to find it immaculate. 'We were starting to think you'd absconded.'

'Why would I do that?' Trina slipped her hand into Rory's and rested her head on his shoulder. 'I love this man more than anything and I'm looking forward to spending the rest of our lives together.'

'How sweet.' Carrington curled her lip as though it was

anything but sweet. 'Let's hope you don't take after your mother. How many times has she been married? Four?'

Trina looked at Rory, wondering if he was going to jump to her defence. Apparently not. 'It's five, actually.'

Carrington's eyes widened before she turned to Rory. 'Good luck. I think you'll need it.' Carrington gave her brother's arm a squeeze before she stalked away.

'Are you really going to let her talk to me like that?' Trina could feel her lip wobbling and feared her eyes would join in any moment and wreck her make-up. The last thing she wanted to do was cry non-happy tears on her wedding day, but it felt like Carrington was always going out of her way to undermine her. Trina had hoped that it would stop once she and Rory were married.

Rory placed his hand on Trina's shoulder and gave it a gentle squeeze. 'She doesn't mean anything by it.'

Trina begged to differ, but now wasn't the time or place to argue her point. 'I suppose not. Shall we take our seats? I think everybody's waiting.'

When the bride and groom were seated at the head table, dinner was served. Trina could barely manage a couple of mouthfuls, both because she was too excited and because her dress was so snug. Winnie and Troy had devised a brutal diet for Trina to adhere to during the lead-up to the big day in order to fit into the minuscule dress they'd deemed appropriate, but Trina hadn't followed it quite as rigorously as they'd have liked. Trina – like much of the wedding plans – hadn't had much say in the dress, but she hadn't wanted to rock the boat with Rory. He was so close to his mother, and Trina feared he would take offence and think Trina was picking at Winnie despite all her help with the wedding. Besides, the dress *was* stunning, even if it had been a bit of a squeeze getting her inside it that morning. Trina had only just fitted into the dress, but who needed to breathe anyway?

'Wasn't it all worth it?' Winnie had asked as she'd

admired Trina that morning. She'd turned to the others in the room – it seemed Trina's room was filled with every female member of Rory's family, plus Troy, as she prepared for the day. 'Honestly, you should have heard her complain! But look at the result! A daughter-in-law to be proud of.'

By rights, Trina should have been stuffing her face with the food presented before her, to make up for the months of eating nothing but seeds and sticks of celery (plus the odd secret, guilt-inducing treat). It had taken weeks – if not months – to finalise the menu, and it all looked and smelled delicious. How annoying that she still couldn't enjoy her food!

'Aren't you hungry?' Rory asked. He'd wolfed his food down without fearing for the seams of his outfit.

Trina pushed her plate away. 'I'm too excited to eat.'

'Thinking about tonight?' Rory winked at his new bride. 'I'm certainly anticipating the night-time activities. The sooner we can get rid of the guests and hole ourselves up in the honeymoon suite, the better!'

'Of course I'm looking forward to tonight, but I'm also thinking about the rest of our lives together.' It was going to be magical. Unlike her mother, who seemed to thrive on clocking up divorces, Trina was in this for life.

'I'll drink to that.' Rory raised his glass and clinked it against Trina's.

Yes, she and Rory would have a very happy marriage. She was sure of that.

THREE

Ruth

After the photos and dinner – which was, quite honestly, the most delicious meal of my life thus far – we came full circle and ended up back in the Great Hall, where the reception could start in earnest. Most of the chairs had been removed, along with the lily-holding plinths, making way for a retro, multicoloured dance floor and a DJ booth. A free bar had been set up where the string quartet had once stood, and it was already being thoroughly abused by the guests. Trina and Rory's wedding may have been a classy affair, but I was pretty sure there'd be a brawl or two before the night was over with all that alcohol being gulped down. Weddings always seem to draw out family feuds, and we were only a few vodka and cokes away from putting on a Jeremy Kyle-style display.

All the boring stuff (i.e. the speeches) had been taken care of during the meal, so we could really let our hair down now. I immediately pulled Jared onto the dance floor, though he didn't need much persuasion. I'd never had a boyfriend who not only liked to dance but was also bloody good at it. In his youth, Jared had dreamed of becoming a professional dancer and although it hadn't worked out for him after an ankle injury, I was reaping the benefits of his dedication now.

'I'm just popping to the loo,' I called over the music. All the champagne and free cocktails were catching up on me. 'Won't be a minute.' I meandered through the Great Hall, following the signs to the toilets which, thankfully, were not in keeping with the ancient castle and were clean and modern.

'Who is that guy you were dancing with just now?' Tori, my cousin and the bride's sister, joined me at the sinks as I washed my hands, reapplying her pillarbox-red lipstick. 'He is *gorgeous*.'

I felt my chest swell with pride. 'That's Jared.' *And yes*, my smug smile continued, *he is gorgeous*. With his blond hair, mesmerising blue eyes and model good-looks, I'd fancied Jared as soon as I'd spotted him, though I'd never have believed he'd find me even remotely attractive back then. I struggled to believe it even now, two years later.

'Which agency did you use?'

My smug smile dropped. 'Agency?'

'Do they still call them escort agencies?' My cousin tinkled a laugh as she ruffled her platinum blonde curls. Tori, Trina and I shared the family's blonde, curly hair gene, though Tori ramped up the shade via expensive salons once a month. 'I wouldn't know. I've never had to use one.'

'I beg your pardon?'

Tori was the kind of relative I only saw sporadically at bigger family gatherings, when she had nothing better to attend, so she'd never actually met Jared before. But still! Her question deflated my pride instantly. I'd never liked Tori. She was nothing like her sweet younger sister, and had been a bit of a cow even when we were kids.

'I didn't *hire* Jared from an agency. He's my boyfriend.'

17

Tori dropped her lipstick into her bag and turned to face me, her eyes wide with the revelation. 'He's your *boyfriend*?' Tori, bless her, wasn't bright (or polite) enough to keep the shock from her voice. I had to feel sorry for the girl. It must have been terribly confusing having just the one brain cell rattling around inside her skull.

'Yes, my boyfriend,' I told her.

Tori crossed her painfully thin arms and tilted her head, eyeing me with a bemused look. 'As in … your actual boyfriend?'

As opposed to what? My make-believe boyfriend?

'Yes, my actual boyfriend.'

'And have you two …?' Tori waved a hand between us. 'You know, *done the deed*?'

Okay, she was annoying me now. I think I'd been generous when I'd assumed she had a brain cell to rattle. 'We live together, Tori. What do you think?'

Snatching my handbag from the side, I left before Tori could enlighten me with her thoughts – if she actually had any floating around in that dense head of hers. Aunt Gloria may have sent her girls to be educated at the best schools in the country, but she clearly hadn't got her money's worth with that one. Who did she think she was, assuming I couldn't possibly bag myself a handsome bloke like Jared? I mean, I had those thoughts myself – constantly – but that was different. Still fuming, I made my way into the Great Hall, but every ill thought evaporated when I caught sight of Jared dancing with the elderly Betty, twirling her around the dance floor and ending with an elaborate dip.

'You've a smashing young chap here,' Betty told me once she was righted again. She gave my arm a squeeze. 'You keep hold of him.'

I fully intended to. 'Don't stop on my account, Betty. Have another go.'

Betty fanned her face with her crooked fingers. 'I'd love to, but I need a fortifying sherry. I'm not as robust as I used to be.' She left the dance floor with a chuckle, but not before she'd given Jared's bottom a squeeze.

'When I'm old, I want to be just like Betty.' I looked across to the bar, where Betty was now chatting up the barman, who was young enough to be her grandson. She reminded me of my friend Mary from yoga. They were both so full of life, refusing to slow down just because they had a few more miles clocked up than the rest of us.

'Are you okay?' Jared and I had wandered towards the edge of the dance floor. He'd ended up being seated across the room from me during dinner so we hadn't had the chance to talk properly until now. 'You were looking a bit flustered during the ceremony. Don't worry – I'm not going to drag you down the aisle, you know. I'm happy as we are.'

'Are you?' Jared sounded surprised.

Shouldn't I have been happy? Was our relationship not as rock solid as I'd imagined? Perhaps it was all a bit shit but I'd been too busy floating around in my happy little bubble to notice.

'Aren't you?'

'Yes, but …' Jared didn't get the chance to continue, as the DJ announced the arrival of the new Mr and Mrs Hamilton-Wraith. They arrived looking completely in love, beaming at one another, adoration shining in their eyes. It was the way I always imagined Jared and I looked when we were together, but now I wasn't so sure.

Yes, but … but what? But I don't want to be with you any more? But I can't put up with your lack of domesticity for another second? But I've found someone else? I turned to Jared to question his statement (in a non-nagging sort of way, of course. There was no need to drive him further away) but his eyes were on the happy couple, applauding as they took to the dance floor for their first dance as a married couple. I clapped along but my heart wasn't in it. It was all right for Trina. She'd secured her man for life, but what about me? Was two years my maximum allowance for happiness?

'Don't they make a lovely couple?' Mum was at my side, sighing right down my earhole. I thought about batting her away like an annoying fly. 'Me and your dad used to be like that, you know. Before you and Stephen came along.'

'So we ruined your marriage, did we?'

Jared gave me a funny look as I snapped at Mum but she didn't seem to notice my harsh tone.

'Gosh, no. It's all this DIY nonsense that has put a spanner in the works. Ha! *Spanner* in the works. DIY!' Mum tittered to herself as she wandered away, but was quickly replaced by someone else. Couldn't I have two minutes alone with my boyfriend? I had an important relationship-wrecking conversation to have here.

Actually, when you put it like that …

'Hello again! Aidan, wasn't it?' I'd never met my dinner companion before that evening, but I wanted to pull him in close, attaching him to my side so that I wouldn't have to have The Conversation with Jared. Besides, he'd been pleasant company earlier. Much better than Mum and her complaints about the caravan.

'Ruth! Nice to see you again. This must be Jared.' Aidan held out a hand, which Jared shook. 'I've heard a lot about you.'

I cringed. I had talked about Jared a lot during dinner; I couldn't help myself. It wasn't very often that I had bragging rights over a boyfriend. But I didn't want Jared to know that if he was about to concoct a list of my faults – or, worse, dump me outright. I couldn't enjoy the rest of the night with this 'yes, but …' hanging over my head. Imagine if I caught Trina's bouquet (which I was determined to do, by the way. That baby was *mine*) but was dumped on the same evening?

'This is Trina's friend, Aidan. We sat together at dinner.'

I decided to sidestep the whole can't-stop-blathering-about-my-boyfriend business. It would be less humiliating that way.

'You're lucky,' Jared said. 'I got stuck with a boring old git who talked about nothing but his yacht.'

'Oh, you mean my uncle Fred,' Aidan said. 'Loves his yacht, does Freddie. It's his pride and joy.'

'Your uncle?' Green Jared was back. 'I didn't mean boring old git in a *bad* way. Just, you know ...' Jared widened his eyes at me, silently begging for help. But I wasn't going to come to his aid until we'd sorted this 'yes, but' stuff out.

'I'm kidding.' Aidan clapped Jared on the back, trying his hardest not to laugh. 'Sorry, I've got a crap sense of humour. I don't really know anybody here apart from Trina.' He looked at the happy couple, who were twirling around the dance floor. When Trina and Rory's spot in the limelight was over, other couples took to the dance floor, including me and Jared. I caught sight of Betty clutching Aidan and, as they whizzed by, Betty flashed me a wink.

'I have no idea who this young man is,' she called. 'But he sure can dance!'

FOUR

Ruth

'I think you've made a friend for life there.' I looped my arm through Jared's as the coach pulled away from the gravel driveway, using my free hand to wave back at Betty. After dancing with Aidan, the insatiable pensioner had grabbed Jared to strut their stuff on the dance floor. 'Let's show these youngsters how it's done,' she'd declared as she'd led Jared by his tie to the centre of the floor. Once she'd tired Jared out, she'd given Aidan another go, only pausing very briefly to refresh herself with a sip of sherry. She'd only stopped when she was told the coach was leaving right now, with or without her.

'Who exactly is she?' Jared asked as the coach – and Betty – disappeared from view. It was late, and the long driveway was illuminated by fairy lights threaded through the trees that lined the road, creating a magically romantic atmosphere.

'I think she's a second cousin of my mum. Or maybe third.'

'She's sweet.'

22

I reached up on my tiptoes to kiss Jared's cheek. 'So are you.' It seemed Jared had forgotten about our 'yes, but …' conversation, and I wasn't about to remind him.

'Nah, it's all a ruse.' We started to move around the castle towards the car park, having already said goodbye to Trina, who was completely sloshed and currently dancing the Macarena solo on the dance floor. There were rooms available at the castle, but as it was only a forty-five-minute drive back to Woodgate (and the room prices were extortionate if you were ordinary and non-super-rich), Jared and I had decided to travel back the same day.

'I'm actually an utter bastard and I'm simply biding my time before I show my true colours,' Jared said as we neared the car.

'I don't believe you.' Jared had never been anything but lovely towards me. He treated me to breakfast in bed on regular, non-special occasions, never complained when I burned our dinner to smithereens, and he made me feel beautiful every single day.

'That's because I'm such a good actor,' Jared said. We climbed into the car and, seeing me shivering, Jared immediately turned the heating on, thus proving my point.

'Keep dreaming. I know you too well. You couldn't keep a secret from me if your life depended on it.'

'Is that so?'

'Absolutely.'

Jared gave a small shrug. I like to think he was admitting defeat to my amazing power to sniff out a secret.

'We'll see.'

We pulled out of the car park and started to move along the road lined with the twinkling of fairy lights. I kept my eyes on the castle as it began to recede as we wound our way out of the grounds. 'It was a wonderful wedding, wasn't it?'

'It must have cost a fortune.'

I stifled a yawn. It had been an extremely long day. 'That's what happens when you have a rich daddy to pay for everything, I suppose.' Aunt Gloria's second husband had been mega-rich and liked nothing more than indulging his daughters (by throwing cash at them, rather than spending actual time with them). He hadn't spared a single penny when it came to Trina's big day.

'Lucky for some.' Jared pulled out of the wide iron gates and onto the street. I twisted in my seat to take one last look at Durban Castle, doubtful that I would ever step into a place as grand ever again.

'I don't know. We're pretty lucky with the families we have. Tori and Trina's dad may like to splash his cash around, but I don't think he had much of a parental role in their lives. They spent most of their childhoods away at school. It's a bit sad, really.'

Jared took one final look at the castle through the rear-view mirror. 'I won't spend too much time feeling sorry for them. By the looks of it, they have plenty of banknotes to wipe away their tears.'

'Is this your bad side emerging?'

Jared grinned across at me. 'I told you I was a bastard.'

I patted his arm. 'Good try, but you'll have to do much better than that.'

I must have dropped off somewhere along the way, as I felt myself being gently nudged awake. We were parked outside our flat with all traces of fairy lights, castles and dancing pensioners well and truly behind us. I dragged my weary body up to the second-floor flat Jared and I had been sharing for the past eight months. I'd been worried that moving in with Jared would be weird, as I'd never co-habited with a boyfriend before, but my concerns were unfounded and I couldn't imagine not living with him now. We had quite different views when it came to living

24

arrangements – Jared liked to wash the dishes as soon as possible while I could leave them 'soaking' for anything up to three days – but it seemed to work well. Or so I'd thought. We still hadn't cleared up that 'yes, but …' niggle.

We moved straight to the bedroom, where I kicked off my shoes and peeled off my navy chiffon dress, abandoning them on the floor while I pulled on a pair of worn, but comfortable, pyjamas. Jared waited until I'd wandered to the bathroom before he scooped up the dress and shoes, depositing them in the laundry basket and the bottom of the wardrobe respectively. It was the same most nights. I didn't mean to be so slothful, but it was a difficult habit to break.

I washed off the make-up I had so carefully applied that morning before pulling out the mass of grips I'd used to pin my hair up. Aidan was a stylist at a posh hairdressers in town and had passed on one of his business cards. I was sorely tempted to book an appointment – who wouldn't want to have their hair done in a salon frequented by celebs? The only thing stopping me was the hefty price tag.

'The bathroom's free.' My face washed and my teeth brushed, I returned to the bedroom, desperate to climb beneath the sheets. The nap in the car hadn't been nearly enough to revive me. 'We need to add toothpaste to the shopping list. It's almost all – what are you doing?'

When I walked into the room, Jared was down on the floor (or, rather, down on one knee. He hadn't collapsed or anything).

'Is that a—?' I gasped and covered my mouth with my hand. This couldn't be real, could it? Surely I was still asleep and would wake up any moment, drooling on the car window as we pulled up outside the flat. Because this *really* couldn't be happening. Jared couldn't be proposing to me here, in our bedroom, while I was wearing my oldest, ugliest (but extremely comfortable) pyjamas.

Could he?

'I wasn't going to ask you tonight. I had it all planned. It would have been way more romantic than this, I promise, but I couldn't wait. I saw how happy Trina and Rory were today, and I want that too.'

He could.

Jared really was going to propose to me!

Why hadn't I slipped into something a bit sexier than my worn-out winceyette pyjamas?

'Is that why you were looking so flustered during the ceremony?' I asked, my happy grin diminishing as I recalled his sickly complexion. It was hardly flattering, was it? The thought of marrying me had brought Jared out in a sweat!

'Hey, it's a nerve-wracking thing, proposing to someone. What if it doesn't go to plan? What if you say no?' Jared gulped. He was starting to sweat again. 'Are you going to say no?'

Why the fluff would I say *no?*

'You haven't even asked me yet.'

Jared took a fortifying breath. This was it, the moment I'd been waiting for since I slipped out of the womb. 'Ruth, will you marry me?'

A grand proposal would have been wonderful. We could have had roses and violins and champagne. There could have been moonlit walks or a trip up the Eiffel Tower. We could have been on a sun-drenched beach with the waves lapping at our feet, or staring up at the sky as a sign billowed from an aeroplane, declaring to the world that Jared wanted little old me to be his wife.

But who needed all that extra stuff? The only thing that mattered was Jared and those beautiful words. Would I marry Jared?

Would I marry Jared?

'Of course I'll bloody marry you!'

FIVE

Ruth

I'd taken to walking around with my left hand outstretched for the remainder of the weekend and even on Monday morning, when I should have been busy working, I was preoccupied, admiring the ring on my finger. I couldn't take my eyes off it. It didn't matter that it was a little loose and I had to clamp my middle and little fingers tight to keep it in place. On TV, engagement rings are always a perfect fit, as though the proposer has super-human ring-sizing capabilities. In reality, Jared's guess had been slightly off, and we would have to get the ring resized. But it was still so beautiful and, more than that, it was so *me*. Jared had made a blinding choice in my engagement ring. It was quite a chunky white gold band set with a princess-cut diamond with a row of pink sapphires at either side. He must have known that a delicate little ring would have looked ridiculous on my finger, and I adored the pop of colour.

'Sally says she's still waiting for the minutes from Wednesday's meeting.' My boss thumped his way into my office, dumping a bundle of papers haphazardly into my in-tray. His presence totally ruined my romantic reverie, and I was forced to tear my eyes away from my finger and at least look like I was doing some actual work. Shoving my left hand under the desk, I grabbed the mouse in my right and swished it around a bit, as if I was busy doing something I was paid to do. I'd worked as the PA to the company's general manager for long enough to have perfected the art of looking industrious when in fact I was doing nothing more taxing than having a daydream.

'She hasn't got them yet? How odd.' I worked the ring off my finger with my thumb, letting it plop into my lap. Jared and I hadn't announced our engagement yet – we'd spent the remainder of the weekend holed up in the flat 'privately celebrating' – and I wanted to keep it under wraps at work until we'd had the chance to tell our friends and family, particularly since I worked with two of my closest friends. Although they worked in the sales and marketing department and reception, gossip travelled like lightning at H. Wood Vehicles. It meant I had to store my beautiful new ring in my purse – moments of admiration aside – until we'd shouted it from the rooftops. Which I would totally do if the mere prospect of standing up on a slippery roof didn't bring me out in a sweat.

'I'll email the minutes over to Sally again straight away.' As soon as I'd actually typed them up, obviously.

'Did I get a copy?'

'Of course you did. I filed it for you.' Kelvin would never check. He didn't touch his filing cabinets unless he thought he'd stashed an emergency Mars bar in there. There were many disadvantages of working as a PA for the extremely lazy Kelvin Shuttleworth, but at least I could bullshit him to mask my own laziness from time to time without any recriminations.

'Right.' Kelvin hitched his trousers up by the belt loops. 'Susan may call later. If she does, tell her I'm in a meeting and take a message. I'm sick to bloody death of hearing about flowers and seating plans.'

I slipped into a daydream, imagining the kind of flowers I'd have for my wedding. Something bright, obviously. Maybe a posy of pink and orange tulips …

'And I'll have a coffee.' Kelvin strode towards his office, but paused on the threshold. 'I'll have just two of my biscuits from now on, though. Until the wedding's over and done with, at least.' Kelvin pursed his rubbery lips. 'Susan's got me on a diet.'

'But it isn't even your wedding.' Kelvin's daughter was getting married in a few weeks and from what I could gather, it was going to be an elaborate affair. On a par with Trina's, at the very least.

'Try telling my wife that. It's bad enough that I have to pay for the blasted thing. Putting me on a diet is a step too far. In fact …' Kelvin strode out of the office, grabbing a fistful of change from his trouser pocket. I took a guess that he was on his way to the vending machine and, sure enough, he returned with a selection of chocolate bars in his hands and a packet of crisps clamped in his teeth. His stride was purposeful, his shoulders back. A few thousand calories would show his wife who was boss!

Kelvin gave me a satisfied nod as he passed, before shutting himself in his adjoining office.

'Don't forget that file for Sally,' he called through to me amid the delightful rustle of wrappers. 'And my coffee.'

Giving my ring one last admiring look, I popped it safely into my purse before heading to the kitchen to make Kelvin's coffee. When I returned, I fished the notes from last week's meeting from my in-tray. I'd get right on it. After a quick Google search of wedding venues.

My head was swirling with wedding ideas by the end of the day. I'd managed to make a list of forty venues in

Woodgate and the Greater Manchester area that seemed reasonably priced. They'd have to be whittled down, of course, but it was a start. Trina's wedding had set the bar high, but I couldn't see me and Jared getting married in a castle. As lovely as the day had been, it was all a bit pretentious and not us at all. Perhaps I could ask Trina for some tips when she got back from her honeymoon, though. I'd had a fun day perusing the internet for ideas, but I really didn't have a clue when it came to organising a whole wedding, and it'd be nice to catch up with my cousin. We hadn't had much time to chat during the wedding as everyone had wanted a piece of the bride.

'What are you looking so chirpy about?' Quinn, the receptionist at H. Woods, asked as I leaned against the desk to conserve energy as I waited for Jared. One of the many advantages of being with Jared – and, believe me, there were many – was never having to catch the bus to and from work again, as we both worked for the same company. We'd met in H. Wood's little kitchen two years ago and since then had been living happily ever after. We were a perfect little unit, travelling to and from work together, saving both petrol and my sanity. Never again would I have to wait in the pouring rain for a bus that never had any intention of turning up. Never again would I have to get lumbered with the local fruitcake (there's one on almost every bus. You've probably sat next to one before and wished you'd had the foresight to walk instead). Never again would I have to deal with a surly driver first thing on a Monday morning or time my journeys so that they didn't coincide with the local delinquents' ride to school. Going to work was no longer something to dread – apart from the actual being at work part, of course, but there was no getting away from that.

'It's the end of the day. Of course I'm chirpy.' I wanted to tell Quinn all about my engagement, and I can't tell you how much it pained me to keep it zipped. As well as being the receptionist at H. Wood Vehicles, Quinn was also one of my best friends and I knew she'd be so happy for me.

Jared arrived and I had to pinch myself – as I so often did – to make sure I wasn't dreaming and Jared was actually my boyfriend. No, no. My *fiancé.* Jared kissed my cheek by way of greeting. Pinch, pinch, pinch!

We dashed home and Jared immediately set up camp in the kitchen while I attacked the sitting room and bathroom. We'd invited our parents over for tea to share our news and I didn't want Linda and Bob's first thoughts at hearing about our engagement to be that their son was marrying a sloth. No matter how true that would be.

'Do we have to listen to S Club 7 again?' Jared groaned from the kitchen as the cheery beat of 'Bring It All Back' started up from the stereo.

'Of course we do.' I couldn't clean without the motivation of a bit of 90s pop. There wasn't much I *could* do without the motivation of a bit of 90s pop.

Once the rooms were clean-ish – I'm not going to pretend to be either Kim or Aggie here – I pulled out the foldaway dining table and set it up with a tablecloth (which I wasn't even aware we owned until Jared alerted me to its presence) and cutlery, which I did my best to ensure matched as best as possible. Our parents arrived, exchanging knowing glances as I led them up to the flat. The food wasn't quite ready, so I settled everyone in the sitting room and poured glasses of wine. This was by far the most formal meal I'd ever had at home. Jared and I weren't a throwing-dinner-parties type of couple and, before living with Jared, I'd shared a house with two blokes whose idea of formal dining was pouring a family-sized packet of crisps into a bowl and sticking it on the coffee table.

'This is nice, isn't it?' Linda – my future mother-in-law – said as we squeezed around the table that wasn't made to seat six. We'd had to improvise with seating and borrow the desk chair and the stool from my dressing table so we'd all have somewhere to sit. It created different levels of seating, but we all pretended it was perfectly fine to be at nose-level with your dinner or towering above it.

'It is, but I'm wondering if there's a reason we're all getting together,' Mum mused, raising her eyebrows.

I took a deep breath. There was no better opening than this. 'Actually, there is a reason.'

I heard a sharp intake of breath – presumably from the mothers – as Jared took my hand from across the table. 'I've asked Ruth to marry me.'

The breaths were released as Mum and Linda squealed, clapping their hands while Dad and Bob, father-in-law-to-be, beamed and shook hands with Jared.

'I suspected as much.' Mum had a smug look plastered over her face.

Linda nodded. 'It was either an engagement or the patter of tiny feet.'

'One thing at a time,' I joked. Everyone laughed, apart from Jared, who looked a little unwell at the suggestion. Kermit was making a comeback, so I decided to bring the real reason for our get-together back into focus.

'Would you like to see the ring?'

Of course everybody did – especially the mothers – so I flashed my gorgeous ring, explaining why I'd had to fish it out of my purse.

'It's stunning, Jared. Did you pick it yourself?' Mum nearly fell off her chair when his reply was in the affirmative. Dad didn't have a romantic bone in his body – or any shred of taste. 'Wow. Well done. Louie, if you ever feel the need to buy me jewellery, come and ask Jared for help. He obviously has the knack.'

'He doesn't get it from Bob,' Linda said. Bob and Dad shared an 'uh oh, they're ganging up on us' look. A swift change of subject was needed before all their faults were dumped onto the foldaway table for all to see. Luckily for the pair, Mum unwittingly came to the rescue.

'So, have you thought about dates yet?'

Phew – Dad and Bob were off the hook, and the rest of the evening passed without too much more husband-bashing. We ate Jared's lovely meal (I told you he was a keeper) and worked our way through a couple of bottles of wine before our parents dragged themselves away. Mum and Linda had been in their element as we bounced ideas around, but it was getting late.

'Congratulations again. I couldn't be happier for the two of you.' Linda pulled her son into a hug, squeezing him a little tighter than was comfortable before repeating the process with me. 'We'll all have to get together again soon and discuss the wedding plans more.'

Jared and I shared a furtive look. How much more was there to discuss? The mothers seemed to have covered everything from an engagement party (Jared and I didn't think one was necessary) to honeymoon destinations (definitely necessary) and everything in between. We'd both agreed that we wanted a medium-sized wedding; big enough to be an actual event but nothing as extravagant as Trina's. As long as our family and friends were there to witness the occasion, we would be happy.

'There's so much to plan,' Mum said, her beaming smile showing how much she was looking forward to getting stuck in. 'The first thing you need to do is decide the date.'

'We really don't want to wait too long, do we?' I turned to Jared for assurance. 'Maybe next spring?'

Mum nodded. 'That's a good timescale. It'll give you just over a year to plan.'

'Will that give us enough time?' If you'd asked me at the beginning of the evening how long I'd need to plan my wedding, I'd have said a few months would suffice, but now just over a year didn't seem like a particularly long time after everything Mum and Linda had discussed. The workload involved in organising one little wedding seemed frighteningly immense.

'Oh, plenty.' Mum gave a dismissive wave of her hand. 'Now, we'd better get going. Give me a call and we'll arrange a time that suits everybody.'

Linda gave my hand a squeeze. 'This is going to be so much fun!'

As she and Mum skipped out of the flat with Dad and Bob trailing after them, I wasn't quite so sure of that any more.

SIX

Trina

Trina had woken at least an hour ago, arranging herself prettily on the crisp white pillows, the sheet riding down just enough to give Rory a peek at her pink silk negligee. She'd been hoping to entice her new husband into a little pre-breakfast honeymooning, but Rory lay still beside her, snoring and snuffling as though his slumber needed announcing constantly. Still, it wasn't as though it was the first time Trina had heard him snore, so she couldn't be *too* annoyed. But was it too much to ask that he'd wake up, ravish her (in a lovely, romantic way, obviously) and then arrange a sumptuous breakfast in bed? It would be lunch in bed at this rate, and Trina had so much planned for the day ahead.

Trina and Rory had spent their first night as a married couple back at Durban Castle, being pampered with champagne and room service until their check-out at noon. Rory had arranged for their bed to be scattered with rose petals, which had been a lovely surprise as he carried her over the threshold of the honeymoon suite. It didn't matter that it had been Winnie's idea; men were notoriously unromantic. Trina had changed into a stunning pale blue chiffon nightgown that she had spent hours shopping for before the wedding. The floor-length nightgown was exquisite, with lace detailing at the back and waist, giving just the tiniest hint of the flesh beneath. Trina had felt truly beautiful as she presented herself to her new husband – and Rory had certainly appreciated the effort she had gone to.

Now, though? Now Rory appreciated his sleep.

Trina gave Rory a nudge with her foot before feigning sleep once more. Nothing. She tried again, slightly harder this time. Not a murmur. It took a swift kick to Rory's calf to rouse the man, but he simply batted her foot away and his snoring resumed immediately.

Trina snatched the sheet away and marched towards the en suite bathroom of their hotel room. After spending a romantic evening at the castle, Trina and Rory had flown to Mexico for their honeymoon. Rory was clearly still shattered from the flight, but perhaps the sound of a running shower would wake him. They would probably have to forgo breakfast in bed now, as Trina had a boat trip scheduled in just over an hour. There would be snorkelling, followed by a picnic on a secluded beach before they returned to the hotel for a couples massage. The honeymoon had been the only part of the wedding Trina felt she had any control over as Winnie wasn't interested in something she couldn't show off to her friends, so she had planned it all down to the minute details.

Trina stepped into the shower. It was huge – able to fit at least four people within its frosted glass walls – and contained an array of luxurious products. Trina lathered and shampooed and conditioned before wrapping herself in a fluffy robe and padding back out to the bedroom. The hotel suite was divine, and managed to be both spacious and cosy, with its plump sofa and chairs facing the fireplace. Not that Trina and Rory needed a fireplace. The sun was already beating down on the terrace beyond the French doors.

'Rory?' Trina adopted what she hoped was a sensual tone as she moved through to the bedroom. 'Ah, darling. You're up.' *Finally.* She was beginning to suspect she'd be snorkelling by herself that morning. 'Wait, don't move.' Trina scurried to the bed before Rory could disentangle himself from the sheets, leaping and landing neatly in her husband's lap.

'Gosh, babe.' Rory groaned as Trina covered his face in kisses. 'Can I expect a wake-up call like this every morning?'

'Definitely.' Trina lay back on the bed, shivering with delight as Rory untied her robe. Or it could have been due to the fact that the air conditioning was cranked up to the max, but Trina wasn't complaining either way. 'But we don't have much time. We're going snorkelling soon.'

Rory, who had been busy nuzzling Trina's neck, paused and propped himself up on his elbow. 'Snorkelling?'

'I told you about it, remember?' Trina had booked the trip back in England, way before the wedding. She'd discussed her plans with Rory beforehand and he'd smiled indulgently and said that he was happy to do whatever Trina wanted. 'And I reminded you on the plane. You said you were looking forward to it.'

'Did I?' Rory saw his wife's face fall. She'd put a lot of effort into planning their honeymoon – it was the only thing that hadn't been meticulously planned by Winnie and Troy. 'Oh, *snorkelling*. Of course! Yes, I'm very much looking forward to it.'

'Really?' Trina's sparkle was back as she smiled up at her husband.

'Really.' Discussion over, Rory resumed his nuzzling.

Trina wrapped her arms around Rory, feeling the taut,

toned muscles in his shoulders and back. All that time he spent at the gym was well worth it. 'You haven't forgotten our couples massage, have you?'

Rory propped himself up again. 'What the hell is a *couples* massage?'

So he hadn't been listening after all.

Their first full day of honeymoon didn't quite go according to plan. After a speedy breakfast of croissants and coffee in the restaurant, they'd hurried to the beach, where the boat was waiting for them. They climbed aboard and set off with the instructor. And that's when it all went wrong.

'But you sail all the time,' Trina said as she rubbed Rory's back. His knuckles had turned white as he clung to the side of the boat, his head hanging over the edge.

'I know. I love sailing. Eugh-euff!' The noise that erupted from Rory as his body convulsed was most non-human. 'I do not love this.'

Rory's seasickness had taken them both by surprise. Rory's father owned a bloody yacht! He'd grown up wearing a lifejacket as they spent so much time on water. Rory didn't get seasick. It was a joke. A cruel joke.

'Poor baby.' Trina circled Rory's back with a gentle touch. 'Do you want to go back to the hotel?'

Rory shook his head. Going back to the hotel would be humiliating. It would be admitting defeat, which was not something a Hamilton-Wraith did lightly. It would take more than a bit of nausea to break Rory.

'No, I'm fine. It'll pass soon. Eugh-euff!'

In the end they gave snorkelling a miss and instead headed straight to the secluded beach. Rory felt much better as soon as his feet hit dry sand, and they set up their picnic. The instructor left them to it, promising to return in a couple of hours.

'I'm sorry about the snorkelling.' Rory took Trina's hand

and gave it a squeeze. He knew he'd let her down. 'Maybe we can try again later in the week, once I've got my bearings.'

'Maybe, but don't worry about it. Do you fancy a swim?' Trina was wearing a two-hundred-quid bikini that her sister had insisted she buy for the trip, and she didn't want to waste it by keeping it covered with a sundress.

'I think I'm recovered enough for that.' Rory jumped to his feet and peeled off his T-shirt. 'I'll race you there!'

It was hardly a fair race, Trina mused as she watched Rory tear off towards the water. She had yet to remove her dress and couldn't seem to drag her eyes away from her husband's magnificent body. She couldn't believe how long it had taken for her to actually notice Rory. She'd seen him around over the years, had even spoken to him on occasion, but she'd never really *seen* him. Not until that night at the golf club dance. She'd been feeling down, as her date had failed to arrive, but Rory had managed to cheer her up. By the end of the night she was smitten.

'Come on, Trina! The water's lovely.'

Shaking herself into action, Trina tore off the sundress and jogged down to the sea to join Rory ... and perhaps partake in a little water-based honeymooning.

The day should have looked up from that point. But it didn't.

'Oh my God, Rory! Wake up!'

The pair had fallen asleep on the sand, exhausted after their splash in the water. The sound of the boat arriving to take them back to the resort woke Trina – and alerted her to the fact that her husband had forgotten to reapply sun cream. The front of his body, including his face, was an angry lobster colour, apart from one patch on his chest that was shaped like Trina's head.

'Mmm, what?' Rory mumbled before attempting to sit up. The screech he emitted sent a shiver down Trina's spine. 'Fuck! Ow! What's happened to me?'

'You're burned. You haven't put any sun cream on since we left the hotel this morning.'

'Why didn't you remind me? Arggghh!'

'I didn't think you'd need reminding.' Rory was an adult, after all. Yes, he still lived at home with his parents – where there were staff on hand to clean up after him and take care of his washing and meals – but that didn't negate the fact that he was a twenty-seven-year-old man.

'So you just let me burn? *Ow!* Christ, it hurts.'

'I did not *let you burn*. I was asleep! I had no idea you hadn't reapplied it until now.'

'Everything okay here?' The instructor had strolled up the beach to meet them. He winced when he caught sight of Rory. 'Ouch. Nasty. That's going to be sore, mate.'

'It already is!' Rory stormed away from Trina and the instructor as best as he could with his agonisingly stiff skin, stalking towards the waiting boat. Trina was left to pack up the barely touched picnic with the help of the kind instructor, who lugged the basket back to the boat. Rory was aboard, sulking – painfully – in a corner. He refused to talk to Trina the whole way back to the hotel, and because of his burned-to-a-crisp skin, the couples massage was out of the question.

SEVEN

Ruth

My pink gym bag slung over my shoulder, I made my way into the local church hall in my leggings and T-shirt, which weren't all that flattering but were necessary. Once upon a time, I'd attempted to lose weight but it hadn't worked out too well. I'd hated every minute of it: the diets, the exercise, the crushing disappointment when I stood on the scales. However, there had been one thing I enjoyed while at the gym, and that had been the yoga class. My gym subscription had long lapsed, but I now took a weekly class at the church hall and while the facilities weren't great (no changing rooms or showers), the instructors were lovely and the class was both invigorating and fun.

I made my way into the hall, saying hello to the others en route, and set out my pink yoga mat alongside Mary, an eighty-two-year-old great-grandmother who had more energy and flexibility than most of the other participants combined.

'Hi, Mary. Good week?'

Mary, balancing on one leg to stretch out her thigh,

released her leg and tilted her hand back and forth. 'So-so, I suppose. I increased my jogging time by two minutes but then I found out one of my old school friends died at the weekend.' She shook her head and switched feet, balancing on her left foot and grasping her right ankle behind her back. 'There aren't many of us left. We're dropping like flies.'

'I'm so sorry, Mary.'

Mary released her foot and gave it a little wriggle. 'You get used to it, dear. But that's why you have to make the most of life while you can. Grab it by the bollocks, girl.' Mary chuckled at my shocked face. 'They say you only regret the things you didn't do, you know.'

I did know, though I didn't entirely agree. I regretted a lot of the things I had done – most notably the ex-boyfriends I'd wasted so much time on in the past.

'That's why I've finally agreed to go on a date with Cecil.' Mary's cheeks turned pink beneath her blue veins at her confession. Her widowed neighbour had been sniffing around Mary since her husband passed away four years earlier, but she'd resisted until now.

'Good for you. I hope you have a good time.' I wanted to share my own news with Mary – with the whole room, actually – but we'd decided to keep our engagement quiet until we'd told those closest to us. Our whole families now knew – Mum and Linda couldn't have kept it to themselves if they'd been gagged – but we hadn't officially told our friends yet. 'Officially' because of course I'd told my best friend, Erin. I couldn't have kept it from her for a second longer and was ready to burst, so it was for health reasons that I'd blabbed, really. Plus, I'd sworn her to secrecy, so it didn't really count. We planned to tell our other friends in a couple of days, at our usual Thursday night meet-up. My ring would hopefully be back from the jewellers by then and sitting snugly on my finger.

And after that I would be free to tell the whole world

that Jared Williams wanted to marry me!

'Good evening, everyone.' Nell, one of the instructors, padded into the room wearing a pair of aqua leggings and a white cropped top that showed off her tanned, toned body to perfection. Normally I would instantly dislike somebody who looked as good as Nell, but she was so lovely that she made it near impossible to harbour any ill thoughts towards her.

'Good evening, guys.' Greg, Nell's husband and fellow yoga instructor, followed, carrying a CD player and a couple of rolled-up mats tucked under one arm. 'Are we all ready?'

Nell and Greg set out their equipment, and soothing tones began to emit from the CD player as they took us through a warm-up before our workout. I hadn't been sure what to make of the husband and wife team when I first started the yoga class. I didn't really trust people who were happy all the time, but Nell and Greg were a genuinely nice couple who were bright and cheery, yet calming.

'Okay. Feet together, hands by your side.' Nell stood on her mat in the position described. 'We're going to start with the mountain pose. Remember: beginners should follow Greg, who will modify each move accordingly, while those who have been with us for a while and feel able should follow me. Are we ready?' Nell took a deep breath and raised her arms above her head. 'We're going to bring our arms down to our sides again on the exhale.' Letting her breath out slowly, Nell lowered her arms, and we all copied. 'Deep breath in. And exhale.'

I went through the movements, which were now so familiar that I could switch my mind to other things while my body went through the motions. My mind automatically returned to my wedding, as it had throughout the day. I'd spent the majority of my time at work researching wedding and reception venues, adding to my already extensive list. There were so many options available, from churches to the local registry office, golf clubs to community centres and hotels to pub function rooms. It was bewildering.

My body moved into the chair pose, my breathing even despite my mind being a hive of activity. The venue was the tip of the wedding iceberg. There was so much to think about and I wasn't sure where to go from here. I'd never planned a wedding before and never thought I'd ever get the opportunity to before Jared, so I'd definitely need Mum and Linda's help.

Cobra pose. I lay on my mat, feeling the stretch. What was I going to do about a dress? I'd had a brief glance at plus-size wedding dresses online but they'd been so horrific, I'd been forced to close the internet browser before I called the whole thing off. Who wanted to get married in a cream tarpaulin? Brides were supposed to feel beautiful and you can't do that sporting a potato sack. I'd (mostly) come to terms with the fact that I was a size 22 (on a good day), but I was conscious of the wedding photos I'd one day show my grandchildren.

'Now let's move straight into the plank,' Nell said in her soothing voice. I followed Greg's lead on this one. No matter how many sessions I attended, the plank was my most dreaded pose.

Speaking of dread, my mind shifted to the guest list. There were certain people who I wasn't all that keen to have at my wedding, people who sucked all the joy out of life and got their kicks from putting others down – and not even behind their backs like normal people do. But I couldn't think of a way to get out of inviting Aunty Pat and her vicious tongue. I'd contemplated – fleetingly – getting married abroad. Imagine getting married on the beach with the sound of waves gently lapping as you exchanged vows with the man you loved. It sounded blissful, but then I could never get married without Mum and Dad there, and I was pretty sure Jared felt the same way about his own parents. There was the option to take our families with us, but that would cost a fortune and we'd be saving for a million years to pay for it.

Downward dog.

I'd been thinking about the theme of the wedding too – as advised by the wedding websites – but I was a bit confused by the whole thing. How did you pick a *theme* for a wedding? Did they mean like Christmas or Halloween? Because I wasn't keen on that in the slightest. Easter could have worked, what with all the chocolate and everything but … no, it all seemed a bit daft to me.

'Let's go back into the mountain pose,' Nell instructed.

I'd tried discussing all of this with Jared, but he wasn't that interested in the wedding. He'd said we had plenty of time to iron out the details, which was true. Perhaps I was panicking too soon, but it seemed like there was an awful lot to panic about and not nearly enough time to do it in.

'Maybe we could have a long engagement?' Jared had suggested. 'If it's all getting a bit much?'

I'd been horrified. I didn't want a long engagement. I wanted to marry Jared as soon as possible, before he could change his mind.

'Take a step back,' Nell instructed and we all followed. 'Arms outstretched.'

My body took itself into the warrior pose while my mind went over wedding plans, to-do lists that I needed to put together, and long engagements.

'Are you all right, Ruth?' Greg asked once the class was over and I was rolling up my mat. 'You seemed a bit tense today.'

I secured the bands to keep my mat in place and tucked it under my arm. 'I'm fine.' My mouth was aching to tell Greg about the wedding, just to see what it sounded like to say it out loud again, but I managed to keep it buttoned.

'Well, if you're sure …' Greg hung around for a moment, waiting for me to speak. I hitched my bag onto my shoulder, which finally convinced him that I wasn't about to offload what was clearly on my mind.

'Are you coming for a drink?' Mary asked as Greg wandered away.

'Yeah, why not?'

Jared was right. There was no point in worrying about this stuff right now. We had months and months ahead of us to sort everything. We hadn't even set a date yet.

Having a drink with the others after yoga managed to calm my mind. Somewhere between my first drink and Mary's impromptu jukebox singalong, I realised that I could do this wedding thing. Other people managed to get married without combusting, so why couldn't I? This would be my one and only wedding, so I needed to keep calm and enjoy the process.

I prepared Kelvin's office for his arrival before settling down to work the following day. I'd decided to take the wedding one step at a time, so today I would be concentrating on honeymoon destinations. There could be surely nothing stressful about planning a holiday! A few clicks later and my theory was proven to be wrong. I knew Jared would love an action-packed holiday – perhaps skiing – while I was happier lying by a pool with a cocktail. Jared would enjoy activities and walks to take in the scenery while I'd need nothing more than a good book and regular siestas. The honeymoon was clearly going to need a bit more time and thought than I'd anticipated.

'I've just been collared by Sally.' Kelvin puffed his way into the office, a film of sweat coating his brow. I had to admit the stairs were a pain first thing in the morning. I was contemplating starting a petition to have a stair lift installed. 'She says she still hasn't had the minutes from you.'

My mouth fell open. 'But I emailed them yesterday. You saw me do it.' This was a big fat lie, but Kelvin didn't pay enough attention to be able to confidently call bullshit. I gave a heavy sigh. 'I'll do it again now. You don't think there's anything wrong with my computer, do you?'

Kelvin grunted. He didn't care about my computer. He didn't really care about the minutes. He simply wanted Sally from HR off his back.

'Would you like a coffee?' Anything to get his mind away from the minutes, in case he decided to stand there and witness me emailing them, supposedly for the second time.

'I can't.' Kelvin spat the words. Actually spat them. I surreptitiously wiped the spittle from my cheek. 'Susan's put me on a detox for the bloody wedding.'

I shuddered. I certainly wouldn't be detoxing before my wedding. I needed coffee and alcohol and junk food to get me through the day. What was the point in living otherwise?

'If she rings, tell her I've dropped dead from lack of toxins.' Kelvin shuffled into his office, grumbling about nuptials and his lack of caffeine while I grabbed the notes from the meeting from my in-tray. I was busily typing them up, for once not consumed by wedding plans, when Kelvin's wife appeared and put me off my stride.

'Is he in?' Without pausing for pleasantries, Susan wobbled towards Kelvin's door but changed her mind and stopped in front of my desk, her chin jutting out as she observed me. 'I'm here to talk to Kelvin about wedding arrangements. Not my own, of course.' Susan tittered and swept a stray platinum curl from her eyes. I think Kelvin's wife modelled her appearance on Marilyn Monroe, but it had gone horribly wrong somewhere along the way. Her look was more gruesome than glamorous, with her shoddily applied make-up and hideously tight clothes, which showed every bump and crevice. 'It's my daughter's. She's marrying a professional rugby player, you know.'

I did know. Susan shoehorned the fact into every single conversation. 'How lovely for her.'

'Indeed.' Susan gave her hair a flick, but it was so heavy with hairspray that it didn't budge. 'It's so strange having an athletic future son-in-law. Nobody else in the family is remotely fit.'

'What about your future daughter-in-law? Erin's pretty athletic too.' I didn't mention that my best friend's athleticism lay in the bedroom only.

As though on cue, Erin walked into the office, freezing when she spotted Susan. Erin had been seeing Susan and Kelvin's son, Richard, for the past couple of years. Susan's lip curled when she caught sight of Erin. She didn't approve of her son's choice of girlfriend, but then Erin couldn't stand Susan either so it was a well-balanced loathing.

'Anyway, I must be getting on. I need to speak to Kelvin rather urgently.' Susan turned to Erin, the lip-curl still in evidence. 'Don't forget we have a wedding meeting on Saturday afternoon. Don't be late.'

'I wouldn't dream of it,' Erin muttered as Susan disappeared into Kelvin's office. She flopped wearily onto the edge of my desk. 'Have you got time for a skive?'

I looked at the half-typed-up minutes, then back at Erin. I could spare ten minutes, surely.

EIGHT

Erin

'So how are the wedding plans coming along?' Erin and Ruth were sitting on a bench in the far corner of H. Wood's car park, which was their preferred skiving spot. It wasn't quite warm enough to sit outside, but they both needed a breather from the office. Despite the coolness, the back of Erin's neck was sticky so she pulled the mass of dark hair away from her collar and secured it with a band on top of her head, creating a messy ponytail. For years, Erin had kept her hair in a short, glossy bob, but she'd allowed it to grow longer recently. Richard, her boyfriend of over two years, said he liked it this way so Erin had kept it, even though the extra length could be a bit of a pain at times. Fiercely independent, Erin was surprised that she'd allowed Richard's opinion to sway her hairstyle choice, but she had to admit that the style suited her.

'It's all a bit overwhelming, if I'm honest.' Ruth tore open the Twix she'd bought from the vending machine on their way out, handing one of the fingers to Erin before biting a chunk off her own. 'There's so much to do and

Jared doesn't seem particularly interested.'

Erin gave a wave of her hand. 'That's just men. They're really only interested in the wedding night. They think with their willies, not their hearts.'

'But Jared's not usually like that. He can think with both.'

Erin and Ruth shared a smirk. 'I can ask if Lindsay's wedding planner is available to help.'

Ruth almost choked on her Twix. 'God, no.' Ruth had heard enough about the wedding planner to know that she was a complete nightmare. Erin had somehow found herself agreeing to be a bridesmaid for Richard's sister and was finding the whole process as arduous as Kelvin was. Erin hadn't been Lindsay's first choice of bridesmaid, and she'd only been asked when one of the other bridesmaids had been ejected from her duties for daring to question Lindsay's taste in wedding dresses. Erin had seen a photo of the dress that had caused all the furore and had to agree with the original bridesmaid. The dress was hideously tacky and had since been scrapped, but the bridesmaid had never been forgiven or reinstated.

Lucky cow.

'It's probably a good thing you're not interested in hiring a wedding planner. Ingrid is costing poor Frank a fortune. You'd think he was a Premiership footballer the way Lindsay spends his money.' Groom-to-be Frank Harper played for their local rugby team, the Woodgate Warriors, but Lindsay was somehow under the impression that she was now a WAG and acted accordingly.

Ruth picked up her cup of coffee from beside her on the bench and blew on it. 'I thought Kelvin was paying for the wedding?'

Erin spluttered. 'You must be joking. I think he offered to pay for his own suit, but that's about it. No, this wedding is all on Frank.' And it was costing him an absolute arm and a leg. As well as wedding planner Ingrid,

Frank was funding eight bridesmaids, partnered with eight groomsmen plus a pageboy and two flower girls. The wedding was taking place in a fancy hotel and promised to be the most garish wedding Woodgate had ever seen.

'I don't think our small savings will stretch to a wedding planner,' Ruth said. 'So it looks like I'll have to do it myself for free.'

Erin placed a hand on Ruth's. 'If you need any help, you know where Quinn is.' She laughed when Ruth stuck her tongue out at her.

'You don't have a romantic bone in your body, do you?'

'Thankfully not.'

'What are you going to do when it comes to your own wedding? Hire Ingrid?'

Erin's mouth dropped open, aghast at the very suggestion. 'Who said I was ever going to get married? You know my views on that.' The thought made her shudder. Erin couldn't think of anything worse than being shackled to a man for life.

'But that was before you found Richard.'

'I can still have Richard without a wedding.' Erin really didn't get what all the fuss was about. A piece of paper and a bit of jewellery didn't prove your love. 'Besides, Richard's already been married, so hopefully Amanda scarred him for life on that front.'

'You don't mean that.'

'That's easy for you to say. You haven't met the woman.' Richard's ex-wife was needy and demanding and if Erin hadn't been against marriage on principle before she met Amanda, she certainly would have been afterwards. 'I know you can't wait to marry Jared and I'm so happy for you, but I just don't feel the way you do about marriage.'

'Not even a teeny bit?'

'Not even the tiniest scrap.' Ruth had spent years listening to Erin's views on marriage and knew there was little point in arguing her point. 'I'm happy as we are.'

Erin pushed the key into the lock, and the delicious smell of home cooking wafted towards her as soon as she opened the door. Before Richard, she had never possessed the key to a boyfriend's house – before Richard, she hadn't really had long-term boyfriends at all – but it had seemed like a convenient step forward in their relationship to exchange keys. Erin had worried she would feel like her personal space could be violated at any moment, but so far it hadn't been a problem and she quite liked how grown-up that small act made her feel.

'I'm in the kitchen,' Richard called as Erin made her way down the hallway, following the spicy scent. Richard was still in his work shirt, but he'd rolled the sleeves up and covered it with a navy and white striped apron. Erin couldn't quite believe she was attracted to a man who would wear an apron, but life was full of surprises.

'What are we having?' Erin dumped her handbag on the kitchen table before reaching up to kiss Richard.

Richard stirred the contents of a large saucepan on the hob. 'Chicken curry.'

'Don't make it too spicy. It was too hot for Ralphie last time.' The poor boy had acted as though he'd needed a fire extinguisher for his mouth and in the end Erin had made him cheese on toast instead. He'd said it was the best meal he'd ever eaten, which was either very sweet or put Richard and Amanda's parenting skills into question.

'I remember. I've made it quite mild. See?' Richard spooned out a little of the curry and held it out for Erin to try.

'Mmm, not bad. I think we may get away with it.'

'I've made sure there's some cheese in the fridge, just in case.' Richard returned to his cooking duties but was interrupted by his mobile. 'Can you keep an eye on this? I won't be a minute.' He fished his phone out of the pocket on the front of his apron and moved through to the sitting room. Erin gave the curry a tentative stir, not really having a clue what she was supposed to be keeping an eye on. Cooking was definitely not her forte. She was temporarily relieved from cooking duties when the doorbell rang and she bolted for the door. Her relief at being excused from cooking, however, was brief.

'Isn't Richard in?' Richard's ex-wife wasn't impressed when it was Erin who opened the door, and she did little to disguise her displeasure. Amanda had taken an instant dislike to Erin and had tried her best to make her relationship with Richard as awkward as possible.

'He's on the phone.' Erin too did nothing to disguise her displeasure. She didn't have to explain herself to Amanda.

'Well, remember the rule.' Amanda raised an eyebrow and placed a hand on her hip. 'No sleepovers while the children are here.'

Erin tried her best not to roll her eyes. Erin's sleeping arrangements had nothing to do with this woman, but she knew she and Richard would follow her rule anyway. It was easier for all involved if they played along with Amanda's little games.

'Whatever.' Erin turned from Amanda and plastered a smile on her face while she addressed Richard's children. 'Hey, kiddos. Are you hungry? Your dad's making a curry.' Erin ruffled Richard's son's hair. 'But don't worry, Ralphie, it isn't too hot this time.'

'His name is *Ralph*.' Amanda put a hand out to stop her children from charging into the house. Erin wondered if her mouth had permanently resembled a cat's arse during her marriage to Richard, or whether it was a habit she'd developed once she'd signed the divorce papers. 'Give Mummy a kiss before you go.' The children dutifully kissed their mother before they skipped into the house, dumping their bags in the hallway before moving through to the kitchen. It had taken a while for them all to adjust to the new dynamics of life with Richard's children, and not because they didn't like sharing their dad with Erin but because Erin wasn't entirely comfortable around kids. She'd always done her best to avoid children, but she could hardly swerve Richard's offspring. Surprisingly, Erin found that she was quite fond of LuLu and Ralph. They were all right, as far as kids go, and were pretty easy-going. It helped that at twelve and nine years old, LuLu and Ralph were fairly independent, didn't require anything gross like nappy changes, and were quite capable of bathing themselves.

'I'll see you after school tomorrow!' Amanda called after the children, but they'd already disappeared into the kitchen – no doubt raiding the biscuit tin while their dad was out of sight. Again. 'I've packed LuLu's PE kit. Please don't forget it in the morning.' Amanda gave Erin a scathing look before she turned and stalked across the garden path without a farewell. Erin closed the door and turned, almost tripping over a Hello Kitty backpack.

'Hey, kids. Why don't you take your things upstairs before tea?' *And before your bags cause an injury?* LuLu and Ralph dutifully trooped back into the hallway – crumbs suspiciously adorning their T-shirts – and picked up their bags. Erin ruffled their hair affectionately as they passed her on their way to the stairs.

'I've got a new pair of shoes for school,' LuLu told her. 'Do you want to see them?'

'Sure.' Erin followed LuLu up to her very pink bedroom and sat on the bed while LuLu pulled out her neatly folded school uniform and hung it in the wardrobe, ready for the following day. LuLu wasn't like Erin at this age. At twelve, Erin had been at the rebellious stage that would take her through her teens. Clothes were strewn across her bedroom floor, shoes flung under the bed, and Erin had been more interested in the Year 9 boys than Hello Kitty. But, from an (almost) parental perspective, Erin much preferred LuLu's way than her own.

LuLu returned to her bag. Out came her PE kit, the purple unicorn that LuLu still refused to sleep without, and a pair of shiny black leather shoes with a jewel-encrusted bow on the front.

'Aren't they cute? Faye has a pair *exactly* like these.' LuLu held the shoes out towards Erin, her face beaming with pride. 'Don't you just *love* them?'

'I do. They're very pretty.'

Beaming wider, LuLu placed the shoes carefully at the bottom of her wardrobe. 'Kayla is going to be *so* jealous because she wanted a pair and her mum said no because there's nothing wrong with her old shoes. She has to wait until they break or they don't fit. She's going to be so mad when I show up with them tomorrow. She thinks she's Faye's best friend, but she isn't really. Faye doesn't even like her.'

LuLu's triumph over her new shoes and popularity was cut short by the sudden squeal of the smoke alarm downstairs. Erin gasped and flew into the hall, but it was too late. The smell of burning was already wafting up the stairs and was no doubt filling the kitchen.

'Oh, shit. I've ruined the curry.' Erin forgot all about Amanda's 'no swearing in front of the children' rule as she tore down the stairs. LuLu and Ralph followed closely behind and the three of them joined Richard in the kitchen. He stood in front of the stove, looking down forlornly at the ruined chicken curry.

'Grab your coats,' Richard said as he removed the pan from the hob. 'It looks like we're going out for pizza.'

Erin shot Richard an apologetic look as they slipped their coats on in the hallway, but when she turned around Ralph was grinning at her. Lifting his hand, he gave her a high-five.

'Thanks for burning dinner. You're awesome.'

'You're welcome?' Erin turned nervously to Richard, but he rolled his eyes and gave her a reassuring smile. This wasn't the first time she'd cocked up in the kitchen, and he was sure it wouldn't be the last. It was a good job he wasn't with her for her cooking skills.

'Erin? Can I wear a bit of your make-up?' LuLu asked as she zipped up her jacket.

Erin gave LuLu's hair a ruffle. 'I'm afraid not, kiddo.' That was most definitely against Amanda's rules.

NINE

Ruth

Before moving in with Jared, I'd shared a house with a couple of blokes. I'd known Billy for as long as I could remember, as he was my brother's best friend. Theo had made up our little trio and although he could be a bit of a knob at times, we'd got along quite well for a few years. When we'd lived together, Billy and I would always watch our favourite sitcom, *A Beginner's Guide To You,* together, and that tradition remained strong even now we no longer lived under the same roof. Somewhere along the way we'd picked up a few more viewers who joined us for our weekly ritual. Jared, Erin and Quinn were now avid viewers, while Richard and Theo joined us when they could. Richard had to drop out occasionally due to parental duties, while Theo only deigned to join us when he wasn't busy with one of his many lady friends.

'Aren't the others here yet?' I asked Billy as he led us into the sitting room, where only Theo and a girl I'd never met before were sitting. She was petite with a mass of brown hair and a lovely olive complexion. She was wearing a pair of tiny orange velour shorts and a matching hoodie and her feet were bare, flashing her co-ordinated orange painted toenails. I took a guess that she was Theo's latest conquest, but it was hard to tell as Theo had a permanent smug look about his chops. He was lounging on one of the chairs, feet slung over the side, and made no attempt to introduce her.

'Nope, you're the first to arrive,' Billy said before indicating the orange-clad girl. 'This is Casey, our new housemate.'

'What happened to Anya?'

Billy glared at Theo. '*He* happened to Anya.'

'What? She was hot.' Theo gave a shrug, as though his sleeping with their housemate couldn't have been prevented. Theo was notorious for sleeping around before losing interest in the girl, often practically at the point of climax. Like I said, he could be a bit of a knob.

'Let this be a lesson to you,' I said to Casey as I plonked myself down on the sofa. 'It's best to keep your distance from Theo.'

'Oh, don't worry about me.' Casey gave a dismissive wave and I noticed her fingernails were also orange. 'I know not to shit on my own doorstep.'

That was a good stance to take, in my opinion. I'd fallen foul of defecating too close to home myself in the past, and it wasn't something I'd recommend.

'Isn't Richard coming tonight?' Jared asked when Erin arrived on her own. He made the effort to come to these evenings for my sake, but he didn't feel entirely comfortable around my old housemates. Having Richard there made it a little easier for him.

'He can't. He has a meeting at the school.' Erin pulled a face. 'They're planning on scrapping the breakfast club. Ralphie doesn't even use the breakfast club, but Amanda has dragged Richard along for moral support.' Erin rolled her eyes. 'Supporting what? Amanda's need to be a pain in the arse?'

We all murmured our disapproval about Richard's ex-wife. As Erin's friends, it was our duty. Luckily, Erin had run out of steam (Amanda-bashing could take up an entire evening at times, depending on what Richard's ex had done) and she nabbed the last seat. It was only an old bean bag that pre-dated any of the housemates, but it was better than the floor, which was all that was available when Quinn arrived.

'My old bones are too rickety for the floor,' Erin said when Quinn tried to switch with her. 'You're a baby in comparison. You'll cope much better.'

'What is it with floors?' Casey asked, tucking her feet beneath her on the chair she'd been lucky enough to bag early. 'I used to lounge on the floor all the time when I was a kid but now I feel ancient, like my body can't possibly lift itself back up again.'

'Hey, you're only twenty-seven,' Billy said. 'Feeling ancient isn't allowed. Come back and say that when you're at least thirty.'

'Thirty is *so old*,' Casey said with a grin. Being almost thirty myself, I bristled, but Billy – who had already galloped through that milestone – grinned back at her.

Hmm, interesting. Was there a little bit of flirting going on here?

'But anyway,' Erin said as Quinn – the baby of the group at just twenty-two – lowered herself onto the rug. 'Let's have a catch up before the show starts. What's everyone else been up to?' Erin gave me a meaningful look and I started, realising it was time. Yes, the day had finally come. Jared and I would be announcing our engagement to our friends and then there would be nothing stopping me from yelling about it for the whole world to hear. Once the ring was placed on my finger tonight (it was back from the jewellers and could now sit snugly on my finger), there would be no taking it off and hiding it away ever again.

'Jared and I have an important announcement to make.' I left a suitable gap to create some all-important anticipation, my gaze shifting from each person in the room, including newcomer Casey. 'We're engaged!'

Quinn squealed and leaped to her feet – and quite sprightly too, despite being down on the floor. She threw her arms around me while Erin put on a convincing act of being totally shocked by the revelation.

'Have you set a date?' Quinn asked once she'd released me from her congratulatory death-grip.

'Not yet, but we're looking at venues at the weekend. We're thinking about next spring.' I grabbed my handbag and fished in my purse for the ring, which earned a round of gasps from the girls as I finally slipped it onto my finger permanently.

'What do you think?' I flashed the ring at Theo, who barely raised his eyes to look.

'Very nice. Are we watching this or what?' Theo pointed in the vague direction of the telly.

'Theo!' Quinn glared at him through moist eyes. 'Ruth and Jared are *engaged*. Don't you think that's more important than a bunch of fictional characters?'

Actually, as fictitious as Meg and Tom were, I was itching to know what was going on in their lives. Last week Tom had announced his own engagement to Parker, an annoying American woman who was – unbeknown to poor Tom – only after a UK visa. She didn't love Tom at all, but then Tom was obviously in love with Meg, even if he didn't realise it himself yet.

'We could always celebrate later. If everyone wants to watch, that is.' I looked around the room, gauging whether everyone was on board or thought I was a complete monster.

Quinn flopped back onto the rug when it became clear that everyone else was in agreement. 'Doesn't anyone have a romantic bone in their body around here?'

'Nobody is saying that TV is more important than my engagement.' Except Theo, perhaps. 'It's just that Tom and Parker are getting married too, so maybe I can pick up some tips from them.' Lord knows I needed some tips, from whoever was offering, whether they were real people or not.

'Hey, maybe you'll get married at the same time as Tom.' This idea seemed to cheer Quinn slightly and she grinned up at me.

'You'll have to hurry up,' Theo said. 'The season finale is in seven weeks and the wedding is bound to happen then. Of course Meg will stop the wedding right at the last minute and pledge undying love for her best friend.' He rolled his eyes at the predictability of it all, yet remained seated, waiting for it to start.

'Seven weeks?' I spluttered. 'I'll need way more than that to plan a whole wedding. I don't think even seven *months* would be enough.'

'It's funny, it feels like I've been hearing about it for a lot longer than seven months already.' Theo grabbed the remote and turned the volume up. 'Now shush and watch.'

'Are you okay with all of this?' The show had long finished and we were getting ready to leave. I'd taken the opportunity to pull Billy aside for a quick chat. 'You know, the engagement and everything?' I waggled my finger at him, enjoying the way the light caught the jewels on the ring.

'Yeah, of course I am. I'm happy for you.' Billy glanced over my shoulder before placing a hand on my arm. 'Jared is a good bloke and he makes you happy.'

'He does.' I couldn't help the grin from spreading across my face. 'And you've got Jane now.'

Billy screwed up his face. 'Actually no, I haven't. We

split up.'

'It wasn't because of …' I couldn't say the rest out loud, so simply waved a hand between Billy and myself. Billy's last two girlfriends had dumped him because he'd been in love with me. Talk about pooping on your own doorstep, eh? Still, that was a long time ago and Billy had assured me that his momentary lapse in sanity had been rectified.

'No, nothing like that. She was offered a job promotion that meant she had to move to St Helens. I know it isn't that far away, but our relationship was never that serious, so we've decided to just call it quits.'

'That's a shame. I liked Jane.' And Billy having a girlfriend helped to ease my guilt over Billy's unrequited crush.

'Yeah, she's great but she's just not for me.' Billy averted his gaze and his cheeks started to turn pink. 'Anyway, I've sort of got my eye on somebody else.'

I gasped, pouncing on the juicy bit of gossip. 'Who is it?'

Billy scratched the back of his neck, still unable to meet my eye. 'I don't want to say. I'm not sure they feel the same way.'

'It's Theo, isn't it? You've finally fallen for his charm.' My joke broke the strained atmosphere and Billy and I grinned at each other. 'Seriously, who is it? It's Casey, isn't it?'

Billy opened his mouth to speak but closed it again when he saw Jared approach.

'Are you ready?'

I nodded and grabbed my jacket. Pulling Billy into a farewell hug, I whispered that I would find out who she was, which made Billy blush again. Saying goodbye to the others, Jared and I made our way out to the car. My engagement ring glinted under a nearby streetlight as I reached for the door, so I stopped to admire it for a moment. Gazing at it would never grow old.

'Erin already knew about the engagement, didn't she?' Jared asked.

I gaped at Jared, preparing to give an affronted speech about trust, but then I thought, sod it. It would be no use lying. Jared knew me too well.

'Yeah, she knew.' I climbed into the car so that I didn't have to face Jared's reaction, but he simply chuckled to himself.

'I knew you couldn't keep it a secret.'

I stuck my tongue out at Jared as he climbed in beside me. 'I can't help it if I'm incredibly excited that I'm marrying the man I love. Aren't you excited too?'

'Of course I am.' Jared leaned across to kiss me. 'I can't wait to marry you.'

I gazed at my beautiful ring once more. I seriously couldn't keep my eyes away from it. 'We're going to live happily ever after, aren't we?'

'I'll make sure we do.'

TEN

Trina

Trina stretched out her foot, straining to catch a tiny ray of sunlight with her toe, but it seemed that would be a stretch too far.

'Darling.' Reaching out, Trina's fingers brushed against Rory's thigh. He snorted once before his regular snoring resumed. 'Darling.' Her tone sharper this time, Trina gave her husband a poke.

'Hmm?' Rory stretched his arms above his head, wincing at the pain the movement caused. He was still sunburned from the beach a few days earlier, his skin taut and pink.

'Do you think we could do something?'

'We are doing something, babe.' Rory flung his forearm over his eyes and stifled a yawn. 'We're relaxing.'

Relaxing. That's all Rory had done since their disastrous outing on the boat. Trina had been sympathetic to begin with. Rory's skin was so tight, and it had even started to blister in places, so any form of movement was agonising. She'd drawn him cool baths and applied after-sun creams with a gentle touch, and she hadn't even complained when Rory refused to leave the safety of their hotel room. But Trina's patience was wearing dangerously thin. It was their honeymoon and they were wasting their precious time together. Once they were home, normal life would resume and their time would be consumed with work and family commitments.

'But don't you want to go out?'

'We are out.' Rory's voice was already thick with sleep.

Technically, this was true. Rory had finally emerged from their hotel room but hadn't made it more than a foot away from the building. They hadn't even joined the other holidaymakers by the pool, and had instead dragged a couple of sun loungers to the safety of the shade under a huge tree. Rory had taken the precaution of wearing a pair of baggy jogging bottoms (they were two sizes too big but there hadn't been much choice in the hotel's gift shop) and a long-sleeved T-shirt with the hotel's logo emblazoned on the front. He wore a floppy hat and layer upon layer of factor fifty. He wasn't taking any chances.

'I meant, don't you want to go on excursions and things? Or even have a wander along the beach?'

Rory propped himself up on his sun lounger and glared at his wife. 'Are you kidding? Do you know how agonising sunburn is?'

Trina had a pretty good idea. Rory had been very vocal about the experience.

'But it's getting better now.' Rory's skin had started to peel, much like a snake shedding its skin. Bits of dried-up flesh wasn't what Trina had envisioned waking up to on her honeymoon, but it was what she'd been treated to so far. 'It doesn't seem to be causing you too many problems any more.'

'Well, that shows how much attention you pay.' Rory dropped back down onto his sun lounger. 'I happen to be in excruciating pain. Speaking of which, can you pass me the sun cream? It's time to reapply.'

'But you only put it on ten minutes ago.' And there wasn't much skin on display to slather the cream onto, anyway.

'Do you *want* me to burn again?' Rory's voice was so sharp it made Trina jump. 'Is that it? You actually *want* me to be in pain?'

'Of course not.' Trina picked up the factor fifty and handed it to her husband. 'I just don't think it's necessary yet.'

'Just like you didn't think it was necessary to remind me to top up last time.' Rory gave the bottle a violent squeeze, sending a jet of cream onto the palm of his hand. It was way too much for the three centimetres of uncovered skin. 'I'm not in any hurry to take your advice. Mother says I should stay out of the sun and that's what I intend to do.'

'Your mum? When did you speak to her?'

Rory slathered his face with the cream. 'On the day it happened, of course. You clearly didn't know what you were doing so I phoned Mother while you went in search of the after-sun cream.'

He'd phoned his mother? 'Oh.' Trina didn't know what else to say. She'd assumed – possibly naively – that he'd stopped running to his mother whenever he'd hurt himself years ago.

'She also said I should drink plenty of water.' Rory swapped the sun cream for a bottle of water, taking a lengthy gulp. 'And rest. Which is what I intend to do.' Rory placed the bottle of water on the little table he'd dragged over from the poolside and settled down once more. Defeated, Trina looked out towards the pool, which was bright and alive with the laughter of joyful holidaymakers. She longed to strip off her sarong and submerge herself in the water, basking in the glorious sunshine. If she spent any more time under that damn tree she was going to return home with a vitamin D deficiency.

'Rory, darling?'

'What now?'

Trina tore her eyes away from the pool. Should she ask? Yes, she should. This was her honeymoon too, and she should be able to enjoy it. 'Would you mind if I went for a little swim? I won't be far away and I'll only stay in the pool for a few minutes. I'll be back before you know it.'

Rory waved his hand. 'Do what you want. I'm going to have a sleep.'

'Are you sure?'

Trina's question was met by a snuffle, which she took as confirmation. Whipping off her sarong and flip-flops, Trina burst forth from the shade and joined the revellers. She wouldn't be long. Ten minutes, tops. Being on their honeymoon didn't mean that she and Rory had to spend every single second clamped together. There would be plenty of time to do romantic things together later.

ELEVEN

Ruth

'Have we got everything?' Jared paused in the doorway of the flat, patting his pockets to check he had his car keys. The pocket of his jeans made a reassuring jingle.

'I've got the list of venues.' I held up the notebook I'd purchased specifically. It had a pale pink cover made from the softest leather with a heart embossed on the front. So far it contained an extensive list of venues within the Greater Manchester area, whittled down to a shortlist of ten, plus a page dedicated to practice runs of my soon-to-be new name and signature. *Ruth Williams. R. Williams. Mrs Ruth Williams.*

'Where is it we're going first?' Jared asked as he started the engine.

I paused in my doodling of 'Jared's wife' in the practice run page of the notebook and consulted my list, though I knew it off by heart by now. I'd mapped out our itinerary for the day and had studied it seriously. 'Woodgate Registry Office. They're expecting us in twenty minutes so we'd better get going. I was speaking to my mum, and she said we had to be quick before everything gets booked up.'

'There's no rush though, is there?' Slowly, Jared pulled away from the kerb, as though demonstrating his relaxed state through the medium of his vehicle. 'Not if we're planning on next spring. That's still what you want, isn't it?'

'Yeah, spring will be lovely for a wedding. Why? Have you changed your mind?'

Jared made a noise somewhere between a laugh and a splutter. 'Of course I haven't changed my mind. You know I want to marry you.'

'I meant about spring.' Oh God. *Had* he changed his mind about the wedding? Did he want to postpone it? Or break it off completely? Perhaps he'd changed his mind about me in general. Oh God, he was going to dump me on the way to the registry office!

'Ruth, are you having an internal wobble?'

'Yes.' I could barely breathe. 'How can you tell?'
Wheeze, wheeze, wheeze.

'Just a hunch.' Jared smiled at me. 'You need to relax. We're going to get married and live happily ever after, remember. That's a good thing.'

It certainly was, if only I could put my wobbles aside. I'd have to ask Mum if it was normal for brides-to-be to regularly imagine they were being jilted. Jared had declined my offer of porridge that morning, saying he was fed up of the bumper pack we'd been working through. I took the normal, 'we've been eating porridge for days on end' reply to symbolise our relationship. I suddenly became the porridge in Jared's life that he was fed up of, and instantly panicked. I hadn't been able to eat the porridge either after that, and now I was starving. Why couldn't I put aside the idea that I wasn't good enough for Jared and enjoy these moments?

The registry office was a red-bricked Victorian structure

with steps leading up to a pretty columned porch decorated with large planters of early spring flowers, which would make a fantastic setting for photos.

'What do you think?' I asked as we climbed out of the car and gazed up at the building.

Jared nodded his head. 'It's lovely.'

'It's really nice, isn't it?' I dug my notebook and pen out of my bag and scribbled a few notes. 'Shall we go inside?'

We made our way up the steps, pulling open the heavy oak doors that were framed by hanging baskets. I imagined myself emerging from the building as Jared's wife, pausing for photos on the steps. The thought sent a delicious tingle up my spine. We were met in the reception area by a solid woman in a navy trouser suit, a clipboard tucked under one arm. She wore her glasses perched on top of her greying curls, and her red lipstick was a couple of shades too bright for her skin tone.

'I'm Barbara Vincent and I'll be giving you a tour of the building this afternoon.' Her voice was monotone, and she gave a heavy sigh as though she would rather be anywhere else in the world than greeting yet another loved-up couple. Opening the clipboard, she plucked out a handful of pamphlets and handed them to me. 'You should find everything you need in these, but if you have any questions, please ask.' She gave a nod and turned to the huge stone staircase behind us. 'Most of the rooms are upstairs, but if you'd like to take photos here, that would be fine. Confetti isn't allowed within the building, however.'

The wide staircase was flooded by natural light from the multitude of windows and it was quite pretty with a chunky, polished oak handrail entwined with foliage.

'It's lovely,' Jared said.

I nodded. 'Really nice.'

With another nod, Barbara led the way up the steps.

There were about a hundred of them and I was gasping for breath by the time we reached the first floor. That wouldn't be very romantic on the actual day. Perhaps I could have a little break once I reached the top to get my breath back in order to say my vows without sounding like Darth Vader.

'We have three differently sized rooms to choose from, priced accordingly. All costs are in the pamphlet.' Barbara nodded at the stack in my hand. 'How many guests are you expecting?'

Jared and I glanced at one another and gave small shrugs.

'We haven't really talked about it,' I admitted. 'But pretty small. Close friends and family, really.'

'You may be better with our Rose Suite.' Barbara paused in front of a door, turning to us before she swung it open. 'It's our middle-sized room and the most popular.' She swept into the room, and Jared and I followed.

'It's lovely,' Jared said, taking in the simple but perfectly acceptable room.

'Really nice.' What else could I say about a bland room filled with nothing but rows of red-cushioned seats and a heavy desk? Barbara stood against the back wall while Jared and I paced the room. She was hardly selling the place.

'We also have the Owen Suite, which I will show you in a moment. It's our more basic room and seats up to six people only. No exceptions.' Barbara swept out of the room and we scuttled behind her. 'Down in the basement we have our newly refurbished ballroom – the Lavender Suite – which seats up to two hundred guests. We can provide wedding packages with the Lavender Suite, which include a hot meal and a DJ. Have I given you the pamphlet for that?'

I fanned out the pamphlets, sure it was in there somewhere – I had about a million of the things.

'What do you think?' Barbara pushed open the door of the Owen Suite and led us inside.

'It's, um, lovely.' The room was little more than a broom cupboard, but Jared was too polite to say.

I squashed myself against the tiny desk so that Jared could get more than his toes over the threshold. 'Yeah, really nice.'

'But perhaps too small for us?' Jared backed out of the room, sucking in a glorious lungful of air now he was out in the open again.

'I'll take you down to the Lavender Suite so you can see what you think about that.' Barbara closed the door to the Owen Suite and led us back down the stone staircase in silence, the only sound the tapping of her heels. We made our way down a second staircase to the Lavender Suite, which was a large room with a bar set up in one corner and room for a DJ in another. The room could be set up for the ceremony before being transformed for the reception afterwards. The décor was simple but tasteful, and the colour scheme could be adapted to suit our needs.

'Whichever room you choose, you'll need to provisionally book and we can hold the date for up to fourteen days. Payment is required before a final booking can be made. You can book up to two years in advance. All the information is in the pamphlet.'

I scanned the pile in my hands, discovering one dedicated to the Lavender Suite. I took a quick glance but soon closed it when I spotted the price list.

Blimey. Had Will and Kate paid that much for their wedding?

'Do you have any questions?' Barbara looked relieved when we both shook our heads, and she happily led us back up to the exit.

'What did you think?' Jared asked once we were safely back in the car.

I popped the pamphlets between the pages of my

notebook. 'It was lovely. Really nice.'

'But not for us?'

'Not if Babs is going to perform the ceremony. She was a bit …' I struggled to find the words to describe our tour guide.

'Dull? Miserable? Couldn't be less happy in her job if she tried?'

I caught Jared's eye and couldn't help the corners of my lips twitching. 'I was going to say lovely. Really nice.'

Next up was Westbridge Golf Club. From the research I'd already done, I knew, the wedding packages would be a little pricey, but I was sure it would be worth it as we drove along a long, tree-lined road to the main building.

'Hi there. You must be Jared and Ruth?' A young woman in smart black trousers and a white blouse bounced towards us, her long blonde ponytail swishing. 'I'm Cerys. It's so lovely to meet you.' Cerys held out her hand, shaking Jared's hand and then mine before she led us inside, chatting as she went. We were led into the breakfast room, which was bright and airy, the tables set with white tablecloths and white chair covers. 'If you have a particular colour scheme, just let us know beforehand and we can accommodate that for you.' I opened my notebook and added 'colour scheme?' to my long to-do list. 'We have several options for breakfast. All menus should be finalised at least six weeks before the big day. Did you have a date in mind?'

'We were thinking next spring,' I replied.

'Lovely. The grounds are absolutely beautiful during the spring.' Cerys led us further into the room, pointing out the little details, such as the choice of candles for the tables and flower arrangements. We followed Cerys out of the breakfast room and into a long, narrow room lined with chairs. At the end of the room was a table wrapped in a white tablecloth and tied with a green bow to match the chairs. It looked like a giant present.

'Again, the colour scheme can be changed to suit your needs. We're fully licensed to carry out civil marriages and afterwards you'll be permitted full use of the Darlington Suite until midnight. Shall I take you through?'

The Darlington Suite was a large function room, fully equipped with a bar and a little stage that could accommodate a DJ or band.

'There are a few catering options, but the finger buffet is particularly popular,' Cerys told us as we wandered around the room. 'I'll give you a wedding pack with all the information on the way out, but if you have any questions, please do get in touch.'

In the car, Jared and I discussed the golf club. We both really liked the venue, but couldn't deny it was a little out of our price range, which was a shame.

I consulted our itinerary. We had just over an hour before we were due at our next venue. 'Shall we stop for some lunch before we go to the next one?' My stomach grumbled loudly, angry at the lack of porridge that morning.

'Sure. Where are we off to next?'

'Burton Inn. It's a hotel and restaurant. The website looks fantastic.' I had a good feeling about Burton Inn. 'I think this one could be it.'

TWELVE

Ruth

Burton Inn was not it. The building was small and shabby with peeling paintwork, crumbling plaster and threadbare carpets. One room had a suspicious yellow stain in one corner that I tried not to focus on. I wouldn't have been at all surprised to learn the inn was rat-infested by the state of the dining room – if two tables squeezed into a large walk-in cupboard could be described as a dining room at all. There were crumbs all over the floor and a half-eaten bowl of cornflakes congealing on one of the tables, despite it now being after lunchtime. It looked like it should be featured on *The Hotel Inspector*.

The landlord and so-called hotelier wasn't much better than his establishment. He was greasy-haired and wearing a pair of tatty jeans and a T-shirt that had seen better days and his grey pallor and dark-rimmed eyes didn't instil confidence that he would prove to be a good host. He couldn't have been less interested in our big day if he'd tried. He shuffled around his dirty premises in a pair of holey slippers, not bothering to introduce himself beforehand, mumbling about fees and bar tabs, pausing every now and then to scratch his arse or crotch.

'That's about it. Let us know then, yeah?' Tour finished, the landlord – we still didn't know his name – stuck out his hand for Jared to shake. Having seen the man's fingers wedged up his crack and shuffling around his bollocks, Jared flinched away and we scurried back to the car.

The next venue was more promising (let's face it, it couldn't have been much worse than Burton Inn). The Bridgewater was a sizeable hotel in town and, while it wasn't quite high-end, it was clean with friendly, approachable staff. The price per head was a little steep, but if it was a choice between Ratsville Hotel and this, we'd just have to tighten our belts a bit.

'We aren't licensed to hold wedding ceremonies,' the manager – Geoffrey, who was freshly shaven and didn't scratch himself at intervals – told us. 'So you would have to find a separate venue for the actual wedding.'

'That's fine,' Jared said as I scribbled down some notes. We had a few churches to see that afternoon, and there was always the registry office, which didn't seem quite so bland after witnessing the horrors of Ratsville. 'We'll be in touch to book when we have a date.'

Jared and I made our way out of the hotel and climbed into the car.

'What did you think?' I asked as I pulled the seatbelt across my chest.

'It was great. Much better than Burton Inn.'

'*So* much better than Burton Inn.' I gave a sigh of relief, happy that we'd actually found somewhere half-decent and pretty much affordable. 'It's a bit expensive, but doable, right?'

Jared nodded. 'I think so. We'll have to cut back and save as much as we can, though.'

'It'll be worth it.' I clapped my hands, unable to keep the grin from my face. 'Is that it, then? Have we found our venue?'

'I think so.' Jared started the engine. 'But first we have to find somewhere to become husband and wife. Where to next?'

We visited a church that wasn't too bad. It was clean enough, but it wasn't very pretty, and it was a bit cold and damp inside. Plus, the vicar had a whiff of cheese and onion crisps about him. I have nothing against cheese and onion crisps – it's a fine flavour – but I didn't want the smell lingering over me as I took my vows.

But the second church was perfect. The building was quite imposing: it was large and built in a gothic style, but it had lots of pretty arched windows and a set of huge, heavy wooden doors that I could picture myself walking through to become Mrs Williams. The churchyard consisted of well-maintained lawns with tall oak trees and smaller silver birches that would make the perfect setting for photos. There were stone steps at the churchyard's entrance, which led to a pretty wooden lych-gate that would also make a beautiful setting for photos. I could picture us as newlyweds, standing underneath the arch, our guests in the background.

'First impressions?' Jared asked as we made our way towards the heavy doors.

'I adore it.'

This was it, I was sure. I had such a good feeling about this church and knew this would be the place where we took our vows. The feeling intensified when we stepped inside. The interior of the church was just as impressive, and was warm with lots of natural light flooding in from the arched windows. The pews were beautifully polished and I could picture them packed with our loved ones.

'Hi there,' a booming voice called out. A short, round man strode towards us, giving a cheery wave. 'I'm Father

Edmund, but please call me Eddie. Everybody does. Apart from my mother, who always insisted on using my full name. She said if she wanted a son called Eddie, she'd have put that on the birth certificate. But she's dead now, so don't worry about offending the old girl.' Father Edmund chuckled before sticking his hand out for us to shake.

'I'm Jared.'

Father Edmund pumped Jared's hand before turning to me, almost crushing my hand with his enthusiasm.

'And I'm Ruth.'

'Do you prefer Ruth or Roo?' He winked at me before leading the way to a room at the back of the church that was furnished with fat sofas and worn, but cosy, scatter cushions. 'Would you like some tea? Coffee, perhaps?'

'Coffee would be good, thanks.' I sank into one of the sofas and it almost swallowed me whole.

'I'll go and put the kettle on and then we can have a chat.' Father Edmund left us, whistling a merry tune. He returned a few minutes later with a tray laden with tea and coffee and a whole packet of chocolate hobnobs.

I liked this man.

'I usually have a lady to help with this kind of thing, but I sent her home early. She's useful, Mrs March, but she does go on a bit at times. I wasn't in the mood for hearing about her rheumatic knee today, so I sent her home to rest it. She wanted to stay, of course, being a bit of a martyr, but I insisted.' Father Edmund set the tray down on the coffee table and threw himself onto the opposite sofa, flinging one leg over to rest on his knee. 'So then. You want to get spliced?'

'Yes.' I grasped Jared's hand and he gave mine a reassuring squeeze. 'And we'd love to get married here.'

'And why not? It's such a beautiful building.' Father Edmund reached for the packet of biscuits and tore it open. 'We'll go through all the boring facts and figures later, but did you have a date in mind?' He slid a biscuit out of the packet and bit off a chunk, wafting away the crumbs that fell onto his chest.

'We were thinking about next spring,' I said. We were edging towards the end of February, so we'd have just over a year to prepare.

'How lovely!' Father Edmund returned the packet of biscuits to the tray. 'Do help yourself. I'll only eat them all if you don't. They're my favourite.' He chuckled to himself while reaching for an iPad on a little desk to his left. He opened an app, sliding his finger across the screen. 'Bear with me. I'm not so good with all this techno gubbins, but you have to move with the times, don't you? Mrs March says it's unchristian, so I gently remind her who the boss is around here. And I'm not talking about the big guy upstairs.' Father Edmund chuckled to himself again as he continued to swipe his finger across the screen. 'Oh. Oh dear.' Father Edmund paused and looked up at us. 'There don't appear to be any dates available for next spring.' He slid his finger across the screen a few more times and gave a sad shake of his head. 'Or even next summer.'

'What about winter?' Winter could work. I could wear a thick red shawl and weave holly and ivy through my hair and bouquet. A festive wedding sounded lovely, actually. I should have thought about it earlier.

'Nope, nothing for winter either, I'm afraid.' Father Edmund slid the packet of biscuits across the tray towards me, and I took one. It would be rude not to. 'We're quite popular, you know. Ah, here we go. The next available slot is in June.'

'*This* June?' Panic made me spray biscuit crumbs, but we all pretended we hadn't noticed. 'But that's only four months away.' We couldn't arrange a wedding that quickly, could we?

Father Edmund chuckled. 'Of course not *this* June.'

'Next June?' Father Edmund shook his head and I

reached for another biscuit. 'The June after that? But that's almost two and a half years away.' A lifetime, practically. We couldn't wait that long. What if Jared realised he could do so much better than me in the meantime and called the whole thing off? 'Aren't there any closer dates?'

Father Edmund returned the iPad to the desk and clasped his hands together on his lap. 'I'm afraid not. Why don't you think about it for a few days and give me a call if you'd like to book?'

I really wanted to get married at St John's, but I didn't want to wait so long. Disappointment made me want to cry. Instead, I reached again for the packet of chocolate hobnobs.

THIRTEEN

Ruth

Jared slipped his hand into mine as we left St John's, and gave it a little squeeze. 'Should we go and see the next church? They might have a closer date.'

I shrugged. My heart was no longer in the search for our wedding venue. I'd practically skipped into the church, but I could barely manage a shuffle on the way out. And it wasn't just because I'd stuffed myself with consoling biscuits.

'You really wanted this one, didn't you?'

I nodded, emitting a sad little sigh. 'It's perfect. What did you think?'

'I liked it, particularly Father Edmund.'

'Eddie.' I managed my first smile since we'd discovered the hefty waiting list. I'd wolfed down four chocolate hobnobs, but they hadn't made me feel any better about the situation. The next four hadn't either. 'I liked him too, but two and a half years is a long time to wait.'

'You could look at it like that.' As we reached the car park, Jared held up his key fob to unlock the car. 'Or we could see it as a blessing.'

Panic began to rise up in my chest. What was Jared saying? That he didn't want to marry me after all, and this was his perfect get-out excuse?

'Stop wobbling, Ruth. I'm not trying to get out of marrying you, you big dope.' Jared knew me so well. 'All I'm saying is that we could use that time to save up even more money for the wedding. We could get married here and have the reception at the golf club without worrying about the price tag.'

I hadn't thought of it like that, but Jared was right. We *could* see this as a blessing. It would give us plenty of time to plan the wedding, meaning I wouldn't have to panic every time I glanced at my ever-expanding to-do list, and the extra time for saving would certainly come in handy. Maybe we'd even manage to scrape together some extra cash for a luxurious honeymoon, like Trina and Rory had done.

'Let's do it.' I turned away from the car and started skipping back up towards the church. 'Let's book it right now.'

Father Edmund was surprised to see us again so soon. He brushed the hobnob crumbs from his clothes as he led us back into the cosy little room. The packet of biscuits was almost empty.

'We'd like to take that booking,' Jared said once we were all seated again.

'Jolly good.' Father Edmund's face lit up and he shook our hands in turn. 'I enjoy nothing more than seeing a young couple in love. Let's get this thing booked then, shall we?'

I felt much lighter as we emerged from the church again. We now had a little more time, and the pressure had been taken off us, so I could truly enjoy the experience of planning our wedding. I couldn't wait to tell everyone that we'd set a date, even if it was three million years in the future. We phoned our parents first, who were obviously thrilled. Mum insisted we pop over for a celebratory roast lunch the following day, and who was I to say no?

I thought Mum had been going a bit over the top whenever she moaned about Dad's caravan – it was a hobby for him, and better than chasing after busty women or buggering off to the pub every night, right? – until I clapped eyes on the monstrosity myself. 'Rusty' and 'run-down' didn't even begin to describe the caravan that sat on Mum and Dad's front lawn, ruining the grass and flowerbeds. The once white paint was bubbled and peeling, revealing orange rust and holes in the panels. The body was covered in layers of grime, and a grubby old net curtain flapped about in the breeze where a window had once been. The house prices of the entire street must have plummeted upon the arrival of this *thing*.

'I'm so sorry.' I flung myself into Mum's arms as soon as she opened the door. 'I didn't know.'

'What is it, love?' Mum pulled away, worry etched onto her face. 'What's happened?'

'*That* happened.' I turned and pointed at the caravan. 'It's horrific. I thought you were being a miserable, moany old cow about it all, but you weren't. It's disgusting. Does he really think he can make it into a gym?'

Mum rolled her eyes as she ushered us inside. 'He really does, the daft old sod. He won't be told. He's even started bidding on gym equipment online. Where he's going to put it in the meantime, I don't know. I've told him he's not cluttering up my dining room with it.' Mum shook her head. 'Hello, Jared, love. I bet you're wondering what you're marrying into, aren't you?'

Mum deposited us in the sitting room while she popped into the kitchen to check on lunch and to put the kettle on. Dad was hunched over his laptop, eagerly watching the last few minutes of a treadmill auction on eBay.

I plonked myself on the arm of Dad's chair. 'You're not seriously buying a treadmill, are you?'

'Of course I am. This beauty's a bargain. Hold on a second.' Dad suddenly became animated, clicking and tapping away. 'You have to wait until the very last second, you see. That way you get the best price. Drat! I've been outbid.' Dad squinted at the screen. 'By less than a bloody quid!' Shaking his head, Dad snapped the lid of the laptop closed and put it down on the coffee table. 'That's the third time that's happened this week.'

'It's the third blessing this week,' Mum called from the kitchen. Dad grunted in response.

'Maybe you should finish the caravan before you start buying equipment.' Or maybe even make a start on the project. From the look of it, he hadn't touched it yet.

'You sound just like your mother.' Dad folded his arms across his chest like a petulant child. 'She doesn't believe I can pull it off. Says it's an eyesore.'

Mum had a point there, but I kept my gob shut. Dad was still smarting from his loss, and there was no need to kick him while he was down.

'She wants me to get rid of it. Wants me to take it to a bloody scrapyard!'

'Enough about that blasted caravan.' Mum joined us with a tea tray. 'Let's hear the latest on the wedding. What's the church like?'

'It's gorgeous, Mum.' I gave a dreamy sigh as I remembered. 'It's a shame we have to wait two and a half years, though.'

Mum smiled at me, not worried by the timescale at all. 'It'll pass quickly enough, trust me.'

'You don't have to wait, you know.' Dad shifted the laptop over so Mum could place the tray on the table.

'Why don't I forget the gym for now?'

'Hallelujah!' Mum couldn't have looked more pleased. I'd never seen her grin so wide, and her hands were thrown up in the air.

'I said *for now*.' Dad turned from Mum to me, so that his shoulder completely blocked Mum from his view. 'As I was saying, I could forget the gym *for now* and turn the caravan into a cosy little chapel. I'm sure you can get licences for this kind of thing.'

Taking both of Dad's hands in mine, I hoped to convey how much his gesture meant to me. 'That's very sweet of you, Dad, really. But I couldn't possibly accept.'

'I don't mind, love. I can always do up the caravan as a gym later.'

I smiled at Dad while I figured out how to phrase my reply. 'It's not that. I can't accept it because – and no offence is meant here, none at all – that caravan out there is a pile of crap.'

Mum gave a hoot while Dad's face fell, making me feel bad. 'I'm sure one day it'll be … not so crap, but I've set my heart on St John's. It's such a lovely church, and I have a good feeling about it. It's where I want to start my married life – and, anyway, it gives us more time to save.'

Dad puffed out his chest. 'You don't have to worry about money, love. That's what me and your mum are here for. It's tradition.'

'It's a tradition I don't believe in.' This was something I felt very strongly about. 'Jared and I will be paying for our own wedding.'

'Can't we help out a little?'

I gave Dad's hand a pat. 'It would really help if you could come up with an excuse not to invite Aunty Pat.'

Dad's sister-in-law was not a pleasant woman. She thrived on putting people down, leaving a path of misery behind her wherever she went.

'If we knew how to get rid of the woman, we'd have

done it a long time ago.' Mum gave a sniff and patted her hair. 'She told me I was going grey the other day. I mean, I know I am, I do own a mirror, but there was no need to point it out. I was hoping to grow old gracefully, but I can't cope with Pat's jibes so I've booked an appointment to have it coloured.' Mum picked up her cup from the tray and blew on her tea. 'But enough about that old crow. How are the rest of the wedding plans coming along?'

'Not that well. I'm finding the whole process overwhelming, but there's loads of time so it'll all come together.'

'Oh no, no, no.' Mum shook her head with vigour. 'Weddings don't simply come together. They take a lot of hard work. Why don't you go and see Trina when she comes back from her honeymoon? They'll be back by next weekend. I'm sure she'll give you some pointers.'

'Isn't it a bit soon? Shouldn't I give them a bit of space to, you know, do what married people do?'

'Argue about the wet towels on the bathroom floor?' Dad asked.

Jared laughed. 'Or about whose turn it is to do the washing up?'

'That one's easy,' Dad said. 'It's always my bloody turn.'

Mum and I glared at the men, not finding their little quips amusing or helpful. Eventually Dad and Jared admitted defeat and dropped their eyes to the carpet, their mouths firmly shut.

'It's never too soon to go and see a new bride,' Mum said. 'Trina will be thrilled to be able to relive the wedding. Talking about her big day will be almost as good as the actual wedding. Better, even, without all the stress.' Mum caught my eye and gave an awkward laugh. 'Not that it's *very* stressful.'

No, of course it's not.

FOURTEEN

Trina

The *fasten seatbelt* sign pinged, earning a sigh of relief from Trina. She couldn't wait to land, to pick up her luggage (okay, maybe she wasn't looking forward to *that* part so much) and go home. She was exhausted – and not just because of the travelling. The last few days of her honeymoon had been action-packed, with snorkelling (and this time it wasn't an ill-fated trip), boat rides to see dolphins, walks along the beach and swimming in the beautiful, clear sea. Trina had been windsurfing, quad biking and had attempted to learn to surf. Her body ached, but she'd had such a fantastic time that it was more than worth it. Who would have thought that her honeymoon would turn out to be quite so fabulous?

She fastened her seatbelt before giving Rory a dig in the ribs. His snore turned into a snuffle but he didn't stir. Trina tried again.

'Ow. What's your problem?' Rory glared at Trina through one open eye. The other remained closed, ready to drop back to sleep.

'Seatbelt.' She pointed at the lit-up sign above them. 'We'll be landing soon.'

Rory grunted. He fastened his seatbelt before settling back down again. He was snoring again within seconds.

Yes, Trina's honeymoon had been fabulous. It was a pity that Rory hadn't been part of it, though. He'd spent their honeymoon dozing beneath a tree with his factor fifty and bottled water. His sunburn had faded, but Rory was still determined to snooze their honeymoon away. So Trina had taken matters into her own hands and left him in the shade. Literally. She'd had a wonderful time, but now she needed a good cup of tea and time to recuperate.

'Thank you for flying with us. Have a good day.'

Trina shuffled off the plane, nodding in acknowledgement to the cabin crew. Rory strode ahead of her, more awake than he'd been since they'd taken off from England. He was fiddling with his phone, eager to catch up with the work he'd missed while they were on honeymoon.

'Can't that wait?' Trina cantered after him, dragging her small wheeled suitcase behind her. 'I'm sure they'll cope without you until tomorrow.'

Rory shot her a withering look. 'I've missed out on far too much already. I'd been hoping to keep up to date while we were away, but the Wi-Fi at the hotel was terrible. My Trip Advisor rating will reflect that.'

'We haven't even picked up our luggage yet,' Trina gasped as she galloped along next to her husband. 'I thought we could spend a bit of time together before you started back at work.'

'We've spent plenty of time together. What do you think the honeymoon was for?'

Trina honestly didn't know. She'd been hoping it would be romantic and passion-filled, but it had seemed that Rory only felt passionately about sleep. They'd eaten breakfast together before going their separate ways, Rory to his shade and Trina to whatever activity she fancied. They'd only met up again in the evenings to eat in the hotel's restaurant. Rory had spent more time with his sun lotion than he had with her.

'Can we at least slow down?' Trina stopped, grabbing her side as a stitch took hold. A couple grumbled as they were forced to go around her. 'Rory, wait!'

Rory turned with a heavy sigh. 'Come on, babe. Don't you want to go home?'

Trina did. Very much. Today would be the real start of their married life as they set up home in the Hamilton-Wraiths' annex. The honeymoon had been a practice – however unsuccessful – but now their lives together could truly begin.

Trina set off again, trundling after Rory as he made his way to baggage claim. With their suitcases loaded on a trolley, they made their way to the exit. Trina turned to head for the taxi rank while Rory veered the other way. All became clear as Carrington flew towards her brother, flinging her arms around him.

'Welcome home!' Carrington released her brother and held him at arm's length. 'Look at you. Where's your tan? Don't tell me you spent the whole time in bed!' Carrington placed a hand on her hip, observing Rory with mock indignation. 'Come along. Ginny's waiting in the car.'

At no point did Carrington address, or even glance at, Trina. She didn't comment on her tan (which Trina actually had. She was golden and glowing) or offer any sort of welcome. Turning with a swish of her sleek ponytail, Carrington marched off towards the exit.

'I didn't know Carrington was picking us up,' Trina whispered as they scurried after her. She was smarting after being snubbed by her sister-in-law, but she knew better than to bring it up in front of Rory. He was fiercely protective of his younger sister and Trina knew she wouldn't come out on top should she push it.

'Mother arranged it.' Rory attempted to manoeuvre the luggage trolley while checking his phone, growling with frustration when it proved unsuccessful. 'She didn't want us taking a cab.'

Gosh, no. Winnie wouldn't want her son slumming it, thought Trina.

They made their way across the car park, where Carrington's car waited to transport them to their new, temporary home. She slipped onto the cool leather seat while Rory and Trina lugged the suitcases into the boot.

'Congratulations! I'm *so* sorry I couldn't make the wedding.' Carrington's best friend Ginny greeted them from the passenger seat as they climbed into the back of the car. Ginny had known Carrington – and therefore Rory – since prep school, and was a familiar face at the Hamilton-Wraiths' house. 'I was called away to the Sydney office at the last minute and only arrived back yesterday. I hear it was a lovely day, though. Carrie says you looked very handsome.'

'Doesn't he always?' Carrington checked her reflection in the mirror, swiping an imaginary smudge of lipstick from the corner of her mouth. 'He has Daddy's genes.'

'Winnie showed me your photos. You looked radiant, Trina.'

Ginny's compliment washed over Trina. 'Winnie has our photos?'

'Yes, wasn't that quick?' Carrington started the engine and pulled smoothly out of the parking spot. 'We were surprised too.'

'But *we* were supposed to pick them up.' And how dare Winnie look at them first! And show them to other people? Who else had seen her wedding photos before Trina?

'Oh, Mother doesn't mind. It was no trouble.' Carrington flashed a reassuring smile through the mirror. 'She sent Mrs Timmons.'

The *housekeeper* had picked her photos up from the photographer? Had *she* had a good look at them too?

'How very thoughtful.' Rory gave Trina's hand a squeeze. 'That's one less job for us to do.'

Trina's eyes filled with tears. Rory made it sound like a chore, but she'd been looking forward to picking up the photos. She'd planned a whole day around it. First, she and Rory would go somewhere nice for lunch before they picked them up from the photographer. Then they would go home and pore over them together, taking time to study them and remember their day. She'd bought a gorgeous album for them, and she'd been looking forward to choosing their favourites for the oversized frame they'd hang in the hall.

But that special day had been snatched away from her.

'Mother says you're to have supper with us tonight,' Carrington informed them. 'She didn't think Trina would be in the mood for cooking after the flight. Mrs Timmons has left some sliced ham in the fridge and stocked up your cupboards in case you get hungry before then.'

But Rory had already switched off from the conversation and was tapping away at his phone.

'That's very nice of Mrs Timmons,' Trina said.

'She's such a doll.' Carrington swung out of the car park and drove Trina and Rory home to start their married life.

FIFTEEN

Ruth

My cousin Trina and her new husband Rory were starting their married life in the annex of Rory's parents' property. They hadn't lived together before the wedding, so the annex was a temporary measure until they found their dream house. Now, I know what you're thinking – or at least what *I* was thinking. Annexes – or granny flats – are little single-storey buildings tacked on to the side of a house. They're quite dainty but contain everything the occupant or visitor may need.

Trina and Rory did not live in any sort of annex I had imagined. Far from it.

'Did you find us all right?' Trina asked. 'Those country lanes can be a bit tricky.'

Tricky was an understatement. The bus had dumped me in a little nearby village and I'd had to navigate my way along the roads (some of which were little more than dirt tracks) until I found the Hamilton-Wraiths' property tucked away behind an orchard.

'I would have picked you up in the village, but

Carrington's car is in for a service and Rory said she could borrow mine.' Trina led me along the hallway towards her sitting room. The hallway was wide, with an oak staircase leading to the upper floor. Four doors led off the hallway – the kitchen, dining room, sitting room and downstairs loo. Yes, Trina's 'annex' was better equipped than my flat – and the downstairs alone was quadruple the size.

'Come on through.' Trina led me into the sitting room, and I stared at it in awe. The room was light and airy, with French doors leading out to a decked area and garden beyond. The garden stretched so far into the distance, I wasn't sure where it ended and the countryside began. 'Can I get you something to drink? Diet coke? Tea? We did have some champagne left over from the wedding but Rory's sister and her friend polished it off.'

'Diet coke will be fine, thank you.'

The so-called annex was so grand, I assumed Trina would summon a butler to fetch the requested drinks, but it was Trina herself who toddled off to the kitchen. I sat on one of the sofas – there were three set around the fireplace – and took in my surroundings. I suppose this was quite normal for Trina. Aunt Gloria had accumulated quite a lot of money through her several marriages and divorces, so Trina was used to the finer things in life. Not that Trina was a snob. Unlike her older sister, Tori. Trina had always been sweet and down to earth, and I'd loved spending time with her when we were younger. Since I was eight years older than Trina, she'd looked up to me, trusted me, and basically thought that I was the bee's knees, which was a nice feeling. I'd take Trina (and Tori, if I really had to) to the local playground whenever they visited, or we'd hang out in my bedroom, listening to music and giggling. I didn't have a lot of friends growing up, so I liked having Trina around, even if she was just a little kid. We didn't see a lot of each other once she went away to boarding school, so it was a relief to see she was still the same Trina

I'd known and loved whenever we did meet up again.

'I'm so glad you've come to see me.' Trina joined me on the sofa, placing two cans of diet coke on the coffee table before pulling a MacBook onto her lap, pulling her bare feet under her skinny-jean-clad bottom. 'I was thrilled when Mum phoned to tell me you were engaged. I'm so happy for you, Ruth. You'll love getting married. It's the best!' Trina opened the MacBook. Her wedding photos were already set up, the slideshow ready to begin with the tap of a finger. 'You'll be the first person in my family to see these photos.'

'Haven't Aunt Gloria and Tori been round to see them yet?'

'Ha! As if!' Trina gave a little giggle, but I couldn't help feeling sorry for her. I knew for a fact that we wouldn't be able to stop Mum visiting as soon as Jared and I were back from our honeymoon. She'd probably be waiting on the doorstep for our arrival. 'Mum's on a Caribbean cruise with potential ex-husband number six and Tori's sulking. She thinks, as the older sister, she should have married first.'

I sort of understood Tori's point. I'd been more than a little peeved that my younger cousin was getting hitched before me.

'Tori hasn't even got a boyfriend, never mind a fiancé. Was I supposed to wait forever?' Trina shook her head, her wavy blonde hair flapping around like a shampoo commercial. Her hair had turned almost white in the sun and her skin was a lovely golden colour.

Trina tapped at the MacBook and the slideshow began. 'These photos are a mix of the professional photos we had taken and family snaps.' The first photo was obviously taken very early in the morning of Trina's wedding, judging by her groggy eyes and unruly hair as she emerged from her bedroom.

'I meant to take that one out. Tori took it just to be

cruel. Oh! Here's Aidan working his magic.' Trina's hairdresser friend was pinning her hair and they were laughing about something, eyes crinkled and mouths wide, completely uninhibited. I found my own mouth stretching into a smile, the joy they felt at the time spreading all these weeks later. 'He really is great. How he managed to turn that bedhead into such a stylish do I'll never know.'

'Have you known Aidan long?' The photo changed to one of Trina and Aidan toasting the successful hair-do with champagne.

'He's been my stylist since I was sixteen. I was his very first paying client. Somewhere along the way, we became friends. He's such a sweetheart.'

The slideshow continued, telling the story of Trina's big day, from a sumptuous breakfast to the beautiful ceremony and ensuing celebrations. The slideshow then moved on to Trina and Rory's honeymoon.

'It looks gorgeous.' I took a sip of coke as I watched one photo morph artistically into the next. 'But you and Rory don't appear to be in many photos together.' I'd counted two so far: a selfie taken at the airport on the way out and another as they prepared to come home again.

'Rory didn't venture out of the hotel much. He said it was too hot so he spent most of the day under the shade of a tree with his book. I did a lot of sightseeing, though, and I met some really interesting people.'

Mostly young, bronze-skinned men with sculpted bodies, judging by the photos.

'Are you looking forward to your big day?' Slideshow over, Trina closed the MacBook and placed it on the antique coffee table in front of us. 'You're going to make such a stunning bride. You've got such a pretty face and excellent style.'

I suspected Trina had been hitting the champagne a bit too hard since the wedding and impaired her judgement. 'I'm not sure about that, but I am looking forward to the wedding. There's so much to do, though, and I haven't even scratched the surface yet.'

Trina placed a hand on my arm. 'I completely understand. I'm lucky that I had a super-efficient wedding planner, but even then everything seemed to take forever. The waiting list for Durban Castle is at least five years, but luckily Mum had connections.' Did she have any connections with St John's church in Woodgate, by any chance? 'I'm so grateful Winnie hired the wedding planner for us. I wasn't too keen at first – Troy and Winnie completely took over and made most of the decisions for us – but they did put a lot of work into it.'

'I don't think a wedding planner is quite within our budget.' It would take more than a two-and-a-half-year engagement to save up for such an extravagance.

'I still have the file from my wedding if you want to borrow it. It has all the notes and plans Troy made.'

'That would be wonderful, thank you.'

Trina beamed at me before she hopped off the sofa. She left the room, returning a few minutes later with the file. It did nothing to ease my qualms at all. Rather than the slim manila file I was expecting, it was in fact a huge lever arch file stuffed to the gills. How was I supposed to sift through all of that and create a wedding of my own? I don't say this very often, but Mum had been right; the two and a half years to wait didn't seem sufficient all of a sudden.

'Thanks for this. I really appreciate it. Oof.' Trina dropped the file onto my lap and I was sure I heard something crack. It'd be a trip to A&E I'd require, not the church, at this rate.

'It's no problem at all. Keep it for as long as you need.' Trina giggled. 'I certainly won't need it again. Unlike Mum, I only plan on getting married once.'

I opened the file and had a quick scan through the first couple of pages. There was so much to take in. 'Do you have any advice?'

Trina toyed with her sun-lightened hair as she mulled over the question. 'Go to as many wedding fairs as you can. There's so much on show under one roof and you can make loads of useful contacts. I was really looking forward to going to some, but Troy already knew everything so I didn't need to.' Trina looked momentarily glum but soon brightened. 'But choosing a dress is so much fun! You'll feel like a princess, I swear.'

I struggled to my feet with the hefty file. How was I going to lug this home on the bus? 'I should be getting home. But thank you, Trina.'

'You're welcome. Come and see me any time. Rory works so much, it gets quite lonely out here at times.' I pulled my cousin into a hug, promising I'd see her soon, before I dragged myself (and the file) back through to the village and onto the three buses that would take me back to the flat, which now seemed tiny and inadequate after I'd spent the afternoon in the annex.

SIXTEEN

Erin

It always amazed Erin every time she stepped into her boyfriend's parents' house. Not because it was huge and flashy (which it was), but because the house belonged to Kelvin Shuttleworth, the general manager of H. Wood Vehicles. If you'd told her a few years ago that she'd be spending her Saturday afternoons at the Big Boss Man's house, she'd have laughed in your face. Mind you, she would have laughed her socks off if you'd told her she'd end up with the Big Boss Man's son too. As much as she loved Richard, there was no denying that he wasn't her usual type. Erin didn't normally go for straight-laced ginger men with stalker-ish tendencies, but life was funny like that.

And Richard wasn't really stalker-ish. He simply had fabulous taste in women and a stubborn streak. As Erin's manager in the sales and marketing department of H. Woods, Richard had chased her relentlessly until she eventually caved in and agreed to a date. Inexplicably, she'd then agreed to another date, and another, until eventually she found herself at the Shuttleworths' home to discuss wedding plans. Yet again. It seemed as if they'd gathered in Susan and Kelvin's dining room every weekend since Lindsay had announced her engagement. The dining room, though quite large, was packed with wedding participants, with most of them standing as the chairs had all been taken by Lindsay and her parents, the groom's parents and Susan's sister (who wasn't even part of the wedding party but had invited herself along anyway to be nosy). Ingrid, the wedding planner, had been offered a seat, but she'd declined. Probably because she didn't feel quite so powerful and able to lord it over the others while seated.

'I've set up a meeting with the photographer for Wednesday at seven o'clock. Frank will make *that* meeting, won't he?' Ingrid cast a severe glance in Lindsay's direction, who cowered slightly under her glare. Ingrid wasn't pleased that the groom had missed a 'crucial' meeting, while Erin thought what a lucky bastard he was to have given it a swerve. As well as Erin and Richard and the bride and groom's parents (plus Richard's nosy aunt Diane), the other seven bridesmaids and groomsmen had been summoned by Ingrid, who was holding court in the Shuttleworths' dining room, clipboard in hand, while she barked out her orders. As Lindsay and Frank's wedding drew closer, Ingrid's voice became harsher. Right now, with a month to go, she was at Drill Sergeant level – who knew where she'd end up by the big day? Somebody ought to slip the woman some Strepsils or something.

'I'm not sure.' Lindsay's voice was low and her eyes darted everywhere, not wanting to meet Ingrid's glare. 'Frank has a very busy training schedule. I'll have to speak to him about it.'

'You do that.' Ingrid consulted her clipboard. 'Did you and Frank manage to decide on your wedding vows?' She arched an eyebrow, as though silently adding *Or is Frank's training schedule too important for that too?*

'I bet their vows are beyond cheese,' Erin whispered to Richard. Lindsay and Frank had decided to write their own vows, which she could only imagine were going to be cringe-inducing.

'Don't worry. When we get married, we'll go with some old-fashioned pre-written vows.'

Erin hoped Richard was joking. She'd made it pretty clear that marriage wasn't for her. The fact that she gagged every time the W word came up was a big indicator. Plus, she'd said several million times that she never, *ever* wanted to get married, which was a whopping, elephant-sized clue.

'I've mocked up a seating plan, as per your specifications.' Ingrid pulled a sheet of paper out of the clipboard and unfolded it on the table in front of Lindsay. Susan whipped it away before Lindsay could get a look, and squinted down at it. Her nose was practically touching the paper in a bid to see what was printed on it. Susan was supposed to wear glasses but refused to, due to vanity. Erin thought her lack of sight explained some of her fashion choices.

Susan shook her head, a satisfied smirk on her face. One of her favourite pastimes was finding faults and pointing them out, especially when it came to Lindsay's wedding. She seemed to resent Ingrid's involvement and tried to trip her up whenever possible. As amusing as it was for Erin to see Ingrid thwarted, it did make these meetings drag on even further.

'You can't put Brian and Hugh together,' she said, jabbing a finger down on the seating plan.

'Why not?' Lindsay asked. 'They're brothers.'

'Because Hugh is now married to Brian's ex-wife, Marcia.' Susan scanned the seating plan again, grinning when she spotted another flaw. 'And you can't put Great Aunt Rosamund that close to the bar. There'll be no drink left for the rest of us. And why is my mother seated so far away from the top table?' She turned to Lindsay with wide eyes. 'Don't you want to share your big day with your grandmother?'

What all this had to do with the bridesmaids and groomsmen, Erin didn't know. Richard was missing out on spending precious time with the children for this. Amanda had almost rubbed her hands together with glee when he'd had to cancel their afternoon together.

'We really cannot make any further changes after this.' Ingrid made a few notes before she folded the seating plan and returned it to her clipboard. 'A hair and make-up consultation has been scheduled for Sunday morning.' Sunday morning? Sunday mornings were made for lie-ins and leisurely sex, not fannying about with hair and make-up. '*All* the bridesmaids must attend.' Was she looking directly at Erin when she said this? 'Plus the mothers of the bride and groom, flower girls and of course the bride herself.' Ingrid ticked that point off her agenda before continuing. 'The final dress fittings for the bride, bridesmaids and flower girls is in *two weeks*. Please don't miss it *under any circumstances.*' Ingrid eyed the bridesmaids, her look seeming to linger on Erin before she consulted her clipboard once more. 'The suits will be ready for collection next weekend. The best man will be taking care of that, yes?' Ingrid's beady eyes roamed the dining room. 'Where is the best man?'

'He's also training,' Lindsay said. She looked as though she'd quite like to slip under the table and spend the remainder of the meeting there in safety.

Ingrid looked as though she was about to explode. 'Does he at least have the address?'

'I think so.' Erin wouldn't have been surprised if Lindsay had popped her thumb into her mouth for comfort as Ingrid gritted her teeth and fiercely scribbled something on her agenda.

'I have good news,' Ingrid went on. Somebody should have told Ingrid's face this, as it was still pinched and lined with a scowl. 'I've booked the harpist for the ceremony, plus the band have agreed to play at the reception.'

Lindsay gave a squeal and clapped her hands together, suitably cheered after her fright just moments earlier. 'They're *so good*. They made the *X Factor* final a few years ago and everything!'

Ingrid didn't look impressed by this unnecessary nugget of information. But then neither did anybody else. The band Lindsay had been desperate to book for her wedding had long ago sunk into obscurity. No wonder they had agreed to play at the reception – they were probably in dire need of bookings to pay the rent.

'Moving on, I've liaised with the designer. All the flower arrangements have been finalised, the seating covers and table runners have been sourced, and the favours and decorations are sorted. The only problem is with the arch for the top table, but I've discussed this with Lindsay already.'

On and on Ingrid went. In the end Erin switched off. This meeting and all the fuss that went with it was the perfect example of why she was so set against marriage.

SEVENTEEN

Ruth

Pressing print, I sank back in my chair, emptying my lungs in a huge sigh of relief. Those meeting minutes had been like a bloody albatross around my neck, but they were finally typed up and I would no longer have to concoct increasingly elaborate excuses for why Sally hadn't received them. Gathering the document, I stapled the pages together before taking them personally, as requested, to the HR office. The HR girls were all gathered around Sally's desk when I arrived. I handed over the minutes with a suitably apologetic look on my face.

'I'm sorry it's taken so long to get these to you. I don't know what's happening with my email. I've got the IT guys looking at it, but even they're stumped.' *Lies. All lies!*

'Don't worry about it. Thanks for printing it off.' Sally took the document and it was a relief to have it off my hands. *Fly, albatross, fly!*

'What's this?' I asked, pointing at the card open on Sally's desk.

'It's card for Stuart Accrington.'

'Oh? Is it his birthday?'

'No, he's getting married on Saturday so we were just about to do the rounds with a card and collection tin.'

What? Stuart from Accounts was getting married? That was so unfair! Stuart had never committed to anything other than a favourite football team and he was getting married before me? Why should Stuart, who had never shown any interest in marriage or even a long-term relationship, get to go first? What next, Erin and Richard sprinting down the aisle? Or Jared's little sister? It wouldn't have surprised me if Aunt Gloria had moved on to husband number seven by the time Jared and I made our vows.

'Would you like to sign the card?' Sally held the card out to me and I could hardly refuse, could I? Or worse, throw it on the ground and put the heel of my shoe through it.

'Of course.' I smiled serenely as I signed the card while inside I wanted to puke on the sentiments already penned. 'Send Stuart my best wishes, won't you?' I almost gagged as I said the words, but being bitter was not a trait I wanted to project. I left the HR office, making a detour down to reception to have a moan to Quinn. There would be no point chatting to Erin about it, as she wouldn't understand.

'You'll never guess what.' I slumped on the reception desk, my mouth downturned. 'Stuart from Accounts is getting married. On Saturday.'

'That's so unfair!'

I *knew* Quinn would get it.

'He's *hot*. Lucky cow, whoever she is.'

That wasn't quite what I had in mind, but never mind. Besides, Stuart from Accounts *was* pretty hot. Not as hot as my Jared, obviously, but it was a shame for the single population in the Greater Manchester area. Many of whom Stuart had encountered on drunken Friday nights already.

'What do you think their wedding will be like?' Quinn had the dreamy look she adopted whenever weddings – or any kind of romantic gesture – were mentioned. I found it bizarre that the girl was still firmly single. Not only was she extremely pretty and sweet, like a human-sized Tinkerbell, she was also lured towards romance like I was lured towards chocolate cake.

'It'll be a quick wedding, I should imagine. It can't be long before his fiancée is due to give birth.'

Quinn's dreamy look increased tenfold. Her eyebrows almost lifted off her face while her mouth grew pouty. 'He's going to be a daddy too?'

I gave a shrug. 'Why else would Stuart from Accounts be getting married?'

'Love,' Quinn sighed. 'The only reason is love.'

Stuart from Accounts' upcoming wedding played on my mind for the rest of the day, even as I attempted to reconcile myself with our longer engagement. Two and a half years wasn't that long, if you really thought about it, and there was so much to organise in the meantime, as evidenced by Trina's file, which was now safely nestled under my bed, where it felt a bit less daunting. I'd pretty much convinced myself of the merits of waiting for so long as I made my way into my weekly yoga class.

'Hi, Mary. How did your date go with Cecil?' I placed my mat next to Mary's and unrolled it. Mary was already carrying out an initial stretch on her own mat, but she stopped to chat.

'Lovely, thanks. He took me out to a sweet little restaurant and then we went back to his for dessert.' Mary winked at me and I almost collapsed onto my pink yoga mat.

'Dessert? You mean like cake or ice cream?' *Please let*

her be talking about cake or ice cream.

'No, dear. I'm talking about sex.'

Thud. 'Sex?' I whispered the word, hoping to all that was good and holy that I'd misheard.

'Yes, sex. It's been a while, you know, since my Gordon passed, but it was lovely. Cecil is rather good.' Mary chuckled at my aghast expression and relief washed over me. She was only pulling my leg (and her own, as she resumed her stretches). 'You youngsters think you invented sex. I was getting my jollies off long before you were born, and the desire is still there, you know. It was a bit dusty, but Cecil soon sorted that out.'

Gah! She was serious, and that image wouldn't leave my brain for a long, *long* time. I'd have welcomed thoughts of Stuart from Accounts and his rapidly approaching nuptials back with open arms.

'Hey everybody. I hope you all had a good weekend.' Nell waltzed into the hall, a couple of rolled-up yoga mats under her arms. From the beatific smile on her face, she hadn't heard the Cecil story. I'd have quite happily switched brains with the woman. 'Greg and I have some lovely news that we'd like to share with you.' Nell hurried her husband over, clearly about to burst if she didn't spit their news out soon. Greg reached her and looped a hand around her waist. 'A few weeks ago, we found out that we're pregnant!' Nell paused while the group gave a collective *aah* and we offered our congratulations. 'We've kept it to ourselves, but on Friday we had a scan and the baby is happy and healthy and thriving. Show them, Greg.'

Greg pulled a scan photo from the pocket of his shorts and passed it around the class. When it arrived in my hands, I couldn't help thinking that it looked like a kidney bean with tiny stumps attached. Nothing to get too excited about, at any rate.

'At least that's one thing I don't have to worry about.' Mary leaned across to look at the photo. 'Although I did make Cecil wear a johnny. You never know what you might catch these days.' Mary beamed up at Greg as he came to retrieve the photo. 'Congratulations. You're going to make marvellous parents.'

The class began but I found it pretty difficult to concentrate, what with my raging jealousy of Stuart from Accounts, worry about my own wedding, and the image of Mary and Cecil going at it swirling around my poor brain. I was in the warrior pose when an upbeat mobile ringtone broke my limited concentration. With horror, I realised it was my own ringtone. I must have forgotten to put my phone on silent before the class. Oopsies.

'Sorry,' I whispered as I dodged the sea of yoga mats and made it to the edge of the room where my bag was. I didn't recognise the number, so I ended the call before switching the phone off and tiptoeing back to my place.

'Great session, everybody,' Nell said at the end of the class as we all rolled up our mats.

'We should go out and celebrate your news,' Mary called out. 'Who fancies a quick drink?'

There was unanimous agreement, so we all gathered our things and trooped into the nearby pub, taking over our usual corner. We made a toast (with both Nell and Greg's glasses filled with orange juice, which had nothing to do with the pregnancy – they were both just freakishly healthy).

'To Nell and Greg.' Mary raised her glass of port. 'Congratulations on your pregnancy.'

'Congratulations!' we all chorused, raising our own glasses. We took it in turns to personally give our best wishes to the couple and, when it came to my turn, Greg quickly spotted my engagement ring.

'What's this?'

I explained about my engagement and told him that I'd decided to keep it quiet as I didn't want to steal their spotlight (and it had killed me to keep my gob shut, believe me).

'Don't be silly.' Nell grabbed my hand before turning to the rest of our group and raising her voice. 'It looks like we have a double celebration tonight, guys. Ruth is engaged!' Nell lifted my hand for everyone to see, and I was showered with congratulations and a toast of my own. Suddenly all thoughts of Stuart from Accounts and Mary and Cecil left my head as I finally let go and started to enjoy the fact that *I was actually getting married!* A few drinks later, I made my way home, my mood still jubilant, so I was more than willing to play along when Jared practically pounced on me as soon as I walked through the door.

'Oh, hello. It's like that, is it?' Giggling, I kicked the front door shut and kissed Jared, but when I attempted to pull him towards the bedroom, his feet refused to move. 'What is it? What's happened?' I was hit by a sudden sense of dread, noticing the stricken look on my boyfriend's face. How could I have mistaken it for arousal?

'We need to talk.' Jared attempted to lead me through to the sitting room, but now it was my turn to refuse to budge. This was it, wasn't it? The moment I'd been dreading since our first kiss. Jared had realised what an utter bollocks he'd made of his love life when he'd – bizarrely – taken a fancy to me, and now he was finally coming to his senses.

With a firm tug, Jared pulled me out of the tiny hallway and settled me down on the sofa before taking both of my hands in his. This was it. Dumpsville, here we come.

'You're wobbling again, Ruth. Stop it.' Jared kissed me, but it was a peck and not at all like the reassuring, 'I still fancy the pants off you' snog I needed. 'I know you don't always believe it because of your past, but I love you. Never, *ever*, doubt that, okay?'

Jared was right – my past did blight my relationship with him from time to time, but when you're bullied relentlessly during your school years because of your weight, you start to believe you really are as worthless as your tormentors tell you.

Jared gave my hands a squeeze. 'Father Edmund phoned earlier.'

That was it? *Father Edmund had phoned?* Big whoop! But then it dawned on me why Jared's face looked so pinched as he delivered the news, and my eyes pooled with tears.

'He's cancelled our wedding, hasn't he? Is it because we're heathens who never go to church?' Without pausing to allow Jared to speak, I jumped to my feet and started to figure out a plan of action. I'd thought Father Edmund had been a little unconventional when he hadn't insisted we join the church or sign up for a pre-marriage course before we booked the date. 'We'll have to start attending. Quick, phone him back and tell him we promise to go to church every single Sunday from now until we die.'

'Calm down. The wedding hasn't been cancelled.' Luckily Jared delivered the good news before I dropped to my knees and started to pray. 'It's the opposite, really.'

'Thank God for that.' I sank back onto the sofa and let out a puff of air, thoroughly relieved that I could continue to enjoy Sunday lie-ins. 'I had a phone call while I was at yoga. I wonder if it was Father Edmund? I didn't answer as we were in the middle of our session and I was so embarrassed I just switched it off.' I reached into my bag and, bypassing long-forgotten lipsticks, balled-up tissues and crumpled receipts, I pulled out my phone. It was still switched off. 'What did Father Edmund say?'

'He phoned because somebody else has called their wedding off. The couple split up after the groom-to-be found his wife in bed with her brother-in-law. That's her sister's husband, by the way, not the groom's brother. I don't see what difference it makes who she was in bed with, but Father Edmund was keen to clarify. Worryingly, he seemed to relish passing the information on.'

'And that's why he phoned?' I asked. 'For a gossip?'

'Not entirely.' Jared took my hands again, squeezing with uncomfortable enthusiasm. 'Father Edmund said he really liked us as a couple and could see that you were upset at having to wait, so he's offered us the cancellation.'

'What?' I leaped up out of my seat, my hands covering my suddenly hot cheeks. 'We can get married earlier? That's brilliant news!' For us, not the cheated-on groom, obviously. I did a little jig on the spot, while Jared remained motionless on the sofa. 'So when is it?'

Jared pulled a face. 'It's in six weeks.'

'Six weeks?' I dropped back onto the sofa, the happy jig knocked out of me. '*Six weeks?* But that's insane.'

Jared's shoulders had been hunched up around his ears, but they relaxed when he saw the panicked expression on my face. 'It's too soon, isn't it? I thought so too.'

'Is it even possible to plan a wedding in six weeks?' I thought about Trina's wedding file under my bed. It would take at least six weeks to read through that alone. 'Although …' I thought again about the file under my bed. Yes, it was humongous. Frighteningly so. But my wedding wouldn't be nearly as big as Trina's had been. We could cherry-pick the bits we actually wanted, and all the painstaking research had already been done and was sitting right there. 'This could actually work. It'll be a mad rush. It'll be hectic. But it'll be worth it, won't it?'

Jared rose from his seat and began pacing the small sitting room. 'We'll be married in six short weeks, in the church we want.' Pace, pace, pace. 'You know what? This could be perfect.'

'It could be, couldn't it?' A giggle burst from me rather suddenly. Married! In six weeks! 'What do you think?'

Jared paused in his pacing to look at me, a mixture of

stomach-churning panic and 'little kid at Christmas' painting his face vividly. 'I think I want to marry you in six weeks.'

'I think I want to marry you in six weeks too.' I leaped at Jared and this time there wasn't a hint of resistance. Jared and I were getting married in six weeks. Six tiny, minuscule weeks! This was either an utterly romantic or a terribly foolish plan. I wasn't sure which one it would turn out to be.

EIGHTEEN

Ruth

Six weeks! I was getting married in *six weeks*. I couldn't quite believe it, and even feared I'd dreamed the whole thing when I woke the following morning. But no, it was true – the wedding was booked for six short weeks away. I lugged Trina's file from under the bed, convinced it was growing by the day as it seemed heftier every time I picked it up. There were tabs for everything inside, from cake designs to make-up mood boards, seat covers to bridal lingerie, and wedding favours to buffet options. There was even a whole section dedicated to sequins. Sequins!

As lovely as Trina's wedding was, it wasn't the kind of gig I was aiming for as a) we didn't have the funds for such extravagance, b) there wasn't nearly enough time to pull off something like that, and c) a huge, flashy affair like Trina's wedding wasn't really me. I wanted a wedding that was simple, yet fun. I didn't care about seat covers with matching table runners and tiny heart-shaped table confetti scattered just so. I wanted people to come to my wedding and have a blast. I didn't want three-hour-long speeches that made you pray for death. I wanted laughter and for people to feel that they were at the best party ever.

'Are you ready?' Jared popped his head around the bedroom door. 'We should be setting off soon.'

Closing the file, I toed it back under the bed. 'I'm ready.'

We were going to Jared's parents' house for lunch, where we would be sharing our news. We'd already told my parents the day before, and while they'd been shocked by the sudden haste (Dad had suspected I was pregnant. I assured him I was not), they were happy for us.

'You'd better get your skates on,' Mum had told me. As though I didn't know that already! I'd already made a dozen lists of things that needed to be done, which, quite frankly, was a scary amount.

'Do you think we should do away with the speeches?' My ever-ready notebook was on my lap as we drove over to Linda and Bob's. Every spare second would now be dedicated to planning the wedding, including car and bus journeys and any time Kelvin was away from my desk.

'You mean we won't have any?'

'They're always a bit of a snooze-fest, aren't they?'

Jared shrugged as he indicated to turn right. 'Sometimes, I guess. I think your dad might want to say something, though.'

'Hmm.' I put a question mark next to 'speeches' in my list. 'I definitely don't want a top table. I don't want there to be a hierarchy at our wedding. Everyone should be equal.'

'Even the bride and groom?'

'Okay, we can be a *teeny* bit more special. But I still don't want a top table.'

'Fair enough.'

'Do you mind not having one?' I didn't want to come across as a bridezilla who wanted everything her own way, but Jared wasn't giving me much in the way of preferences.

'Not at all.'

We pulled up outside Linda and Bob's house and I reluctantly put my notebook away. There was so much to do that any time away from the notebook felt like I was squandering vital planning opportunities. The house was full, as it usually was whenever we visited. Linda and Bob had a house that always seemed so alive, whether the whole family was squeezed into the sitting room or fragmented into smaller groups throughout the house. Growing up with only Mum, Dad and Stephen, it was a bit of a change for me, but I'd soon grown to adore Jared's chaotic family. The eldest of four, Jared had three younger sisters, the youngest being seventeen-year-old Jimmy. Ally and Freya were in their early thirties, and sat in the middle of the Williams family sandwich. Ally was married to Gavin and together they had an adorable toddler son (though, as adorable as Noah was, it was usually him who caused the majority of the chaos at the Williams' house). Sure enough, as soon as we stepped into the house we were welcomed by Noah's sticky hands reaching out for a cuddle. Jared scooped him up and blew a loud raspberry on his little pot belly, not caring that Noah was smearing him with melted chocolate buttons. Hefting Noah onto his hip, Jared strode into the sitting room, where the rest of the family were gathered.

'We have news!' Jared had decided to make the announcement sooner rather than later. If important business wasn't attended to quickly in the Williams household, it would be forgotten as tea and cake took precedence (it was why I liked visiting Jared's parents so much).

'Let me guess.' Ally grabbed Noah and pounced on him with a handful of wet wipes. 'Ruth's pregnant!' Ally widened her eyes at her son, already envisioning a little cousin for Noah.

'No!' Jared and I answered quickly, dismayed at the suggestion. I hoped my ovaries weren't listening to all this pregnancy talk and getting ideas. Let's not get ahead of ourselves here.

'It's about the wedding,' Jared clarified. 'It's been brought forward slightly. We're getting married in six weeks.'

'Six *weeks*?' Linda's mouth fell open. 'That's an awfully short time to plan a wedding.'

'What's to plan?' Freya gave a nonchalant shrug. 'They've booked the church. All they have to do is buy a dress and a suit and they're good to go.'

Ally shook her head at her sister. 'You can tell you've never planned a wedding. There's so much to think about. Not that I'm saying you can't do it in six weeks.' Ally panicked that she'd offended us, but I quickly assured her that she hadn't. There *was* so much to think about. This wasn't breaking news.

'And we don't have much in the pot, so we have to plan it on a small budget,' Jared added. We'd been expecting to save up for at least a year, then over two, so the small timeframe had put our funds in jeopardy. 'We don't want to get into debt so we haven't got a great deal to play with.'

'But that just means we have to be creative.' I'd decided that 'being creative' (code word for cheap) would make the whole process fun rather than filling us with debilitating fear. Time would tell how that theory would pan out.

'I think it's romantic,' Linda decided. I added 'romantic' to my list of deluded buzz words. 'And if you need me and your dad to chip in financially, we'll do what we can.'

'That really isn't necessary.' I was horrified at the thought of Linda and Bob thinking we'd come begging for cash. 'We'll manage. If we have to make cutbacks, we will.

The marriage is the important bit, not the wedding.'

'That's true, but the offer is there.' Linda looked across at her husband and her eyes went soft. 'You know, Bob and I had a very small wedding. Only our parents and our closest friends and family were there. Mind you, it was a bit of a rush job, what with Jared being on the way. We weren't fussed, but my parents were livid and practically marched Bob down the aisle.'

'Not that I needed any encouragement.' Bob's chest puffed out a little. 'I loved you and wanted to spend the rest of my life with you.'

'Dad, behave yourself.' Freya made gagging motions but I thought it was sweet. *We could do this. It would be a breeze. Sort of.*

It was our weekly *A Beginner's Guide To You* night and we had all gathered at Billy and Theo's. The house was full of the usual gang, plus Richard and newbie Casey. We waited until the end of the episode before we made our announcement. Erin, of course, already knew. I couldn't help telling my best friend.

'I think it's great,' Richard said as he shook Jared's hand. I wasn't sure whether Erin had already told him. She'd sworn to keep it to herself, but everybody knows that partners don't count. 'If you love someone, of course you should get married as soon as possible.'

'Don't you be getting any ideas,' Erin warned.

'Nah, I don't buy it.' Theo gave himself a thorough scratch, which, as you can probably imagine, was pleasant viewing for the rest of us. Why did we bother with the lives of Meg and Tom when we could witness Theo giving his nethers a good old rustle? 'Are you up the spout?'

What was it with the pregnancy thing? 'Nicely phrased, Theo, but no, I'm not pregnant.'

Quinn gave a dramatic sigh, along with a Disney-princess-style eye fluttering. 'I think it's ever so romantic. I wish someone would propose to me. Everyone's getting married but me.'

'I'm not.' Theo gave himself another scratch. Was it any wonder there weren't any girls dragging the dude down the aisle?

'You don't count,' Quinn replied.

'And why not? Am I not good enough for you or something?'

'Don't get huffy. You wouldn't want to marry me either.'

Theo shrugged. 'I might. You're well fit.'

'Oh.' Quinn's Disney eye fluttering was back.

'And I bet you make a cracking bacon butty, which everyone knows is the best quality any wife can have.'

'Are you looking for a wife – or a maid?'

Theo grinned and I held in a groan. I'd lived with Theo for long enough to know what was coming. 'Aren't they the same thing?'

'You're such a pig.' Quinn was no longer channelling demure Disney princesses as she launched a cushion across the room at Theo.

Theo caught the cushion and positioned it behind his head. 'But I'm a lovable pig.'

'I wouldn't be so sure about that, Theo,' I said, though I'd heard just how lovable the man could be through my former bedroom wall on too many occasions. 'Anyway, let's move away from this conversation before Theo ends up wearing our snacks.' I pulled the bowl of crinkle-cut crisps towards me before Quinn got any ideas. 'And get back to what we came here for. To talk about my wedding!' I grinned at the group, but I wasn't kidding. Those guys may have been under the impression that we'd gathered to watch TV, but for the next six weeks we had far more important things to do. 'We don't have long to save up for the wedding, so we've got a tight budget we need to stick to. That means we won't be having the reception at the golf club as originally planned. Unless our guests want to party in the car park and eat gravel, of course.' I looked around the room, but nobody seemed keen on that idea.

'Why don't you have the reception at Cosmo's?' Billy suggested. Cosmo's was a local restaurant run by an old friend of ours. 'I'm sure Cosmo will give you a great deal, with mates' rates and everything.'

Leaping out of my seat, I threw myself into Billy's lap, ruffling his already unruly mop of brown curls. 'Billy, you're a genius. I knew there was a reason you were one of my best friends.' I turned to Jared. 'What do you think?'

'Sounds good to me.'

'Great! I'll speak to Cosmo tomorrow then.' I removed myself from Billy's lap and returned to my seat. 'Good work, Billy. And speaking of work, I'm going to need all of your help. There's a wedding fair on at the weekend and I need you all to come with me. Many hands make light work, and all that. So, what do you think?'

As if my friends had a choice in the matter!

NINETEEN

Trina

'Where the hell have you been?'

Aidan took a protective step back as Trina lunged at him, panicking as she threw herself over the threshold with arms outstretched and ready to grab him. But instead of walloping him as he suspected she was about to, Trina pulled him into a rib-crunching hug, burying her face in his T-shirt. Aidan hesitated for the briefest of moments before he wrapped his arms around her and hugged her back almost as fiercely.

'Hey, what's the matter? I haven't been anywhere.'

Trina gave a sniff before she attempted to pull herself together. 'You haven't been *here*. I've been back for *days.*'

'I thought I'd give you and Rory a bit of alone time.' Aidan led Trina inside, silently marvelling at the spacious annex. 'You know, to do what newlyweds do.'

'Ha! If only.' Trina shuffled into the sitting room and slumped onto the sofa. She was too miserable to play the perfect hostess and offer drinks and snacks. 'Rory is too busy working or playing golf. He hasn't been home before ten o'clock since we arrived home, and even then he's usually got a hanger-on with him. Do you remember his buffoon of a best man from the wedding? Ferguson?' Aidan shook his head and Trina waved her hand. It was inconsequential, really. The fact was, Rory insisted on bringing these people home with him every night, meaning they hadn't had a minute of time alone together since their honeymoon. 'He's been here almost every night, scoffing everything in sight. We didn't even get to spend our first evening here alone. Rory invited his sister and her friend back to guzzle the last of our champagne.'

'So it hasn't been quite the wedded bliss you were expecting?'

Trina's eyes pooled with tears, but she didn't bother to swipe them away. If she couldn't cry in front of Aidan, her closest friend, who could she cry in front of? Certainly not Rory. He wouldn't notice if her eyes spurted out the contents of Lake Windermere.

'I've just been so lonely, Aidan.' It wasn't like this before the wedding. Rory had always been so attentive, so loving. Now he barely noticed Trina was there at all. And although Trina had adored her job, Rory had talked her into giving it up, claiming they'd be able to spend more time together this way. Ha! 'I've been sitting here, on my own, day after day. The only person who has visited me is my cousin, Ruth. Mum's still on her cruise and Tori's still insisting that she's the ugly sister who will never get married.'

'I'm sorry, Trina. I had no idea.' Aidan felt awful. He'd thought he was doing the right thing by staying away for a while. 'You know you could have called me, don't you? I'm always here for you. *Always*.'

The tears that had been threatening to fall spilled forth, bringing with them an unattractive amount of snot. Trina grabbed a tissue from the box she'd been working her way through since she arrived back from her honeymoon, and blew her nose.

'I just never expected it to be like this.'

'I know, sweetie.' Aidan pulled Trina into his T-shirt, not minding at all that it was now smeared with tears and gook. 'But it will get better, I'm sure.'

'Do you really think so?'

How could Aidan answer in anything but the affirmative when Trina looked up at him through wide, child-like eyes, her eyelashes damp with tears? 'Of course I do. This is all new to both you and Rory.'

'It *is* new. And scary. I feel like I'm doing something wrong.' Trina looked down at her hands, her fingers scrunching up the tissue. 'Like I'm not being a good wife.'

'Oh, Trina, sweetie.' Aidan removed the tissue from Trina's fingers so that he could hold her hands. 'You love Rory. That's all you need to do.'

'Really?'

He gave Trina's hands a quick squeeze. 'Really. Now, dry those tears. I'll put the kettle on and you can show me your wedding photos. I know you're dying to.'

Trina bit her lip, trying to keep a smile from sliding onto her face, but it was no use. Aidan knew exactly how to make her feel better. 'They are pretty spectacular photos.'

'There you go then. Get them ready.'

Trina pulled out her MacBook while Aidan made the tea. They squished up on the sofa and watched the slideshow, laughing at the funny photos (Aidan trying to foxtrot with some aging relative of Trina's) and aahing at the sweet ones (Rory's little cousin kissing Trina's little second cousin on the cheek).

'Look at how handsome you are in this one.' Trina paused the slideshow. She couldn't believe how debonair Aidan could be when he wanted to be.

Aidan shifted on the sofa so that he was facing away from the laptop and observing Trina instead. 'Are you saying I'm not usually handsome?'

Trina gave him a nudge. 'You know what I mean. You're not usually so … groomed.' With his tattoos and piercings, Aidan usually had a rough-around-the-edges look about him.

'I'm a stylist. I'm always groomed.'

'Polished, then.' Trina gave him another nudge and resumed the slideshow. 'You know what I mean. Anyway, I like your look. It's *you*. I'm just saying you scrub up well.'

'So do you.' Aidan nodded at the image on the MacBook. Trina was sitting at her dressing table, a glass of champagne at her smiling lips. Aidan was off-camera. He'd just finished styling her hair and had said something amusing. Trina wished she could remember what.

'Look how hot Rory is!' Trina pulled the MacBook closer. She couldn't believe she'd actually married the man on her screen.

Aidan pulled himself up off the sofa. 'Do you fancy another cup of tea?'

Trina felt much better by the time Aidan left. He'd managed to calm her down with copious amounts of sweet tea and allowed her to pore over her wedding photos for ages. Being reminded of their beautiful wedding allowed Trina to put things into perspective. Yes, Rory worked hard, but that had always been the case and he was working hard for their future together. And of course Rory would want to bring friends over to the house. It was his home too, after all. Trina was starting to feel pretty ridiculous. What must Aidan think of her, sniffling away like a spoiled two-year-old?

Trina was putting too much pressure on her marriage. It was only a couple of weeks old, just a newborn marriage, really. She had to give everything a chance to settle down and realise that fairy tales were a thing of fiction, whereas reality needed a bit more work.

Pulling on a pair of boots, Trina slipped out of the annex and hurried over to the main house in search of Mrs Timmons. She found the housekeeper in the kitchen, busily scrubbing at a hefty pan.

'Hello, dear.' Mrs Timmons wiped the suds from her hands with a tea towel as Trina approached, shooing away the family's aging dog as he attempted to clamber up Trina's thighs. 'If you're looking for Mrs Hamilton-Wraith, you've just missed her. She's gone to visit Mrs Goleman and won't be back for an hour or so. Would you like me to pass on a message?'

'No, that's okay. I popped over to see you.'

'Me?' Mrs Timmons was surprised to hear this, but she hid it quite well. 'What can I do for you, dear?'

'I was wondering if you had a recipe for that chicken dish you make. The one Rory loves?' Trina was going to stop snivelling and be proactive. If she wanted a little romance in her marriage, she was going to have to be the driving force on this occasion. She would make Rory his favourite meal, which they would enjoy over candlelight – even if they had to eat it late at night once all their guests had gone home.

'Would you like me to make it for you? It won't be any trouble. I'll bring it over this evening, before Rory gets home.' Mrs Timmons tapped the side of her nose. 'He'll never know. It'll be our little secret.'

It was tempting. Very tempting.

But no.

'That's very kind, Mrs Timmons, but I wanted to make it myself.'

'Oh.' Mrs Timmons couldn't hide her surprise this time. Trina – or any other member of the household – had never shown any inclination to cook for themselves. Since arriving home from their honeymoon, Trina and Rory had been surviving on meals prepared and frozen by Mrs Timmons. All they'd had to do was defrost and reheat them.

'I want to be a good wife for Rory.'

'Oh, darling.' Mrs Timmons reached out to cup Trina's chin with her still slightly damp fingers. 'You *are* a good wife. Don't you let any of them tell you otherwise.' Mrs Timmons quickly dropped her fingers and turned away from Trina, shuffling in the pocket of her polka-dotted apron for a pen. 'I don't use a recipe, but I'll write one out for you. Would you like a cup of tea while you wait?'

One cup of tea and a home-baked iced ginger biscuit later, Trina returned to the annex with a list of ingredients and a step-by-step guide. After a quick trip to the supermarket, Trina rolled up her sleeves, set her mouth in a determined line and began her task. It took a lot of effort and a not-too-serious burn, but Trina eventually pulled the dish out of the oven. Remarkably, it resembled Mrs Timmons's creation, if you squinted a little bit. Mrs Timmons had assured Trina that the meal would keep well if kept in its dish and reheated later on, so Trina took herself up to her en suite for a long, luxurious soak.

Yes, her marriage would work. Trina wouldn't hop from one husband to another like her mother, she was sure of that. She just had to get used to Rory's ways, that's all. To be doubly sure, Trina selected a sheer black nightie with matching robe to entice Rory. The way to a man's heart may be through his stomach, but turning him on couldn't hinder the marriage either, so Trina had both bases covered.

Wrapped in the robe, Trina floated down the stairs to select music for the evening. She wanted something soft and romantic to set the mood. She was halfway through devising her playlist when the phone rang. Her heart lifted when she heard her husband's voice. He rarely bothered to phone her any more, so this was a good sign.

'Hey, babe. I'm just phoning to let you know that Carrie and Ginny have invited us out for dinner. I won't have time to come home after work, so you'll have to meet us at the restaurant.'

Trina's heart dropped again. 'But I've cooked.'

'This will be way more fun. Ginny's managed to book the Blue Llama!' The Blue Llama was an incredibly pretentious restaurant endorsed by a celebrity chef. Rory had been keen to sample its supposedly exquisite cuisine, but the waiting list was stupidly long. You'd have more chance of sitting your arse down on the moon than you would getting a table at the Blue Llama.

Could Trina really deny Rory this one tiny pleasure?

'What about the meal I've cooked?'

'Feed it to Leo.' Rory's comment was throwaway, but it hurt Trina. She'd tried so hard to cook that meal for Rory and he wanted to feed it to his family's *dog*?

'I don't really feel like going out to eat tonight.' Trina looked down at her nightie and robe. She was hardly dressed appropriately.

'Oh. Never mind, then.' Rory didn't sound nearly as disappointed as Trina had expected. Perhaps the Blue Llama wasn't as important to him as she'd thought. 'Maybe next time.'

'You really don't mind?'

'Of course not. We'll all go together another time. Or maybe just the two of us?'

'I'd like that.'

'Great. I'll get us on the waiting list.' So they may get to eat there around Rory's retirement. 'I have to get back to work now, but I'll see you later.'

'I love you,' Trina said, but Rory had already hung up. It didn't matter, though; Rory was coming home to eat her meal instead of dining at the Blue Llama, which was irrefutable proof that he loved her. Trina quickly finished off the playlist before popping the dish back into the oven to warm up. She set the table and lit the candles, butterflies fluttering deliciously in her tummy as she anticipated Rory's arrival. Unfortunately, those butterflies would have quite a flight ahead of them, as it was almost midnight before her husband returned home, squiffy, dishevelled and full of exquisite food – courtesy of the Blue Llama.

TWENTY

Erin

Everyone gathered at Billy's house early on Saturday morning, apart from Richard who was taking the children bowling. With a day of parading around a hall full of wedding paraphernalia and couples radiating everlasting love ahead of her, Erin wished she was joining them. And Erin hated bowling. It was sweaty and noisy and she *always* broke a nail in those stupid holes in the stupidly heavy balls, but it was preferable to the vomit-inducing wedding fair.

'Don't you *ever* want to get married?' Quinn asked her. She couldn't understand Erin's views at all. She couldn't wait to walk down the aisle and marry the man she loved. She just had to find that man first.

'Nope. Witnessing Lindsay's wedding preparations is enough to put me off for life.'

'How are the plans coming along?' Ruth pulled out her ever-ready notebook, pen poised to make a few notes.

'Horribly.' Erin still wasn't sure how she'd ended up

getting herself tangled up in the whole thing. 'It's so tacky and over the top. They're having a horse and carriage for the bride.' Erin wanted to gag, while Quinn practically swooned at the mere thought.

'But that's so lovely. Seeing brides riding along in a carriage always makes me think of Cinderella.' Quinn sighed dreamily. 'It's utterly romantic.'

'If you say so. I think a hearse is more apt.'

'Wow, you're really not into weddings, are you?' Quinn asked and Erin shook her head.

'Not even a little bit. Marriage is such an outdated concept. Who wants to be shackled to the same man for a lifetime?'

Ruth raised her hand. 'I do.'

'Oh, sorry.' Erin cringed. She really should learn to be more tactful in her aversion to nuptials, at least until after Ruth's wedding, and she vowed to try harder. Ruth was so excited to be marrying Jared and Erin didn't want to bring her down, no matter what her personal views on the subject were.

'It's okay.' Ruth tapped her notebook with her pen. 'So, Lindsay's wedding?'

'Is hideous. You should see the bridesmaid dresses.' Actually, Erin was thankful that her friends *wouldn't* see the bridesmaid dresses. 'And we have to drive to the hotel in a pink limo.' Erin pretended to gag. It didn't take much acting skills to pull it off, as the thought was utterly repellent to her.

'But I love pink limos,' Quinn said. Erin slung an arm around her.

'You would. You're cute and romantic.'

'Whereas Erin is hard and cynical.' Ruth nudged her friend to show that she was kidding – almost – before she popped her notebook and pen into her handbag and clapped her hands. 'Right, everybody. We need to get as much covered today as possible, so I've put everybody into pairs with specific areas I want you to look at. Take plenty of photos, business cards and leaflets, and we'll swap notes at the end.' Ruth pulled a sheet of paper out of her pocket and unfolded it. 'Billy and Casey will be working together on flowers, table decorations and favours.' She looked at Billy and Casey in turn, waiting until she had a nod of approval before moving on. 'Theo and Quinn will be looking at transport and hair and beauty.'

'Hair and beauty? Me?' Theo couldn't believe he'd been given such a girlie role. He should have been given a more masculine job to do like ... oh, forget it. There was nothing manly about weddings.

'Theo, you use more hair products than all the women here put together, you great vain git.' Ruth consulted her list, moving swiftly on before Theo could attempt to fabricate an argument. 'Erin was supposed to be with Richard but as he can't make it, you can pair up with my cousin, Trina.' Ruth had invited Trina along as she hadn't had the opportunity to attend any fairs for her own wedding and Ruth felt a bit sorry for her. She should have been euphoric after marrying the man of her dreams, but she'd seemed a bit down when Ruth had visited. 'She should be here any minute. You'll be looking at cake and sweet treats and wedding stationery. Jared and I will take care of bridal gowns, suits, bridesmaid dresses and photographers. Does anybody have any questions?'

Theo raised his hand. 'Is your cousin fit?'

Ruth folded the sheet of paper and returned it to her pocket. 'Trina's gorgeous. She's also married, and if you even look at her in a non-gentlemanly manner, I will twist your bollocks off. Okay? Good.'

As though on cue, there was a dainty knock at the door, signalling Trina's arrival. Theo's eyes almost bulged out of his sockets when he clocked her, but one warning look from Ruth was enough to temper his desires. Ruth made the introductions and then it was time to go.

'We'll meet up for tea and cake at the catering area at three o'clock to compare notes. Ready? Let's go!'

The wedding fair was being held in a venue that resembled nothing more than a huge grey box, but inside it was a hive of activity with stalls, information stands and a catwalk that would host a fashion show of bridal wear in the afternoon. While Erin would rather have tap-danced naked in the centre of the Arndale shopping centre than attend such a corny event, Trina was taking the whole thing almost as seriously as the bride-to-be herself, and had a notebook and pen at the ready before they'd even stepped inside the building.

'I didn't get to go to anything like this for my own wedding,' she explained. 'My wedding planner took care of everything.'

Erin rolled her eyes. 'Don't get me started on wedding planners.' The thought of Ingrid made Erin shudder. 'At least we got the best category.' Erin couldn't believe her luck that she'd landed cake and sweet treats, which ranged from wedding cake to heart-shaped cupcakes and chocolate fountains and everything delicious in between. 'We get to eat as much cake as we want while supposedly doing Ruth a favour.'

'Oh, no. I can't actually sample any of it. I'm on a diet after seeing my honeymoon photos.'

Erin looked Trina up and down. The girl was so skinny that she could hide behind a tall blade of grass. 'More for me then, I guess.'

The pair shuffled along the slowly moving queue before finally making it through the doors, where they were immediately bombarded with noise. Goody bags were thrust into their hands, which was quite exciting until they realised they were crammed mostly with leaflets. There was also a key ring advertising the venue as well as a pen printed with 'Choco Fountain, for all your celebrations!', which wasn't all that thrilling.

'Ooh, a free pen!' Trina was far more impressed with the goody bag's offerings than Erin was, but then Erin wasn't really interested in anything at this wedding fair unless it was crammed full of sugar. They headed for the nearest confectionery stall, which hired out cute wooden carts filled with jars of sweets. This was definitely Ruth's kind of thing so Erin took a photo with her phone.

'Would you like to take a leaflet?' the owner of the stall asked, homing in on the possible interest. 'Our carts are really popular and we can adapt the theme to suit your requirements.'

Erin had a quick flick through the leaflet, where she could see a couple of the themes on display as well as the price list. Wow. That was a pretty hefty price tag for what was essentially jars of dolly mixtures, marshmallows and cola bottles. Erin doubted this would fit into Ruth's tight budget, no matter how delightful it was.

The next stall they found was full of delicious-looking treats. It was a cacophony of sugar and colour, with chocolate swirl lollipops arranged artfully in jars, sherbet dips in champagne flutes, a rainbow of macarons arranged in a giant heart shape, mini jars of jellybeans and Smarties tied with ribbon, and tiny cupcakes with frosting of every colour known to man. It looked as though Willy Wonka had thrown up on the table.

The stall's owner was quick to pounce. 'We can set up a sweet station package for you or we can create wedding favours for your guests.' She handed over a cellophane bag of three mini macarons tied elaborately with swirls of ribbon. 'This is just a small selection of what we do. You should check out our website.' She handed over a business card before she uttered the words Erin had been hoping for. 'Would you like to try a sample?'

Yes, Erin would very much like to try a sample, thank

you. By the time they made it to the chocolate station halfway through the exhibition, Erin had tried many samples. The sight of the chocolate fountain, pulsing thick chocolate over and over again, made her feel queasy. And the fountain was only the start of the delights displayed. There were chocolate mousses set in cocktail glasses, a pyramid of chocolate fondant cakes with sickly pink icing piped on top to form little hearts, millionaire's shortbread with gold leaf detailing, and mugs of hot chocolate with heart-shaped marshmallows bobbing on the surface.

'Would you like a sample?' the stallholder asked and Erin started to turn green. If she had one more sample, it wouldn't be only Willy Wonka throwing up rainbow treats.

'No thank you. We'll just take this.' Trina grabbed a leaflet from the stack and moved Erin away from the stall. 'It's nearly time to meet the others. Shall we call it a day?'

'Yes please.' Erin grabbed hold of Trina and leaned heavily on her as they made their way towards the catering area. Quinn and Theo were already there and had secured a table. Erin flopped gratefully onto a chair, clutching her stomach. She really shouldn't have eaten so much. Perhaps Trina's strategy of swerving the samples had been the right way to go. Damn you, hindsight, you smug little shit!

'How's it been?' she croaked.

'It's been a nightmare.' Quinn glared across the table at Theo. 'He was bored after two minutes and spent the whole time whining. It's been like shopping with a toddler, only this toddler has tried it on with every passing female. And most of them have been brides-to-be.'

'Like that's ever stopped Theo before,' Erin pointed out, which Theo took as the compliment it was not.

'I have to challenge myself. Being this good-looking can get a bit boring at times.' Theo winked at Trina, who waggled her wedding band at him.

'I'm afraid even your obviously superior good looks

and, erm, *charm*, aren't enough to sway me into unfaithfulness.'

Theo leaned back in his seat. 'The day isn't over yet.'

Trina smiled sweetly at him. 'And neither is my marriage.'

TWENTY-ONE

Ruth

I was stupidly excited as we pulled into the car park of the wedding fair venue, my feet itching to race inside to see what was on offer. Instead – rather heroically, I think – I hung back to make sure the others had arrived and checked again that they knew what their duties for the day were. I wouldn't have put it past Theo to talk the others into skiving off to spend the day in the pub instead, but they all dutifully arrived and confirmed the jobs I had set for them.

After I'd confirmed that my team were all on board and raring (ish) to go, I marched towards the back of the scarily huge queue before it grew any longer. I had just shy of six weeks to plan my wedding, and it looked as though I'd be spending three of those queuing outside the fair.

'Remember to meet up at three at the catering area. Whoever's last has to buy the cake.' The others followed me and together we shuffled along the queue until the entrance came tantalisingly into view. I pulled Billy to one side, whispering so the others didn't hear, 'You're welcome, by the way.'

'For what?'

I nodded towards Casey. 'I paired you up on purpose, so you get to spend the day with her on your own.'

'Oh. Thank you?'

'Like I said, you're welcome.' I grinned, satisfied with my cunning plan. Chuck a nappy on me and call me Cupid!

Shockingly, we made it inside the building before Jared and I were due to take our vows and while the promised goody bag was a bit shit – who wants a key ring of some random venue? – the rest more than made up for it. Displayed before us was every bride's dream. Whether you wanted a traditional or a quirky wedding, it was all there, spread out in all its glory.

'Look at it.' I turned a full circle to take in the madness before us. The noise was deafening, the space crammed with bodies, stalls and displays. It was truly wonderful. 'Aren't you excited?'

Jared appeared less than thrilled to be there, however. I hadn't been expecting him to perform cartwheels – there wasn't room even if he was inclined to do so – but he didn't have to look like he was being led to his execution.

'Yeah. Of course I am.' Jared attempted a smile. It was a piss-poor effort and I was about to pull him up on it when I was distracted by a rail of wedding dresses. I bounded over, tugging Jared with me, but my enthusiasm dampened a little as I examined the dresses. They were all beautiful, of course, but they all looked the same. They may have had a slightly different neckline or bits of lace or pearl buttons sewn onto them, but they were essentially the same dress, repeated.

'They're a bit boring, aren't they? I feel like I'm drowning in a sea of white.'

The stallholder's jaw dropped as though I'd just admitted I drowned fluffy kittens for fun. I moved on quickly, pulling Jared along with me.

'They're not really me, are they?' I wore bright colours and prints, not plain and white. Which was unfortunate, given the long-standing tradition of wedding dress design.

'You don't have to wear white,' Jared pointed out.

'I know, but I don't want any old dress off the high street. It's got to be special, hasn't it?'

'Oh my God, Mum. Look!'

Jared and I were pushed aside as an over-excited bride-to-be barged past us and snatched a swathe of ivory from a rail of dresses. She emitted an ear-piercing squeal as she pressed the fabric to her chest. 'It's just like the one I saw in the magazine. Isn't it lush?'

The mother fawned over the dress and I couldn't help feeling a little down, despite my surroundings. This girl knew what she wanted. Had known what she wanted before she'd even arrived at the fair, but I didn't have a clue what I was looking for. But I'd know as soon as I saw it. I would know my dress.

Wouldn't I?

We had a bit more luck with the bridesmaid dresses, which were bolder in colour and more my style, but they were so expensive and would push us way out of our budget. I knew bridesmaids weren't essential for a wedding, but I did want my loved ones to be part of my wedding. I'd already asked Erin to be my maid of honour (and as she hadn't gagged as she'd accepted, I felt I couldn't take it away from her now). Quinn, Jared's little sister Jimmy and my niece Riley were on board to be bridesmaids and would need to be clothed (obviously). My brother and his family lived in New York and I'd already spoken to Riley about the kind of dress she would like to wear over Skype. She was super-excited (Riley's words, not mine) about dressing like a princess and, as her aunt and the woman who had dangled the carrot, I had to fulfil that dream. She would have a dress worthy of a princess, just not from here.

Our mission to find a photographer was much more successful, particularly when we met Sadie Alexander, a young photographer I felt an instant connection with. She showed us a portfolio of her work and I knew then that I wanted her to document our big day. Her photos were stunning without being staged. She'd managed to capture the essence of the couple and their guests – a cheeky kiss as a newly married couple, laughter over the best man's speech, a couple of children whispering and giggling under a table. Her pictures depicted real weddings rather than staged shots under picturesque trees with false smiles after three hours of posing.

'We really should be going.' I reluctantly closed the portfolio. We were due to meet the others, and my stomach was already rumbling at the thought of cake. 'But can I take your details?'

'Of course.' Sadie handed over her business card. 'My website is listed on there if you'd like to have a browse at some more samples of my work.'

'Thank you. Hopefully we'll see you again soon.' I slipped the card into my handbag before Jared and I made our way towards the catering area at the back of the huge hall. We were the last to arrive, which meant we would be footing the bill – but then that was the least I could do after the help I'd received. There was no way Jared and I could have made our way around the fair on our own.

'No cake for me, thanks,' Erin said as I placed the order. She was looking a bit green after apparently overindulging in the sweet treats. But who could blame her? I'd have done the same.

'So? How did you get on?' I sat down at the table crowded with tea, coffee and cake. I couldn't wait to find out what the others had discovered.

'These sweet stations look pretty popular.' Erin handed

me her phone, where she'd taken photos of cute little carts filled with jars of sweets and tables laden with goodies. I loved the idea of a sweet station – it was certainly fun, which was what I was aiming for – but I did not love the prices.

'Most of the wedding favours work out pretty expensive too.' Casey handed over her phone, which displayed the snapshots she'd taken. 'But I bet you could make some of them yourself much cheaper. Like this one.' Casey reached over, swiping her finger over her phone until she reached a photo of a mini plant pot. 'These are pots of herbs with the guest's name printed on a tag. It's a really simple idea if you think about it, but it looks so cute.'

'I'm not sure we'd have time to grow herbs,' I pointed out. *Less than six weeks, people.* 'But I do like the idea of getting creative and making our own favours.'

'How about this one?' Casey swiped her finger across the screen again, pausing at a photo of a cupcake in a cellophane bag tied with pretty ribbon. The cupcake was covered in pink icing topped with a Love Heart sweet. 'They look easy enough, and they'll be pretty cheap to make. Plus, you can personalise each by attaching a tag to the ribbon.'

It was certainly something to think about. 'Thanks, everyone. You've been a great help. I feel more confident that we can have a fabulous wedding on a budget. Especially now we have the reception venue sorted out.' I turned to Billy and told him about my meeting with Cosmo. Billy had been right about Cosmo offering us a fantastic deal. Plus, the restaurant would be perfect, as I wanted our wedding to be fun and informal and Cosmo's had a lovely relaxed atmosphere. 'Cosmo said there'll even be room to squeeze a DJ or something in there.' I'd already started to jot down a playlist in my notebook – mostly tracks by the Spice Girls and S Club 7, naturally.

We finished off our cakes and decided to call it a day as

we were all exhausted. We passed the fashion show taking part on the catwalk as we made our way to the exit – and that's when I saw it. My dress. It was fifties-style, cut below the knee with a full, netted skirt, a halter-neck top made of ivory silk and overlaid with polka-dotted organza, and nipped in at the waist with a pink organza sash. I stood and stared at the dress. It was so me! I could picture myself wearing that dress, teamed with a pair of ivory peep-toe heels.

'Quick!' I called to the others. 'Find that designer!'

TWENTY-TWO

Ruth

As soon as Jared and I got back from the fair, I began updating the notes on my wedding plan spreadsheet, making sure I referenced all the photos Erin and the others had emailed over (FYI, my friends are *amazing* and super-duper-efficient). I had my own wedding file now – though it would never quite reach the proportions of Trina's – to which I added the leaflets and business cards we'd collected. Jared was out at the pub with Gavin (discussing the important matter of the stag do, no doubt), so, at a loose end, I decided to pop over to Billy's once I'd finished my task. We'd lived together for over a decade – in a non-sexual manner (apart from one, ill-judged encounter, which we both tried our hardest to forget) – and it was still strange not seeing him every day. Things had been a tad awkward between us after our little friendship mishap (aka our one-night stand. 'Friendship mishap' doesn't sound quite so seedy), but that had been a couple of years ago and we'd soon sorted ourselves out. Our friendship was too important to throw away over a quick fumble.

Being a Saturday evening, I was hoping that Theo and Casey would be out, being young and free, allowing Billy and me to have a proper catch-up without the others, but I was out of luck as the pair were at home. And, not only that, Quinn was there too.

'What are you doing here?' I didn't mean to sound quite so rude, but it was a surprise to see Quinn curled up on the sofa. She hadn't even known Billy and Theo until she started joining in with our *Beginner's Guide* nights a few months earlier.

Quinn shrugged. 'I just felt like hanging out. I haven't been home since the fair.'

'We can't seem to get rid of her,' Theo said. 'We tried leaving the front door open as a hint but she didn't take it.'

Quinn unfurled herself. 'I'll go if you want me to.'

'Nah, I like having fit birds around the place. It's why I let Casey move in.'

Quinn's and Casey's eyes met, rolling in sync. Theo was a good-looking bloke but his so-called charm needed a lot of work. Being an ex-housemate, I'd been privy to this information for a long time and didn't know whether to be shocked or utterly devastated in humanity whenever Theo managed to convince a girl he was worthy of their time or – worse – their emotions.

'Anyway.' I decided to change the subject before Theo ended up wearing the contents of the open bottle of wine sitting precariously close to Quinn. 'Did you guys think Jared was acting funny today?'

'In what way?' Billy asked.

'He was very quiet while we were looking around the fair and he doesn't seem to have an opinion on anything wedding-related.'

'I don't blame him.' Theo stretched and scratched, not minding at all that he had an audience. 'Being trapped with all that wedding crap would have any normal bloke running for the divorce courts.'

'Why would he run for the divorce courts when they're not even married yet?' Quinn asked.

Theo pulled a face. 'Whatever. Just cut the bloke some slack. Men don't get wet over weddings like you women do.'

'You don't think he's changed his mind then?' The wobbles were refusing to do one, no matter how much I willed them to bog off.

'After today, it's highly likely.'

'Shut up, Theo,' Billy, Casey and Quinn all cried.

Billy turned to me. 'Jared hasn't changed his mind.'

'He's mad about you,' Quinn added.

'Do you really think so? Shut up, Theo.' Seeing my ex-housemate open his mouth, I decided to cut him off, knowing that the words that were about to leave his mouth would be the most unhelpful – and possibly offensive – words he could think of. 'You've never been in love, so your opinion doesn't count.'

'Have you really never been in love?' Quinn asked.

Theo shook his head, a smug look on his face. 'But I have *felt* the love of many women.' He winked at Quinn, and I felt a bit queasy.

'Love and sex aren't the same thing,' she told him and a heated debate ensued. With Quinn's uber-romantic view on life opposing Theo's misogynistic piggish ways, I figured it could take a while before they burned themselves out so I took myself off to the kitchen to put the kettle on.

'Jared loves you, you know.' Billy joined me in the kitchen and hopped up to perch on the counter while I busied myself making tea and coffee. 'He hasn't changed his mind, I'm sure. Why would he?'

'Bless you, Billy.' I stretched out and gave his hair a ruffle. I could always count on Billy to make me feel better about myself. 'How are things going between you and Casey?'

'It's going well. She's a great housemate and we've got

loads in common. We're going to the cinema tomorrow.' He mentioned a comic-based film and I was suddenly immensely grateful that Casey was in our lives and I no longer had to endure those films with Billy myself.

'Quinn and Theo seem to be getting on well too.' I finished making the drinks and handed one to Billy. 'You don't think something's going to happen between them, do you?'

'I hope not.' Billy hopped down from the counter. 'There is a bit of flirting going on, but Theo will only use her until he gets bored.'

'Which we both know won't take long.'

'Exactly.' Billy lowered his voice as we started to head back into the sitting room. 'Quinn's too good for Theo.'

'Way too good.' We joined the others and settled in for a nice evening of chat and laughter. I felt much better by the time I left. My friends were right. Jared did love me. He wouldn't have asked me to marry him if he didn't.

Jared's love for me was cemented further in my mind as we stood in Mum and Dad's front garden the following weekend, peering at the heap of crap that had once been a caravan. Dad's chest was inexplicably puffed up with pride as he showed it off. Mum's face was explicably pinched.

'It's nowhere near ready,' she hissed at me as Dad wrestled with the rusted door. When it eventually opened, it almost came off altogether in Dad's hands but he didn't seem surprised that it was hanging off its hinges. 'And he's already bought a blasted treadmill and cross-trainer. They're cluttering up my dining room. I nearly break my ankle every time I try to eat a meal. Look.' She stuck out a slippered foot, revealing a heavily bruised calf. 'You know, most men spend their spare time hiding from their wives down at the pub or chasing loose women, but your father has to tinker with this pile of junk.'

'But you'd rather he was here with *this*.' There really wasn't any better way to describe the former caravan without resorting to insults. 'Wouldn't you?'

Mum placed a hand on her forehead and emitted a weary sigh. 'I don't know, love. I really don't.'

'Are you coming in or not?' Dad had bravely stepped into the caravan, but he'd stuck his head out when nobody had followed him. Jared braved the rickety old vehicle and I winced as he stepped over the threshold. 'Careful there, Jared. The floor can be a bit unpredictable.'

I peered around the doorway (I wasn't brave or stupid enough to actually step inside myself) and had to hand it to Dad. He had optimism, that was for sure. Where Dad described the floor as unpredictable, I'd have described it as rusting and half-missing.

'It's a work in progress,' Dad said.

'A work in progress?' Mum gave a hoot. '*A work in progress?*'

I stepped back as Dad's head popped out of the caravan. 'Yes, Vee. A work in progress. A bit like your roast chicken. How many decades have you been working on that, and it still comes out as dry as a nun's you-know-what?'

'Well.' Mum's chest puffed out but I could tell by the stony expression on her face that it wasn't with pride. I expected to see steam sputtering from her ears. 'This is the first I've heard about it. Why haven't you complained before if it's so bad?'

'Tact, dear. It's called tact.' Dad disappeared back inside his pride and joy while Mum marched back into the house, giving the door a good slam to show that she was royally pissed off.

Yep, Jared must have really loved me to put up with this. Not only was he standing in the middle of a domestic between my parents without batting an eyelid, but he was doing so while risking his life in a rusty bucket on wheels. I checked. Yes, it did still have wheels.

'Aren't you going to go and say sorry?' I popped my head back into the caravan. Good lord, there was a gaping hole in the corner. I could see next door's cat licking his arse on the other side of the fence. 'Mum looked really upset.'

'*She's* upset? What about me?' Dad thumped a fist on his chest. 'She puts my caravan down every day. Every minute of every day, in fact.'

And who could blame her?

'But she doesn't have your vision, does she? She can't see it how you do. All she sees is a load of rusty crap in her garden.' As would any sane person. 'She doesn't have your artistic flair.' Dad's chest puffed up once more. 'She won't get it until it's finished. Do you want to fight until then?'

Dad shook his head. 'Was I too harsh?'

'It depends. Do you want Mum to cook for you ever again?' Dad nodded. I don't think he'd made more than a ham sandwich during their entire married life. 'Then go and grovel. And make it good.'

Dad rushed into the house while Jared stepped gratefully back onto solid ground.

'Promise me one thing,' I said as we headed back towards the house. 'We'll never end up like that when we're married.'

Jared slung an arm around my shoulders. 'Cross my heart. I will never, *ever* tell you just how bad your cooking is.'

I gave Jared a nudge, but I was relieved by his promise. If Jared was marrying me for my cooking skills, we'd never make it down the aisle.

We found Mum in the kitchen, her arms folded across her chest as she looked down at Dad. The daft sod was actually on his knees on the lino.

'Your chicken's lovely, you know that. I was hurt and

angry and lashing out. Please forgive me.'

'Oh, get up, you fool.' Mum grasped Dad by the collar and hauled him back up to his feet. 'You're making a show of yourself in front of Jared.'

'I don't care. I only care about your forgiveness.'

Steady on, Dad. He was laying it on a bit thick.

'Make me a cup of tea and I'll think about it.' Mum winked at me as she passed and I followed her into the sitting room while Dad leaped at the kettle. Mum and I settled down on the sofa while Dad clattered about in the kitchen, with Jared staying for moral support.

'Stephen phoned last night,' Mum told me. 'They've booked the flights for the wedding. They won't get here until the day before, though.'

I would have liked more time to catch up with my brother before the wedding, but I was just glad he and his family could make it over from New York at such short notice. I'd been a bit worried that they wouldn't make it, and I couldn't imagine getting married without Stephen being there.

'How are the wedding plans coming along?' Mum asked. 'Linda told me she's making the cake. I didn't know she baked.'

'Yeah, she makes gorgeous cakes.' The first time I'd tasted her chocolate cake, I'd wanted to move into Linda's kitchen permanently. If I hadn't already been smitten with Jared, I'd have fallen for him just for his mum's cake. 'Since when do the two of you chat?'

'Since your engagement. We swapped numbers. It's an important job being mothers to the bride and groom. We need to compare notes.'

'Right.' I wasn't sure I quite approved of this new alliance. What if Mum mentioned the caravan/gym and Linda questioned what her son was marrying into?

'So what else have you planned?'

I updated Mum on the wedding fair and the cost-saving

measures we were putting into place. As well as accepting Linda's offer of a cake, I'd saved some much-needed cash by printing off invites at work while Kelvin dashed off for an 'impromptu meeting', which had clearly been a sneaky chocolate break. The Curly Wurly sticking out of his pocket had been a dead giveaway.

'I'll need some addresses for the invitations.' I pulled out my notebook while Mum toddled off to locate her address book and I jotted down the contact details of our family. 'Do I really have to invite Aunty Pat?'

'Can you imagine the fallout if you didn't?'

Mum and I exchanged a glance before I scribbled down the address in my notebook. Great. It looked like I was inviting the Wicked Witch of the West after all.

TWENTY-THREE

Erin

Sunday mornings were made for lengthy lie-ins or lazy sex or even propping yourself up with pillows while you read the papers, if you were so inclined. Sunday mornings were not made for dragging your zombie-like carcass to a salon in the city centre. But that was exactly what Erin was doing.

'You owe me. You do know that, don't you?' Erin scowled across at Richard, who was singing along to the radio as they drove along.

'*I* owe you? It isn't my wedding you're practising for.'

'No, but it is *your* sister's.' Erin slumped in her seat. She would rather be doing anything else right now. But mostly sleeping. Sleeping was good and healthy and didn't have anything to do with Lindsay and her stupid wedding.

'You can't blame me for my sister's lack of taste.'

Erin could, and she would. 'You don't have to look so pleased about it, though.'

'I'm not.' Richard tried to keep a straight face, but failed. 'I'm just excited about the game, that's all.'

After dropping Erin and LuLu off at the salon, Richard was taking Ralph to watch a rugby match, the lucky bastard. Erin didn't follow rugby – she wasn't a fan of any sport, no matter how hot the players were – but she'd take it up if it meant she could avoid the *TOWIE*-athon that was about to occur. The salon came into view, and it was far worse than Erin could ever have imagined. Nestled between a greasy-looking kebab shop and a closed-down pawnbrokers, the salon was overly pink with a bubble-gum neon sign with the word *Sparkle* glowing against the dull morning. The whole façade offended Erin's eyes.

'Please don't make me go in there.' Erin grasped hold of Richard's arm, stretching her eyes to Bambi-like proportions. 'I'll come out orange.'

'They're only doing a trial run of your hair and make-up.' Richard cut off the engine and unclasped his seatbelt. He hopped out of the car to open the passenger door for LuLu.

'I think it looks lovely. Like a pretty palace,' LuLu said as she joined her father on the pavement. But then she would. LuLu still had a toe firmly in the Disney Princess phase, which was another difference between her and Erin. At twelve, Erin had thought anything Disney was totally uncool and babyish, but LuLu still lapped it up and Erin wasn't in any hurry for her to lose that innocence.

'We'll pick you up later.' Richard kissed first LuLu and then Erin on the cheek before he slipped back into the car. 'Have fun.'

Erin's middle finger itched to flick up at Richard's cheesy grin but she refrained due to the children. Plus, she needed Richard to drive her home later.

'Come on, kiddo. Let's get this over with.' Erin looped an arm around LuLu's shoulders and guided her into the sickly pink salon. Her eyes were assaulted by yet more pink as they stepped inside, from the pink-and-white checked flooring to the pink chairs, pink-edged mirrors and the pink uniforms of the beauty therapists.

'Welcome to Sparkle!' A beauty therapist descended on them, glossy pink lips set in a wide grin. The whiteness of her teeth was blinding. 'Are you with Lindsay's party?'

Yes, unfortunately. 'I'm Erin, one of the bridesmaids, and this is LuLu.'

'I'm going to be a flower girl.' Pride oozed from the girl. 'Can I have my hair twisted up like yours?'

The corners of the beauty therapist's lips turned down. 'I'm afraid Lindsay has already picked out all the styles.'

Then why the hell were they wasting a perfectly good Sunday morning if all the decisions had already been made?

'Would you like to come with me?' The beauty therapist held out a hand for LuLu before turning to Erin. 'If you take a seat over there, someone will come and collect you shortly.'

Erin wandered over to the (pink, obviously) squashy sofa by the window and flopped down. If she'd known she was going to be sitting around, she'd have snoozed her alarm for a bit longer.

'Erin?' Another beauty therapist – this one with a cleavage up to her chin – had approached the seating area. 'I'm Samantha, and I'm going to be doing your hair today. Would you like to come this way?'

Erin wanted to shake her head – she wanted to do anything but 'come this way' – but she forced herself to her feet and followed Samantha to her station at the back of the salon. She felt like a fool by the time Samantha had finished pinning her hair into a giant bun on top of her head. With an oversized pink bow attached to the front, Erin looked like a show dog.

Next came the make-up, the theme of which seemed to be 'thick and swirly'. Liquid eyeliner was applied freely, looping out from the corner of her lids in an intricate pattern that was enhanced with pink sequins and glitter.

Ostrich feather-sized false eyelashes had been applied. (Eyes can, like, totally disappear on the photos if you don't wear them, apparently. Funny, not one photo of Erin – or anybody she knew – had ever turned out eyeless.)

Erin felt like a berk.

'Don't worry,' Dena, Erin's assigned make-up artist, said when she caught Erin's look of horror in the mirror. 'You look stunning.' Erin didn't trust a word that make-up artist Dena spouted. She was clearly as thick as pig shit, judging from their earlier conversation.

'Your skin colour is *gorgeous*,' Dena had gasped as Erin plonked herself in the pink seat earlier, trying to avoid glimpsing her hair in the mirror. 'Do you use sunbeds?'

'No, it's my Sri Lankan heritage.'

Dena's brow had attempted to furrow (but was thwarted by her overuse of Botox). 'Is that, like, a fake tan? Can you get it from Boots?'

No, Erin wouldn't be trusting Dena's judgement any time soon.

'Wow, look at you all!' Lindsay had wandered into the centre of the salon and was turning in a circle to take in everyone's appearance. She placed her palms as close to her cheeks as she could without smudging her make-up. 'You look *amazing!*' She clapped her hands, truly thrilled with the results. But then she would, as she looked half-normal with her subtle, understated make-up. (She didn't want to overshadow her dress. Erin had seen the dress and, if anything needed to be overshadowed, it was that monstrosity.)

'Wow, LuLu. You look like a real princess.' Lindsay gave her niece a careful hug so she didn't smudge her make-up or dislodge any hairpins. At least LuLu had emerged from the process looking vaguely like herself. Her hair had been loosely curled and held back off her face with dainty diamanté-encrusted butterfly-shaped clips. She was only wearing a dab of lip gloss as Lindsay had strict instructions from Amanda regarding make-up. It was probably the only point Erin and Richard's ex would ever agree on.

'I can't wait to show Dad my makeover,' LuLu said. 'Can you?'

Funny, Erin wasn't quite as enthusiastic as LuLu was when it came to revealing her so-called makeover to Richard. She could already hear his laughter.

TWENTY-FOUR

Ruth

Quinn flipped the driver's seat forward to allow a grumbling Erin to crawl into the back of her car. Erin hated sitting in the backs of cars, but she didn't have much choice unless she wanted my vomit slicked down the back of her neck. I didn't actually suffer from travel sickness, but it was a great excuse for avoiding squeezing into the back seat.

'Couldn't you find a smaller car? I feel like an elephant.' Erin tucked herself in, her knees up to her eyeballs in Quinn's tiny car.

'You could have offered to drive, you know.' Quinn righted the driver's seat and slipped into it.

Erin folded her arms and glared out of the window, shooting daggers at an innocent shrub. She couldn't argue with Quinn on this one, but that didn't mean she couldn't sulk.

Quinn pulled her seatbelt across her chest before starting the engine and checking her mirror for traffic (and smudged lipstick) before pulling away from Erin's flat. I fiddled with the radio until I found a decent song ('Wannabe' by the Spice Girls, FYI). Butterflies took flight as we drove along, reminding me of the momentous day ahead of us. I'd managed to track down the wedding dress designer from the wedding fair, so we were travelling to the village where her shop was located. Luckily, Hartfield Hill wasn't far away so we wouldn't have to put up with Erin's gloomy chops for too long.

'I just need to make a quick detour,' Quinn said as Mel B serenaded us. 'I think I left my purse at Billy and Theo's last night.'

I caught Erin's eye in the rear-view mirror. With the slightest head movement, she indicated that I should jump in. Erin had temporarily ceased sulking in order to intervene in Quinn's assumed madness.

'About that.' I squirmed in my seat. Why did intervening fall under my jurisdiction? 'Since when did you start hanging out there on your own?'

Quinn gave a shrug, keeping her eyes conveniently fixed on the road ahead. 'Not that long. I get on pretty well with Casey. She reminds me of my sister.'

'Yeah, *that's* why she hangs out there.' Erin caught my eye in the mirror again. 'It has nothing at all to do with Theo.'

'As if!' Quinn took her eyes – momentarily – off the road to shoot Erin an aghast look through the rear-view mirror. 'I do not fancy Theo.'

'Not even a little bit?' I'd lived with Theo for two irritating years and even though the thought of smooching a bloke *after* I'd tugged his hairs out of the plughole on a regular basis was enough to make me shudder, even I could (silently) admit that he was a good-looking bloke.

'Okay, I *did* fancy him a little bit at first.' It pained Quinn to admit this – and rightly so. 'But he's such a big flirt and not my type at all.'

'How long is it since you've had sex?' Erin asked.

Quinn winced. 'Too long.'

'Then you don't have a type. Unless desperate counts. Hey, I'm kidding. Don't crash the car or anything.'

Quinn's knuckles whitened as she turned her eyes back to the road, her hands gripping the steering wheel. It was taking all her effort not to turn back around with a retort, but Erin was right – about both crashing the car and her sex drought. Still, it took a moment before her fingers relaxed and she was composed enough to speak.

'Theo is not my type – shut up, Erin, or I'll flip the car over. As good-looking as he is, I don't go for uber-groomed guys.'

'Then why all the flirting?' I asked.

'There's nothing wrong with a bit of flirting.'

'But that's how it all starts. A giggle here, a hair flick there. The next thing you know, your knickers are dangling from Theo's lampshade and your self-respect has flown out of the window. I've seen it happen many times.'

'You watch Theo having sex?' Quinn met Erin's eye in the rear-view mirror and they both sniggered, mini-squabble forgotten. 'I always knew there was something dodgy about your relationship.'

I wanted to gag at the thought of a front-row seat as Theo performed. Hearing it through the wall had been bad enough. 'Whatever. Just be careful. Theo's an all-right mate—'

'Don't go overboard with the compliments, will you?' Quinn said, but I ploughed on with my words of wisdom.

'But he's a selfish arsehole when it comes to women.'

'It's a good job I'm not interested in him like that, then, isn't it?' Quinn asked as she pulled into Oak Road and parked outside Billy and Theo's. 'I'll only be a minute. Do you want to come in or wait here?'

'I'll wait here.' Erin pulled out her phone and started tapping away, no doubt texting Richard. She had – against her will – become one of those people who couldn't go thirty seconds without some sort of communication with their partner.

'I'll come in and say hello.' *And make sure there's no untoward flirting happening*. I wasn't usually such a party-pooper, but Quinn was a nice girl and Theo really was a pig. Unfortunately, my surveillance was compromised as I received a phone call as soon as I stepped over the threshold.

'I have brilliant news!' Mum cried as soon as I answered. I gave a quick wave to Billy, Theo and Casey and pulled an apologetic face.

'Has Dad's gym/caravan given up and crumpled into a rusty pile in the garden?'

'Not that brilliant, love.' Mum gave a long sigh, no doubt imagining the rusty pile in the garden. She'd be dancing a celebratory jig on top of it while organising a skip to take away the debris. 'But it is good news. You know Marie McDermott from two doors down? Her niece is a florist and she said she'll do the flowers for your wedding super-cheap. Her words, not mine, obviously.'

'Really?' That *was* good news. Much better than Dad's caravan going kaput. 'Do you have her number?' I grabbed my ever-ready notebook and pen and scribbled down the niece's phone number. By the time I'd finished, Quinn had retrieved her purse – thankfully not from Theo's bedroom – and we were heading back out to the car.

'Are we ready to go and find your wedding dress?' Quinn asked once we were buckled back up.

The butterflies took flight again, but I was more than ready.

Libby Collinson owned a wedding dress shop in the quaint Peppersmith Square within the village. We made our way along the cobbled courtyard, with Erin grumbling about her heels suffering on the cobbles, and into the shop. The exterior was painted a sage green, and two large windows displayed flowing white dresses on shiny mannequins. A bell announced our arrival as we trooped inside, our eyes roaming around in awe. Sumptuous dresses lined the shop, with soft sofas arranged in the centre facing a large ornate mirror.

'Hello, can I help you?' Libby joined us from a room at the back, a lilac tape measure around her shoulders.

'Hi, I'm Ruth. We spoke on the phone.'

Libby's face broke out into a wide smile. She was surprisingly young – mid-twenties at the very most – and very pretty with strawberry blonde hair and a smattering of pale freckles across her nose. 'Of course. You wanted to see the tea-length dress with the polka dots, yes?'

'That's right.' I was so excited at the prospect of seeing the dress again that when Libby nipped out to the back of the shop and returned with the dress from the fashion show, I had to suppress the urge to do a little wee on the spot.

'Here it is.' Libby presented the dress and I felt myself falling in love with the sweep of ivory silk and organza.

'It's perfect. I love it.' Would Libby mind if I threw my arms around the dress and hugged it tight? Possibly. 'The only problem is, I'm getting married in a month.' There was no way the tiny-waisted dress in Libby's hands was going to fit me, even if I wired my mouth shut until the big day.

Libby placed the dress in Quinn's arms and pulled the tape measure from around her shoulders. 'We'd better get you measured then.'

Taking my measurements for the dress didn't take too long. The majority of our time in Libby's shop was spent picking out the fabric for the sash. When Libby mentioned that I could choose the fabric to suit my colour scheme –

which I had yet to make a decision on – I knew we were going to be a while. Libby took me into the room at the back, which doubled as her sewing room. A table was set up in the centre with a sewing machine and all the paraphernalia she needed, while shelves around the perimeter housed reams of fabric. I was like a kid in a sweetie shop as I moved along the shelves, finally deciding on a sunshine yellow with large white spots. Libby said she was more than happy to make a matching wide ribbon to hold my hair back instead of wearing a veil or a tiara.

'I have your number, so I'll let you know when the dress is ready for your first fitting,' Libby said, making a few final notes. We said goodbye and – reluctantly – I left the shop with my friends.

'You're going to look stunning,' Quinn said as we stepped back onto the cobbles.

'The dress certainly will.' I spotted a restaurant across the courtyard and linked my arms through Quinn's and Erin's. 'I'm starving. Let's go for a celebratory lunch.'

Over a delicious lunch of chicken and avocado ciabattas followed by Black Forest cheesecake, we discussed the dress – and the wedding in general.

'How do you feel about vintage for the bridesmaid dresses?' I asked.

'It depends,' Erin replied. 'By vintage, do you mean actual vintage or just second-hand?'

Well, the budget *was* tight. 'How can you be so picky? At least I'm not making you wear the dress Lindsay has picked for you.'

'Why? What has she picked?' Quinn hadn't had the good fortune of seeing Lindsay's bridesmaid dresses. I'd only accidentally caught a glimpse of a photo on Erin's phone, but that had been hilarious enough.

'Never mind that.' Erin shot me a warning look. If I described the dress to Quinn it would be at my own peril. 'You know I was only kidding about the second-hand thing anyway. It's your wedding. I'd wear a potato sack if you wanted me to.'

I screwed up my nose. 'Nah, it won't go with my beautiful dress.'

Quinn scraped the last of her cheesecake onto her fork and popped it into her mouth, closing her eyes to savour the taste. 'That was the best cheesecake ever.'

'Speaking of cake.' I looked mournfully at my empty plate. My own cheesecake had been inhaled within seconds. 'I can't decide what kind of cake I want for the wedding, so Linda is doing a taste test next week. Do you want to come and help me decide?'

Quinn placed her fork on her plate. 'What sort of a question is that? Free cake? I'm there.'

'Me too,' Erin said. 'That cake she made for your birthday last year was gorgeous.'

'So you're both coming. Great.' I made a note in my book and looked at the next point on my to-do list. 'Now, wedding lingerie. Who fancies a shopping trip soon? I'll need to go before my first fitting with Libby.'

'I'm in,' Quinn said.

'Me too.' Erin pushed her plate away, half of her cheesecake still begging to be eaten. 'Did you know that Lindsay has supplied all her bridesmaids with underwear? She didn't say anything; it just turned up one day. I thought Richard was being a bit kinky when it came in the post until I read the note. I'm not sure I like the idea of my boyfriend's sister buying me lingerie.'

'How did she know your size?' I wasn't really asking Erin the question. My eyes were fixed on the half-eaten cheesecake.

'I have no idea. How creepy is that?' Erin shuddered.

'At least *somebody's* buying you underwear,' Quinn said. 'I have to buy my own. I don't think I'll ever get a boyfriend again.'

'Weddings are a great place to meet men,' I told the

cheesecake. 'I could set you up with somebody. Ooh, how about Jared's friend, Paul? He's so lovely.'

'I don't usually go for lovely. I always seem to pick the mean guys who treat me like shit.'

I tore my eyes away from the cheesecake. It hurt. 'Perhaps it's time for a change, then. Just look at Erin. I'd have never pictured her with somebody like Richard.' I'd never have pictured Erin with anybody for longer than an hour or two before Richard. 'But look how happy they are. I bet I won't be the only one getting married in the near future.'

'Oh, don't you start.' Erin shook her head. 'There isn't even the slightest possibility of me and Richard getting married.'

I grinned at Quinn. 'I think the lady doth protest too much.'

'The lady can't protest enough,' Erin said. 'Why can't people accept that I don't want to get married?'

'Because you love Richard?' I suggested.

'But love doesn't equal marriage, though. Plenty of people are trapped in loveless marriages.'

'Luckily, that's never going to happen to me and Jared.'

'Of course not. You and Jared are destined to live happily after ever,' Quinn said.

'Permission to be smug?'

'Permission granted,' Quinn said while Erin mimed sticking her fingers down her throat.

'Erin?' I asked, in my nicest voice. 'Are you going to eat that cheesecake?'

TWENTY-FIVE

Trina

The highlight of Trina's day so far had been sifting through the mail that had landed on the mat mid-morning. Amongst the bills, unsolicited credit card applications and takeaway menus was a postcard from her mother, who was still enjoying a Caribbean cruise with her latest beau. Dumping Rory's mail on the little table in the hall, Trina had turned the postcard over to read the message.

Hello, darling! You probably won't even read this as you will be far too busy consummating your marriage to that GORGEOUS new husband of yours (which is how it should be!!!) but I thought I would scribble a quick note to let you know I am well and will see you soon. Yuri sends his love. Your loving (and super-tanned!) mother xxx

Trina had shoved the postcard on the mantelpiece, her cheeks burning as she realised there was a high possibility that the postman had read it before he'd popped it through the letterbox. Gloria may have had no problem flaunting herself and her sexual needs, but Trina was much more discreet and private.

And also – who the hell was *Yuri*? Hadn't her mother sailed away with a banker called Barry? Shoving her boots on and grabbing her handbag, Trina had left the annex and climbed into her car. Being cooped up was driving her mad.

'Have you thought about going back to work?' Trina, with nowhere to go in the middle of the day, found herself in Aidan's chair, her freshly washed hair hanging around her shoulders. She hadn't planned on having an actual cut – a cup of tea and a sympathetic ear would have done – but her friend had managed to squeeze her in, and her hair *had* taken a beating in the hot sun during her so-called honeymoon.

'I'd *love* to go back to work, but you know what Rory's like.' Trina met Aidan's eye in the mirror and pulled a face. 'They're a very traditional family. Husband goes out to work while wifey stays at home, going out of her mind with boredom. Winnie's trying to persuade me to join one of her committees, but I'd rather boil my own head in dog wee than hang out with her snooty friends.'

Aidan paused, his scissors in mid-air. 'Didn't you grow up around your mum's snooty friends?'

'Exactly!' Trina didn't want her life to revolve around lunches and designer handbags. There was more to her than that. Besides, she'd loved her job (or 'little job' as Winnie referred to it). She'd worked as a dog groomer since she'd left school and she missed the dogs – and their owners – terribly.

Perhaps it was why she and Aidan got on so well; he styled humans while she styled their pets.

'Have you spoken to Rory about all this? Since the wedding, I mean?'

'Not really.' Trina had barely spoken to Rory about

anything since the wedding. He was usually too busy with work and she'd been sulking since the whole Blue Llama mix up and the subsequent row once he'd returned.

'But you said *you* didn't want to go. You never said anything about me,' Rory had pointed out. Which, while technically true, didn't make it right. But although she'd been fuming that he'd gone off to stuff his face with posh food after she'd slaved away at Mrs Timmons's recipe, Trina had tried to remain cool. This coolness, however, soon vanished once it became clear that Rory didn't give a toss that she'd made an effort to please him, to get their marriage securely on the right track. He didn't seem to realise their marriage had veered from the track at all, even once all of Trina's grievances, worries and fears poured out. She hadn't uttered more than a handful of words to him since. Not that Rory had noticed. Or cared, Trina suspected.

'Why don't you talk to him, then? Tell him how you feel.' Aidan resumed his snipping. 'He'll want you to be happy, won't he?'

Trina wasn't so sure about that, but she promised to talk to him anyway.

It was two days after her haircut – which Rory had failed to notice – before Trina had the chance to chat to him about returning to work. Rory had been incredibly preoccupied with work – even more so than usual – and hadn't got home from the office until way after midnight, leaving again shortly after six. Rory worked for the family's business, which operated a hugely successful chain of betting shops across the UK, with Rory steering the online side. Trina had known Rory worked hard before they got married, but she wasn't prepared for these extreme levels. But Rory was forced to take time off from work at the weekend when Winnie insisted he and Trina join the family for dinner. It was Carrington's birthday so Winnie was hosting an intimate dinner party at the house. Carrington had been most put out that her birthday hadn't warranted a more elaborate venue, but she kept her sulking to a minimum (i.e. she only slammed three doors, stamped up one flight of stairs, and delayed confirming the evening's menu until the day before). Although it was supposed to be a family dinner, she'd managed to wrangle an invite for Ginny (who was practically part of the family anyway and had known them all far longer than Trina had, and *she* was invited, Carrington had whined).

The dinner was to take part in the Hamilton-Wraiths' grand dining room. Although Mrs Timmons had cooked, Winnie had hired a couple of waiters for the occasion. Trina was seated between Rory and Ginny, who had so far insisted on conducting a conversation between themselves as though Trina wasn't there at all. She felt completely out of place and unwelcome, especially as Carrington was shooting daggers at her from across the table. Stuck between her parents, Carrington felt she was missing out on the fun at the other side of the table. At either end of the long table sat Rory's regal-looking grandmother and grandpa, who were visiting from Cyprus, where they had retired several years before. They hadn't made it to the wedding, but had flown over to wish their granddaughter a happy birthday. And yet Carrington still wasn't grateful.

'So, Katrina. What do you do, dear?' It was the first time Cecilia – or Grandmother, as she insisted on being addressed – had spoken to Trina.

'I'm a dog groomer.' Or used to be. Now she was a bored layabout who'd spent far too much time in the company of Phil, Holly and the gaggle of loose women on the telly.

Carrington unsuccessfully muffled a giggle with her hand. 'I think Grandmother meant what do you do with your spare time? Committees and things. Like Mother.'

Because why on earth would Trina work for a living when she had a husband? 'I'm not on any committees. I'm thinking about going back to work. I know Rory isn't keen, but I feel so useless at home. It isn't like we have children for me to look after.' Trina gave Rory a sideways glance. He didn't look too impressed with the idea – his lips were pursed like a cat's arse. 'What do you think?'

'I think this is something we should have discussed in private.'

Yep, Rory was mad. Really mad, judging by the vein attempting to vacate his skull at his hairline.

'You're a *dog groomer*?' Grandmother had been too shocked to speak until now, but all heads turned towards her as she spat out the question. She spoke as though Trina had announced she wrestled in dog poop for sport.

'Yes. A dog groomer.' Trina lifted her chin. She'd adored her job, and she wouldn't allow herself to be belittled by this snobby little woman who had probably never worked a day in her life.

'But her father is chief executive of Elswood Spas.' Winnie was quick to jump to Trina's defence – or, rather, to defend her son's choice of wife.

'Elswood?' Grandmother looked suitably impressed. Elswood Spas was a worldwide chain of luxury spas and hotels. 'How delightful.' Grandmother twitched her lips in an attempt at a smile in Trina's direction. She couldn't *quite* forgive the rather unsavoury dog-grooming business. 'We have an Elswood not far from our Florida villa.'

Trina wasn't sure what to say to that. Should she congratulate the woman? Or perhaps offer her a family discount? Luckily, their first course arrived and the conversation moved on.

'Did you have to embarrass me like that in front of Grandmother and Grandpa?' Rory leaned in towards Trina to hiss his question. 'What will they think of us now? We should have discussed this in private.'

'I tried.' Trina's voice was pathetically weak. 'But you're always working. I didn't get the chance.'

'I work so many hours so you don't have to.'

'But I *want* to. I'm so bored at home. What do you expect me to do? Hang out with your mother's snobby friends?'

'Why not? Maybe you'd learn a thing or two from them.'

Trina gaped at her husband. What was *that* supposed to mean? But she didn't get the chance to ask as Grandmother called for her grandson's attention.

'Your mother has just told me that you're off to New York tomorrow. I believe your Aunt Beatrice still has an apartment in SoHo. You should get in touch with her. It would be so much cosier than staying in a hotel. Unless, of course, you're planning to stay at an Elswood.' Grandmother smiled indulgently at Rory. Trina glared at him.

New York? Tomorrow? Why was Trina only hearing about this now?

Rory was going to New York and he'd left it until the night before to let Trina know. Or, rather, he'd left it to his grandmother to spill the beans the night before. When Rory would have divulged his plans if it had been left to him was anybody's guess. As he packed his bags? Or via a quick last-minute text as the plane taxied along the runway?

'Of course I was going to tell you.'

Trina had waited until they were safely out of earshot in the annex before she aired her grievances. Rory liked to conduct their conversations in private, after all.

'But it was all very last-minute. I didn't find out myself until this morning.'

Which was fair enough, until you factored his mother

in. 'Why couldn't you tell me when you told your mum?' Or even before. No – what a crazy idea that was!

Rory kicked off his shoes, letting them fall to the bedroom floor with a thud. 'I saw her this afternoon. She was in town, so we met for lunch and it came up. By the time I got home, we were in a rush to get to Carrie's dinner.' He unbuttoned the top three buttons of his shirt before peeling it over his head and discarding it onto the floor with his shoes. Trina had almost forgotten how sculpted her husband's body was. They hadn't had sex since their honeymoon, before Rory burned himself to a crisp and rendered all movement agonising. They shouldn't be fighting over a trip to New York – they should be taking her mother's advice and consummating their marriage. Repeatedly. Isn't that what newlyweds did? Their marriage had got off completely on the wrong foot and it seemed like an uphill battle every single day, but it didn't have to be that way.

'I'm sorry, okay?' Trina unfurled herself from the bed, where she'd slumped on their arrival back at the annex. 'It was just a shock.' She placed her hands on her husband's bare chest. Forget New York. Right now she didn't care if Rory was about to take off for Timbuktu. They'd just have to make the most of the few hours they had left.

'It's all right, babe. I should have told you earlier, but it's been so hectic.' Rory twirled a stray curl around his index finger. It was the most contact they'd had since the sunburn incident. 'But things will get better, I promise. I'll take some time off work after New York and we can start looking for a house of our own.'

'Really?' The annex had always been a temporary measure, but he hadn't made so much as a murmur about moving into their own place since the wedding.

Rory cupped Trina's chin in his hand, lowering his face until they were nose to nose. 'Really. I love you, Trina. You know that, right?'

Trina forgot about New York and the crushing disappointment her marriage had been so far. Rory loved her, as he went on to prove with toe-curling gusto. Everything would be fine. Better than fine. They would find somewhere perfect to live, somewhere of their own where Trina wasn't living under his mother's shadow. They would live happily ever after.

'Do you know what would be so romantic?' Trina snuggled into Rory as he began to drift off to sleep. 'If I came to New York with you. I could try to get a flight in the morning and we could have a second honeymoon.' *It would go some way to make up for the first.* 'What do you think?'

'Sorry, babe,' Rory said through a yawn. 'I'll be working all hours. It won't be a holiday.'

'You'll have the evenings, though. I could keep myself busy during the day and then we could have dinner together.'

'I doubt I'll even have much time for dinner.' Rory rolled away. 'I need to get to sleep now. I have to be up at four.'

So that was that. Rory would be going to New York – alone – and Trina would do what she did best: sit in the annex and wait for him to return.

TWENTY-SIX

Ruth

I tapped away at my keyboard, filling my Word document with random patterns of letters until Kelvin's bulk disappeared from view. Once I was alone, I gave up the pretence of work and switched over to one of my bookmarked wedding blogs. I was busy researching handmade favours, which basically meant weeding out the easy-looking ones to have a go at. I did try Pinterest for a bit of inspiration, but the whole experience left me feeling wholly inadequate and I closed it down in a bit of a huff.

'Oh, hello.' Spotting a possible winner, I reached into my handbag and pulled out my wedding notebook, grabbing a pen from the pot on my desk and taking the lid off with my teeth. I scribbled down 'personalised fortune cookies?' before scrolling down past the photo. This could be a fantastic idea. I could really have some fun with this one. Imagine my dad's face when he pulled out his fortune that told him any continued DIY attempts could lead to divorce. Or Theo's telling him his doo-dah would fall off if he didn't temper his slutty ways.

'Oh.'

There was a recipe for the cookies. I'd have to bake them myself? I'd presumed I could buy a load of empty cookies and slot some printed-out fortunes inside. This looked like far too much hard work. Yep, further investigation revealed this was far beyond my capabilities. I couldn't bake fortune cookies – I couldn't even manage chocolate chip cookies.

It was back to square one then. I returned to the blog and scrolled to the next project. Personalised jars of homemade jam? Not happening. Wooden hearts engraved with our guests' names? Yeah, right. Jog on handmade soap and bath bombs.

Ah, this was more like it. Cupcakes topped with pale yellow icing and finished with a Love Heart sweet, just like Casey had shown me at the wedding fair. Perfect! Even I could bake cupcakes. *Children* baked cupcakes with their grannies on rainy Sunday afternoons. Satisfied with my discovery, I made a note and printed off the recipe, tucking it into my notebook before opening my email to let Jared know the good news. I had just finished my email and was seriously considering doing some actual work when a new email came through. I assumed it would be a reply from Jared, congratulating me on a successful morning, but it was from Stuart from Accounts. Apparently he was back from his honeymoon and wanted to thank everyone for the card and gift voucher. He and his new wife – Bex, it transpired – were touched. He'd attached a photo of the pair, grinning at the camera in their wedding finery. A few weeks ago, that photo would have made me homicidally jealous, but now it only reminded me that I'd be walking down the aisle very soon myself. Plus, their wedding was over and done with, while mine was still on the horizon, tantalising and exciting, rather than dead and buried. In your face, Stuart and Bex!

I was determined to leave all thoughts of weddings at the door of the church hall as I attended my weekly yoga class. I hadn't realised how exhausting planning a wedding would be, and I had a constant ache between my shoulder blades from the moment I woke up (thinking about the wedding) until I dropped off to sleep (dreaming of the wedding).

Yoga was my chance to relax, which meant I had to push aside all thoughts of nuptials for the next hour.

Ha! Fat chance.

'Hi Ruth,' Mary said as I joined her, unrolling my mat next to hers. 'How are the wedding plans coming along?'

'Good, thanks.' I rolled my shoulders to ease the ache. 'There's a lot to do but I'm getting there.'

'I know what you mean.' Mary grabbed her right foot with her left hand to stretch her muscles. 'My Eric got married last year. It's his third go, bless him. I'd have given up after his second wife – awful woman – but my Eric isn't a quitter.' Mary dropped her foot and switched sides. 'She's lovely, though, this new one. She's a nurse. She was ever so good when I injured my knee that time.'

A few months earlier, Mary had taken part in a 5k run to raise money for charity. She'd twisted her knee after two kilometres, but had persevered and finished the run. Her knee had turned purple and was the size of a beach ball by the time she crossed the finishing line. Mary was incredible – like Supergirl but all grown up and a little bit wrinkly.

'His second wife didn't work at all. Claimed she had a bad back. Probably because she spent all day lying on it with her legs in the air, servicing any man who'd have her while my Eric was hard at work.'

'She cheated on him?'

Mary spluttered. 'Cheated? I'm surprised she didn't

give him gonorrhoea, the way she got through men. I always knew she was a bad 'un but my Eric is too trusting. Mind you, that trust disappeared when he found her going at it with the butcher from three doors down. My Eric hasn't been able to stomach steak since.'

'Right.' What else was there to say to that? Thankfully Greg arrived and the conversation came to an end.

'Good evening, everyone.' Greg attempted to wave with the hand holding the CD player. 'I'm afraid it's just me tonight. Nell isn't feeling too good.' He placed the CD player and his mat at the front of the hall and mimed rubbing a small bump at his abdomen. 'She's been feeling quite queasy for the past few days.'

'I completely understand,' Mary said. 'I spent the first six months with my head down the toilet bowl when I was in the family way with my Eric. My husband thought I'd contracted some horrible disease and called the doctor out five times in two days. In the end, the doctor refused to make any more home visits, even when I was in labour and the baby got stuck.'

I gasped, despite knowing it all worked out fine. Eric was alive and well and married to the nurse. 'What did you do?'

'My neighbour came round to help out. She'd given birth seven times herself and had delivered fifteen grandchildren. She just rolled up her sleeves and yanked him out.'

By then, Nell wasn't the only one feeling queasy.

'Anyway, shall we get started?' Greg asked and the whole room, bar an oblivious Mary, nodded in grateful agreement. 'Great! Let's warm up.'

I somehow managed to get through most of the class without thinking about the wedding, and the ache in my shoulders had almost receded by the time I was rolling up my mat.

'Are you coming for a drink?' I asked Mary as I tucked

the mat under my arm and grabbed my pink holdall.

'I can't tonight.' Mary popped her own mat under her arm. 'I've promised to show Cecil my downward dog.' Mary winked at me before leaving the hall with a definite skip in her step.

TWENTY-SEVEN

Ruth

Our wedding plans were (very temporarily) put on hold as my birthday arrived – my thirtieth. How had *that* crept up so fast? Jared, having heard me bang on about Aidan and his hair-styling prowess since Trina's wedding, had treated me to a bit of pampering at his salon before my party. My hair was washed by a surly-looking girl who couldn't have been more than fifteen, yet had several piercings on her face and a tattoo snaking from her wrist, up to her elbow and beyond the sleeve of her black tunic. She looked a bit rough, but her hands were magical as they massaged the shampoo into my scalp.

'Right then, what are we having done today?' Aidan sat me in his chair and swivelled me around to face the mirror. I'd forgotten quite how cute he was with his messy (but styled) mop of black hair and eyes that crinkled whenever he smiled, which was a lot.

'A bit of a tidy-up, please, and I'd quite like it to be sleek.' I'd been blessed with a lovely natural curl, but if Jared was paying a small fortune for this – and believe me, he was – then I wanted something completely different to my usual look.

Aidan grabbed a comb and a pair of scissors and began snipping. 'Is this for a special occasion? Or just a treat?'

'It's my birthday.' I hoped Aidan wouldn't ask which one. I wasn't quite ready to admit that I'd waved goodbye to my twenties.

'Many happy returns. This calls for a celebratory drink.' Aidan turned towards the rough-looking-but-magic-fingered girl and asked her to bring me a glass of champagne. It wasn't even lunchtime yet – how very indulgent!

Aidan worked his magic as I sipped the champagne, snipping away at the split ends before spritzing my hair with something fancy-looking then blow-drying it.

'Have you seen Trina lately?' Aidan asked as he ran some sort of serum through my hair. 'She seems a bit lonely, especially with Rory being away in New York.'

'I had no idea he was away.' I hadn't seen Trina since the wedding fair. Perhaps I should give her a call. Perhaps even invite her to my birthday meal. I was sure we could squeeze another chair around the table.

'He went yesterday. Trina was pretty upset. I'm worried about her.'

I smiled at Aidan through the mirror. 'You really care about Trina, don't you?'

Aidan smiled, but there was a sadness in his crinkly eyes. 'I do. She's my best friend.'

'Aidan.' I placed my glass of champagne on the shelf below the mirror and clasped my hands on my lap. 'Is it more than that?'

Aidan's fingers paused on the crown of my head and our eyes met in the mirror. He opened his mouth to speak – probably to deny any such thing – but, giving a sigh, he closed it again.

'Do you love her?'

Aidan's eyes dropped from mine as he reached for a clip, busying himself with pinning up half of my hair. He didn't answer, but he didn't have to.

Oh my God, he did! He was actually in love with my cousin. How romantically tragic. Quinn would have *loved* this.

'Does she know?'

Aidan grabbed a set of straighteners and let them glide through my hair. 'I thought she did.'

'What happened?' It was none of my business, of course, but I couldn't help myself asking. Aidan was well within his rights to tell me to mind my own, but he didn't. Perhaps he needed someone to unload his feelings onto and I just happened to be nosy enough to ask.

'We've been friends for years. We met here, through Gloria. I thought she was amazing but way out of my league.' Aidan continued to glide the plates through my hair, unclipping and re-clipping at intervals. 'But we became friends and it sort of grew from there. We were supposed to go to this dance at her dad's golf club, our first official date, but I ended up missing it.'

'You missed it?' How could he? If he was supposedly in love with my cousin, why had he buggered up his chance?

'I was involved in a car accident on my way there. Some idiot hit me while he was on his phone. I wasn't too badly hurt, just a bit dazed, but they insisted I went to A&E to get checked out. I tried calling Trina but it turned out the handbag she'd planned to use didn't go with her dress, so she went without one, meaning she had to leave her phone behind.' Aidan met my eye and he gave a genuine smile, clearly loving my cousin and her little quirks. 'By the time I got through to her, it was too late. She'd met Rory.'

'Didn't you fight for her?'

Aidan shook his head. 'She was besotted with him, not me. She made it clear we were better as friends.' Aidan shrugged. 'And she was happy. That's all I want for Trina.

For her to be happy.'

We'd booked a table at Cosmo's, the restaurant where, in just a few weeks, Jared and I would be holding our wedding reception. The restaurant was sweet and cosy, with framed paintings and photographs hung on the exposed brick walls, the tables covered with red-and-white checked tablecloths with flickering tea lights at their centre. My party took up a good chunk of the space as there were eighteen of us, including Trina, who'd been delighted by the last-minute invite.

'Hey, Ruth, love, did your mum tell you how well I'm doing with the caragym?' Dad asked from across the table. I groaned. We hadn't even ordered our starters yet and he was already starting on that little gem. Predictably, Mum tutted at the topic.

'Louie, the last thing I want to talk to my daughter about is that rusty old caravan.'

This wasn't technically true. Mum had struck up many conversations about the caravan since its purchase. All of them complaining about the bloody thing.

'It's coming on a treat, love.' Dad's chest puffed out as he shared his news. 'I'll be working out by the summer.'

'Are you into all that health and fitness stuff?' Linda asked and Dad's chest deflated ever so slightly.

'I will be. I have the equipment ready.'

Mum grumbled about the equipment rendering her dining room a danger zone.

'Maybe Jared can give you some pointers. He's into keeping himself fit.' Linda turned to her son. 'You'll be able to pass on some tips, won't you?'

Jared, bless him, glanced from Linda to Dad and then Mum, his loyalties being pulled in all directions. If he said yes, Mum would be fuming that he'd taken Dad's side, but if he said no, Dad would feel rejected. The poor bloke couldn't win. I decided it was my soon-to-be wifely duty to rescue him with a swift change of subject.

'So, Trina. I hear Rory's in New York.'

And so a conversation about the Big Apple began, with Mum imparting the wisdom she'd learned via Stephen. She'd only been to New York twice, but you'd think she was a Big Apple Greeter the way she was going on. Still, it had saved Jared's bacon, however temporary.

'I propose a toast,' Dad said later as we tucked into our main courses.

'You'd better not be toasting that blasted caravan,' Mum muttered.

'Of course not.' Dad glowered at Mum. 'Although, maybe we should. It's taken a lot of work, you know. It isn't as easy as those TV shows make it look.'

'Louie!'

Dad jumped as Mum hissed at him, and he almost sloshed the drink he was holding over the pretty checked tablecloth. 'I'm messing with you, woman. Do you really think I'd propose a toast to a bloody caravan? In front of all these people?'

'I wouldn't put it past you, you daft old sod.'

I wouldn't either, but an intervention was needed. Mum was starting to turn purple with rage. 'Why don't you just propose your toast, Dad?'

Dad cleared his throat, looking around the table bashfully. 'Yes. Good idea.' He raised his glass. 'I'd like to propose a toast to our Ruthie, my little baby girl who is all grown up now.'

'To Ruth!' our table chorused, raising their own glasses.

'The next time we all meet here, we'll be toasting Ruth and Jared as newlyweds.' Dad grabbed his napkin and dabbed at his eyes. Mum's face lost its purple hue as she took Dad's hand in hers and gave it a squeeze, all thoughts of caravans and gym equipment forgotten. For the time being.

TWENTY-EIGHT

Trina

It was dark by the time Trina left Cosmo's, but it was still only late afternoon in New York so she gave Rory a ring from the back of the taxi. She'd had a lovely time with Ruth and her friends, and it was nice to see her Aunt Vee and Uncle Louie again. Trina hadn't grown up with a close family like Ruth had; her mother was always too busy being wooed by potential suitors, her father didn't seem to care for anything but work, golf and women, and her sister wasn't a people person at all, unless you were an adoring rich man. Sex and money, that's all her family seemed to care about. Luckily Trina now had Rory and although they'd had a bit of a rocky start, she was sure their marriage would flourish once he was back from New York.

'You're through to Rory Hamilton-Wraith. Leave a message!'

It had been the same ever since Rory had left. Whenever Trina phoned Rory, she was met with his voicemail, but then he had told her he would be incredibly busy. It was why she hadn't joined him on the trip, after all.

'Hi, babe. It's me, Trina. I just thought I'd call and see how you are. Phone me back. No rush.' She didn't want to feel like she was pressurising her husband. It seemed all she'd done since their honeymoon was moan and nag, but all that was going to change. 'I love you.'

Popping her phone back into her handbag, Trina settled back in the taxi as it trundled towards the annex. She wasn't relishing the thought of spending the night there alone again, but Rory would be home in a couple of days. She'd already gathered information for a few potential properties for when he returned, and she was jolted with a flutter of excitement whenever she thought about their new home. It wasn't that she was ungrateful for the use of the annex, but it wasn't very romantic living on the doorstep of your in-laws, was it? The annex was already furnished, so Trina hadn't been able to choose her own fixtures and fittings or put her own stamp on it. While the annex was roomy and tastefully decorated, it was rather old-fashioned.

'It's the smaller building on the right,' Trina directed the taxi driver as they entered the Hamilton-Wraith estate. Winnie waved as they made their way past the main house and scurried over to greet Trina as she stepped out of the vehicle.

'Been anywhere nice?'

Trina paid the driver and stepped out of the way as the cabbie set off again, happy with his healthy tip. 'It's my cousin's birthday so she invited me out.'

'How lovely for you.' Winnie smiled at Trina but her eyes were far from friendly. 'Rory's away working hard and you're out partying all night. I'd feel guilty about enjoying myself while my husband was slaving away, but we're all different, aren't we?' She gave a false chuckle. Neither of them bought it.

'I wasn't partying all night. We went to a restaurant.' Trina thought about the Blue Llama. There had been no fake chuckle or guilt about *that*. 'And I *do* want to go back to work.'

'Well, that just wouldn't do, would it?' Winnie's mouth twisted. She was *this close* to 'tsk'ing at her silly little daughter-in-law. 'What if Rory needed you and you were too busy cleaning muck off a filthy old dog? Hardly an aspiring role, really, is it? *Dog groomer*.' Winnie gave a haughty laugh. And running betting shops is something to be proud of? Trina thought, but wasn't brave enough to voice it. 'I'm sure it was fun while you were younger, but it's time to grow up now. You're a wife. Soon you'll be a mother.'

'Mums can work too, you know.'

Winnie straightened, seeming to grow taller than her five foot three frame. 'Not if they are Hamilton-Wraiths!' Piercing Trina with one final glare, she turned on her heel and marched back to the main house.

'Not if they're Hamilton-Wraiths,' Trina mimicked as she wandered into the annex. So that was what Winnie expected of her: wife and mother. Full stop. It was clearly what Rory expected of her too, but that wasn't going to happen. If Rory wanted a wife who was willing to mooch around at home all day (because Hamilton-Wraiths did not look after their own children or homes. They had nannies and housekeepers for that) and look pretty on his arm at social events, he should have married a woman like her sister. Tori had no ambitions or drive beyond marrying a wealthy man, but Trina wasn't like that at all. She'd married for love and if Rory loved her too he would support her choices. She vowed to speak to her husband and make it clear that she intended to return to work as soon as possible. Grabbing her phone, she dialled Rory's number. Part of her expected to hear the usual voicemail message, but Rory himself answered this time.

'Trina, babe. I was about to phone you. I'm just leaving the office now.'

Trina could hear the commotion of Manhattan life in the background, and yearned to be there with him. She'd always loved New York but they hadn't experienced it together yet. 'I'm sorry I haven't been able to get back to you. I've been so busy.'

'It's okay. I understand.' Trina took a deep breath. This was her chance to let Rory know her intentions. What was the worst that could happen? 'I need to speak to you about something.'

'Just a second, babe. I'm about to get in a cab.'

Deflated but slightly relieved, Trina listened as a muffled Rory gave an address to the driver before coming back to her. It struck Trina as slightly worrying that she was afraid of speaking her mind to her husband, but she quashed the feeling.

'Are you going back to your hotel?' Poor Rory. It must have been terribly lonely for him, being out in a bustling city all by himself. At least Trina had Aidan and Ruth – and Rory's family, if she was feeling really desperate for company.

'Not yet. I'm going to grab some dinner first.'

'Alone? Wouldn't it be easier to get room service?' Trina couldn't think of many things worse than eating alone in a restaurant, but Rory wasn't one for grabbing a burger on the go.

'I'm meeting someone.'

'Oh, that's good then.' Trina should really get back to the subject of her employment status, but she found herself avoiding it for just a moment longer. 'Who are you meeting? Someone from the office?'

Rory cleared his throat. 'Can I call you back? It's just I'm almost there and you know how rude I think it is when people talk on their phones in restaurants.'

Trina had never heard Rory object to this, but she could

see his point. 'I guess. It's just that I had something important to tell you.'

'You're not pregnant, are you?' The harsh tone of Rory's question shocked Trina. They hadn't been actively trying for a baby, but they both wanted to start a family and they were married now, so it wasn't something to sound so alarmed at.

'No, I'm not.'

Rory breathed a sigh. 'Thank God for that.' A relieved laugh spluttered from his lips. 'You had me worried there for a minute.'

Worried? Why would a baby worry him? Yes, it would be a little sooner than planned but it would be a nice surprise. Wouldn't it? Plus, it would give Trina something to do while she was stuck at home all day.

'What was it you wanted to talk to me about then?'

This was it. Fortifying breath. 'I want to go back to work. Sooner rather than later.'

There was silence from Rory, the only noise coming from the city as he emerged from his cab. Trina held her breath as she waited for his reaction.

'How soon?' Rory's voice was slow and measured.

'As soon as possible. I can't be the kind of wife who sits at home all day. I enjoyed my job, Rory, and I miss it.'

There was a whoosh of air down the phone, and Trina prepared herself for a tirade, prepared to defend herself and her decision, because defend it she would. The annex was slowly suffocating her. She needed to get back out into the real world and become a useful member of society again.

But Rory didn't say a word. Instead it was a woman's voice Trina heard over the line.

'Hey, Rory. Guess who? Gosh, I'm so sorry. I didn't realise you were on the phone. I'll meet you inside, yes? So sorry.'

There was an awkward silence between them as the

woman's embarrassed giggles faded into the background. Trina finally found her voice – or one that was vaguely like her own.

'Who was that? Why do I recognise her voice?' Trina's first thought was Carrington, but then she recalled seeing her sister-in-law that evening, just before she left for the restaurant.

'I told you I was meeting someone for dinner.'

'But who is it?' She definitely recognised the voice. Was it someone from the UK office, someone she'd met at a function?

'Relax, will you?' Rory's tone was smooth, as though he didn't have a care in the world. Not one teeny, tiny little concern. 'It's only Ginny.'

'*Ginny?* What is she doing there?' Had they travelled to New York together? Gone on a nice little jaunt behind her back? No wonder Rory hadn't wanted Trina to accompany him!

'She got here yesterday. Work have sent her. I didn't have a clue she'd be here, I swear.'

'So it never came up during Carrie's birthday dinner?' Trina found that incredibly hard to believe; the pair had barely paused for breath that evening.

'No, not at all. Ginny phoned me yesterday to say she'd landed at JFK. She's never been to New York before so I offered to show her around a bit.'

'*Show her around a bit?*' Now he really was taking the piss. 'How can you show her around when you're so busy you can barely stop to eat? Isn't that what you told me? Isn't that why I'm still here at home?'

'Trina, calm down. You're overreacting.'

Overreacting? Trina rather thought she was *under*reacting, given the circumstances. He'd refused to take Trina with him as he was so important and busy, yet had time to share cosy little dinners with Ginny and show her around the city! Trina was so angry the phone was trembling in her hand.

'I can't talk to you when you're being like this. Go and have a bath and calm down and I'll call you back later.'

Trina stared at her phone as Rory ended the call. He'd hung up on her so that he could go and enjoy dinner with his little friend! Dropping the phone, Trina curled up on her bed, tucking her knees in tightly. Surely marriage wasn't supposed to be like this?

TWENTY-NINE

Erin

Erin sometimes wondered if she really was in love with Richard. Before they got together, she'd hopped from one man to the next with boundless energy, barely getting beyond a second date. It had been a case of 'the more men the merrier', as far as Erin was concerned. Who wanted to settle down with one man when you could have fun with as many as you liked? Call Erin greedy – she'd been called far worse over the years – but settling down just wasn't in her DNA.

But then she'd given Richard a chance after he'd worn her down and now – miraculously – they'd ended up as a couple. An actual, bona fide couple. And she was happy with what they had. She could have done without Amanda sticking her beak in, obviously, and she wouldn't have chosen Kelvin and Susan as in-laws, but Erin doubted any relationship was truly perfect.

But was it really possible that she *loved* Richard?

Erin prised her eyes open, one at a time, and regarded herself in the full-length mirror.

Yep. Definitely love. Why else would she be trussed up like a complete knob-head?

'Get some bubbles down your throat!' One of the other bridesmaids – Becca or Megan, Erin had yet to learn their names properly – thrust a glass of champagne into her hand before she tottered away. Erin observed the glass in her hand. There wasn't nearly enough alcohol in there to make her outfit any less hideous.

'Are you ready for this, everyone?' Helen, the maid of honour, waved her hands in the air and almost toppled over. The glass in her hand was empty, the champagne sloshing happily in her stomach with the rest of the bottle she'd guzzled while they'd waited. Erin didn't know much about Helen, but she did know that the girl was fond of a drink. Any event was fair game for a piss-up, especially if it involved her best friend and her wedding. Lindsay and her female entourage had squeezed into the boutique for their final dress fittings and now Lindsay was emerging from the curtained-off dressing room at the back of the shop.

'Well? What do you think?' Lindsay gave a twirl, and an appreciative applause started up. The champagne had clearly been a little too free-flowing.

Good lord.

'You look stunning, darling.' Susan waddled over to her daughter and reached up to give Lindsay's cheeks a squeeze. 'Absolutely stunning. I'm so proud of you!'

'You look amazing,' one of the bridesmaids piped up. Erin wondered how much champagne she'd consumed. 'Too much' was the answer.

'Frank is going to *die* when he sees you,' another cried. Erin could believe that. Death by laughter, most probably.

'The fit is incredible,' a third bridesmaid said, which was certainly true. The dress – what little of it there was – moulded to Lindsay's body like a second skin. 'Snug' was an understatement. As was 'tasteless' and 'tacky'. It was the most horrific wedding dress Erin had ever seen. The skirt barely covered Lindsay's crotch, while the sleeveless bodice was made of some sort of feathery material interspersed with pink diamantés. She wore a gaudy six-inch tiara with an attached floor-length veil, which was also adorned with pink diamantés.

Unfortunately, the bridesmaid dresses were just as gruesome, if not more so. Erin was wearing a black-and-pink basque with a short pink tutu and matching pink strappy sandals. She *must* love Richard to agree to wear such tat.

'Ow. It's hurting my arms.' LuLu stepped out of the cubicle next to Lindsay, rubbing her arms. She was the only one who looked vaguely normal, in a pretty pink dress and matching ballet pumps. The only thing spoiling the look were the attached fairy wings, but Erin would take them over the tutu any time.

'Hmm, the sleeves are a bit tight.' Ingrid strode across the room and tugged at the fabric slicing into LuLu's upper arms. 'Your arms are a bit podgy. Do you think you could go on a little diet?'

'Hey, hey, hold on a minute.' Erin dumped her glass of champagne on a shelf and rushed across to poor LuLu, whose eyes had pooled with tears. 'Her arms aren't podgy at all. Her arms are *normal*. It's the dress that's the problem. It needs adjusting.'

Ingrid tutted. 'Do you think we have time to adjust any of the dresses now? This is the *final* fitting.' She tapped at the schedule on the ever-present clipboard.

'And this is your final warning.' Erin took a step closer. If Ingrid didn't shut her gob, she'd be carrying her clipboard permanently up her arse.

'Let's calm down, shall we?' Susan stepped between the women, though she was no threat as the top of her platinum bouffant barely reached their bosoms. 'Erin is right. It's the dress that needs fixing, not our beautiful LuLu.'

Erin wasn't sure who was more shocked, Susan for sticking up for Erin or Erin for finding an ally in Susan.

'LuLu's perfect, aren't you, babe?' Lindsay stroked her niece's hair and LuLu gave a wobbly smile.

'I didn't mean anything by it. I'll see what I can do.' Sticking her chin in the air, Ingrid stalked off in search of the boutique's owner.

'Go and get changed, LuLu.' Erin guided the girl back into the changing room. 'Don't worry, we'll get it sorted, okay?' LuLu nodded, so Erin swished the curtain closed and joined the others. When Ingrid returned, her face was even more pinched than usual.

'We *may* be able to get the dress altered in time.' She made a note on her clipboard, refusing to meet anybody's eye. 'It's going to mess up our schedule, but if that's what you want …'

Erin wanted to argue that what they wanted was for was LuLu to feel comfortable. That they wanted her to feel beautiful and special and not feel as if she had to go on a diet at twelve. But she bit her tongue. She'd already won the battle. She didn't need to incense Ingrid further.

'What shall I do with my dress?' LuLu emerged from the cubicle wearing her jeans and a T-shirt. She held out the dress on its hanger.

'Give it to her.' Erin pointed at Ingrid. 'We're going out for big, fat ice creams.'

Erin caught Ingrid's eye but the woman wisely kept quiet. Erin changed quickly before taking LuLu's hand and leading her out of the boutique. There was a park not far away with an ice cream van parked outside the play area. Erin bought two double cones with lashings of raspberry sauce and marshmallows, which they ate on a bench.

'Are my arms really podgy?' LuLu asked, though she didn't seem overly concerned, judging by the ice cream she was enjoying.

'No. Ingrid was talking shit.' Amanda was dead against

swearing in front of the children, but sometimes it was necessary.

'I don't like Ingrid.'

'Me either.' Erin grinned down at LuLu, and they both giggled.

'Do you think you'll marry my dad?' LuLu asked. 'Then you'd be my step-mum.'

'But step-mums are horrible and nasty and witchy. A bit like Ingrid.' Erin nudged LuLu and they giggled again.

'Seriously, though, having you as a step-mum would be pretty cool.'

Erin licked her ice cream, wondering how to explain it to a child. She couldn't seem to explain it to herself, so she didn't stand a chance with LuLu.

'I don't really want to get married, sweetie.'

LuLu's brow furrowed. 'What, never?'

Erin shook her head. 'That doesn't mean I don't love your dad. I do. Very much.' So much that she was willing to dress up like Chav Barbie to please his sister. 'But marriage just isn't for me.'

'But *all* girls want to get married and dress up like princesses.'

Even Aunty Lindsay? That dress was as far from princess-y as you could get, even if it was topped off with a tiara. 'Not me, kid.'

'Why not?'

Erin placed an arm around LuLu's shoulders and pulled her in tight, resting her head on LuLu's. Perhaps it was because she'd witnessed the utter breakdown of her parents' marriage as a child and had been let down by her father monumentally ever since. How could she ever trust a man so completely when she'd seen the mess her father had left behind? Marriage wasn't a guarantee to a 'happily ever after', and Erin refused to fall under its spell.

'I'm happy as I am.' It was the easiest explanation – and the truth.

THIRTY

Ruth

'I have been *dreaming* about today.' Quinn rubbed her hands together, her face a picture of pure joy as we made our way up the path towards Linda and Bob's house. 'Is Linda really as good as you say she is?'

I nodded. 'She's like a younger version of Mary Berry.'

'Wow.' Quinn adopted a dreamy look on her face. 'I love *Bake Off*, don't you?'

'Nah.' Erin couldn't have looked any less interested if Quinn had asked her opinion on the Vietnamese football league. 'I've never actually watched an episode. I like to eat cake, not watch it being made. What's the point in that?'

'Because it's *Bake Off*.' Quinn's voice had a faint tremble to it, as though she could burst into tears at any moment.

'Have you ever watched an episode of *Embarrassing Bodies*?' Erin asked.

Quinn shook her head, the joy well and truly wiped from her face. 'No, it's gross.'

'Me either, but plenty of people do.' Erin gave a shrug. 'People like to watch different things.'

'You can't compare *Bake Off* to *Embarrassing Bodies*. *Bake Off* doesn't have any infected willies on it for a start.' At the exact moment Quinn uttered the words 'infected willies', the door swung open, revealing Jared's mum. Quinn suddenly took great interest in the doorstep as she studied it intensely, her cheeks bright beneath her curtain of blonde hair.

'She doesn't watch *Bake Off*.' Quinn thrust a finger in Erin's general direction as though it explained everything.

'Oh, well, nobody's perfect.' Linda stepped aside and allowed the three of us to troop inside. She led us into the kitchen where Jared's sister and nephew were sitting at the table, plates of cakes tantalising them from the centre.

'You've got some willpower,' I told Ally as I joined her at the table. 'There would have been nothing but a plate of crumbs remaining if I'd been left in here unsupervised.'

'Believe me, I wanted to scoff the lot, but Mum would have killed me.'

Linda gave a tut as she filled the kettle. '"Killed" is a bit extreme. Maimed a little, perhaps.' She turned away from the sink to grin at us. 'If you could just hold on for two more minutes, I'll make us all a drink and then we can start tasting.'

Linda had made three cakes for us to sample to help me decide what I wanted for the wedding: a Victoria sponge with vanilla buttercream and raspberry jam, a lemon drizzle cake, and an orange sponge with chocolate buttercream and marmalade filling.

'Hello again, Noah.' Quinn, who had met Jared's nephew at my birthday dinner, was making silly faces at the boy. 'Aren't you being a good boy?'

'He's being very patient while we wait for our cake,' Ally said, looking pointedly at her mother.

'Okay, okay, I'm going as fast as I can.' Linda finished

making the drinks before she cut the cakes, placing a small slice of each in front of us. 'I can ice and decorate the real thing to make it look fancier. Have you had any ideas for the kind of design you'd like?'

I shook my head, my mouth too full of lemon drizzle cake to answer. I'd spent an entire evening poring over Trina's wedding file, looking at the cake designs there. They were all beautiful but – dare I say it? – boring. White icing was traditional, but it wasn't my style at all.

'These are amazing,' Quinn told Linda. 'You really are as good as Mary Berry.'

'Oh, I don't know about that.' Linda waved away the compliment but it was clear she was chuffed with the comparison.

'It's true, Mum. I know we're supposed to be helping Ruth, but I can't choose.'

Quinn shook her head. 'Me either.'

I couldn't be swayed by any of the cakes either. They were all delicious in their own way, and choosing just one was going to be tough. I'd need to test at least another slice of each.

'Do you know what I used to do when I was single and couldn't decide between three men to date?' We all turned to Erin as she shared her words of wisdom. 'I'd date all three. Why deny yourself pleasure?'

I held my breath. Where was Erin going with this in front of my future mother-in-law? Erin had calmed down since getting together with Richard Shuttleworth, but before that she could be pretty filthy and I was afraid of the memories she was about to unleash in Linda's kitchen.

'You know, I think you're right.' Linda nodded as she observed her cakes. 'I could make a three-tiered cake descending in size. One of each cake.'

'I like the sound of that.' Why deny yourself pleasure?

'I could use traditional white icing or vamp it up a little with colour. Pink for the Victoria, yellow for the lemon drizzle, and orange for the orange sponge.'

I didn't need to think twice about the second suggestion. 'Definitely the coloured icing.'

'I thought so.' Linda picked up her cake knife. 'So, who wants another slice?'

We naturally started to talk about the wedding as we worked our way through yet more cake. It was quickly becoming my only topic of conversation lately, and the more word spread about my upcoming nuptials, the more people I got to chat to about it. I'd run into one of the girls from payroll in the loos a few days earlier and we'd spent almost twenty minutes discussing garters in front of the sinks. Cheryl from IT had stopped by for a chat each morning, sharing a host of new tips each day, from the supplier of her invites to the best place to convert your currency for the honeymoon. I didn't have the heart to tell her that Jared and I weren't actually going on honeymoon as every scrap of our savings was going towards the wedding. There wouldn't be enough left over for a day trip to Blackpool, never mind a full-blown holiday.

'I'm trying to work out what I want for the evening entertainment,' I told the others now. 'There won't be a great deal of room at Cosmo's. Jared suggested a DJ, but I want something with a bit more of a fun element. Within budget, of course.' There had been plenty of ideas on the wedding blogs I frequented, but most were far too costly for our shoestring wedding.

'Have you thought about karaoke?' Ally asked and my eyes widened at the suggestion. Of course! For Freya's thirtieth birthday, Ally had organised a karaoke party. The host was outrageous, with his over-the-top innuendo, and his dress sense hadn't been anything to aspire to, but it had been so much fun.

'I think that would be perfect.'

'Do you want me to get the number for you?'

'That'd be great, thanks.' I reached into my handbag

and pulled out my notebook to jot down Ally's suggestion. The notebook was now jam-packed with ideas and to-do lists and I was sure it wouldn't make the tiniest bit of sense to anybody else who happened to stumble across it. Even Jared had trouble deciphering my notes, and it was his wedding too.

'Have you had any luck with the favours?' Linda knew I was keen to make my own, but I'd had some difficulty finding something easy enough for my limited capabilities.

'I was thinking about making some cupcakes topped with Love Hearts sweets.' It was by far the easiest option I had come across.

'Give me a shout if you need any help.'

I thanked Linda for her offer, but I was sure I wouldn't need it. How difficult could baking some simple cupcakes be?

I wasn't much of a baker – understatement! – but with the Spice Girls blasting from the sitting room, I weighed out the butter and sugar and creamed them together using the electric whisk I'd borrowed from Linda (I did need a little bit of help from her, after all). All was going well until I added the egg, which curdled the mixture and ruined it. Later, when it was far too late, I learned that the situation could have been easily remedied by mixing in a little flour, but I assumed the mixture was a Ruth-disaster (and was surprised it had taken so long to occur) and consigned it to the bin before starting again. This time, the eggs behaved themselves and I was pleased – and more than a little shocked – when I ended up with a respectable cake mix. I spooned the mix into cake cases and popped them in the oven.

Hurrah! Miracles *do* happen.

I gave the bowl a thorough licking before I moved into the sitting room. While I waited, I had a look through

Trina's wedding file to make sure I hadn't missed anything vital. The wedding plans seemed to be coming along nicely, but I didn't want to walk down the aisle and realise I'd forgotten to buy the rings or anything important like that. Trina's plans were extensive but I could skip a lot of it since we weren't planning on having a wedding breakfast or midnight barbeque or a mass release of Chinese lanterns – or any of the many extras Trina and Rory had opted to include. I was feeling pretty pleased with the progress I'd made as I flicked through the file, but my eyes started to grow heavy. Stifling a yawn, I turned the page, landing on a section dedicated to plinths. Having no use for this section, I turned the page, stifling another yawn. Wedding planning was *exhausting*.

A piercing noise jolted me awake and it took me a moment to figure out what was going on. I remembered sitting down with Trina's wedding file after …

'Cripes!' Leaping to my feet, not caring when the file flipped through the air and landed in a heap on the carpet, I scuttled towards the kitchen and flung open the door. Thick smoke was snaking from the oven and starting to fill the room, which was causing the smoke detector to screech its warning.

'Shit, shit, shit.' I didn't know what to tend to first – the cakes or the alarm. 'Shit, shit, shit.' Frantically waving my hands in front of me to try to dispel the smoke, I stepped into the kitchen and turned the oven off before opening the door, coughing and spluttering as I was met with a cloud of smoke. The cakes were black. No amount of wafting was going to change that (although I did give it a go with a tea towel). I opened the window as wide as I could before standing on a chair to reset the smoke detector. Why had I allowed myself to fall asleep?

'Oh no.' I returned to the cakes and gave them a prod. There was no way to save them. Silver Spoon couldn't produce enough icing sugar to mask the lumps of charcoal before me. I would have to start again. For the third time.

'Sod it.' Who had I been kidding? I couldn't bake! I'd have to scrap the cupcake idea and come up with something else. Something that wasn't a fire or health hazard. Piling the dishes in the sink – I would do it later, honestly – I settled down on the sofa with a bar of chocolate (I needed the sugar after my shock) and my *Beginner's Guide* box set. I'd watched two and a half episodes and the chocolate was long gone by the time Jared got home.

'How did the cake testing go at Mum's?' Jared flopped down next to me on the sofa and pulled me close for a cuddle. I nestled into his body, relaxing into its familiar contours.

'Great. We've settled on a three-tiered cake of Victoria sponge, lemon drizzle and orange sponge.'

'Sounds good.'

'How did the stag night plans go?' While I'd been sampling cake, Jared had been at the pub with his brother-in-law, who was also his best man, discussing Jared's final night as a single man.

'Good, I think. I've told Gavin I just want a quiet night in the pub. A few drinks, a game or two of pool. Nothing tacky like strippers.'

'Theo will be disappointed.'

'I don't care. I don't want to turn up at my wedding with a raging hangover. I want to enjoy the best day of my life.'

I shifted my position so that I could kiss Jared, partly hoping he was saying such sweet things just to get into my pants.

'Ruth?' Jared pulled away and smoothed a stray strand of hair away from my forehead. 'What is that smell?'

'Oh. That.' I cringed. I'd been hoping the smoke would have dissipated enough to go unnoticed, but it looked like I would have to explain.

'I feel like such a failure,' I said once I'd told him about my baking disaster. I expected Jared to laugh when I told him about the burned-to-smithereens cakes but he simply gave me another squeeze.

'Let's order a takeaway and, while we wait, we'll have a look on the internet for something else to make. All this favour-making business needs is a bit of teamwork.'

This was why I was marrying the man.

THIRTY-ONE

Erin

Erin loved her flat. It was small, but light and airy, and everything in it was hers. She'd chosen everything from the wallpaper to the bathroom suite, the cushions on the sofa to the rug on the hardwood floor. It was her space, the place she could shut out the world and truly relax.

But there was one place she loved more than her little flat, and that was her mother's house. Erin had been almost ten when they'd moved to the small terraced house, and the memory of finally feeling safe as she stepped through the doors was still fresh in her mind. They were starting again – Erin and her mum – and the bruises from their former life were already healing. Erin still felt that same sense of relief and security as she stepped over the threshold now, over two decades later.

'Richard not with you?' Ann asked as she led her daughter into the sitting room. The room was warm and filled with memories: hot chocolates as Erin and Ann snuggled under a blanket to watch a video, games of Monopoly, Frustration and Mouse Trap, dancing and giggles and good advice and gossip. This home was full of love. It had been their fresh start after the divorce, just Ann and Erin and a lifetime of goodness ahead of them to erase the bad that had gone before.

'He's with LuLu and Ralph.' Amanda had been quite clear that her children shouldn't mix with Erin's family as it 'may confuse them'. Everybody knew that it was nothing more than another ploy to keep some control over her ex-husband, but Richard went along with her rule as it was easier that way.

'You really shouldn't let that woman push you around,' Ann said. 'They're Richard's children too, and you're part of his life now. Stand up for yourself, Erin. Always.'

Erin smiled at her mum. Ann was the strongest woman Erin knew, but that hadn't always been the case. Once upon a time Ann had been meek and timid, crushed under her husband's rule, but Ann had finally escaped and forged a new life for herself and her daughter, and she would never stop encouraging Erin to be herself, no matter what.

'I know, but anything for a quiet life, eh?'

'Quiet? You?' Ann gave a hoot. When had her daughter ever kept her mouth shut about anything she believed in? Ann couldn't have been prouder of the woman she had raised.

'New partners are important.'

'I know that, Mum. But you know what Amanda's like. It's nothing personal against me – she'd be like this with whoever Richard was with.'

'I wasn't actually talking about you and Richard.' Ann fidgeted with the hem of her cardigan, inspecting it for bits of fluff. 'I was talking about me.'

'You?'

'Yes, me.' Ann plucked a piece of imaginary lint from her cardigan and searched for more. 'And Alistair.'

'Who?'

Ann gave up the lint charade and finally looked at her

daughter, although she didn't quite make eye contact. 'You know Jacqui?'

Jacqui was Ann's best friend. They'd worked together eons ago, when Erin was little and they'd lived in their old house. It had been Jacqui who'd finally convinced Ann to leave her abusive husband, Jacqui who'd provided them with a bed to sleep in until they'd sorted themselves out. She'd phoned the police when Erin's dad had turned up at the house and tried to kick the front door in, had held Erin and Ann as they shook with fear as he was taken away. She'd been there for Ann and Erin over the years and neither of them dared to imagine where they'd be without her.

Ann took Erin's hand, unintentionally squeezing it a bit too hard. 'Jacqui has a brother. I don't know if you remember him?'

Erin shook her head while Ann took a fortifying breath.

'Anyway, I always thought Alistair was rather dishy.'

Erin couldn't help the giggle that escaped. Dishy? Her mum thought a man was *dishy?* Nobody used that term any more for a start and, besides, her mother had sworn off men after she'd divorced Erin's father. She'd said that her relationship with him had been enough to last her a lifetime – and as far as Erin was aware, she hadn't been on one date since.

Ann decided to ignore the giggle, however hurtful the sound was. Ann was still a woman, no matter how out of practice she was at romance. 'We met again at Jacqui's grandson's christening last year and got chatting. He asked to see me again and I said yes.'

Erin's eyes widened. 'You went on a *date?* An actual date?'

'More than one. We've been seeing each other for a few months.' Ann cleared her throat. 'Just over a year, actually.'

'A *year?*' Erin was about to rise with indignation and

ask how her mother could keep such information to herself, but then she realised she hadn't been completely honest about her relationship with Richard in the beginning. It had been new and scary and Erin had to be sure she was comfortable about it all herself before she shared it with anybody else. 'Wow, Mum. That's great.'

'Do you really think so?'

'Yes, as long as you're being careful.'

Ann gave Erin's hand a pat. 'Oh, I am. Don't worry about that. Alistair is *nothing* like your father. He's about as threatening as a stick of celery.'

'That isn't what I meant. I mean *be careful*.' Erin sighed when it was clear her mother wasn't getting it. 'I hope you're using protection, Mum, because there's all sorts going around and you don't want to find yourself riddled with nasties.'

Ann's cheeks burned bright at the implication. 'Well, yes. Thank you for the advice.' Ann cleared her throat. She was *mortified* at the way the conversation had turned out. 'Shall I put the kettle on?'

'The kettle? A moment like this calls for champagne, surely.'

'Oh, I don't know about that.' Ann resurrected her lint-hunt. 'It's not like he's proposed. Yet.'

'You think he's going to ask you to marry him?' Blimey. Five minutes ago, Erin had been under the impression her mother was happily, *permanently* single. Now she was talking about the possibility of getting hitched to a man Erin couldn't recall ever meeting.

'I don't know. Maybe.' Ann smiled shyly at her daughter. 'We've talked about … you know … the future.'

'And you'd marry him?'

'Yes, love. I would.' Ann took Erin's hand once more. 'I let your father rule my life for far too long, even after I'd left him. I've wasted so much time. But not any more. Alistair makes me happy, and I think I deserve to be.'

'You do, Mum. Of course you do.' Erin pulled her mum into a hug, like the many they'd shared in that very sitting room over the years. 'But before you marry him, do you think I could meet him?'

Ann laughed. 'He'd like that very much. And so would I.'

THIRTY-TWO

Trina

'Am I overreacting?' Trina looked down at the giant mug of hot chocolate topped with whipped cream, marshmallows *and* chocolate sprinkles, sitting proudly next to a huge slab of sticky ginger cake with lemon frosting. Overloading on sugar in one of her favourite independent coffee shops was usually her favourite way to indulge on a rainy afternoon, but her heart just wasn't in it today. Her heart hadn't been in anything but turmoil since she'd discovered that Rory had a travelling companion. But she trusted Aidan to tell her the truth about the situation, even if she couldn't look him in the eye as he delivered it.

'I don't know, Trina. I really don't. I mean, it *is* pretty shitty of him to be playing tour guide to this girl when he told you he'd be too busy to hang out with you over there, but that doesn't mean he's cheating on you.'

Trina's eyes snapped away from the hot chocolate. 'You think he could be cheating on me?' The thought had – fleetingly – crossed her mind, but Rory wouldn't do that to her. He may have been a bit of a pig about the whole New

York thing but he wouldn't be unfaithful, would he? They'd only been married for five minutes!

'No!' Aidan reached across the table to take Trina's hand in his. His sudden outburst earned him a few curious glances from the other patrons of the coffee shop, but Aidan didn't notice. 'I thought that was what you were thinking. I was trying to put your mind at rest. I clearly suck at it.'

Trina managed a small smile, which was a major feat. She hadn't felt like smiling since her latest phone call with Rory, where she'd ranted and raved like a mad woman while Rory sighed and tutted and told her to calm down. Which she hadn't, of course. His words had only riled her further.

'That's better. I don't like to see you looking so sad.' Aidan gave Trina's hand a squeeze before he released it. 'You should always be smiling, and I hate to say it, but Rory is a prick for making you feel like this. Has he been in contact since?'

Trina nodded as she swiped a finger into the hot chocolate's cream and licked it off. 'He's phoned a couple of times, but I haven't answered. Do you think I should have?'

'That's up to you.'

Trina groaned. 'Don't do that. Tell me what to do. Please! Because I haven't got a clue.'

'I can't make these decisions for you.'

'But you know me so well. You know what's best for me.'

Aidan observed Trina for a moment, watching her intently as he gathered his thoughts. She started to feel quite warm under his gaze and squirmed in her seat. She still wasn't really in the mood for her hot chocolate, but she picked it up and took a sip anyway to break the intense eye contact.

'I think you should talk to Rory.'

'I should?' Trina's shoulders drooped. She wasn't quite sure what she'd been expecting Aidan to say, but his advice felt a little flat.

'You can't sort this mess out if you don't talk to each other.'

That made sense, and she had calmed down after the initial shock. She could talk to Rory and give him the chance to explain. Maybe Rory had been right and she *was* overreacting. So he'd met up with a friend while he was away. So what? It was hardly Rory's fault that Ginny had turned up, and he was only being gentlemanly by taking her under his wing.

'You're right. I'll phone him later.' Trina gave Aidan's foot a nudge under the table. 'See, I told you you'd know what was best for me. What would I do without you?'

Trina felt a tight knot of apprehension in her throat as she picked up the phone later that evening. Her finger hovered over the call button as the knot tightened further, seeming to squeeze the breath from her. Phoning her husband shouldn't feel like this. This wasn't how she'd imagined her life with Rory would be at all. She'd quickly fallen for his charm, agreeing to marry him after only a few months together, but did she really know him? And did he know her? It had only been a little over a year between the golf club's dance and their wedding day, after all. They both seemed intent on moulding the other into their idea of the ideal spouse, but it shouldn't be like that. Trina should be able to be herself. She shouldn't have to tiptoe around her husband, quashing her own desires so that she wouldn't disappoint him. And Rory wasn't the only one to blame here; Trina had known how passionate Rory was about his work, yet she expected him to cut back now that they were married. It was about time they started to compromise. Trina would try to get her job back at Pooch

Couture and if Rory could accept that – which she hoped he would once the whole New York fiasco had been sorted – then she would accept Rory's workaholic tendencies. This marriage would work with a little bit of give and take – on both sides.

Pressing the call button, Trina tried to relax into the sofa but her shoulders were still taut with tension. They tensed even more when Rory picked up.

'I didn't think you were ever going to speak to me again.' Rory's voice was guarded. 'You know there's nothing going on with Ginny, don't you? She's just my little sister's best friend who happens to be here at the same time that I am.'

'I know.' Even still, Trina was glad to have that confirmed. 'I was just upset that you were there with her, and not me.'

'*You* were upset? What about me? I've been accused of getting up to all sorts.'

'I didn't actually accuse you of anything,' Trina said but Rory wasn't listening.

'I am allowed female friends, you know. I don't have a problem with you spending time with Aaron.'

'It's Aidan,' Trina corrected but again, Rory wasn't listening. He'd wanted to get all this sorted out immediately but Trina hadn't had the decency to speak to him until now, so he had a lot of pent-up frustration to release.

'You're always with him, gossiping and giggling, and I don't say a word. Mother says I should put my foot down and end your friendship now we're married, in case people get the wrong idea. She was quite adamant until I pointed out he's a poofter.'

'Aidan isn't gay!' He certainly wasn't a 'poofter'. Trina's lip curled at Rory's choice of word. 'Aidan's straight.' Very much so, judging by the kiss they'd once shared. It was still Trina's most thrilling memory, although she would never admit it.

'Come off it.' Rory spluttered at the very idea. 'He's a *hairdresser*.'

'He's a hair *stylist*, actually. And he's straight.' An image of Aidan's hands in her hair as they kissed popped into Trina's mind. He was definitely straight.

'Don't be so naïve. The man's a bender!'

Had Rory always been so offensive? Had he kept it to himself or had she been blinded to it?

'Why do you think I keep my distance when he's around? You can't be too careful with his sort. They'd have your underpants around your ankles before you could blink.'

Where had her charming husband disappeared to? The sweet Rory who she'd often felt had stepped out of the pages of a fairy tale?

'Believe me, you're not his type at all,' she told him.

Rory snorted. 'Likes the squeaky, mincing ones, does he?'

'No, he likes *women*. In fact, Aidan and I were quite … close before we got together.'

That shut Rory up for a moment. Trina closed her eyes and scrunched up her face. She shouldn't have let that slip. She and Aidan had agreed to forget all about their almost dalliance long ago, deciding their friendship was too important. Aidan may not have wanted Trina in the romantic sense, but he wanted her as a friend, and she was willing to accept that. Friendship was better than nothing, although she may have put a spanner in the works just now with her big gob.

'You slept with him?' Rory's voice was a mix of disbelief and outrage. He'd been convinced Aidan had been checking him out every time they met, but had he been checking out his wife instead? The sneaky little bastard!

'No, it didn't get that far. We kissed, that's all.' But what a kiss! Trina had been harbouring feelings for Aidan for quite a while but was afraid of making the first step, so it was a blissful moment when Aidan had kissed her. It had been the most romantic thing that had ever happened to her. More romantic than Rory's very public proposal, more romantic than their flash wedding (which neither of them had had much input in). When Aidan had kissed her, it had been unexpected but real, full of passion and promise. Or so Trina had thought at the time.

'You hypocrite!' Rory couldn't believe his ears. 'You've been whinging about Ginny being here – when absolutely nothing has happened between us – and yet you're friends with *him*.' Rory felt like such a fool! Had people been laughing at him behind his back? There he was, allowing the friendship to continue, blithely unaware of what was really happening under his nose. 'How dare you humiliate me like this?'

'Humiliate you? I haven't done anything wrong. It was just one kiss and then I met you.'

'Rubbish!'

'It's the truth.' Trina had been gutted when Aidan had failed to show up for their first date. She'd been crushed when she realised he must have changed his mind about her, but then Rory had arrived and somehow put a smile back on her face. He'd been charming and attentive, which was exactly what Trina needed after her rejection. Deep down, she'd still hoped Aidan would have a valid excuse for not turning up, but none had been forthcoming when they saw each other afterwards. In fact, he'd agreed that they should forget about the kiss in order to keep their friendship intact, and Trina was more than happy to bury the whole thing and claw back a little dignity. She'd gushed about Rory at every opportunity to prove she didn't have any romantic feelings for Aidan, but then Rory deserved to be gushed about. At least he had back then.

'Truth or not, you can't be friends with him any more.'

Trina laughed, because Rory was kidding, right? Aidan

was a massive part of her life. He was her best friend and she couldn't just toss him aside on her husband's say-so.

'I mean it, Trina.' Rory's voice was low and controlled, but Trina could still detect his anger from across the Atlantic. 'It's him or me.'

THIRTY-THREE

Erin

The coach trundled along the motorway, its occupants jubilant as they drank champagne, excited about the fun weekend ahead. But if you looked closely enough, you would notice one passenger who wasn't having as jolly a time as the others. This passenger was slumped by the window, her small suitcase resting on the seat beside her to prevent anybody trying to buddy up with her. Her knees were drawn up, resting on the back of the seat in front, and anybody could see she would rather be anywhere else than right there, on that coach of joy.

'Hey, you. Where's your hat?' Lindsay had been working her way up the aisle of the coach, topping up the glasses of her hyped-up bridesmaids with champagne while tooting on the pink whistle attached to a ribbon around her neck. She wore a pink, glittery cowgirl hat at a jaunty angle, which she now patted as she stood next to Erin. All members of the party had matching hats and whistles, which they tooted in response every time Lindsay blew hers. Erin wanted to shove the bloody whistles – all sixteen of them – up Lindsay's arse.

'I must have left it behind.' Erin gave an apologetic shrug as she delivered the great big lie. The hat was currently sitting underneath her suitcase, crushed beyond redemption.

'Never mind.' Lindsay waved her hand before giving three sharp toots of her whistle. A chorus of toots responded. 'Hey, Annie! Pass down one of the spare hats.' Lindsay grinned down at Erin. 'I knew they'd come in handy!'

The hat was passed down the coach like a crowd surfer moving along a mosh pit until it reached Lindsay's gleeful hands. 'There you go.' She plonked the hat on Erin's head with a little more force than was necessary. 'Now you fit in.'

Great. Just what Erin had always wanted – to fit in with a bunch of airheads.

'Do you need a spare whistle too?' Lindsay gave a toot of her own and the coach was filled with the ear-piercing response.

'No. Thanks.' Erin grabbed the beribboned whistle from under her bag and dutifully looped it around her neck. So that was seventeen whistles to shove up Lindsay's arse then.

Lindsay brandished a bottle of champagne. 'Top-up?'

God, yes. Alcohol was Erin's only hope of getting through this weekend. Because Lindsay wasn't content with torturing Erin for one night. Oh no! Lindsay wanted a whole flipping weekend for her hen night. *Greedy cow.*

Lindsay moved along after filling Erin's glass, tooting on the whistle. 'Who wants a little sing-song?'

Erin groaned as Lindsay's suggestion was met with enthusiasm and the coach was filled with drunken warbling. Erin gave serious thought to suggesting to the driver that they find a ginormous tree and plough into it at top speed. She was pretty certain he'd agree to it.

Finally, after a medley of Abba, Madonna, Kylie and Girls Aloud, they reached their destination and the coach pulled up beside the hotel and spa that they'd be spending the next two nights at (all paid for by Frank, of course). Erin, with her second hat 'accidentally' left behind, trudged off the coach. She paused when she caught sight of the driver. He looked as traumatised as she felt.

'Were you grey before we set off?' She indicated his head of grey hair and the driver managed a small smile.

'No.'

'Sorry.'

The driver gave a shrug. 'No problem, love. At least I get to rest my ears until Sunday evening when I pick you lot up again.'

'Lucky you. Do you think I could sneak a ride back home now?'

The driver chuckled. 'Curl up under one of the seats. I'll let you know when they're out of sight.'

It sounded like a marvellous idea to Erin, but Lindsay had other plans. Seeing that she was missing a bridesmaid, she marched to the coach's open door and bellowed at Erin to hurry up.

'Come *on*. We have to get booked in.' She practically wrestled Erin off the coach, smiling sweetly at the driver over her shoulder and giving a cheery little wave as he pulled away. 'Do you really have to flirt with every man? He had to be at least sixty.'

'What? He was cute.' Erin waited until Lindsay turned and marched away before she stuck her tongue out at her back.

'Come on, girls!' Lindsay marched into the hotel but luckily she refrained from blowing her whistle. The others followed, oohing and aahing as they made their way into the reception hall. It was a nice place, and Erin would love it if she were here with anybody but Lindsay and her band of merry women.

'This is well posh, isn't it?' fellow bridesmaid Lillian gasped as she ran a hand along a leather wingback chair. 'Come on, everybody. Let's take a selfie!' She took out her phone, ensuring everyone – including a cringing Erin – was squeezed on or around the chair before she captured the image. Erin knew that it would be plastered all over Facebook and Instagram within seconds.

Once they were booked in, the women made their way to their rooms, with instructions to meet back at reception in fifteen minutes. Erin was sharing with Rita, Frank's cousin and fellow bridesmaid. Erin wished she was there with Richard instead. They could have pushed the twin beds together and made this weekend worthwhile. She wondered what he would be doing as she sat miserably on one of the beds. Probably cooking for the kids. She hoped he'd remembered the project LuLu was working on that was due in on Monday. Erin had printed off a load of info for her, but she'd left it by the printer in Richard's study. What if he didn't find it?

'We should get going,' Rita said as Erin pulled her phone out and started to tap out Richard's number.

'I won't be a minute. I'll meet you down there.' Erin waved a reluctant Rita away, her phone pressed against her ear. Richard didn't answer. She was about to try again when there was a knock at the door.

'Erin!' It was Lindsay, barking like a Rottweiler from the hallway. 'Everyone is waiting in the bar. We're having welcome cocktails.'

A cocktail would be more than welcome after that coach trip, thought Erin.

After the cocktails, Erin returned to the sanctuary of her room to unpack. According to Lindsay's itinerary, she had twenty minutes to unpack and freshen up before the group was to meet back in the bar for pre-dinner drinks.

The party of bridesmaids would be staying at the hotel and spa for two nights and it seemed that every single minute was allocated to an activity. There were only two spots marked as 'free time', but Erin was going to need much more than that just to get over the headache the coach journey had caused.

Kicking off her shoes, Erin sank onto the bed she had claimed earlier. Her unpacking could wait. She had more important things to take care of first. This time Richard answered quickly and Erin felt herself sinking further into the mattress, her body relaxing with the relief of hearing his voice. What the hell had happened to her? Not so long ago Erin had prided herself on her inability to commit, and now she was pining for her boyfriend after being parted for a couple of hours!

'How is it?' Richard asked and Erin choked down the urge to burst into tears. It was awful and she missed Richard already.

She really did have it bad.

What a loser!

'It's fine.' She couldn't tell Richard the pathetic truth, could she? 'What are you up to?'

'We're just about to sit down to dinner and then we're going to watch a film.'

'*Frozen* again?' Erin asked and Richard laughed.

'What else? I've promised Ralph he can pick next time.'

'LuLu *always* gets to pick,' Erin heard Ralph whine in the background. Erin smiled, picturing the scene that would shortly unfold: Ralph would squeeze himself into the corner of the sofa, arms folded stubbornly across his chest and his eyes narrowed slits. This act of defiance would last around thirty seconds before he was singing about building a snowman.

God, Erin missed them.

'Don't forget LuLu's project. I've printed some stuff out for her. It's in your study.'

'What would we do without you?' Richard asked, but this time it was Erin questioning what *she* would do without *them.* It was a scary question, and not one she had ever expected to be asking. Everything was changing and Erin wasn't sure how she should be reacting. Did she go with it or fight it? First her mother – who had sworn off men indefinitely – was loved up with Alistair, and now Erin was turning into one of those ghastly, needy women she'd always looked down on.

'Hello!' Rita came bounding into the room, the pink cowgirl hat still planted on her head. 'Isn't this place *amazing?* I've just been to Becca and Megan's room and it has a balcony overlooking the lake. It's stunning.' Rita flopped – uninvited – onto Erin's bed. 'Did you see the barman downstairs? Hot or what? I hope he's still there when we go for pre-dinner drinks.'

Erin just hoped they were going to be extremely large pre-dinner drinks.

'Oh, gosh.' Rita slapped a hand over her mouth. 'You're on the phone. I'm so sorry. I'll leave you in peace.' Clambering off the bed, Rita skipped into the en suite, humming a Girls Aloud song. Erin experienced an unwelcome flashback from the coach ride.

'Sorry about that,' Erin said once she was alone again.

'No worries. I have to go now anyway. I think the pasta's about ready. Have fun!'

Erin doubted she would, but she added some pretty convincing false cheer to her voice. 'I will. You have fun with the kids. Give them a big kiss from me.'

Once she'd hung up, Erin flopped back onto the bed with a groan. What the hell was happening to her?

THIRTY-FOUR

Ruth

I sat cross-legged on the carpet, a pile of sealed, addressed envelopes to my right and a list of crossed-out names in front of me. Just one name remained, and I was loath to carry out the job.

'Do we really have to invite Aunty Pat?' I asked, picking up a blank invitation. Most of the wedding plans were now in place. I'd confirmed the menus with Cosmo, booked the DJ and karaoke host, and made arrangements with the florist. The rings had been ordered and we'd picked hymns and verified the order of service with Father Edmund. After several rather lengthy discussions, Jared and I had agreed on a song for our first dance as a married couple. I'd put my (substantial) weight behind '2 Become 1' by the Spice Girls, which Jared had argued against vehemently.

'Isn't that a song about having sex?'

'*Safe* sex. It has a positive message.'

'But it's still a song about sex, safe or otherwise.'

'Don't be such a prude!'

We'd argued back and forth, but Jared had refused to

budge and in the end we'd settled on Etta James's 'At Last'. It was a lovely song and everything, but it wasn't the Spice Girls, was it?

Jared and I had scoured the wedding blogs for favours and had settled on some pretty handmade boxes filled with the Love Hearts sweets I'd bought for my failed cupcakes. Over a couple of nights we made the matchbox-style containers out of lime green card with white polka dots and printed each guest's name on a pink heart, which we'd stick to the top of the boxes and finish off with ribbon once we had the RSVPs back.

Most things had now been arranged. The only thing lagging was the invitations, which we still hadn't sent out. It should have been a task nearer the top of the list, underneath booking venues, but it had somehow ended up being a last-minute job. At this rate we'd be getting married without any guests at all.

Looking down at Aunty Pat's name, that wasn't such an unappealing option …

'I'm afraid we have to invite her,' Jared said. 'She's family, and all that.'

Pulling a face, I scribbled 'Raymond and Patsy Lynch and Family' (yes, we had to invite my horror cousins too, it seemed) on the envelope and shoved an invitation inside. Copying out the address Mum had provided me with, I added the envelope to the pile to be posted.

'That's that, then. She's invited.'

Jared gave my shoulder a squeeze. 'You never know, she may be busy.'

'Fingers crossed.' I gathered the envelopes and placed them on the coffee table so I wouldn't forget to post them later. First, we had a meeting with the photographer, who had arranged to meet with us at home so she could get a proper feel for us.

Sadie Alexander looked like she'd just stepped out of a celebrity magazine, with her waist-length blonde hair and clear complexion. She looked effortlessly glamorous in skinny jeans, a white T-shirt and a floral scarf resting against her collarbones.

'It's so lovely to see you again.' Sadie shook our hands before she settled into a chair. Her glamour was at odds with our worn furniture, but Sadie didn't seem to mind and seemed perfectly at home. 'Not long until the big day! You must be so excited.'

'We are.' I couldn't help grinning as I replied. I still had to pinch myself to make sure I wasn't dreaming.

'I have a few questions I'd like to ask, just to get a sense of who you are and the feel of the photos you'd like.' Sadie pulled a notepad from her bag and rested it on her lap before reaching out to take a jammy dodger from the plate on the table. Good girl! I awarded the photographer three million Brownie points and took a biscuit myself.

The questions didn't take very long at all, but by the end I felt like I knew myself and Jared better than I had before Sadie's arrival. She showed us her portfolio again, which we could take our time over away from the bustle of the wedding fair. Sadie's photos were beautiful, but also very real, and I couldn't wait to see the results of our own wedding.

'I'm really looking forward to working with you,' Sadie said as she returned the portfolio to her bag, and I believed her. She wasn't just spouting superficial crap to score a booking.

The intercom buzzed and Jared went to answer it. Bizarrely, it was Theo, who had only visited the flat once in the whole time I had lived there, and that was only because I'd blackmailed him into helping me move in.

'Quinn asked me to drop this off—' Theo stopped mid-sentence, the bag he'd been waving at me suspended in mid-air. I hoped he hadn't peeped inside – it was my wedding lingerie, which I'd accidentally left in the boot of

Quinn's car.

Theo's eyebrows shot up his forehead as he spotted Sadie. *Yes,* I wanted to tell him. *There is a beautiful woman sitting in my flat. And no, you cannot touch her.*

I plucked the bag from Theo's fingers. 'Since when do you run errands for Quinn?' Since when did he run errands for *anyone*? And what had Quinn been doing with Theo? As if I couldn't guess!

'I was just passing this way.' Theo gave me a cursory glance before he sauntered towards an unsuspecting Sadie. 'Hi, I'm Ruth's very good friend, Theo.'

Very good friend? Pah!

'Hi, it's nice to meet you. I'm Sadie, Ruth and Jared's wedding photographer.' Sadie rose from her seat and stretched out a hand towards Theo. Poor, naïve woman. I felt like I had to act, and jumped between the pair before contact could be made.

'Thanks for bringing this over.' I patted Theo on the back before turning him away from the beautiful Sadie and propelling him towards the door. 'I'll see you soon, okay?'

'But—' Theo tried to protest as I shoved him out of the door.

'Do not ruin my chances of having Sadie as my photographer,' I hissed before shutting the door in his bewildered face. I plastered on a smile before I returned to the sitting room. 'Sorry about that. He had to rush off. He's so busy, our Theo. Always rushing around!'

'Never mind. Maybe we'll get a chance to chat at the wedding,' Sadie said and I nodded, while silently vowing that I'd never allow that to happen. Not until the photos had been taken, at least. 'Anyway, I think that's everything. I'll see you on your big day.'

After showing Sadie to the door, I did a little victory lap around the sitting room before collapsing on the sofa. This wedding was really coming together. I had my first dress fitting scheduled for the following weekend, and I knew that once I was wearing my dress it would be real. I would actually believe that I was getting married.

After Sadie had left and I'd recovered from my sprint around the sitting room, I got ready to go out, then gathered the invitations to post on the way to the bus stop. I'd arranged to have lunch with my parents, but Jared couldn't make it as he'd already made plans with Gavin. They were working on some sort of surprise for me for the wedding. I was pretending I didn't mind being kept in the dark, but all the secrecy was driving me mad. I'd grilled Mum and Dad about it, but if they knew what Jared was cooking up, they hid it well and claimed they didn't know what I was talking about.

'Do you want to see what I've done with the caragym?'

I'd barely put my bum on the sofa before Dad was trying to manhandle me out of the door again.

I looked at Mum but she simply rolled her eyes.

'Sure, Dad. I'd love to see it.' Moments later I was standing in front of the caravan, feeling rather disappointed. It looked exactly the same as the last time I'd seen it. Dad hadn't even cleaned it.

'Look!' Dad swung the door open and I peered inside, my expectations rising.

They plummeted pretty rapidly.

'It looks the same.'

'It does not.' Dad shook his head at me, genuinely baffled. I was too. 'The hole in the floor! It's gone!'

I dropped my eyes to the floor. Sure enough, the hole had been patched up and I could no longer see what had once been Mum's lawn. 'Oh. Yes. Well done, Dad.'

Dad's chest puffed out as he gave a satisfied nod. 'Isn't it marvellous?'

'It is, Dad. You'll be jogging away on the treadmill in no time.'

Dad slung his arm around my shoulders and together we wandered back into the house. I put the kettle on before we settled in the sitting room.

'I spoke to Stephen on that Skype doo-da last night,' Mum told me. 'I couldn't get his face up on it, but I could hear him well enough.' Stephen had been living in New York for over a decade, but Mum still had trouble chatting to him when Dad wasn't around to set up the laptop.

'How is he?' I missed my brother terribly. The distance never got any easier, no matter how many years had passed.

'He's okay. Busy at work and everything, and he's been looking after the little ones as Aubrey isn't feeling too good.'

'What's wrong with her?' Selfishly, I was worrying about the wedding. I didn't want Stephen and his family to miss it.

'Stephen says it's just a stomach bug.' Mum pressed her lips together for a moment. 'Anyway, he was calling about the wedding.'

My gut tightened. He was going to miss it. Aubrey was too ill to fly over and my big brother was going to miss my wedding. I *knew* everything was running too smoothly!

'As you know, they won't be arriving until the day before the wedding, so Aubrey has suggested they buy Riley's bridesmaid dress over there and bring it over with them to make sure it fits. You know what American sizes are like.'

'So they're still coming?'

'To the wedding?' Mum asked. 'Of course they're still coming to the wedding. They're not going to miss it, are they?'

'But I thought Aubrey was ill.'

'Oh, yes. The *stomach bug*.' Mum's lips pressed together again and she raised her eyebrows a fraction. 'I'm sure she'll be fine by the wedding.'

Thank cupcakes for that! The thought of getting married without Stephen being there was a horrible one.

'So, the dress? You are still getting them from the high street, aren't you?'

I nodded. 'Unless we win the lottery between now and the big day.'

'Right. So if you let Aubrey know the specifications, they can sort it out at their end.'

I didn't really have any specifications for the bridesmaid dresses, as long as the wearer was comfortable, but I would email Aubrey with a budget.

'I'll also let Aubrey know about the hen night plans.' I hadn't wanted to have my hen night on the night before my wedding, as I wanted to enjoy my big day without being in the throes of a hangover, but time restraints meant I had little choice. The only upside was that Aubrey could now attend.

'About your hen night.' Mum squirmed a little in her seat. 'Aren't I bit old for that sort of carry-on?'

'You're never too old for fun, Mum. Besides, Dad's going to Jared's stag do.'

'And I'm looking forward to it too.' Dad rubbed his hands together. 'It'll be the only chance I'll get to see a woman in the nip these days.'

Mum and I glared at Dad.

'I hate to disappoint you, Dad, but there aren't going to be any strippers.' I didn't hate it at all. I was glad, the mucky old sod. 'Jared just wants a few drinks in the pub.'

Dad spluttered. 'Of course he's going to say that. Do you think I told your mother what I got up to on my last night of freedom?'

I was appalled but Mum simply gave a tut. 'Don't listen to the silly old fool. On his last night of freedom, he had a couple of pints with your Uncle Ray and was tucked up in bed by nine. Your gran told me, and that woman would have cut off her own tongue before she told a lie.'

Dad folded his arms across his chest. 'Well, luckily our Jared has a bit more to him than this old sap. If he doesn't have a stripper, I'll eat my hat.'

I decided the best course of action was to ignore Dad and attempt to wipe our conversation from my memory. Unfortunately, the image of my father salivating over a woman young enough to be his offspring while she twiddled tassels stuck to her nipples was a difficult one to erase.

THIRTY-FIVE

Erin

With a groan, Erin rolled over in the garden-gnome-sized single bed and picked up her phone to squint at the time. 8:35 am. Whoever was banging on her door could bog right off. It was the weekend and Erin had sleep to catch up on. Wasn't it enough that she'd endured a coach trip from hell? That she was trapped in this spa with a gaggle of bimbos without having so much as a foot rub, never mind a full-on massage? She was owed a decent sleep, at the very least.

'Erin, are you in there? You're going to miss breakfast if you don't get a wriggle on.'

Sod breakfast. In fact, sod this whole arsing hen weekend. Erin didn't want to spend the morning with a bunch of women she barely knew. Especially when those women were armed with pink bloody whistles.

'Erin?'

Whoever was out there was persistent. Couldn't they understand Erin's need to recuperate after their night out?

Whichever obstinate bastard was out there had stumbled back to the hotel in the stupidly small hours just as much as Erin had. Why couldn't they be normal and bog off back to bed until a more reasonable hour? Lunchtime, for example.

Erin lifted her head a painful millimetre to squint at the neighbouring bed, but it was empty. Rita was already up – or hadn't gone to bed in the first place; Erin couldn't be sure. There'd been a bit of a boozy get-together in one of the other rooms when they'd returned from their night out, but Erin had declined the offer and had climbed into bed while she was still capable. She'd gone to sleep in a blissfully empty room and had only woken because of the bellend banging on the door.

'Erin, are you in there?'

It was no use. Erin was going to have to have a conversation with this person. And by 'conversation', Erin meant she was going to have to yell at them to back the fuck off and leave her to sleep off the hangover that was gurgling in her stomach and thumping in her head.

Erin didn't usually regret a hangover, as it usually signalled a bloody good night out, but this one felt like such a waste after spending the night with Lindsay and her cronies. After dinner, the group had piled into a convoy of taxis – thankfully minus the pink whistles and cowgirl hats. The taxi had taken them into the nearest town, which had been a crappy, mainly deserted gathering of prehistoric buildings. The maid of honour had booked the VIP area of the town's only club with champagne on tap. Lindsay had acted like she really was a VIP (Very Ignorant Piss-taker, judging by the way she clicked her fingers to grab people's attention as she lorded it about the place). She told everyone who would listen about her famous rugby-playing fiancé – and even those who wouldn't. Erin had found herself stuck with Whitney, the youngest bridesmaid. At sixteen, she shouldn't even have been in the club, and Erin was one Harry Styles anecdote away from shopping her to the bouncers just to give her ears a rest.

Lindsay and her friends spent the night necking champagne and dancing provocatively with each other while Erin hid in dark corners to avoid Whitney. Erin enjoyed a good night out as much as anybody else, but right then she'd much rather have been at home with Richard and the kids watching *Frozen* with a huge bowl of popcorn wedged between them, which was a sobering thought. What was happening to the fun-loving girl she used to be? In an act of revolt, Erin had decided to outdo the others with the champagne consumption and was now paying for it dearly.

'*Erin!*'

'All right, all right.' Erin forced herself from the bed, whimpering as her stomach sloshed with the movement. 'I'm coming. No need to bloody shout.'

Erin made it across the hotel room without spewing on the plush carpet and opened the door to find Lindsay standing in the hall, hands planted firmly on her hips. She was plastered in make-up, which Erin guessed was to mask the fact that she felt as crap as she did.

'I don't care about breakfast.' Erin would have appreciated an hour longer snoozing more than a plate of bacon and eggs. Her stomach gurgled just thinking about food.

'You need to eat,' Lindsay told her. 'You'll need the fuel for this morning's activity.'

Erin wasn't fond of horses. They were okay at a distance – like on the telly – but up-close they were smelly and mean-looking. Erin especially didn't like riding on them – if she was going to sit astride something, it would be a man, thank you very much.

'That was so much fun!' Becca, Whitney's slightly older sister, bounded from the stables with flushed cheeks. 'Wasn't that the *best*?'

No, Erin thought as she hobbled back towards the hotel. That hadn't been fun at all. The girls had spent the morning having a horse riding lesson at a nearby stable, which was possibly the worst activity to endure when there was a vineyard's worth of champagne swishing around your stomach. As well as a thumping head, Erin could now add burning arse and thigh muscles to the mix.

And Becca thought that was *fun*?

'Come on, guys.' Lindsay marched on ahead, sucking in the so-called fresh air (what was fresh about air clogged with the smell of horse shit?) as she swung her arms jauntily. 'Let's get back to the hotel. You should have just enough time to shower before we meet in the orangery for lunch.'

After her shower, Erin's appetite had – surprisingly – returned and she wolfed down the leek and potato soup served with warm, crusty bread followed by lemon posset and summer fruits. She would have quite happily eaten a second helping, but Lindsay's itinerary didn't allow such luxuries. Luckily, the next activity was a much more pleasant one and wouldn't involve any farmyard friends. Had Erin known about the after-effects of horse riding beforehand, she probably would have opted for an arse-cheek massage for her first treatment of the weekend, but they'd booked their treatments weeks in advance, when she had been blissfully unaware of the other planned activities. Still, the Indian head massage was heavenly and more than welcome, and she was glad of the block of 'free time' afterwards. Hobbling back up to her room, she sank into a hot bubble bath and settled herself in for a long soak. Afterwards, her wrinkled body nestled in a fluffy robe, Erin curled up on the bed and phoned Richard for a catch-up. He didn't answer, which probably meant he was out somewhere with the kids. They'd probably gone to the park with the kite and a football. Erin had once thought kite-flying was the most dull and pointless activity known to man, but that was before Richard and the kids showed her how much fun it actually was. They could spend hours at the park on a good kite-flying day, and they'd warm up afterwards with hot chocolates in the café.

Simply because she had nothing better to do, Erin forced herself out of the robe – which would definitely be making the trip back to Woodgate in her suitcase – and pulled on a pair of jeans and a T-shirt. She tried Richard again, but there was still no answer. Throwing her phone on the bed, Erin marched from the room. She would go down to the bar for a drink or two before dinner. She could survive without Richard. It would be easy.

'So I said to Megan – you know Megan, don't you? She's staying next door with Annie? – I said, "You *can't* draw a moustache on Lillian while she's pissed up. She will *kill you*. Actually kill you dead." So do you know what Megan did?'

Erin should have packed a pair of earplugs. She wondered whether it was worth calling down to reception to ask if they had any.

'Did she draw a moustache on Lillian, by any chance?'

Rita giggled to herself, keeping a cheesy grin on her face as she ever so slowly applied her lip gloss. She thought she was being such a tease, making Erin wait for her answer. The trouble was, Erin didn't give a badger's arsehole what Megan and Lillian had got up to last night. She didn't give a badger's A-hole about any of this hen weekend.

'Nope. She did not draw a moustache on Lillian.' Rita pouted at her reflection in the dressing table's mirror, still tittering to herself. 'She drew a *penis* on Lillian's cheek. A penis! Can you believe it?'

Erin stifled a yawn. She was missing seeing LuLu and Ralph to spend the weekend with a bunch of women whose idea of fun was drawing willies on their friends' faces with a Sharpie pen?

'Lillian was not impressed. Not. At. All.'

'But I saw Lillian this morning.' At least Erin thought it had been Lillian. She hadn't really made an effort to get to know the other bridesmaids so it could have been any of them, really. 'At the horse thing. She didn't have a knob on her face.'

'That's because she washed it off.' Rita gave Erin a look that suggested she wasn't quite the full shilling. 'Who would walk around with a you-know-what drawn on their face?'

'She washed it off? How?'

Rita gave a shrug and returned to pouting in the mirror. 'I think she uses those cleansing wipes with grape extract.'

Erin grabbed the pillow from her bed. She wanted to scream into it. Or smother herself. 'No, I mean *how* did it come off? I thought Sharpie pens were permanent.'

Rita twisted around and gave Erin the look again. 'It wasn't a Sharpie pen. It was an eyebrow pencil.'

Erin hugged the pillow to her chest, trying her hardest not to give in and cut off her oxygen supply. 'Megan drew on Lillian with an *eyebrow pencil?*'

What was the bloody point in that? If you're going to behave in a puerile manner, at least do it properly!

'Yes. Isn't she hilarious?' Rita giggled to herself as she twisted back towards the mirror, checking her complexion for any imperfections.

Erin dumped the pillow back on the bed and headed for the door. 'I need a drink. I'll meet you downstairs.'

Erin had spent the remainder of the afternoon in the hotel's bar and had only popped upstairs to change before the evening's activities, but had been stuck listening to

Rita for the past forty-five minutes. She had ten minutes until she was scheduled to meet the others in reception, which was plenty of time to top up her alcohol level in preparation for dinner and whatever plans maid-of-honour Helen had up her sleeve. The itinerary simply said 'The Show'.

'Come on, Erin. We're all waiting.' Lindsay beckoned to her from the entrance to the bar. Erin hadn't even managed to perch herself on a stool, never mind order a drink. She had ten minutes until the designated meeting time, and Erin thought she was entitled to spend those ten minutes with a drink in her hand.

'*Erin*. Come *on*.'

Erin caught the barman's eye but decided it was best to follow Lindsay's instructions. It didn't seem worth facing the bride's wrath over a vodka and coke.

'All right, all right.' Erin lumbered after Lindsay, joining the others crowding the reception area. Rita waved to catch Erin's attention before pointing at Lillian and mouthing 'no penis' and giving two thumbs-up. Erin really, *really* needed that extra vodka and coke.

A parade of taxis transported the girls into town, where they had a pleasant enough meal with plenty of wine, which was more than welcome. The whistles had thankfully retreated since the coach trip, but they made a return as the party piled out of the restaurant.

'Are we ready, ladies?' Helen distributed the whistles and began striding along the pavement, eager to reach their destination. She gave a hearty toot, which was, of course, returned at high volume.

Lindsay linked her arm through Erin's as they ambled along after Helen. 'Don't worry, I won't tell Richard if you don't tell Frank.'

'Tell them what?' Erin asked, but there was no need to answer. The group had stopped in front of a building with blinding neon lights promising male flesh. And lots of it.

'Strippers?' Erin asked. Her mouth watered at the thought of a room full of hot, sweaty men with rippling abs and bulging G-strings. Now this – finally – was an activity Erin could get on board with.

THIRTY-SIX

Ruth

'Good evening, ladies!' Nell bounced into the church hall, her high ponytail swinging to the beat of her jovial mood as she passed the rows of yoga mats. 'I hope Greg has been taking good care of you while I've been away.'

'He's been a treasure,' Mary said from beside me. 'Although we're glad to see you up and about again. How are you feeling?' Mary patted her own slightly rounded tummy, as though reminding Nell of her pregnancy.

'I'm pleased to let you know that all signs of morning sickness have vanished,' Nell said. I tried to picture this goddess of a woman with her head stuck down the toilet but the image was not forthcoming. 'I'm feeling positively radiant! In fact, I wouldn't know I was pregnant if my boobs hadn't ballooned to double their size and I wasn't craving a McDonald's strawberry milkshake.' She certainly didn't *look* pregnant. There wasn't a hint of a bump on her lithe body. 'But I haven't stepped foot in a McDonald's in almost a decade and I'm not about to start now.'

'Wait til she gets piles,' Mary said quietly out of the

233

side of her mouth. 'Then she'll bloody know she's pregnant.'

'Good evening, ladies.' Greg lumbered into the hall, two rolled-up mats tucked under his arms and the CD player dangling from his fingers. 'I bet you're glad to see Nell's back to take charge.'

'I don't know about that,' Mary said, still speaking to me out of the side of her mouth. 'I quite like a man to take charge. Don't you?'

Nell began the session and although I was trying to concentrate on her instructions, my mind was elsewhere. My first wedding dress fitting was scheduled to take place at the weekend, and I couldn't help worrying that I'd look like a polka-dotted blimp in it. The last thing I wanted was to have Jared bottling it and legging it up the aisle when he saw me waddling down it towards him.

'Now take a breath in, bring your palms together and rest your thumbs lightly on your sternum.' We all copied Nell and Greg, bowing our heads slightly as they did. 'Great session, ladies. We'll go straight into meditation, so if you get yourself into a comfortable position, we'll begin.'

This was the time to really clear my mind and allow my body to relax, but my thoughts were still firmly on the dress. I'd been so excited about the fitting but now I was filled with anxiety and there was no breathing technique that could remedy it.

'Before you all go, I have an announcement to make,' Mary said as we were packing away our things at the end of the session. 'At the weekend, Cecil proposed and I said yes!' Mary held out a wrinkled hand to show off the huge antique rock sitting proudly on her finger. The group gathered to offer their congratulations, gasping and murmuring appreciatively at the enormous sparkler. How the hell had I missed *that* shining up at me from Mary's mat?

'Who wants to join me in the pub for a celebratory

piss-up?' Mary asked, and we all rushed to gather our things before trooping out of the church hall and walking en masse to the pub across the road. I scurried after Mary and linked my arm through hers.

'So, when are you planning on getting married, then?'

I thought I'd asked the question in a casual manner, but Mary saw straight through me and gave my arm a reassuring pat. 'Don't you worry, my love. I won't be beating you down the aisle. I haven't even met Cecil's daughters yet. Mind you, we don't want to leave it too long. We're both getting on, and the last thing we want is one of us keeling over at the altar.'

'Don't say that.' I rested my head against Mary's grey curls. 'There's plenty of life left in you yet.'

'I hope so, love, but I'm not taking any chances. That's why I live my life to the full, as they say. I want to squeeze every bit of life out of this old dog before it's too late.'

'I'm sure you and Cecil will have many happy years together.'

'We'll certainly give it a go, my love.' Mary released me and charged towards the pub's door. 'Come on, folks. First round's on me!'

My stomach gurgled with a combination of excitement and anxiety as Jared called out to me and Quinn as we left the flat, instructing us to have fun. Today was my dress fitting and I hadn't managed to overcome my misgivings despite my yoga and meditation session – and our session in the pub afterwards.

'We will!' Quinn called over her shoulder. I wish I'd had her confidence. 'Isn't this exciting? It's a shame Erin can't be here.'

Erin wouldn't be coming to the fitting as she was currently at Lindsay's wedding, trussed up in a tutu and basque. I'd have loved my best friend to be with me, but we were on such a tight deadline that there had been no room for manoeuvre. We were cutting it fine as it was.

'Do you think Erin and Richard will ever get married?' Quinn asked as we drove towards Hartfield Hill and the dress shop.

'I don't know.' I gave a frustrated sigh. 'They're perfect for each other, but Erin is a bit weird when it comes to marriage. She doesn't believe in it.' I knew Erin and her mum had been through some tough times – Erin didn't like to talk about her childhood much, but I did know her father had been violent, so I could kind of understand her reluctance to marry.

'I can't *wait* to get married.' Quinn gave her own frustrated sigh. 'I just need to find someone who wants to marry me.'

'I hope you're not pinning any hopes on Theo fulfilling that role.'

Quinn screwed up her nose. 'Not even a little bit.'

'So you're not still harbouring feelings for him?'

'I have never harboured feelings for Theo. He's not my type, especially now I've seen how he operates up-close.'

I shifted in my seat, eyebrows raised. 'How up-close?'

'Not *that* up-close.' *Phew.* 'Apparently he hooked up with some girl last weekend and she hasn't stopped calling since. He gets Billy to answer so he doesn't have to deal with her.'

I nodded, not in the least bit surprised. I'd lived with the man for almost three years, after all. 'He's a pig.'

'And why would I be interested in a pig?'

'Plenty of women are.'

'But not me.'

I eyed Quinn as she drove, trying to gauge whether she was protesting too much or just enough. It wasn't an easy task, and I still hadn't made my mind up by the time we arrived in Hartfield Hill. Chatting with Quinn had made me forget about my anxieties, but they came rushing back as soon as I stepped inside Libby's boutique. Even the sight of the stunning dresses on display wasn't enough to put me at ease. My body was not the size of the mannequins wearing the dresses. Far from it.

'Hello again.' Libby stepped out of her room at the back, her tape measure again draped over her shoulders. 'I've got your dress ready. Do you want to come through?'

Libby was lovely as she helped me into the dress, chatting away as she made adjustments with pins. There was a mirror on the wall opposite but I kept my head down, afraid of what would greet me in the glass.

'I won't be a minute.' Libby made one final adjustment before she stood back, a smile spreading across her face. 'Wow. You look amazing. Here, have a proper look.' Before I could protest, Libby had grasped me by the arm and tugged me closer to the mirror. I didn't want to look, but it would be rude to refuse. I prepared a few pleasantries in my head as my eyes lifted towards my reflection.

'Oh my flipping *God!*' In the mirror, my eyes widened in surprise. I *did* look amazing! I was looking radiant despite wearing the bare minimum of make-up and my hair being a bit scraggly, so imagine how fabulous I would look with full-on slap and my hair done. 'You're a genius! I can't believe it.' I turned this way and that, determined to find some sort of flaw, but I looked bloody good from all angles. This was obviously a magical dress, and so worth the huge chunk of our budget it would cost.

'Shall we go and show your friend?'

Quinn was waiting out in the shop, browsing through a stack of bridal magazines, but they were instantly forgotten as Libby and I stepped out from the back room. She rose from the purple wingback chair with a gasp.

'Oh my God. Look at you!' Quinn rushed towards me, her eyes scanning me from top to bottom. 'Give us a twirl.'

I dutifully twirled, rolling my eyes but secretly loving her reaction.

'Could you take some photos to show Erin? Here, use my phone.' I passed Quinn my bag.

'Is that okay?' Quinn asked Libby.

'Of course it is. As long as you don't show the groom.'

I posed for the photos, my grin genuine and taking up at least half of my face. This was it. I was really getting married!

It was such a wrench having to take the dress off, which was a nice change from the negative thoughts that had been plaguing me all week. But it had to come off and I was soon dressed in my regular clothes and saying goodbye to Libby.

'You'll be back soon.' Quinn put her arm around me, partly for comfort and partly to guide me out of the shop.

'I know, but it's such a gorgeous dress. And I'm not being biased because it's mine.' I reluctantly stepped out onto the pavement and spotted the restaurant across the square. 'Do you fancy lunch? My treat?' My mouth was already salivating at the thought of another slice of the Black Forest cheesecake.

'I'm sorry, I can't. I have plans.' Quinn flashed me an apologetic smile. 'But next time, yeah?'

'Deal.' We wandered across to Quinn's car and climbed inside. 'So what are these plans? Anything exciting?'

Quinn struggled with her seatbelt for a moment before answering. 'I'm going shopping with my sister. I told you her baby's due in a few weeks, didn't I? Anyway, she's totally panicking because she hasn't bought enough vests or something. Apparently she can't go shopping on her own in case she goes into labour.'

'Baby shopping is so lovely, though, isn't it?' Not that I'd know. I'd bought my niece and nephews a few bits and pieces, but I didn't make a habit of it as it was awkward having bulky things shipped over to New York. I usually transferred money for birthdays and Christmas instead.

'It isn't with our Orla,' Quinn said. 'She'll have me

carrying everything as she's "with child". She hasn't so much as put her own knickers on since she found out she was pregnant.'

I couldn't fault the woman. I'd milk it for all it was worth if I was pregnant too.

'I'll see you tomorrow then,' I said as Quinn dropped me off at home. 'Have fun shopping.'

Quinn pulled a face. 'I'll try.'

I headed up to the flat, updating my wedding plans as soon as I was inside. My plans weren't quite up to the standard of Trina's – in fact, it was just my notebook and a few printed lists tucked inside my file – but they were looking healthy.

'Jared?' I called as I ticked 'dress fitting' off my to-do list. 'Did you pick the suits up?'

'Yes, and I took them over to Gavin's so they're ready.' Jared emerged from the bedroom in his running gear. 'Can you believe we're getting married in just two weeks?'

'No, I can't. Mad, isn't it?' I ticked 'suits' off the list. 'Are you going for a run?'

'You don't mind, do you?'

I shook my head. It'd give me an hour or so to gaze at the photos Quinn had taken of me in the dress. I'd made her take one from every angle.

'See you soon.' Jared kissed me on the top of my head before he left. I wandered over to the window to let some air in, and as I did I saw Jared climbing into his car. I assumed he'd left his iPod in there until the engine roared into life and he drove away.

If he was going for a run, why was he taking the car?

Dismissing the thought, I rifled through my handbag for my phone, but I couldn't find it, even after I'd emptied everything onto the sitting room floor. Damn! I must have dropped it in Quinn's car. I'd definitely had it in there, as I'd had a quick look at the dress photos as we drove back.

Using the landline, I phoned Quinn to ask about my

mobile, and when she answered I could hear Billy and Theo ribbing each other in the background. Baby shopping with her sister, my arse. The little minx! She'd gone round to see Theo after everything she'd said earlier! So much for Theo being a pig.

'I was just about to leave for Orla's,' Quinn said when I pointed out her location – and her expanding Pinocchio nose. 'I only popped over to Billy and Theo's for a minute. I thought I'd left something behind while we were watching *A Beginner's Guide* the other day.'

'What did you leave behind?' I probed, knowing full well that she was telling great big porkies. She hadn't left anything behind in that house but her sanity and good sense. But I was interrupted by the flat's buzzer before Quinn had the chance to answer, and she insisted that we would chat later. She had baby shopping to do, remember?

Hmm.

I hung up and wandered over to the intercom, my mood instantly lifting when I heard my cousin's voice. I buzzed Trina in, but as she skipped into my flat, looking her usual immaculate self, I started to spot all its flaws: the patch of chipped paint on the doorframe where Jared and Theo had bashed it while carrying my dressing table in on moving day, the mass of letters and bills cluttering the mantelpiece, and a mini-collection of mugs on the coffee table. Nothing major – not by my standards, anyway – but Trina didn't live like this. Her home was luxurious and show room-y, a far cry from my poky little flat.

'I hope you don't mind me popping round. I was at a loose end and I realised it's only two weeks until your wedding, so I thought I'd check how you're getting on.' Trina plonked herself on the sofa. The old, cracked leather didn't suit her glamour but she didn't seem to notice. 'How are the plans coming along?'

'They're good.' I spoke to Trina but my eyes were

scanning the room for abandoned bras or knickers. 'Can I get you a cup of tea or coffee?'

'Coffee would be great, thanks.' Trina smiled sweetly at me while I prayed we had a pair of mugs that weren't chipped. And that were clean. The flat had never seemed so cramped and cluttered and I suddenly understood Mum's frantic cushion-plumping every time she knew Aunt Gloria would be visiting.

'I'm afraid Rory can't make the wedding,' Trina said when I returned with the drinks. 'He has to go away on business again. Only to London this time, but he'll miss it. Sorry.'

'Don't worry about it.' I reached out to give Trina's hand a reassuring pat because she looked devastated. I snatched my hand away when I noticed my flaky pink nail polish and scraggly cuticles. I hadn't paid any attention to Trina's digits, but I was sure they were perfectly presented.

Trina suddenly burst into tears. I forgot all about my inadequate nails and put my arm around the trembling girl. 'Hey, don't worry about it. It's our own fault, really. We haven't given people much notice, especially with the invitations only going out last week.'

'It's not that.' Trina gave a little sniff and reached into her handbag for a tissue. It seemed so grown-up to have tissues to hand. All I had in my handbag was my purse, a couple of crusty lipsticks and several crumpled-up receipts. 'It's Rory. And Aidan. And everything!' Trina buried her face into her hands as she began to sob in earnest. I rubbed her back and made soothing noises until she'd calmed down enough to speak coherently.

'It's not been how I expected it at all. Marriage, you know?' Trina dabbed at her eyes with a fresh tissue. A mound of soggy tissues had formed on the coffee table during the course of her bawl. 'Rory's never at home, so I hardly see him. He expects me to sit at home all day looking pretty.' Trina pulled a face, disgusted at the notion. It seemed like a spiffing idea to me: no dragging my carcass out of bed on Monday mornings. No dealing with Kelvin and his coffee-and-biscuits addiction. No pretending to work hard.

'And now he says I can't be friends with Aidan any more.' At this revelation, Trina broke down once again, and added several more soggy tissues to the collection.

THIRTY-SEVEN

Trina

The mound of sodden tissues grew on the coffee table until Trina's supply ran out and she was forced to use loo roll instead. Trina took a moment to compose herself as Ruth dashed off to grab a wad from the bathroom. She shouldn't have come here. It wasn't fair; Ruth was getting married in a couple of weeks and she didn't need Trina and tales of her disastrous marriage taking the shine off.

She should apologise and go before she ruined everything.

'I brought the whole roll.' Ruth popped the roll next to Trina. 'Just in case.'

'I'm so sorry about this.' Trina unwound a hefty chunk of loo roll and blew her nose. 'It's just that I don't really have anybody else to talk to. Mum's still on her cruise and Tori is – well, Tori.' Trina and Ruth shared a knowing look. Trina's sister wasn't the most sympathetic person on the planet, and wasn't fond of discussing matters that didn't revolve around herself. 'And obviously I can't talk to Aidan any more, as Rory won't let me.'

'Trina, sweetheart.' Ruth took Trina's hand with a firm grasp. 'I know Rory is your husband and you love him and all that, but no man can tell you who you can or can't be friends with. That's not right. It's controlling, and we all know where that sort of behaviour ends.'

Trina shook her head, her wet eyes wide. 'No, it isn't like that. *Rory* isn't like that. It's just that Aidan and I have a past. Sort of. Nothing sordid. We haven't slept together.' Although Rory still didn't believe that. 'We were supposed to go on a date once, before Rory.'

'I know.'

'You do?' Trina's voice squeaked in surprise. 'How?'

'Aidan told me.'

'You've spoken to Aidan?' Trina hadn't, not for a whole agonising week. Aidan was her best friend and she missed him, but it must have been worse for Aidan because he didn't even know why Trina had cut off all contact. She was too chicken to tell him the real reason, so she'd simply avoided his calls and – shamefully – she'd hidden in her bedroom on the occasions when he'd visited, leaving him on the doorstep.

She was a terrible human being and an even worse friend.

'He did my hair on my birthday.' Ruth hadn't told Trina at the time. Aidan hadn't wanted Trina to think Ruth was inviting her to her birthday meal through pity. 'And he told me about the date.'

'Did he tell you that he stood me up?' Trina stuck her chin in the air. She may have been a terrible friend, but Aidan hadn't always acted admirably either.

'Yes. But that wasn't his fault.'

'Then whose was it? *Mine?*' Trina had been devastated when Aidan had failed to turn up for their date. She'd thought they were on the cusp of something really special, but clearly Aidan hadn't shared her feelings. It was such a humiliating experience, standing there waiting for the man she'd fallen in love with (not that Trina would ever admit that now. She'd been embarrassed enough, thank you very much) only for him to lack the decency to turn up. Thank goodness Rory had taken pity on her and asked her to dance!

'I'm pretty sure Aidan blames the arsehole who smashed into him,' Ruth said.

Trina blinked slowly at her cousin, dislodging another tear. She swiped it away. 'What do you mean, smashed into him?'

'Well, not him physically, but, you know … his car.'

'No.' Trina shook her head. 'I don't know. What are you talking about? What car?'

'Aidan's car. The reason he didn't turn up to that dance thing.'

'Aidan didn't turn up because he'd changed his mind about me. About *us*.' Trina could recall the conversation clearly. He'd phoned her the next day – *the next flipping day* – to explain. Trina had quickly got in first, letting him know all about the wonderful man she'd met. She wasn't going to let Aidan know she was heartbroken. No way! She was mortified about being stood up, so she had to save face and pretend it hadn't fazed her at all. Not in the slightest. No, she'd had a grand old time with Rory Hamilton-Wraith and he was taking her sailing on his father's yacht. Beat that, Aidan Miller!

'He didn't tell you about the crash?' Ruth asked.

Trina dumped the sodden loo roll on the pile of tissues. 'I honestly have no idea what you're talking about.'

So Ruth repeated what Aidan had told her about that night, about the car accident and the lack of phone.

'But why didn't he tell me this at the time?' Trina asked.

Ruth gave a shrug. 'You'll have to ask Aidan that yourself.'

Trina was torn. Should she go and see Aidan and demand answers? Or should she respect Rory's wishes and stay away from him? It was all so confusing. In the end she decided to return home so that she could think things over rationally. Everything would all work out in the end. It had to.

Dread washed over Trina when she realised the door to the annex was unlocked. A couple of weeks ago, she'd have skipped over the threshold, pleasantly surprised that her husband was home, but now her feet were sluggish. Rory being home was no longer thrilling, as it meant rows and unbearable tension. Trina was considering backtracking, sneaking back out of the house unnoticed – but where would she go?

'You're home early,' she called through to the sitting room as she hung her coat up in the cupboard under the stairs. Although it was the weekend, Rory usually worked until late and, if he wasn't at the office, he was being kept busy schmoozing on the golf course.

'Darling!' It wasn't Rory who was home after all, but Trina's mother. Gloria appeared in the doorway, tanned arms flung wide. Trina ran into them, yet more tears bubbling to the surface. If she continued on this blubbering path, she'd become dangerously dehydrated, she thought.

'Mum! I'm so glad to see you.' Trina held on to Gloria with a vice-like grip. 'When did you get back?'

'Very late last night.' Gloria peeled Trina away from her bosom so that she could observe her daughter. Her hands were cool as she placed her palms on Trina's flushed cheeks. 'Is everything okay, darling?'

'I'm just happy to see you.' Trina swiped at the tears that had managed to worm their way down her cheeks. 'How did you get in?'

'The housekeeper. Lovely lady. She made me a *gorgeous* cup of tea. There's nothing better when you get back from a trip, is there?' Gloria led the way into the sitting room and arranged herself on the sofa. 'I had a *fabulous* time. I didn't want it to end! Yuri wanted to take me home with him, the little devil.'

'Who *is* Yuri?' The postcard her mother had sent was still propped up on the mantelpiece.

Gloria waved a hand, jangling the charm bracelet she'd bought herself after her first divorce. She added a new charm with each divorce, and it was filling up fast.

'Oh, Yuri was just a fling.'

'And what about Barry?' Gloria had been dating Barry for three months before they went away on the cruise – funded by the man in question.

'He wasn't so keen on seeing me being flung by another man, so that's over.' Gloria gave a dismissive wave. 'So how was the honeymoon? Did you make it out of the bedroom?'

Eventually, after being confined there due to Rory's sunburn. 'It was … nice.'

'Nice?' Gloria's spine straightened as she observed her daughter. '*Nice?* What is *that* supposed to mean? Picnics are nice. Visiting grandparents is *nice*. Your honeymoon is supposed to be delicious and sensual and downright filthy!'

Trina pressed her lips together, but it was no use. She was about to jump right back on the blubber train. 'Oh, Mum.' Yep, here were the tears, thick and rapidly spilling onto her cheeks. 'I think I've married the wrong man!'

THIRTY-EIGHT

Erin

Erin groaned as the alarm evicted her from a deep sleep, and she fumbled to reach it to make the noise stop. But the room was silenced before she could make contact. Beside her, Richard gave a groan of his own as he stretched.

Ooh, Richard. Erin wasn't supposed to be here. She was supposed to be waking up in her own flat, yet there she was, cocooned with Richard. Amanda wouldn't be pleased at all, what with the children sleeping only a wall away. No sleepovers while the children were staying over, that was the rule. Which only made it all the more delicious.

'Morning.' Richard opened his arms and Erin found herself nestled into his chest, a stupidly serene smile on her face. 'We don't have to get up yet, do we?'

'I'm afraid we do. Lots to do today, and Lindsay will flip if we're late.' The day Erin had been dreading was upon them. It was Lindsay's wedding day, which meant Erin was on bridesmaid duty.

Such joy.

Erin hadn't seen Lindsay – or the other bridesmaids – since the hen weekend, which had ended as gruesomely as it had begun when Rita sneaked one of the strippers into their room and Erin had been forced to either listen from the next bed or top-and-tail with Lindsay. Talk about being stuck between a rock and a shit place. In the end, Erin had chosen to squeeze in with Lindsay.

'You're right.' Richard reluctantly pulled himself into a sitting position, rubbing his eyes with vigour. It was going to be a long day. 'I really don't want to face the wrath of my sister if we're late. You go and wake the kids and I'll make a start on breakfast.'

Fastening Richard's robe around her – why did Richard's robe always feel so much cosier than her own? It was the same with his slippers, even though they were far too big – Erin made her way along the landing, knocking gently on first LuLu's and then Ralph's door. LuLu emerged almost immediately, eager for her flower girl responsibilities to begin. Erin wished she shared the girl's enthusiasm for the day ahead, but couldn't bring herself to feel anything but deep hatred for the slutty ballerina outfit she'd be sporting.

After a quick breakfast, the family – for that was what they were, no matter how hard Erin and Amanda had fought against it – dressed before heading out to their respective meeting points. Richard dropped Erin, LuLu and Ralph at his parents' house before driving on to Frank's flat where the groom's party were gathering.

The Shuttleworths' house was in chaos when Erin arrived. The other seven bridesmaids were in differing stages of dress – some already tipsy on the champagne doing the rounds – and Lindsay looked like Miss Hannigan as she tottered around the house in her lingerie and curlers, a glass of champagne in each hand. Ingrid was stalking about the place, clipboard in hand and barking orders, while one of the bridesmaids sat in a heap on the bottom step, sobbing away, apparently overcome by the emotion of it all.

'What's up with Annie?' Erin asked Ingrid, who ignored the enquiry. If it wasn't on her agenda, Ingrid didn't have the time or inclination to trouble herself with it.

'You two need to be in the dining room.' She jabbed a pen towards Erin and LuLu. 'The girls from Sparkle are set up in there. Pageboy, you need to go upstairs. Susan has your suit ready. One of the Sparkle girls will sort your hair out when they get the chance.'

Ingrid snapped her eyes away from her clipboard and marched away, yelling about flowers and shoes.

'Erin, darling!' Erin was set upon by Rita before she'd even reached the dining room. Rita threw her arms around her and gave her a drunken squeeze. 'It's so good to see you again.'

'Erm, yes, you too.' Rita had formed quite a bond with Erin during the hen weekend, but at least today she wasn't waving her arse in Erin's face, as she had done on the coach trip home. For their final day at the spa, Helen had organised a twerking lesson with a so-called professional, which the girls had found *hilarious* and had practised their new skill for the entire journey back home.

'What's wrong with Annie?' Erin peered along the hallway, where Annie was still howling, as she repeated the question she'd asked Ingrid moments ago.

'No idea. She's been like that since she got here.' Rita pulled a brief sympathetic face before brightening and shoving a glass of champagne towards Erin. 'Celebratory drink?'

'God, yes.' Erin took the glass and took an immediate gulp. She was going to need several of those to get through the day.

Three hours later, the bridal party was finally ready, filing out of the house amid excited chatter. A horse-drawn carriage and a pink limo waited outside, the sight of which upped the excitement level by a million per cent. Erin and the children hung back to prevent being stampeded into the hallway carpet, so they were one of the last to emerge from the house. Only Annie and Ingrid were behind them.

'I can't believe this is happening.' Annie had managed to stem the flow of tears for long enough to get dressed and have her make-up reapplied, but a fresh wave threatened to burst forth.

'Will you get a grip?' Ingrid barked. She was clearly a fan of tough love, but it worked. With a final sniff, Annie straightened up and stepped over the threshold with her head held high. Ingrid waited for Erin to join her, cocking an eyebrow ever so slightly as she hesitated.

Was she really expected to step out in public wearing a tutu? She felt like an utter fool inside the house – she would surely expire of embarrassment out in the open.

'Are you going to start snivelling too?' Ingrid's lip curled. She couldn't deal with such soppy women. It wasn't like it was *their* wedding – and even if it was, there was only so much she could tolerate.

LuLu took Erin's hand. 'We'll go out together. No one will even notice you when they see Aunty Lindsay anyway.'

Erin kissed the top of LuLu's head. She hadn't even conveyed her concerns to the kid but she'd still picked up on Erin's discomfort. 'Come on, then.' She turned to Ralph and took hold of his hand too. 'You look handsome, kiddo. Just like a miniature version of your dad.'

Ralph pulled at his tie. 'I don't want to look like Dad.'

'He wants to look like Harry Styles,' LuLu said.

Ralph pulled at his tie again. 'Shut up. I do not.'

Ingrid gave a weary sigh from behind them, prompting the trio to finally make the leap over the threshold and out of the house. The bridesmaids were shrieking about how gorgeous the carriage was as Lindsay sat inside it, waving

251

regally to her adoring fans. Annie stood to one side, struggling with a packet of tissues as mascara streaked down her face.

'Come on, ladies!' Ingrid clapped her hands and directed the bridesmaids into the limo. Erin helped the children inside before she climbed in, followed by Annie, who was given a helping shove from Ingrid.

'I can't do this!' Annie wailed as the limo set off. She held a crumpled tissue, but it was ignored as the tears were running too fast and free to control. Rita gave her a pat on the knee but she was mostly overlooked as another bottle of champagne was opened and the women filled their glasses (or, in the case of Whitney, drank straight from the bottle). Undeterred, Annie sniffled for the entire journey.

'Oh my God, the paps are here!' Whitney squeaked as the limo pulled up outside the hotel. Erin spotted a lone photographer on the pavement, who it later turned out was a reporter from the local free newspaper. Still, it didn't stop the bridesmaids pouting at him, and even Annie bucked up enough to have a photo taken on the grand steps leading up to the hotel where the wedding would take place. The reporter lost interest in the bridesmaids as the groom arrived, and instead snapped shots of Frank as he emerged from his car.

Annie burst into tears again and flung herself into Rita's arms. 'It's not fair! He was supposed to be *mine*! That bitch stole him from me!'

Rita made soothing noises as she stroked Annie's back. 'But you and Frank had only been dating for eight months, and you'd broken up before he got together with Lindsay.'

'For two *days*. She *knew* I was in love with him!'

'Ssh now. You and Frank are ancient history, and Lindsay has been your best friend since you were five. You want her to be happy, don't you? Frank's marrying Lindsay because he loves *her* and she loves him.'

This only made Annie even more unhappy and she broke down again, throwing her head back and making mooing noises.

'Will you get a grip?' Lillian, the eldest bridesmaid, marched towards Annie, slapping her hard across the face. 'Lindsay will be here any minute, and you're going to ruin her day.'

'Fuck Lindsay. She's a selfish *bitch*.'

Lillian slapped Annie again, even harder this time, which managed to knock the girl out of her pity party. But instead of calming Annie, it only incensed her, and she retaliated by grabbing a fistful of Lillian's hair and tugging with all her might. Lillian howled like a strangled cat. The reporter was busy snapping away as the exchange took place.

'What do you think you're doing?' Ingrid waded into the cat fight and prised the pair apart. 'Get inside now and sort yourselves out. You.' She glared at the reporter as she marched the girls past him. 'Don't you dare print those photos.' She dragged the still sniping bridesmaids into the hotel foyer, ordering the rest of the party to follow. 'I want this silliness to stop *right now*. Lindsay is on her way and the last thing she wants to greet her is a pair of bridesmaids brawling in the street.'

'What's going on?' Richard had been waiting in the foyer and now joined Erin and the children, who were gripping Erin's hand with a painful ferocity. He looked handsome in his suit and he showed what impeccable manners he possessed when he didn't so much as smirk when he saw Erin in her ridiculous costume.

'Annie's just overcome with happiness,' Erin said. Rita was trying to drag Annie into the loo, while Helen attempted to fix Lillian's hair. Her extensions had been wrenched loose, giving her hair a roadkill look.

'It's a bit of a palaver, isn't it?' Richard asked. 'We won't have all this when we get married, will we?'

'Don't start all that. Right now, I'm ready to disown you and your crazy family. Apart from you two.' Erin put her arms around LuLu and Ralph and gave them a squeeze. 'You two are the best.'

'Speaking of crazy family ...' Richard pulled Erin to one side, out of earshot of the children. 'Amanda's here.'

THIRTY-NINE

Erin

Of all the people on the planet, the very last person Erin wanted to see her trussed up like Ballerina Barbie On Crack was Richard's ex-wife.

'What's she doing here? Lindsay can't stand her.' Apart from Richard, it was possibly the only thing they had in common.

'Mum invited her.' Richard gave an apologetic shrug. 'She says she's still family.'

Susan and Amanda were still on friendly terms and often met up for coffee, which Susan delighted in relaying to Erin. Amanda was like a daughter to her, apparently, and it didn't seem to matter that it had been Amanda who'd left Richard and started divorce proceedings. The woman was a saint in the (treacherous) eyes of Richard's mum.

'Can't I call it quits and go home?' Erin looked down at her outfit. Amanda was going to *love* this.

'I think you look great.' Richard gave another apologetic shrug when Erin caught his eye. 'Okay, not great. Quite ridiculous, really.' Richard chuckled as Erin nudged him with her elbow. 'But beautiful. *Always* beautiful.'

'You have to say that. You're my boyfriend and you'd also quite like to have sex sometime this century.'

'But it's also true.' Richard wrapped his arms around Erin and kissed her (but not too passionately. His children were present and they didn't want to see *that*).

'She's here!'

There was a flurry of tutus as the bridesmaids charged towards the door to get a glimpse of the bride as she arrived in her carriage. Even Annie popped out of the loo to have a gander, although her face was filled with rage rather than wonder. Ingrid took charge, bellowing orders as she arranged everybody in their rightful places. Lindsay and Kelvin stepped into the foyer and Erin instantly felt better about herself. Lindsay's dress was definitely worse than her own, especially as Lindsay had added a diamant*é*-encrusted garter, which was on show thanks to her minuscule dress.

'Places, please!' Ingrid marched up and down the rows of bridesmaids and groomsmen, nodding her approval or making adjustments as she went along. 'Very good. Straighten that sloppy tie. No gum! Spit it out *immediately*. Very nice. Lovely.' With a final nod, Ingrid threw open the doors of the ceremonial room and stepped aside to allow Lindsay and Kelvin to glide down the aisle towards Frank to the gentle sound of the harp. Timing it to perfection, Ingrid sent the bridesmaids and groomsmen couples down the aisle at intervals. Erin grasped Richard's arm as they followed the bride, her eyes roaming the congregation. There she was. Amanda. Suppressing a giggle into a lacy handkerchief when she clapped eyes on Erin.

Bitch.

The ceremony began, with hymns (several) and readings (too many) before maid of honour Helen and one

of the groomsmen made their way to the front. The intro
to 'Endless Love' began and the pair began to sing. It was
so cringe-worthy, it made Erin's entire body itch, but then
how could she judge anyone, dressed as she was?

Finally, the vows were exchanged (written by the bride
and groom themselves and corny beyond belief). Luckily,
Lindsay and Ingrid knew how to throw a decent, alcohol-
filled party and once the essentials had been carried out –
the throwing of confetti and three million photos of every
conceivable combination of guests – the wedding party
moved through to the hotel's bar for pre-dinner drinks and
nibbles. A video booth had been set up in an alcove, with
instructions to share a story about the bride or groom or
give advice for a long and happy marriage, and a basket of
mini bottles of bubbles invited guests to 'fill the room with
bubbles and love'. Every surface was covered with ribbons
or balloons or sequined hearts – or all three.

Erin and the children found a vacant table, while
Richard went to the bar. He would be a while, judging by
the crowd; there had been a mass exodus to the free
alcohol as soon as the doors had opened. Annie had been
first in the queue.

'Are you hungry?' Erin asked the children. There were
various 'stations' dotted around the vast room: a fruit
station to make your own fruity kebabs, a crisps and dip
station, an ice cream bar to create your own sundaes, a
fish and chips station with mini portions in newspaper
cones, as well as popcorn and candyfloss-makers.

'I want ice cream,' Ralph declared, jumping to his feet.

'I want pink candyfloss.' LuLu was about to pop out of
her seat, but a hand on her shoulder held her in place.

'No sugar before dinner.' Amanda guided her son back
to his seat while glaring at Erin. 'Are you *trying* to ruin my
children's health and teeth?'

Erin was very aware of her absurd outfit, but she
decided to brazen it out. 'It was just a little treat. We *are*

at a wedding.'

'That's no excuse!' Amanda stalked the area, narrowed eyes scoping the room. Her nude six-inch heels made her legs appear to go on forever. Richard's ex may have been a bitch but she had amazing pins. 'Where's Richard?'

'He's at the bar.' Erin pointed him out. He was still nowhere near being served, unfortunately.

'Typical!' Amanda placed a hand on her hip. Her long nails were painted a chilling blood-red, and Erin suppressed a shudder. 'I place my children in the care of the two of you and what do you do? You load them up with junk while you get plastered. Ever heard of responsibility?'

'Ever heard of relaxing and having a good time?' Erin knew she shouldn't rise to the bait, but she couldn't seem to bite her tongue. 'All this stress can't be good for you, Mandy.'

'My name is *Amanda*. And I wouldn't be so stressed if I knew I could trust Richard to take proper care of our children.'

'He takes excellent care of the children!' How dare she state otherwise? Richard loved his children and would do everything in his power to keep them safe and happy, including putting up with their gobshite mother and her ridiculous rules.

'By your standards, maybe.' Amanda's nostrils twitched as though she'd got a whiff of dog shit in the air but was too polite to point it out. 'But my children mean the world to me. I want nothing but the very best for them. You wouldn't understand, not being a mother yourself.' Amanda lifted her chin in the air. 'Come on, you two. You can sit with me so I can keep a proper eye on you.'

Erin watched as LuLu and Ralph dutifully followed their mother, all hope of the coveted ice cream and candyfloss vanishing. They would have to make do with a fruit kebab. And what could Erin do about it? Amanda was their mother and Erin was – well, just Erin.

Richard eventually arrived with a tray of drinks, frowning when he found Erin alone.

'Where are LuLu and Ralph?' His eyes flicked to the food stations, but the children were nowhere to be seen.

'With Amanda.' Erin pointed at a table as far away from her as Amanda could find. Amanda, sitting with the children and Susan, gave a triumphant flick of her hair when she spotted Erin looking in her direction. 'I made the mistake of saying LuLu and Ralphie could have ice cream and candyfloss. *No sugar before dinner.*' Erin adopted a high-pitched mocking tone for the latter part.

'But what's wrong with that? It's a special occasion.'

'You know what she's like.' Erin picked up her drink – a diet coke, as it happened – and took a sip. 'She doesn't think I'm suitable to supervise her children.'

'She said that?'

'No, but it's why she causes all this fuss. You'd be better off if I wasn't on the scene. It'd be simpler for you all.'

'Not for me.' Richard held out a hand to Erin. 'Come on, I've had enough of this.'

Erin scurried after Richard as he strode off towards his ex-wife. Amanda gave a sweet smile as they approached.

'Richard, how lovely of you to come and see your children.' Amanda turned to LuLu and Ralph, who were picking at a fruit kebab with little enthusiasm. 'Say hello to your dad.'

'Don't do that, Amanda.' Richard's authoritative tone surprised them all. He'd never stood up to Amanda, either in their marriage or out of it. 'Don't speak to me as though I'm some shady, absent father. LuLu and Ralph are supposed to be with me today.'

'Supposed to be, yes.' Amanda folded her arms across

her chest and cocked her head to one side. 'But that doesn't entail getting drunk while they're in your care.'

'Getting drunk on those soft drinks over there, you mean?' Richard pointed at the cokes still sitting on their table, but Amanda wasn't knocked off her course.

'I still think they're better off with me – under the circumstances.'

'What circumstances?'

Amanda eyed Erin, arching an eyebrow threaded to within an inch of its life. She didn't say anything. She didn't have to.

'This stops now, Amanda.' Richard didn't raise his voice, but his tone conveyed his anger. 'I am not playing your games any more. I'm with Erin and it's about time you accepted that.'

Amanda gave a hoot. 'You think I'm *jealous?* I divorced you, don't forget. Erin is welcome to you, but my children will not suffer. *I* am their mother and I know what's best for them. *She* is nothing.'

'Erin is my girlfriend.' Richard threaded his fingers through Erin's and pulled her close. 'And you cannot dictate to us how we live our lives. If I want Erin to stay over, she can. If we want to take the children to a family function, we will, without you lording it over us. I am their father. I also know what's best for them, and your bitterness isn't it.'

'Bitter?' Amanda placed a hand on her chest. 'I'm simply looking out for my children's welfare. And that girlfriend of yours is detrimental to that.'

'Actually, Amanda.' Susan leaned towards her former daughter-in-law. 'From what I've seen, Erin has always been very good to the kiddies.'

Amanda's mouth dropped open. She closed it. Then opened it again. 'You're *defending* her?'

Susan leaned back in her chair and held her hands up. 'I'm just saying it how it is. No need to attack me for that.'

Amanda tittered. 'I'm not attacking you, Susan. I'm surprised, that's all. I didn't know you were so chummy with Erin.' There was panic in Amanda's eyes. She was losing her ally. How else was she supposed to keep up to date with Richard without his mother being on her side?

'We're not chummy, but we're not enemies either.' That was news to Erin. 'I think she's good for Richard. And for LuLu and Ralph.'

Susan must have been hitting the champers hard. She'd never had a nice word to say about her son's girlfriend before.

'Well!' Amanda, for once in her life, was lost for words.

'Let them live their lives, Amanda. You didn't want Richard. Why can't he be happy with someone else?' Susan patted Amanda's arm before she turned to her grandchildren. 'You two don't seem very interested in those. How about an ice cream instead?'

'Can I have candyfloss?' LuLu asked.

'Candyfloss it is.' Susan ambled after the children, who tore off towards the confectionery before it was snatched away from them again. Richard sat in his mother's vacated seat and faced his wife.

'We need to sort this, once and for all.'

'I don't want her near my children.' Amanda wasn't ready to give up yet, no matter how many she was battling against.

'I'm afraid that isn't up to you. Erin is part of my life. She loves me and she loves those children.'

'They are not hers to love!'

'But she loves them anyway, and she isn't going away. Don't make our children suffer.'

Amanda pursed her lips. 'I could take away access like *that*.' She snapped her fingers, a self-satisfied grin spreading across her lips, but it dimmed slightly as Richard shook his head.

'No, Amanda. We are not playing this game again. If

you stop me from seeing them, we'll go to court to agree on a more formal access arrangement.'

Amanda narrowed her eyes. 'You always said we'd keep them out of court.'

'That was because I trusted you to do the right thing. You take them away and I'll have no choice. Think about that.'

Richard rose from his seat and, taking Erin by the hand, led her back to their own table. LuLu and Ralph soon joined them with their candyfloss and ice cream, while Amanda made her excuses before slinking away.

FORTY

Ruth

Erin grumbled as she switched from the passenger seat of Quinn's car to the back to accommodate me and my 'travel-sickness'.

'You do know I'm well aware that you don't get travel-sick, don't you?' Erin asked as we set off for Linda's house to pick up Jimmy. The four of us were going shopping for bridesmaids' dresses and accessories. Great fat butterflies took flight in my tummy and it was nothing to do with being in motion. In thirteen days I would become Mrs Williams.

'You will let me know in plenty of time if you're going be sick, won't you?' Quinn asked, no doubt worrying about her car's interior. I didn't blame her – who wanted to drive around in a vomit-mobile?

'She isn't going to be sick.' Erin shifted in her seat, ensuring her knees jabbed into my back through the seat.

'I deserve to sit in the front.' I didn't bother to deny my lack of motion sickness – I wasn't pulling the wool over Erin's eyes, so what was the point? 'I *am* the bride-to-be.' I turned to stick my tongue out at Erin. 'So there.'

'Behave, you two.' Quinn gave a weary little sigh. 'You're supposed to set a good example to young Jimmy, and you're behaving like a couple of toddlers.'

'Sorry, Mum.' I turned to smirk at Erin as we both chimed the words.

Quinn, ignoring us, drove towards Linda's house, where we picked Jimmy up before heading into town. There wasn't a great deal left in the wedding fund, but it could just about stretch to bridesmaids' dresses from the high street.

'What do you think of this one?' I pulled a blue draped jersey dress from the rail, but Quinn shook her head.

'It's a bit … boring.'

'After the dress I wore yesterday, boring isn't always a bad thing,' Erin said. I couldn't wait to see the photos from Lindsay's wedding, just for a laugh. Erin had vowed that nobody who knew her would ever get a glimpse of them, but I would find a way.

'But we want something a bit more special.' Quinn threw an arm around me. 'It is Ruth's big day.'

'What do you think?' I asked Jimmy. She looked up from her phone with a slightly bewildered look on her face.

'That dress? Yes, it's nice.'

I replaced the dress. Quinn was right. 'Nice' wasn't good enough for my bridesmaids.

'How about this one?' I plucked a coral midi dress with a thin gold belt from the rail, but soon put it back when it received three firm head shakes.

'What's Riley wearing?' Quinn asked as we moved to the next section.

'It's a baby-pink party dress with a ruffled bodice and netted skirt.' Aubrey had emailed me a photo of Riley wearing the dress, and she'd looked adorable.

'Maybe we should wear something pink too,' Quinn

suggested, running her fingers along the assortment of fabrics.

'But not baby pink.' Erin was adamant about that. She was not a baby-pink sort of girl.

'What's wrong with baby pink?' Quinn was firmly in the baby-pink camp.

'Nothing. If you're a baby.' Erin moved along the section, pausing for a moment before selecting a raspberry-pink chiffon maxi dress with a halter-neck. Quinn pounced on it immediately, holding it up against her before she rifled through the rail to find her size.

'Special enough?' I asked and Quinn nodded.

'*Definitely* special enough. What do you think, Jimmy?'

Jimmy nodded. 'I like it too.'

'I *love* it.' Quinn, having found her size, skipped off towards the changing rooms. Erin and Jimmy grabbed their sizes and followed. Twenty minutes later we left the shop laden with shopping bags and with another item ticked off my to-do list.

'That was easy enough, but I think it's time we stopped for an energising tea and cake break. My treat.' Shopping always made me hungry, even when I wasn't shopping for myself.

'Do you mind if I head off?' Jimmy asked. 'I said I'd meet somebody.'

I met Erin's eye and couldn't help smirking. 'Is "somebody" a boy?'

Jimmy's cheeks matched the raspberry pink in her shopping bag. 'Maybe.' She bit her lip. 'You won't tell Mum and Dad, will you? Or Jared?'

'Of course not.' Jared was clearly keeping secrets from me with his little wedding day surprise (which I still hadn't managed to coax out of him), so why shouldn't I keep one of my own? 'Will you be okay getting home afterwards?'

'I'll get the bus.'

'With your friend?' Erin asked and I nudged her as

Jimmy's cheeks turned an alarming shade.

'Have fun,' I said and Jimmy nodded shyly before shuffling away. We watched her until she disappeared into the crowds.

'Wouldn't you love to be that young again?' Quinn sighed.

'You practically *are* that young,' I pointed out. *And no, I wouldn't go back to my teenage years for anything.* 'Shall we go and eat? I'm starving.'

We headed to a cute little tearoom just off the high street and ordered giant slabs of carrot cake. It was too late for any wedding diets now – and I hadn't even started one in the first place. I wasn't a fan of dieting; I'd been there, done that and I still didn't fit in the T-shirt.

'This is exactly what I needed.' Erin stabbed her cake and shoved a forkful into her mouth.

'So how was Lindsay's wedding?' Quinn asked. 'Was it as tacky as you feared?'

Erin chewed furiously and took a sip of tea. 'It was so over the top. They had lawn games and the cake had about ten tiers. When they made a toast, they brought out champagne and the flutes were engraved with each guest's name. And you should have seen the favours. They weren't so much favours as goody bags. Mine had a Yankee candle, a mini bottle of champagne, bath salts and a CD of love songs.'

'That sounds amazing,' Quinn said.

I thought it sounded expensive.

'There was a sort of quiz for us to fill in between courses too. It had things like "where did Frank propose?" and "what shall we call our children?"' Erin looked at Quinn. 'You'd have loved it.'

Quinn adopted a dreamy look. 'I so would.' She turned to me then. 'I can't believe there are less than two weeks until you and Jared get married. You must be so excited.'

I nodded. 'I am. Really excited. But I'm also a bit

nervous.'

'Are you scared you're going to mess up your vows and make a complete knob of yourself in front of all your friends and family?' Quinn asked. 'That happened to my cousin. She got so muddled up, she got her own name wrong. She was so embarrassed, she started crying and the priest had to start all over again.'

How reassuring. 'No, that's not what I'm worried about.' Although I was sure I would start to worry about that now too.

'But I'm sure that won't happen to you!' Quinn grinned at me and I tried to return the gesture.

'No, I'm sure it won't.' *Gulp.* 'So the wedding went well then, Erin? No hiccups or humiliation?'

'Not for the bride.' Erin pulled a face. 'But there was some drama. One of the bridesmaids kicked off. It turns out she was with Frank first and she was still in love with him.'

'No!' Quinn and I were wide-eyed, wishing we'd been there to witness the events unfold. It sounded like an episode of *Corrie*.

'And then Amanda turned up.'

'No!' Still wide-eyed.

'I'm afraid so. But Richard stood up to her and told her she had to stop being a dick. He was quite masterful.' Erin shivered with pleasure.

'Do you think she'll listen, though?' Amanda struck me as the sort of woman who didn't like being told what to do.

Erin shrugged. 'Who knows with that one? But she left soon after, so we got to enjoy the rest of the day. It wasn't so bad, really, once I'd got used to the humiliating dress. The food was lovely and you should have seen Richard and LuLu dancing. It was so sweet.'

'Ah.' I met Quinn's eye and we both smiled. 'Look at our Erin all loved up and enjoying family life. She'll be getting married and popping out babies any minute now.'

'Piss right off.' Erin forked a huge chunk of cake. 'That is so not happening. I'm not ripping my fanny to shreds for anything.' She stuffed more cake into her mouth. My cake was no longer quite so appetising.

I knelt, lowering myself so that my forehead rested on the cushioned pink mat while my arms rested at my sides. Taking a deep breath, I ignored the swirl of nerves in my stomach. It had set up camp at the beginning of the class and was refusing to abate. This would be my last yoga class before the wedding. The next time I would be in this room with half a dozen other women (and Greg), curled up on our mats, I would be Mrs Williams.

I'd started to think of everything in lasts: my last hair cut before the wedding (I'd had a trim. Not with Aidan this time, but my regular, more reasonably priced, hairdresser), my last minutes to type up (fingers crossed. There were no more meetings scheduled before the wedding, anyway), my last episode of *A Beginner's Guide To You.* I was counting down the coffees I would have to make for Kelvin and the number of times I'd have to lie to Susan on the phone so he didn't have to speak to her (a rough estimate of sixteen coffees and twelve fibs). There were four more wake-ups (not including waking up on my actual wedding day), twelve meals (plus additional snacks), and one final dress fitting.

It was all scarily close.

'Don't forget to breathe,' Nell instructed from the front of the class, which had always struck me as pretty ridiculous – how could you *forget* to breathe? – but I actually found the reminder helpful that evening. I released the pent-up breath from my aching lungs and took in a fresh inhalation. 'After this next breath, place your palms in front of you on your mat, stretch your legs back and rise into the plank.'

There was a collective groan. The plank was not the class's favourite pose.

'Come on, ladies. You can do it.'

Following Nell's instructions, we moved from the plank – with a collective sigh of relief – into downward dog and then the warrior. As Nell rose to her feet, you could see she was starting to show, very slightly. While her stomach was once completely flat, it now looked like she'd swallowed a grain of rice without chewing.

'I don't know how she does it,' Mary said as we packed up our things after the class. 'I could barely move when I was carrying our Eric. Mind you, I was camped out in the outside lav for the first six months.'

'Didn't you have an indoor toilet?' I knew Woodgate was hardly the height of sophistication and we were going back a few decades, but still.

'We did, but my husband didn't like the smell of vomit, you see. If he got even the slightest whiff, he'd have been heaving his guts up too and I had enough to deal with cleaning up after myself.'

With that lovely image in my head, we started to wander out of the church hall, our feet automatically heading towards the pub. The others were going that way too, apart from Nell and Greg, who were forgoing the post-class drink.

'I need to get home to bed,' Nell had said, patting her grain of rice. 'We need our rest.'

We piled into the pub and arranged ourselves in smaller groups. Mary and I ended up in a corner by ourselves, and we naturally began to discuss my wedding. It had once been my very favourite subject, but now thinking about it brought a wave of nausea. Where was Mary's outdoor privy when I needed it?

'So, how are the wedding plans coming along?'

'They're good. Most things are sorted now, and I've got

my final dress fitting tomorrow.'

'How lovely. I adored my dress when I got married. It was a hand-me-down from my sister-in-law but it was beautiful. I felt like a princess.' Mary sighed at the memory. 'I don't suppose I'll bother with a fancy dress this time around. Both of us are too old and knackered and you know what they say: you can't polish a turd.'

I spluttered, choking on my drink. 'You have to wear something nice. It's your wedding.'

Mary gave a wave of a liver-spotted hand. 'Nah, I don't want to make a fuss. I'll get married in my slippers if I can get away with it. Besides, I'm not even sure there'll be a wedding now.'

I sat up straighter, my nausea briefly receding. I can't deny that the respite was most welcome, even if it was replaced with worry for Mary. 'Why? What's happened?'

'I met Cecil's daughters at the weekend.' Mary pursed her wrinkled lips. 'Pair of stuck-up cows. They reckon I'm after Cecil's money, which would be fine if the bugger had a penny to his name.' She stretched out her hand, displaying her shimmering rock. 'This ring was his mother's and it's the only thing of value he has, bless him. His daughters think it should go to them, but Cecil assures me their grandmother never said a dickie bird about them inheriting it.' Mary shook her head. 'I'm too old to be putting up with their drivel, and if Cecil thinks he can sit there while they tear me to shreds, he can think again.'

'Is that what he did? Sit there while they slagged you off?'

Mary shook her head. 'No, the little madams were too clever for that. They waited until he was out of the room before they started. But I told him about it later, so it's up to him to sort it out. I've told him I want an apology from both of them before I'll even consider marrying him.'

'Good for you.'

'I've put him on a sex ban too. That'll put a rocket up

his arse to sort them out.' Mary winked at me. 'Here's a tip for you before you start married life: men always, *always* think with their willies.'

FORTY-ONE

Trina

The atmosphere in the annex was strained, so it was fortunate that Rory had decided to spend even more time at the office. Trina hadn't thought this was possible, but her husband was willing to prove her wrong. He left before six each morning and it was way after midnight before he returned. In the end Trina stopped waiting up for him. What was the point? They only argued whenever they happened to be in the same room and conscious.

Trina had yet to see or speak to Aidan, both because she didn't want to rock the already capsizing boat of her marriage by going against Rory's wishes and because she wasn't sure where it would lead. If what Ruth said was true and Aidan had been in some sort of accident on the night of the dance, then he hadn't stood her up on purpose at all. But why hadn't he said anything at the time? Trina needed answers, but she feared that seeing Aidan would have cataclysmic consequences for her marriage, and she wasn't ready to face that just yet. Her mother had been little use on the matter – as far as Gloria was concerned, there was no 'right' man for marriage. You got what you could from each union before you scarpered unscathed. And now Gloria was out of the country again, being swept off her feet by Yuri in Paris.

'Darling, you'll be fine,' Gloria had assured her before she dashed off for the airport. 'Rory doesn't beat you. He doesn't drink or gamble away your housekeeping. You'll figure it all out, I promise. We'll chat again when I get back, all right, my love?'

Gloria loved her daughters, but she'd never been very good at putting them first. Neither of Trina's parents had been very good at that, but Trina had hoped that by marrying Rory, she'd always have somebody by her side. Somebody to love her.

But Trina had never felt so alone.

Grabbing her laptop, Trina clicked on her wedding photos, hardly able to believe that they had been taken just a few short weeks ago. It seemed like a lifetime ago, when she'd been so full of love and hope for the future. She and Rory were going to live blissfully ever after, filling their lovely home with children and laughter. But where was the laughter? They didn't even have their own home, lovely or otherwise, and it didn't appear that they would any time soon. Despite Rory's promise before he left for New York, he seemed quite satisfied and settled in his parents' annex. He'd barely glanced at the property details Trina had collected and Trina couldn't bring herself to push for the move.

Shutting down the laptop, Trina went in search of food. It was getting late, but she no longer prepared dinner for herself and Rory – what was the point, when half of it only made it as far as the kitchen bin? There wasn't much in the fridge and the bread bin was empty. Trina decided to go for a walk into the village to stock up and clear her head.

Pulling on her boots and a jacket, Trina left the annex, but didn't make it to the shop after all. Parked on the

Hamilton-Wraiths' drive was Rory's car. Making her way across to the main house, Trina slipped into the kitchen where she was greeted by an enthusiastic Leo. The dog had always been the most welcoming Hamilton-Wraith. She gave him a quick rub behind the ears before going in search of the family.

The Hamilton-Wraiths lived in a large Tudor property that had been in the family for generations. Trina made her way along the plush red carpet in the hall, past the ornate staircase and original fireplace, following the sound of chatter to the dining room. There came the unmistakable booming laugh of Mr Hamilton-Wraith, followed by Rory's more reserved chuckle. Knocking on the door, Trina pushed it open, frowning at the scene before her. It shouldn't have come as any great shock that the family were eating in the dining room – it was its purpose, after all – but she hadn't expected to see her husband merrily tucking into his meal with them.

'Katrina!' Winnie beamed at her daughter-in-law, failing to show any hint of surprise to see her standing in the doorway. 'Do come and join us. I'm sure Mrs Timmons can rustle you up some leftovers, and there are still plenty of bread rolls left.'

'No, thank you.' The reluctant invitation didn't sound genuine to Trina, and the offer of leftovers and bread hardly filled her with warmth. 'I just wanted a quick word with Rory.'

'Oh. Very well.' Winnie turned to her son and pursed her lips. 'Don't take too long, dear. Your meal will grow cold.'

Trina backed away from the room, leading Rory to the sanctuary of the kitchen. The only ears listening there belonged to Leo.

'What are you doing here?' Despite their audience of one, Trina kept her voice low.

Rory hesitated. Was this a trick question? 'I'm having

dinner.'

Without me? Trina wanted to cry, but thought that would sound far too needy and desperate.

'And do you often dine with your family?' Perhaps those late nights hadn't been spent slaving away at the office after all. Perhaps he'd been with his family, laughing and joking while Trina spent her evenings alone.

Rory leaned against the worktop, folding his arms across his chest. 'Not often, no. Sometimes, yes.'

Sometimes. So this wasn't the first time Rory had popped over for a cosy little dinner with his family – plus Ginny, who Trina hadn't failed to notice at the table – without her. Trina felt a stab in her gut. She'd been left out – and all while she was just yards away in the annex.

'Maybe we should talk about this later? At home.' Trina didn't trust herself to not burst into tears, and she wouldn't give any of them the satisfaction.

'I won't be back until late.' Rory straightened and started to head towards the kitchen door. 'Carrie's invited me to a party. It's nothing big. Just a few old friends.'

Something else Trina wasn't invited to.

'Why did you marry me?' Trina hadn't meant to ask the question, mainly because she was afraid of the answer. But there it was, out in the open.

Rory sighed, long and heavy. 'Why do you think?'

'I don't know.' Trina shrugged. 'I thought it was because you loved me, but now I don't think you even *like* me. You never include me in your life, you're never home and you let your family bully me.'

'Bully you?' Rory scoffed. 'What do they do? Rough you up behind the bike sheds when the teachers aren't looking?'

'Bullying doesn't have to be physical,' Trina pointed out. 'But that isn't even the point. I asked a question and you still haven't answered. Why did you marry me, Rory? *Do* you love me or was I just an accessory? The next item on your to-do list?'

'I don't have time for this,' Rory said, already moving away from her. 'My dinner's getting cold and I have a party to get to.'

'When did our lives become so separate?'

Rory paused in the doorway before turning back to face his wife, giving a small shrug. 'You have your friends, Trina. I have mine.'

Whistling a merry tune, Rory returned to his meal, which Trina hoped was now stone cold. The problem with Rory's statement was that, because of him, she didn't have her friend at all. Well, that would change – tonight. She would go and see Aidan – and perhaps she would get some answers too.

FORTY-TWO

Ruth

There was something about my office chair that transformed me into an obsessive clock-watcher. Whenever my arse made contact with that chair, my eyes were compelled to swivel towards the clock – either the little one on my computer screen or the bigger one on the wall – at thirty-second intervals. But today, my clock-watching took on new levels of intensity and my eyes ached from their constant movement. Today was Dress Day. I would be picking up my lovely, gorgeous, flattering, *amazing* dress from Libby, and five o'clock couldn't arrive quickly enough.

Of course that meant that five o'clock took *forever* to arrive. (Seriously. I was convinced time was going *backwards* at one point.) However, eventually that blessed stage known as Going Home Time rolled around and I switched off my computer with glee. I dashed from the office before Kelvin could task me with something urgent, which he had a tendency to do (and which usually turned out to be not that urgent after all). I skipped down to reception to meet Erin and Quinn, grateful to see they were already waiting for me. I was so eager to put the dress on again that I feared I'd burst if I had to wait a minute longer than absolutely necessary.

'Are you ready?' Quinn asked.

I nodded, then pulled a face, my emotions battling it out. 'Yes. No. I don't know.' I was so bloody excited – it was *Dress Day* – but I couldn't rid myself of the spike of apprehension prodding at my gut. It was like my body *wanted* me to be miserable and was rugby-tackling any feelings of contentment before they could fully reach me.

'Come on, you nutter.' Erin linked her arm through mine and marched me out into the car park. 'You'll be fine, I promise you.'

'I hope the dress fits,' I said, the spike of apprehension prodding away at me again like a pokey little bastard. 'Otherwise it'll be a race against time to get it sorted before the wedding.' There were only a few days to go – so few, in fact, that I was almost ready to start counting down the hours rather than days. 'Oh God, what if it isn't ready?'

'Then you'll have to get married naked.' Erin deposited me beside her car (she wasn't willing to squish herself into the back seat of Quinn's car again). 'You can call it a theme. We'll all go as Mother Nature intended.'

I needn't have worried about the dress. Libby had done a wonderful job and it fit perfectly. It was even more beautiful without the pins – and this time I got to take it home.

'Good luck for Saturday,' Libby said as we left the shop, the dress draped lovingly over my arms. I wouldn't have held a newborn baby as gently as I held that dress.

'Thank you, for everything.' I couldn't thank Libby enough. Instead of walking down the aisle resembling a meringue-like blimp, I would be decked out gorgeously and in a dress that fit my usual style.

We headed across the courtyard to Erin's car, but I didn't feel like going home straight away. Surely a celebration was in order – and nothing said celebration like a huge slab of cake.

'Do you fancy going for something to eat?' My arms were full of dress, so I nodded towards the restaurant, my mouth already watering. I was desperate to have another go at that Black Forest cheesecake. Quinn and Theo had thwarted my chances last time, but she wouldn't do that to me again. Would she?

'I can't. I'm having dinner with my family.' Quinn shot me an apologetic look. 'It's been planned for ages, sorry.'

'And I've got my salsa class tonight,' Erin said. 'But another time, yeah?'

I couldn't help feeling disappointed. Hartfield Hill was out of the way and we had no reason to return now I had my dress. Who would travel all that way for a slice of cake?

Oh, who was I kidding? *I* so would!

Once home, I hid the dress at the back of the wardrobe. It was encased in a protective bag, but I didn't want to run the risk that Jared would get a look.

'Jared?' I moved through the flat in search of my soon-to-be husband. I'd flown straight into the bedroom to put the dress away so I didn't even know whether he was home or not. 'Jared?'

I found him in the kitchen. In his running gear yet again. He'd spent every night pounding the pavements of Woodgate for the past couple of weeks and, while I knew he was keen on fitness and all that, I couldn't help feeling put out. We'd hardly spent any time together lately, what with the wedding plans going into overdrive and Jared's freakish desire to be healthy.

'Oh. You're going out.'

'You don't mind, do you?'

I did mind, very much, but I didn't want to start putting

my foot down just yet. We had vows and a legally binding certificate to sign before I could do any foot-putting-down.

'No, of course not,' I simpered. 'I'll see you later then.'

Jared kissed me before leaving the room, only to pop his head back round the door. 'How did the fitting go?'

'Great. Perfect, in fact. Looks like we're all ready to get married.' The spiky bugger was back in my gut. *Prod, prod, prod.*

Jared grinned at me. 'It looks like it.'

I was too excited to sit still – even with a slab of chocolate and the *A Beginner's Guide To You* box set – so I found myself heading over to my former home to see if Billy would chat to me. With my fiancé and best friends otherwise engaged (so to speak), I was beginning to feel a bit abandoned.

Pushing open the gate, I noticed that the sitting room curtains were closed, which was odd as it was still quite early and light. And wait a minute, wasn't that Quinn's car parked out on the street? All became clear when the door was answered by a sweaty, dishevelled Theo.

I adopted what I hoped was an uber-casual tone. 'Is Quinn here?' I knew full well what the answer was. Her car was parked right within sniffing distance.

Theo scratched the back of his neck. 'No. Why?'

'Because her car is over there.' I pointed out the car, crushing Theo's great fat lies. 'What about Billy? Or Casey?'

'They've gone out.'

'Out?'

'For dinner.'

'On a date?' *Interesting.*

Theo gave a shrug. 'I suppose.'

'So you're here with Quinn? Alone? Can I come in?'

Theo closed the door a fraction, blocking me. 'No. You can't. We're busy.'

I bloody well knew it! All that 'I don't fancy Theo' was

crap. Quinn *did* fancy Theo and had fallen for his charms. Plus, she'd lied to me about her plans – twice. Dinner with family? Pah!

I left them to it. Who was I to stand in Quinn's way if this was truly – inexplicably – what she wanted? I'd warned her plenty of times, but Quinn was a grown woman and capable of making her own decisions. Even if some of those decisions were stupid and I would have to twist Theo's bollocks off when he hurt her. Which he would.

I returned home and put the kettle on. I'd have a nice cup of tea and a few pieces of chocolate (aka a whole family-sized bar) and wait for Jared to come home. Maybe we could snuggle up on the sofa with that *Beginner's Guide* box set.

I was just getting started on the box set when the flat's buzzer interrupted the moment when Meg is about to reveal her true, albeit drunken, feelings for Tom. It was my favourite episode from season one, and never failed to make me smile. If my fiancé and friends were too busy jogging or dancing or having sex to entertain me, at least I could always rely on good old Meg and Tom.

Pausing the DVD, I answered the door. My cousin trooped into the flat, shoulders hunched, and not at all her usual perky self. When she looked at me, I could see her eyes were pink and swollen.

'What's the matter?' I guided Trina to the sofa and settled her amongst the scatter cushions. If I'd had a blanket handy, I'd have draped it over her. 'What's happened?'

Trina gave a sniff and her bottom lip trembled as she spoke. 'I think my marriage is over.'

FORTY-THREE

Trina

She felt bad immediately, even before the tears started to cascade down her cheeks, pooling on her trembling chin before she swiped at them with the sleeve of her cardigan. She shouldn't be burdening Ruth with her marriage woes – again – but where else could she go? Her mum was away with Yuri and she hadn't seen or heard from her sister since the wedding. And it wasn't as though she could rock up on Aidan's doorstep with a suitcase of her possessions. Not now. She trusted Ruth and she'd always made her feel better when she was little and feeling sad and lonely.

'How can it be over?' Ruth asked. She hadn't failed to notice the suitcase, abandoned in the hallway. This wasn't a silly little flounce after a row. Trina was serious. 'What's happened?'

And so Trina regaled the (latest) sorry tale of her marriage. The exclusion from family meals, the separation of their lives, going to see Aidan, and then the kiss.

'I feel so stupid.' Trina unravelled a clump of loo roll – Ruth still hadn't got round to buying actual tissues, and

Trina had exhausted her own supply – and gave her nose a hearty blow. 'Why did I marry Rory?'

She'd asked Rory why he'd married her – but now she had to face the question herself.

'Because you love him.' Ruth had no doubt about that. She'd seen the way her cousin had looked at Rory. She adored him.

Trina shook her head. 'I'm not sure I do, not properly. It was all such a whirlwind, you know. I was feeling a bit bruised after being let down by Aidan, and I've always felt like something was missing, that I'm somehow unlovable, so I was grateful that someone like Rory was interested in me.' Although she now knew the truth about what had happened that night. She'd been to see Aidan and he'd told her everything.

'Why didn't you tell me?' she'd demanded when she learned about the accident. Some idiot had ploughed into Aidan while he was on his phone. Luckily neither had been seriously hurt, but Trina couldn't bear to think about what could have been.

'I tried to, but you didn't have your phone with you. By the time I got through to you, it was too late. You'd met Rory and were completely head over heels. You couldn't stop praising the wonderful Rory long enough for me to explain, and I guess I didn't want to look like an idiot. There I was, gutted that I'd let you down, but you weren't bothered in the slightest.'

But Trina had been. Very much so. She'd sung Rory's praises loud and clear so that *she* didn't look like an idiot. 'Weren't you injured, though?'

'I came away with a few cuts and bruises. Nothing serious.'

'How did I not notice?'

'You went away.' Rory had taken Trina sailing on his father's yacht for the weekend, and when they returned they'd been inseparable. It must have been two weeks before she'd remembered there were other people in the world besides her new boyfriend.

'When you didn't show up, I thought you'd changed your mind.'

'Not even a little bit. I was crazy about you.' Aidan had dropped his gaze to his lap. 'I still am. It kills me that you're with him and not me.'

'Why didn't you ever *say* anything? Why did you let me marry him?'

Aidan's head snapped up, and he frowned. 'Because I want you to be happy, even if it's with someone else. All I've ever wanted was for you to be happy.'

'I'm not happy, Aidan.'

Trina couldn't remember a time when she'd been less happy. Aidan was in love with her and she was pretty sure she was still in love with him too, but she was married to Rory now. Everything was such a mess.

'I'm so sorry for coming here,' Trina said now, unravelling another wad of loo roll and dabbing at her eyes. 'I'm not a very good advertisement for marriage, am I? But it's different for you and Jared. You truly love each other.'

'Is there no way back for you and Rory?'

Trina shook her head and emitted a weary sigh. 'No. Too much has happened. There's no trust between us.'

'Maybe that kiss was a one-off. A silly mistake.'

Ah, the kiss. The final nail in the coffin of Trina and Rory's marriage.

'But that's the thing,' Trina said. 'I don't actually care that much about the kiss. I'm embarrassed more than anything.'

Trina had left Aidan's place the previous night as confused as ever. She'd returned to the empty annex and climbed into bed, her mind churning over everything she'd learned that evening. Was her marriage a complete sham? Could it be salvaged? Trina wasn't sure she had the energy to fight for it any more, but did she want to follow in her mother's failed-marriage footsteps? She and Rory had been married for just a few short weeks – they deserved a proper chance, didn't they? But when she thought about Aidan, her heart raced like it had never done for Rory.

Did she stay and fight, or did she listen to her heart?

Trina's answer had arrived a couple of hours ago, via a text message from her sister-in-law. The photo – accidentally forwarded, according to Carrington – depicted her husband and Ginny at the party Trina hadn't been invited to. The photo showed them kissing – but who knew what that kiss had led to …

'Was it an actual affair?'

Trina shrugged. 'Rory says not. Says it was just a kiss. They were drunk, apparently. But it doesn't matter.' Of course it still stung – Rory *was* her husband and that kiss had destroyed all her hopes for her marriage. But hadn't they been destroyed anyway?

'His sister must be a real bitch to send you the photo.' Ruth couldn't believe that somebody could be so vindictive. Not even Tori would stoop that low.

'Carrington's never liked me,' Trina said. 'Maybe I was stepping on her best friend's toes. Who knows?'

Trina found she didn't care that much. A kiss or full-on bedroom action – it didn't matter because she was no longer fully invested in their marriage. They were over, and Trina was quite relieved that the decision had been taken out of her hands.

'What does this mean for you and Aidan?' Ruth asked.

Trina really had no idea.

Trina was grateful when Ruth let her stay over at the flat. Gloria would be home in a couple of days, so Ruth insisted Trina stay with her until then.

'We only have the sofa, I'm afraid,' Ruth had said, but Trina was eternally grateful.

'Are you sure you don't mind?' she'd asked Ruth and Jared.

'Absolutely not,' Jared had assured her. 'In fact, you can help me with Ruth's surprise if you're up for it. I needed another person, but nobody else would volunteer.'

So Trina was kept busy working on Ruth's surprise, which was a welcome distraction. Aidan had been in touch, but she'd asked for a few days to sort her head out. Rory had not been in touch, although his mother had.

'It happens, dear,' Winnie had told her over the phone. 'Do you think Rory's father has been faithful to me all these years? I know perfectly well what he gets up to, but I also know how lucky I am to be married to him.'

'I don't feel very lucky to be married to Rory.' *Quite the opposite, in fact*, Trina thought.

'Well, you should! Rory provides for you and he'll make an excellent father.'

'In what way? By working every hour? Fathers should be there for their children. Husbands should be there for their wives.' Trina felt a surge of courage as she spoke to her mother-in-law. She was sure that her bravery was due to their conversation taking place over the phone. Had they been face to face, Trina was sure she would have shrivelled before the woman and transformed into a simpering fool.

'Grow up! You are not in a fairy tale. This is real life, dear.'

'You're right. This isn't a fairy tale and Rory and I won't be living happily ever after. Not together, at least.'

'Hamilton-Wraiths do *not* get divorced, my dear.'

'But I'm not a Hamilton-Wraith. Not for much longer, anyway.' Trina had hung up the phone. And it had felt bloody fantastic.

Now Trina was on her way home. Not to the annex, but to her mother's house. Her suitcase was in the boot of her car and the rest of her belongings were already ensconced in her old bedroom. Carrington had taken great delight in packing up her stuff and sending it to Gloria's house. Trina was just grateful she hadn't had to return to the annex to do it herself.

'My darling girl.' Gloria greeted Trina with a hug and a large measure of gin with a dash of tonic. 'Welcome home. Let's put all this mess behind us and move on. It's the best way.'

Trina lugged her suitcase up the stairs to her old bedroom and sat on the bed. It looked exactly the same as she'd left it as a single woman. The last few weeks may as well have not happened at all.

If only they hadn't.

Trina looked down at her left hand. Her wedding band and engagement ring still sat on her finger, but she eased them off now. She'd post them back to Rory. She had no need for them now.

There was a gentle knock at the door. 'Trina, darling? Would you like another G&T?'

Trina shoved the rings in the drawer of her bedside table. 'Yes, I think I will.'

The door opened and Gloria appeared, a topped-up glass in each hand. 'I was hoping you'd say that.' She passed one of the glasses to Trina and clinked her own against it. 'To new beginnings, darling.'

Trina managed a smile 'To new beginnings.'

'Good girl.' Gloria took a large sip of her drink, encouraging her daughter to do the same before she took the glasses and placed them on the bedside table. She took Trina's hands in hers, noticing the absence of the rings but not commenting on them. 'You know, I felt exactly how you do after my first husband left me. Yes, darling, *he* left *me*. I know I don't tell it that way, but you can keep a secret, can't you?'

Trina nodded, too shocked to speak.

'I was a little bit younger than you and I thought we were going to live happily ever after.'

'Sounds familiar.'

Gloria gave Trina's hands a squeeze. 'But do you know what happened next? After I picked myself up? I met your father.'

Trina snorted. 'We both know that didn't end well.' The walls of the house practically still shook from the arguments that had taken place twenty years ago.

'No, but I ended up with you and Tori, didn't I? And no matter how miserable your father made me – or how miserable I made him – we still had you two, and that is the best thing either of us has ever done.' Gloria cupped Trina's face in her hands. 'My darling girl, you will pick yourself up and you will find happiness. I promise you. Now.' Gloria released Trina and handed her a glass from the table. 'Drink up and then I'll pour you another one.'

'No, thank you.' Trina put the glass down. 'I don't need another drink. But I will pick myself up. I'll sort my life out.'

'Good girl.' Gloria picked up both glasses and drained them. *Waste not, want not, and all that.* 'Oh, and don't you even *think* about giving those rings back, young lady. Pawn them and treat yourself to something pretty. That's what I always do.'

FORTY-FOUR

Ruth

I'd continued my countdown until the wedding, but now, with the wedding just one day away, it had morphed into 'this time tomorrow'. Fridays usually limped along frustratingly slowly, but this particular Friday took the biscuit (and not even a good biscuit like a party ring, but a … nope, sorry. There are no bad biscuits). I was constantly clock-checking (seriously, my eyes barely left the bloody thing), adding to my 'this time tomorrows':

I'll be claiming I'm too excited to eat breakfast this time tomorrow (as if!).

I'll be getting into my fabulous dress this time tomorrow.

I'll be heading to the church this time tomorrow.

The clock was plodding along to five o'clock – I'll be at the reception at this time tomorrow – when my small office filled with people from various departments. Jared was there, looking as bewildered as I felt as he was pushed to the front and made to stand by my side.

'What's going on?' Kelvin stuck his head out of his

office, propelled into rare action by the commotion.

'Jared and Ruth are getting married tomorrow.' Sally from HR appeared to be the spokesperson for the group. 'So we've put together a little contribution to the honeymoon fund.'

Kelvin grunted as Sally presented us with a card signed by all the staff and an envelope that was nice and fat. I didn't point out that a honeymoon hadn't been in the budget. We'd keep hold of it until our bank balance allowed such indulgences again.

'Thank you so much,' I said while Kelvin grumbled about 'bloody weddings' and 'I'm sick of the damn things' and 'cost a bloody fortune'. He retreated into his office, still muttering to himself.

'We really appreciate this,' Jared said, putting his arm around me and giving me a squeeze. Sally gave us each a kiss on the cheek and my office filled with the sound of applause. Kelvin was probably grumbling further about the fuss next door, but he couldn't be heard over the congratulations. The employees, seeing that it was now five o'clock and officially home time, started to filter away.

'This time tomorrow we'll be married,' Jared whispered in my ear and I couldn't help the grin spreading across my entire face. We'd done it. We had actually – shockingly – planned an entire wedding in six short weeks, and tomorrow we would be husband and wife!

'Hey, enough of that canoodling. You're not married yet.' Erin had remained in my office and we enjoyed an impromptu group hug. 'Right, I'll see you tonight, lady. Don't forget to put your dancing shoes on.' Erin untangled herself and backed out of the room, blowing us a noisy kiss before she disappeared from view.

'Are you ready to go?' Jared asked. Ha! It was one minute past five. Of course I was ready to go! But before I could skip out of the office, Kelvin called me into his. I groaned. What did he want? An 'urgent' email sending that could actually wait until Monday? A cup of coffee and plate of biscuits to tide him over until his wife fed him at home?

'Yes, Kelvin?' I popped my head around the door, not committing fully by stepping over the threshold.

'I just wanted to say, um …' Kelvin cleared his throat and shifted his considerable weight in his seat, the leather creaking beneath his arse cheeks. 'You know, um, good luck for tomorrow.' Cough. 'And, um, congratulations.'

'Oh.' I was stunned. I didn't think I'd ever heard Kelvin say something pleasant to anything other than a Mars bar (it had been beautiful and velvety, apparently. Kelvin had no idea I could hear his sweet nothings through his open door). 'Thank you.'

Kelvin gave a nod, coughed a bit more and shuffled a few bits of paper on his desk so I backed away, saving us both embarrassment.

'What was that about?' Jared asked as we made our way down to the car park.

I pulled a face. 'He tried to get me to do some filing before I left, but I told him I had plans.' Kelvin's reputation as a miserable killjoy would remain intact. I felt I owed him that much.

Once home, Jared quickly changed and packed an overnight bag. I'd been hoping we could eat together before we went our separate ways – a last supper, if you will – but Jared was heading for the door before *Granada Reports* had even had the chance to begin its headlines for the evening.

'I know it's early, but I said I'd meet up with Gavin and the others and have something to eat first,' Jared said as he slung his holdall over his shoulder. 'You don't mind, do you?'

I did mind, but it was too near the wedding to put my

foot down. I didn't want to fall at the last hurdle and scare him away. 'It's fine. Go and have fun.' I kissed Jared before giving him a stern look. 'But not *too* much fun.'

'No way.' Jared took my hand and dropped a gentle kiss on my fingers. 'Just think – the next time we see each other, we'll be about to get married.'

Jared's words sent a flurry of butterflies in my stomach. 'I can't believe it.'

'Believe it.' Jared kissed me for one last time as Ruth Lynch and then he was gone. The butterflies continued their flight as I paced the empty flat. My party of hens wouldn't be here for another couple of hours, so I had some time to kill. I couldn't keep pacing – there'd be no carpet left at this rate – so I picked up the phone and dialled my parents' number instead. I was about to ask if Stephen and his family had arrived yet, but the sounds of rioting in the background told me that they had. Stephen and Aubrey had three children – twelve-year-old Riley, ten-year-old Austin and four-year-old Ryder – and while they were adorable and I loved them ferociously, they could be a handful.

'We're all fine here, love.' Despite the noise, Mum was in her element. She missed Stephen and hated the fact that she had to see her grandchildren grow up over Skype, so she'd happily take the din they created. 'Riley has shown me her dress and it's gorgeous. She looks like she's off to prom! Do you want to speak to your brother?'

I had a quick chat with Stephen, not wanting to keep him long as he should have been on his way to meet Jared and the others for the stag night. At a loose end again, I decided to go through my plans one last time to make sure everything was as it should be. I knew my plans were watertight but it would put my mind at rest to be doubly sure. The florist assured me that everything was on track and the flowers would be delivered first thing in the morning, and Cosmo told me everything was going to plan.

'It's all going to be perfect, I promise you. Would I let you down?'

I knew that Cosmo wouldn't. We'd been friends for a long time and I knew he would do everything in his power to give me the reception I wanted.

'Thanks, Cosmo. I really appreciate it.' Taking my mobile with me, I moved through to the bathroom to run a bath. 'Mum and Linda will be there early to set up if that's okay?'

'Of course, *tesorina*. If I'm not there, my staff will be more than happy to help.'

I added a good dollop of bubble bath and gave the water a swirl. Saying goodbye to Cosmo, I moved through to the sitting room and checked my notebook again. Dialling the photographer's number, I checked on the bath, making sure it wasn't about to overflow.

'Hi, Sadie. It's Ruth Lynch.' I tested the water, turning down the cold ever so slightly. 'I was just calling to check that everything is still okay for tomorrow.'

There was a pause. I wondered whether Sadie was still there, and checked the screen to make sure we were still connected. Finally, Sadie spoke.

It was not good news.

'Oh, didn't I tell you?'

I wasn't immediately worried, as Sadie's tone was bright.

'I can't make your wedding after all.'

Okay, now I was worried. Very worried.

'Whoops, silly me. I could have sworn I'd told you.'

I was confused by Sadie's tone. It was still bright, but now had a dash of flippancy to it. I didn't understand. She was cancelling our booking the night before our wedding and she was being *chirpy* about it. What the fluff?

'What's going on?'

The chirpiness vanished from Sadie's voice. 'Maybe you should ask your friend, Theo.'

Theo?

'What's he got to do with it?' Dread started to snake its way into my gut, suffocating the happy little butterflies. I thought back to our meeting with Sadie, of how well it had gone. And then Theo had turned up. But he hadn't spoken to Sadie. I'd turfed him out of the flat before he could cause any damage.

'Just ask him.' Sadie slammed down the phone and I stared at my mobile, unable to compute what was happening. I was getting married tomorrow and the photographer had just pulled out. *Because of Theo.* Turning off the taps, I perched on the edge of the bath and dialled Theo's number, my foot tapping against the lino.

'Theo!' I barked as soon as he answered. I was determined to get to the bottom of this without any bullshitting around. 'Did you sleep with the photographer?'

'Who?' Theo – the complete shit – yawned as he asked.

'The photographer for my wedding. Sadie Alexander.'

'Oh. Her. Yeah, I did.' Another yawn.

I leaped up from the side of the bath and started to pace the tiny bathroom. It didn't take much effort: two steps forward, turn, two steps back. '*When?*'

'I dunno. A few weeks ago.'

'But how?' I didn't understand. I'd kept them apart – for this very reason.

'I waited for her downstairs and we got talking.'

I was going to throttle him. Slowly.

'She's a right psycho, though. She won't leave me alone. Has she started bugging you now?'

I closed my eyes, imagining my hands tightening around his scrawny little neck. 'No, she hasn't started bugging me. She's cancelled our booking. I don't have a photographer for my wedding. Because of you!'

'Hey, this isn't my fault. How was I supposed to know she'd go all bunny-boiler-ish?'

'You could have *not* slept with her!' I was so enraged I started seeing spots in front of my eyes. This was not good, I was sure. 'Why did you have to sleep with my photographer?'

'She was hot.' Theo's voice was so small, I almost felt sorry for him. Almost, but not quite. I was still going to throttle him.

'Did you sleep with anyone else I should know about? The vicar, perhaps?'

I hung up the phone and then that's when I really started to panic. We didn't have a photographer. We were getting married in less than twenty-four hours and we didn't have a photographer to record the beautiful day!

FORTY-FIVE

Ruth

'It'll be fine. Honestly, it will.'
I'd phoned Jared in a flap, and he was doing his best to soothe me. He'd had a battle on his hands. I'd cried, threatened violence (against Theo, not my darling Jared) and cried some more.

'We'll get everyone to take photos on their cameras and phones and upload them. It'll be more real this way, just like you wanted.'

That was true, I suppose.

'We can put them online and share them. Maybe on Instagram. Or Pinterest! You *love* Pinterest. Plus ...' Jared paused, about to use his trump card. 'We can put the photographer's fee towards a honeymoon. With the money from work, we should be able to have a weekend away soon.'

I did like the sound of that. Forgoing a honeymoon had been a huge sacrifice, so a bit of time away with my new husband sounded good.

'Are you going to be okay?' Jared asked and I assured

him that I would be. I was calmer now that we had a plan in place. Jared was right. Simple photos taken by family and friends was the sort of look I was going for. It would work out fine.

'I'll be fine now. I'm going to get in the bath and get ready for my hen night. I'll see you tomorrow.'

'I'll see you tomorrow, Mrs Williams.'

I tried to relax in the bath, but it was impossible. Despite coming to terms with the fact that our guests were going to act as unpaid photographers at the wedding ('coming to terms with' is quite mild, actually. I loved the idea and wondered why we hadn't thought of it in the first place. Screw you, Sadie Alexander!), I was still shaken up by the drama of it all. Besides, the bath was tepid by the time I sank into the water and my heart was no longer in it enough to top it up with more hot water. I washed and dried my hair before changing into a hot pink skater dress, teaming it with a pair of nude peep-toe heels and chunky pink and navy beads. A navy headband with an oversized polka-dotted bow swept my blonde curls away from my face and completed the look. I'd just managed to make the flat look presentable when the first guests arrived (I couldn't really think of them as hens, as it made me picture my friends and family bobbing around the sitting room, pecking at the carpet).

'Wow, Ruth. You look amazing.' Trina enveloped me in a tight hug before she stepped into the flat, followed closely by her sister. Tori chose not to hug me – which I was totally fine with. She was my cousin but we had never been particularly close – and instead popped her head into the sitting room, pulling a face when she saw that it was empty.

'Are we the first to arrive? How sad is that?' Tori flopped onto the sofa with a sigh, frowning as she plucked a stray pen from underneath her.

I flashed an apologetic smile as I took the pen and

gathered my wedding plans from the coffee table. 'Can I get you a drink?'

'I'll have a vodka and pomegranate juice.' Tori's eyes were flitting around the flat. Judging it, the snobby cow. 'If you have it.'

'I have vodka but no pomegranate. Will cranberry do?'

Tori glanced up at the ceiling, clearly holding in a sigh. 'Yes, I suppose it will.'

'I'll come and give you a hand.' Trina followed me into the kitchen, whispering apologies for Tori as we made the drinks. I was suddenly delirious with gratitude that only the first portion of the hen night would be taking place at the flat, as I was already stressed. Tori could sink as many vodka and pomegranate juices as she desired once we were in town. It wasn't as though I'd even invited the woman – she'd piggy-backed on Trina's invite, claiming she 'had nothing better to do'. If I wasn't such a wuss, I'd have told her to do one.

'I don't suppose you have ice, do you?' Tori called from the sitting room.

'Of course.' I pulled an ice cube tray out of the freezer and popped a couple into Tori's glass. Grabbing a bottle of white wine from the fridge, I poured a glass for Trina and myself. 'So, how are you getting on?'

'Oh, you know.' Trina gave a wave of her hand and, though she was smiling, I didn't quite believe it. 'I've been better, but it's a relief to be back home. It was the right decision to leave Rory.'

'Rory's a prick.' Tori had obviously been listening to our conversation as she added her opinion from the sitting room. 'He's probably screwing that Ginny right now.'

Trina and I chose to ignore her input. 'Have you heard from him since?'

Trina shook her head. 'Not a word. You'd have thought he'd have been a bit miffed that I'd left him, wouldn't you? I'm not asking for him to fight for me, but it could have ruffled his feathers a *teeny* bit.'

It was only common courtesy, I'd have thought.

'What about Aidan?'

'He's phoned a few times – more than a few, actually – but I haven't been up to talking to him yet. I'm just so confused.'

'Sleep with him,' Tori called from the sitting room. 'Get it out of your system.'

I closed the door connecting the kitchen and sitting room and Trina smiled gratefully.

'I'm not sure if I want him out of my system. Part of me thinks we could be really good together, but I've just left my husband, you know?'

I opened my mouth to speak, but the door was wrenched open. 'What are you doing? I thought this was a hen party, not an "exclude Tori" party. Where are the other girls anyway? You haven't just invited us, have you?' *Technically, I haven't invited you at all.* 'How sad!'

'I've invited other people,' I said, my skin prickling with indignation.

Tori grabbed the glass of vodka and cranberry, necking half of it in one go before she hopped up onto my kitchen counter. 'Has Trina told you she's going back to work? Tell her how mad she is. Rory's loaded. She'll bag herself a small fortune in the divorce. Why bother going to work when you're due a payout?'

'Because I *want* to work. I loved my job before I got married.' Trina's face lit up as she told me about her job. It was the happiest I'd seen her since her honeymoon. 'I'm so lucky that my replacement didn't work out. My boss at Pooch Couture almost wept when I asked if I could come back. I start on Monday and I can't wait.'

'I still think you're mental.' Tori slipped off the counter, draining her drink before helping herself to another.

The intercom buzzed, signalling the arrival of Erin, Quinn and Casey. I made the introductions – they remembered Trina from the wedding fair and my birthday meal but they'd yet to have the pleasure of meeting Tori – before arranging more drinks. Mum arrived soon after, and I was surprised to see her alone.

'Where's Aubrey?' Mrs Flack from next door had offered to babysit so that she could join us too.

'I think Aubrey has doubts about Mrs Flack being up to it.' Mum removed her jacket and hung it up in the hallway. 'Not that I blame her. Mrs Flack is ninety-four and those kiddies are a bit of a handful. I offered to stay behind with them, but Aubrey said she wasn't feeling up to a night out. She claims it's jet lag but I suspect we'll be welcoming a new member to the family soon.' Mum tapped the side of her nose before joining the others in the sitting room.

Linda, Ally, Freya and Jimmy arrived a few minutes later, completing the party.

'Who's for a cocktail?' Erin took charge, concocting various cocktails for everyone like a pro. Forming a cramped circle on the sitting room floor, we played a game of 'I have never' in which we took turns to make statements, such as 'I have never been dogging'. Those who *had* been dogging had to take a sip of their drink – thankfully, all drinks went untouched for *that* question. But I did learn some rather unsavoury things about my mother's sex life that I wished I hadn't. Jimmy had decided not to play, which Linda said was a very good idea.

'I'll die if you take a sip for any of the questions,' Linda said.

Jimmy didn't say a thing.

'I have never had sex in a car,' Trina stated. Erin took a sip of her drink – she had for most statements. She was going to be trolleyed in no time – along with Quinn, Linda (my very-soon-to-be *mother-in-law* – aargh!), Freya, Casey and Tori. We were halfway around the circle and Erin's glass was almost empty. Tori's wasn't far behind either, while Trina's and my glasses were practically untouched. I was going to have to start making stuff up if this carried on.

'Hey, Vee.' Linda nudged Mum, a mischievous glint in her eye. 'When Louie gets the caravan sorted, you'll be able to have a go in there. That'd count, wouldn't it?' Linda glanced around the circle while I contemplated emptying my guts onto the carpet.

'Trina said a car. A caravan wouldn't technically count,' Erin said. I glared at her. I wanted this conversation to end. *Now.* 'My turn!' Erin placed her glass down on the carpet and rubbed her hands together. 'I have never had sex in a caravan.'

We all looked at Mum – though I did my best to resist – who paused before finally taking a sip of her drink. The rest of the circle howled with laughter, while I wished for death.

'It wasn't the caragym, was it?' Linda asked.

'Gosh, no. It's still a heap of junk,' Mum said. 'No, this was years ago, back in the late sixties. It wasn't even with Louie.'

'What?' This was an evil game. Every ounce of naivety was being stripped from me. As far as I'd been aware, Mum had only ever had sex with Dad, and I would have liked to have kept that assumption.

'It was before I met your dad. I was only fourteen.'

I dropped my head into my hands. *Fourteen?* No, I didn't like this game one bit.

'He was called Ronald and was staying in the next caravan. Do you remember Great Aunt Violet's caravan in Blackpool?' I'd stayed there on a number of occasions as a child but wished I could remove all memories of it now. 'I was staying with my Aunt Violet and her family for a week. I thought Ronald was a lovely boy. So sweet and handsome. And then I found out he'd also deflowered my cousin Shirley too.'

There was a collective tut from the circle, along with a

chorus of 'men are bastards' before the game – unfortunately – resumed.

After the horrifying game of 'I have never', we remained in the circle for a game of pass the parcel. At Erin's suggestion – she had provided the wrapped parcel – Jimmy was in charge of the music. It soon became clear why when Tori opened the final layer.

'Who needs a man?' Tori waved the sparkly purple vibrator in the air, a look of triumph on her face.

'It's just a pity it doesn't mow the grass,' Linda said, and she and Mum cracked up. *I am never drinking with those two again.*

'Right then, ladies.' Erin, having encouraged Tori to store the vibrator in her handbag (she wouldn't be parted with it completely), clapped her hands together. 'Time to take this party elsewhere!'

Mum and Linda insisted that they were too old to go into town. I was slightly relieved (though of course I hid it well and insisted they came) but they were adamant. Besides, somebody needed to take Jimmy home, and Mum was keen to give Aubrey a hand with the kids, who she was sure would be still full of beans and jet lag.

'We'll see you tomorrow, love.' Mum gave me a peck on the cheek before she took my face gently in her hands. 'I'm so happy for you, my darling girl.' I was sure it was the drink, but we both had swimming eyes as we grinned at each other. 'You go and have fun, but make sure you have a good night's sleep. No amount of make-up can hide a hungover bride.'

With Mum, Linda and Jimmy ensconced in a taxi, the hen night raged on. Erin handed out goody bags, which contained a condom, a travel toothbrush, mini tube of toothpaste and a spare pair of knickers (in case we got lucky, apparently), hen night badges (mine said 'Badass

Bride'), willy-shaped chocolates, a pack of paracetamol (for the morning after) and three envelopes, which we were informed contained dare cards and weren't to be opened until instructed.

I held up the knickers from my bag, stretching them between two fingers. 'What size are these? Barbie?' They were never going to fit. Not that I needed a spare pair of pants. I'd be tucked up in my own bed that night, thank you very much.

'These are delicious.' Tori was already chomping away on a chocolate willy. 'Best cock I've ever tasted.'

I was never drinking with my family again.

We made our way into town, piling into a club that offered the very best in eighties and nineties music, as well as a free shot on entry. We downed our shots before Erin instructed us to open our first envelope, which was marked *Something Old, Something New. Something Borrowed, Something Blue*.

'I'm not doing this.' Quinn held out her dare card and I read it: *Kiss someone over 40.*

Erin read the card too and gave a tut. 'Don't be so ageist.'

'I'm not being ageist,' Quinn said. 'I'm not kissing *anyone*. I can't. I'm seeing someone.'

'Who?' Erin's eyes widened at the prospect of gossip, but I already knew who it was.

'I don't want to say. Not yet.' Quinn stuck out her chin. 'But I'm not doing this.'

'I'll do it.' Casey plucked the card from Quinn's fingers and swapped it with her own – *Collect a blue shirt.* 'I'm involved with someone too but kissing on a hen night doesn't count.'

A debate ensued, with most people agreeing that it certainly *did* count as cheating. In the end, Erin decided enough was enough and held up her hands to silence our group.

'Whatever. It doesn't matter. Casey is happy to do the dare, so let's get on with it.'

'Actually.' Trina raised her hand slightly and turned her card to face the group. 'I can't do mine either.'

'You can't kiss someone under twenty?' Erin asked. 'Why not? We're talking eighteen or nineteen here, not twelve.'

'But I'm *married*.'

'You're separated!' Tori cried. '*Permanently.* Get back on the horse and ride it, baby!'

'No.' Trina folded her arms across her chest. 'I'm not doing it.'

Erin sighed before snatching the card and replacing it with her own. 'Fine. Can you collect a blue sock? Great.'

My own card wasn't too bad. I had to somehow collect a blue pen, which seemed doable and wouldn't compromise my vows before I'd even taken them.

'It's Theo, isn't it?' I asked Quinn while the others were double-checking they were happy with their dares. 'He's the one you're seeing.' Quinn was about to protest, but there was no point. I held my hand up to stop her from wasting her breath. 'I've caught you at the house with him, twice. Why else would you lie to me about where you are?'

Quinn opened her mouth before closing it without speaking. She gave a shrug. 'Fine, then. It's Theo I'm seeing. I can't get enough of him. He's so completely hot.'

'I knew it!' I wanted to jump into the air, triumphant fist held aloft as I whooped. But I didn't. There'd been far too much embarrassment already that evening.

'You won't say anything to anybody, will you?'

I mimed zipping up my lips, my jubilant grin still in place. 'I promise.'

'Are we doing these dares or not?' Erin asked. 'Whoever carries out theirs last has to get the next round in so go, go, go!'

FORTY-SIX

Ruth

Ugh. I thought I wouldn't be able to sleep on the eve on my wedding; I thought my mind would be a hive of activity and excitement would be coursing through my veins. But it turned out it was the waking-up bit that was the problem. My head was glued to my pillow, my eyes welded shut, and no matter how much my alarm heralded the start of a brand-new day – my *wedding day* – they wouldn't budge. I thought I'd been so careful with my alcohol consumption the night before, and we hadn't stayed out that long. The dares had turned out to be a bit of a damp squib, with most people coupled up and refusing to cheat – because we all know that kissing *is* cheating – and I'd wanted to go home before any major damage was done to my well-being. It seemed it was already too late for that. My well-being was trashed.

Ugh. Reaching out, I fumbled around until my stupid alarm shut up. My eyes remained sealed and my head didn't move from the pillow. I would stay here for another five minutes and then I would force myself from the covers and into the shower, where I would emerge refreshed and suitably human. Hopefully. I crossed my fingers and fell back to sleep.

'Ruth?' There was a soft knock at the door. It must have been only twenty seconds since I'd drifted off. 'Ruth?' Another knock, slightly louder this time. 'Ruth, I know you're awake. You're not snoring.'

'Hey!' My eyes flew open. It hurt. A lot. 'I do not snore.'

The door opened a crack and Quinn's face peeped into the room. 'You do. Very loudly. I thought we must be on the flight path for Manchester Airport at first, then I realised it was you.' The door opened fully and Quinn skipped into the room. 'Come on, sleepy. It's time to get up.'

I covered my face with my hands and groaned. I'd only managed to see Quinn through blurry eyes but even then she looked like she'd just awoken from a restful eighteen-hour sleep. Her eyes were bright, and her face didn't have the greyish hue I was sure my own did. There was clearly some sort of witchcraft occurring.

'Do I really have to get up?'

'Yes.' Quinn laughed and tugged at my covers. She was lucky I was wearing pyjamas. I patted myself down. Yes, I was definitely wearing pyjamas. 'You're getting married in a few hours, so come on!'

I thought of Jared, looking handsome – no, *hot* – in his suit, waiting for me at the altar, and the image was enough to put a tiny spring into my step. Enough to help me out of bed and into the bathroom, at least.

'Have you heard from Erin?' I asked when I emerged from the shower, encased in my fluffy pink robe. Quinn had stayed over on the sofa but Erin had met up with Richard after the stag night. It seemed they couldn't be parted for a single night and, once I'd enjoyed my wedding, I would rib her about that relentlessly. The minx was finally, truly, tamed.

'She's on her way.' Quinn led me into the sitting room with a flourish. She'd pulled out the foldaway table and covered it with pastries, fruit and yogurt. 'I popped down to the shop while you were in the shower.'

Oh, sod it. I wouldn't even bother pretending to be too excited to eat. I dived right in. 'I'm really getting married today, aren't I?'

Quinn grinned at me and I grinned right back, not caring that we looked like a couple of gormless tits. 'You are. In a few hours you will be Mrs Williams. You're so lucky.' Quinn gave a little sigh and sank onto one of the foldaway dining chairs. 'I can't wait to get married.'

'You'll be waiting a long time if you keep hanging around Theo.' I helped myself to a mini Danish pastry. Delicious. 'I don't think he'll be settling down any time soon.'

'What? Oh, yeah. No, I don't expect to marry Theo.' Quinn jumped out of her seat and headed for the kitchen. 'I almost forgot.' She returned brandishing a bottle of champagne and a carton of fresh orange juice. 'We have to start the day with a Buck's Fizz. It's the law or something.'

Then the intercom buzzed as Quinn was pouring the drinks, so I let Erin into the flat. She arrived looking flawlessly beautiful, practically glowing. Witchcraft, I tell you.

The flat was soon in chaos as we flew into action. Quinn turned on the stereo, which blasted out a cheery medley of S Club 7 as we flew from room to room, pausing only to sip our drinks (hair of the dog, and all that). I was about to start drying my hair when the intercom buzzed again.

'Looks like I'm just in time.' Aidan appeared in my bedroom doorway, a case of hair-stylist goodies in his hand.

'What are you doing here?' I looked down at my cheap supermarket hairdryer and attempted to hide it. I nudged it with my elbow until it plopped over the side of the dressing table, landing with a not-so-subtle plastic-meets-carpet thud.

Aidan, bless him, chose to ignore my blunder.

'I'm here to do your hair.' He strode into the room and began running his expert fingers through my damp curls. 'Trina sent me. I'm your gift, apparently. Sent here to say thank you for all your help.'

'So you've seen Trina?' That must have been some fast work. I'd only seen her a few hours earlier, climbing into a taxi with Tori and the purple vibrator, which was being waved in the air like a glow stick at a rave.

'Not for a few days, no.' Aidan flashed a sheepish smile as he unplugged my crappy hairdryer and replaced it with his own high-end model. 'She sent me a text last night. It's the most contact I've had with her for days.'

'She's confused, that's all. She's got a lot on her mind.'

'I know, but I miss her. This is why I kept my feelings to myself, so that I didn't ruin our friendship. I've done that anyway now. I should have kept my mouth shut.'

'You haven't ruined your friendship, I'm sure.'

'I hope not.' Aidan pulled a wide-toothed comb out of his case and began running it through my hair. 'So, what are we thinking?'

The hairdryer drowned out the music from the sitting room, but I sang along anyway. There was something soothing about having somebody else tend to my hair. I suppose it reminded me of being a child and having my hair brushed before school. Although Aidan didn't tug quite as hard as Mum and he didn't threaten to cut it all off with the kitchen scissors if I didn't sit still. Aidan kindly offered to do the bridesmaids' hair too, and was almost finished with Erin's when Dad arrived with Riley, Jimmy and our flowers. The rest, he assured me, had been delivered to the church.

Everyone changed and had their hair and make-up done. The bridesmaids each held a single gerbera – pink for Quinn, red for Erin, orange for Jimmy and yellow for Riley – while I had a hand-tied posy made up of all four shades, creating a rainbow of colour.

'Ruthie, love.' Dad held his arms out as I emerged from my bedroom in my dress. 'You look wonderful, you really do. I'm ever so proud.' He pulled me into a tight hug before he released me, holding me out at arm's length. 'Go on, give us a twirl.'

I did as I was told, spinning on the spot and receiving a child-like thrill as the skirt lifted. The dress was just as I'd imagined, resting just below the knee on a bed of netted skirts to give it proper twirlability. The polka-dotted organza overlaying the ivory silk gave my dress the fun feel I'd been aiming for, and was finished off perfectly with the sunshine-yellow polka-dot sash around the waist. Aidan had styled my hair in soft curls that were held off my face with a matching polka-dot ribbon, tied with an elaborate bow to the side. I felt like a fifties starlet.

'Let me get a photo of you all, then.' Dad pulled out his camera and lined us up. I'd told everyone about the photographer (who will be forever known in my family as 'the cruel bitch who tried to ruin my big day'), so Dad, Erin and Quinn had been busily snapping away throughout the morning, chronicling the getting-ready stage of the wedding, which I thought was a nice touch and not something that would have been archived by Sadie, who had planned to meet us at the church.

Finally, it was time and Freya arrived, leading us down to her car, which she'd decorated with ribbon.

'What do you think?'

'I think it looks wonderfully tacky. Thank you!' I felt my eyes brimming with tears, something I'd noticed occurring more and more as the day wore on. First it had been Dad's arrival, looking smart in his suit, then it had been seeing little Riley (who wasn't so little any more) wearing her dress, and then I'd almost burst into floods of tears at the sight of my bouquet. It was so perfect. So *me*. And then I'd put my dress on and there was no stopping the tears. I'd allowed myself a little cry before I mopped up the tears and Quinn redid my make-up.

'I think it's time, love.' Dad went to open the car door but Freya leaped into action, tipping an imaginary cap as we climbed inside. Dad and I travelled with Freya while Quinn drove the others to the church. I didn't think I'd be so nervous, but I was actually shaking as I climbed out of the car. It was handy having Freya there to open the door – she was taking her role as chauffeur *very* seriously – as I didn't think my jittery fingers would have managed.

'I'll just go and find somewhere to park and then I'll see you in there.' Freya gave me a kiss on the cheek before she darted back to the car. I looked across to the church. Jared was in there, I thought with excitement, waiting to become my husband.

We arranged ourselves outside the church's heavy double doors, Dad and I at the front, our arms linked, followed by Riley and Jimmy and then Erin and Quinn. This was it. I was going to marry Jared.

'You look beautiful, love,' Dad whispered as we waited for our cue. Suddenly the doors opened, bringing the sound of the organ loud and clear. 'Ready?'

My life was about to change. Once I stepped through those doors, I would no longer be Ruth Lynch. I would be Ruth Williams, Jared's wife. We would be united in front of our combined families and friends forever.

I couldn't wait.

FORTY-SEVEN

Erin

Ruth and Louie made their way slowly down the aisle towards Jared, the bridesmaids following them. There were rustles and creaks as the congregation turned to get a glimpse of the bride, followed by beaming smiles and the odd watery eye.

Quinn leaned in towards Erin to whisper, 'You can't honestly tell me you don't want this. Imagine it was Richard down there. How would that make you feel?'

'Pissed off. Why is he marrying my best friend? Cheating bastard.'

Quinn's eyes widened. She eyed the congregation for signs that anyone had overheard. 'You can't say that in church.'

'Say what?'

'*That*.' Quinn had another furtive glance. '*Bastard*.'

'You just said it too!' Erin and Quinn bit their lips to stop themselves from giggling. 'Enough now. Be serious.'

Ruth and Louie reached the altar, and the bridesmaids took their places to the side of the bride.

'You look beautiful,' Erin heard Jared whisper.

'You look hot. I can't wait to get you out of that suit.'

So Erin and Quinn weren't the only ones misbehaving in church.

'You'll have to marry me first,' Jared said and that is exactly what they did. The ceremony went smoothly with beautiful, inspiring hymns, and a few laughs courtesy of Father Edmund. Jared and Ruth exchanged their vows in front of their loved ones, emerging from the church united by law. The congregation had been told about the lack of photographer – although Theo's involvement was omitted – so they busily snapped away with their cameras and phones in the churchyard afterwards, with Father Edmund volunteering to act as group photographer so everyone could get in the shot.

'Right, that's enough.' Ruth indicated that everybody should put their photo equipment away. 'This isn't going to be one of those weddings where we stand around for days, posing like a bunch of knobs. Come on, let's go and have some fun!'

With the photos taken care of, Ruth and Jared, and their closest friends and family, made their way to Cosmo's, which had been transformed for the event. The tables were laid with pale pink tablecloths with beautiful rainbow gerbera displays as centrepieces and the sweet box favours Ruth and Jared had made marking each place. Room had been made in the corner for the karaoke later and a space was dedicated for dancing. A rainbow of balloons adorned the room and a row of tables, covered with the same pale pink tablecloths, lined the back wall of the room. Later, in time for the evening guests, a buffet would be laid out on them. In the centre, grabbing Ruth's attention immediately, was Jared's surprise.

'What do you think?' Jared led Ruth to the centre table which was framed by two thick red-and-white-striped columns supporting a pitched wooden roof with rainbow bunting strung between them. The words 'Sweet Buffet' had been appliqued to the front of the tablecloth, and the table was covered with colourful jars of sweets, a rainbow of macarons, fondant fancies and mini cupcakes as well as trays of fruit with chocolate dipping sauce and heart-shaped biscuits iced with Ruth and Jared's initials. Taking centre stage was the three-tier cake Linda had made: a Victoria sponge, a lemon drizzle and an orange sponge.

'I think we should forget about the three-course meal Cosmo has lovingly prepared and dive into this instead.' Ruth threw her arms around Jared, planting a smacker on his lips. 'It's perfect. Who did it all?' Ruth placed a hand on Jared's chest. 'I love you, you know that, but you're no baker.'

'My dad and Louie built the structure and Mum and Vee took care of the sewing and baking.'

'Wow. It's amazing.' Ruth took Jared's hands in hers. 'I don't think I've ever been happier.'

'I know I haven't been.' Jared kissed Ruth, which caused a racket of wolf-whistles and jeering from the room.

'Hey, you two. Leave that for tonight, yeah?' Erin winked at the couple. She was so pleased for her best friend. Nobody deserved happiness more than Ruth.

Cosmo's food wasn't forgotten. The guests located their places and Erin found herself seated with Richard, Quinn and Theo. Ruth had considered barring Theo from the reception for being a git, but Jared had talked her down. Ruth and Jared had enforced a no-speeches rule for the day – they *could* be a bit wanky – so the meal was full of fun and chatter without the embarrassment or boredom speeches could bring.

The food was lovely but the real party began later, once the karaoke machine had been set up and Cosmo's staff had set out the buffet. The rest of the guests would be arriving any minute.

'So how does it feel to be a married woman?' Erin asked Ruth. They hadn't had the chance to chat much since that morning at Ruth's flat. The day had flown by and Erin needed a moment with Ruth, to remind herself that nothing had really changed for them and their friendship.

'It's amazing.' A grin spread across Ruth's face. It would be there for quite some time. 'I can't believe it!'

'I'm so happy for you. You know that, don't you?'

Ruth nodded, pressing her lips together to prevent yet another wave of tears. 'I do know. Thank you.'

Erin took a moment to compose herself. She wouldn't cry in public, even if it was her best friend's wedding. 'Right then! Enough of this soppy crap. Let's dance!'

Keith Barry, the karaoke host they'd hired for the evening, started the music up. The karaoke would start later, once enough alcohol had been consumed to encourage people to sing, but for now Keith would be acting as DJ for the party. Ruth had requested a playlist full of the very best cheesiest pop, and Keith had obviously obliged, as Hanson's 'MMMbop' kicked in.

Erin and Ruth were joined by Quinn on the dance floor, singing along to the cheesy songs until S Club 7's 'Never Had A Dream Come True' slowed down the rhythm and Erin found herself in Richard's arms.

'Hey, you.' Richard pulled Erin in close. 'Are you absolutely sure you don't want all this?'

'Couldn't be more certain, pal. Sorry.' Erin reached out to stroke Richard's cheek. 'Marriage just isn't for me. You know that. But ...' Erin hesitated, not quite sure she was ready to make the leap. She'd been thinking about it a lot lately, but now the moment was here, doubt was setting in. It was her default setting, but she was determined to forge ahead. It *was* what she wanted, no matter how much her brain tried to convince her otherwise. 'How would you feel about moving in together?'

Richard's eyebrows raised ever so slightly. Was this a

trick? 'Are you being serious?'

'You know I don't joke around with this kind of stuff.'

Which was true. Very true.

'Then I think it's the best idea you've ever had.'

Erin's urge to run away from commitment kicked in, but she stood her ground. For once she was going to be brave and allow herself to let go and be happy, just like her mum had.

'Then let's do it. Let's move in together.'

'Shall we finish this dance first?' Richard asked. 'Or will that give you just enough time to change your mind?'

Erin shook her head. 'I'm not going to change my mind. You're stuck with me, til death do us part. So no leaving the toilet seat up – or that'll happen sooner than you think.'

FORTY-EIGHT

Ruth

I'd wanted the reception to be fun, and it certainly was. The dance floor quickly filled as Keith Barry started his set, but I was forced to rest my dancing feet as more guests started to arrive. Jared and I hovered by the entrance to greet them. First up was Aunty Pat, who stepped into the restaurant looking as though she'd stepped in dog poo while wearing her best shoes.

'It's a bit small, isn't it?' she said in lieu of congratulations. 'When Vee said it was being held in a restaurant, I was expecting something far grander.'

'Well, we like it,' I said while imagining ejecting her from the 'small' restaurant with my foot up her arse.

'That's the main thing, I suppose.' Aunty Pat gave my arm a patronising squeeze before dumping her heavy fake-fur coat in my arms. 'Come along, Raymond. Let's see if we can find some champagne. Though I suppose we'll have to make do with sparkling wine.' Aunty Pat trooped into the restaurant, with her husband and devil children, Philip and Lesley, trailing behind. Philip had plucked one of the balloons from the display outside and had sucked in a deep breath of helium. He was singing 'Lesley is a knob-head' in a high-pitched voice as they passed.

I puffed out a breath and smiled at Jared. 'That went better than expected.' She hadn't pointed out that I was fat ('Have you ever thought about losing weight, Ruth? You'd be so much prettier and *healthier* with a little less bulk') or that Jared was clearly out of my league ('Haven't you done *well* for yourself, Ruth? Who'd have thought you'd end up with a man quite so handsome? Who'd have thought you'd end up with a man at all? Ha, ha, ha! I'm just *kidding,* Ruth. Have a sense of humour!') and she hadn't slagged Mum off in her 'I'm just being helpful way' ('Ruth, sweetie. Can you *please* have a word with your mother? Purple really isn't her colour, is it? We don't want her going out looking like that and feeling embarrassed, do we?').

'She didn't tell me I'm thinning on top this time, so I'm happy,' Jared said.

'You do know you're not, don't you?' I was immensely grateful that Jared had married me despite my spiteful Aunty Pat.

'Won't you love me when I'm bald?'

'Of course I will.' I planted a noisy smacker on my husband's (yes, my *husband's* – eek!) lips. 'I'll love you forever. Plus, it'll be handy always having a mirror around with your shiny head.'

'Darling!' Aunt Gloria swept into the restaurant, pulling me into a heavily perfumed hug. 'Congratulations, dear girl. And you.' Aunt Gloria turned to Jared and pulled him into a tight hug. 'You look after our Ruthie.'

'I promise I will,' Jared said and Aunt Gloria gave him a nod of approval before turning to the gentleman she had arrived with. 'Have you met Yuri?'

Yuri was breathtakingly handsome (though not as handsome as Jared, I hasten to add) and at least three decades younger than Aunt Gloria. He held out a manicured hand to Jared and me, and offered his congratulations.

'We met while I was on my little cruise.' Aunt Gloria gazed up at Yuri and emitted a little sigh. I wondered if Yuri would become husband number six. 'He swept me off my feet. Quite literally. He took me off to his bed and my feet didn't touch the deck again until we docked back in England. He's *fabulous* in bed. Simply *fabulous*.'

Yuri gave a small shrug, neither confirming nor denying his sexual prowess.

'Shall we go and grab a drink?' Aunt Gloria asked him. 'I see Pat's already found the bar. She'll have sucked it dry by the time we get over there. Dreadful woman!'

Aunt Gloria gave my arm a squeeze before she led Yuri into the restaurant. Trina and Tori followed, offering their well wishes, and then I used the lull to store Aunty Pat's coat in the allocated cupboard next to the kitchen. When I returned, Jared was greeting Billy's dad and step-mum.

'Brian, Pearl. I'm so glad you could make it.' I enveloped them in a hug before pointing them in the direction of the bar, and Billy. It had been a while since I'd seen the pair and I couldn't wait to catch up, but it would have to wait as the next wave of guests had arrived.

'I'm exhausted already,' Jared joked but there was no chance of a rest. Nell and Greg from my yoga class were full of enthusiasm for married life and offered us some titbits of advice. Nell's pregnancy was clearly progressing well, as she now looked as though she'd swallowed a marrowfat pea.

'Congratulations, dear!' Mary swept into the room, tugging a short, plump man with her. His head was shiny and free of hair, apart from a small tuft of grey fluff behind each ear. I pressed my lips together to smother a giggle as Jared caught my eye and surreptitiously indicated the mirror-like surface of his head.

'I'm so happy for you.' Mary pulled me into a hug, planting a noisy kiss on each cheek. 'You must be Jared.' Mary repeated the greeting with my new husband before turning to the man hovering awkwardly beside her. 'This is my Cecil. We'll be getting hitched ourselves, won't we, dear?'

'Hmm?' Cecil rubbed at his ear and leaned in further towards Mary, who shooed him away towards the bar.

'You've sorted everything with Cecil's daughters then?' I asked.

'Oh, yes.' Mary's eyes travelled towards Cecil who was ambling towards the bar, her eyes shining with pride. 'He gave them a proper ticking off. I didn't think he had it in him. It was quite a turn-on, I can tell you.' Mary shivered with delight before she pulled herself together. 'Anyway, I wanted to tell you what a lovely ceremony it was. You look radiant, my dear.' Mary gave my hands a squeeze before she scurried after Cecil.

I turned expectantly towards the door and was pleased when I saw Aidan shuffling in. I wasn't sure he'd turn up, but I'd been pretty adamant in my invitation that morning. It was the least I could do after he'd used up his free time to do my hair at the last minute.

'Are you sure this is okay?' Aidan's eyes darted from Jared and me back to the door, plotting his escape. I grasped hold of his arm before he could flee.

'Of course it is. I invited you, didn't I?'

'But what about Trina? Is she okay with me being here?'

I hoped so. I hadn't told her yet.

'Ah, Betty! Hello again.' Swerving the question, I moved past Aidan and took hold of the little old woman Jared and I had met at Trina's wedding. It turned out Betty was a cousin of my grandmother, who, sadly, was no longer with us.

'What did I tell you?' Betty asked as she hugged me

fiercely. 'I told you you'd be next, didn't I? I'm always right about these things.' She released me and eyed Aidan, who was still hovering by the door. 'And I remember this handsome young man.' She poked out a foot, swivelling it in front of her. 'I've got my dancing shoes on, so don't go too far.'

Aidan held out an arm. 'How about I get you a drink and then we'll have a boogie?'

Once all the guests had arrived and had had the chance to grab a drink and mingle, Keith Barry paused the music while Jared and I made our way to his little stage.

'We promised there would be no speeches at this wedding,' I said into the microphone. 'And you'll be pleased to hear we're sticking to that.' There was a murmur of a cheer from the middle of the room. I suspected Theo. 'But we just wanted to quickly give out a few gifts.'

I'd ordered necklaces for each of the bridesmaids with a tiny rose pendant. Each bridesmaid's rose matched the colour of their gerbera, and a silver leaf carved with their initial hung beside it. We'd ordered bouquets of gerberas for our mothers – pale pink and lemon for Mum, and raspberry and orange for Linda. For our fathers, we'd bought engraved key rings, as neither Dad nor Bob was the cufflink-wearing sort.

With the gift-giving over, Jared and I signalled for Keith Barry to start up the music again, but Linda held up her hand and rushed to the front.

'Not so fast. There's one more gift.'

I looked at Jared, biting my lip. Who had we forgotten?

Linda grabbed the microphone and held up what looked like a pamphlet. I took a closer look and saw on it a photo of a little stone cottage surrounded by pretty trees and foliage.

'I have a gift here for Jared and Ruth, on behalf of both sets of parents. We've booked you into a little rental cottage in the Lake District for a week. Don't worry about work – Erin has sorted the time off with HR.'

From the crowd, Erin gave a little wave, and I pressed my lips together so I didn't start to blubber in front of everybody. The cottage was gorgeous and looked like the perfect setting to start married life with my new husband.

'Wow, thank you.' I searched the crowd for Mum, Dad and Bob, and beamed at them all. I turned to Jared, to see if he was as thrilled as I was, but he was seemingly showing his appreciation by stripping off his tie. He'd already shrugged off his jacket and was now starting to unbutton his shirt. Was he going to do the full Monty? How much champagne had he quaffed during the meal?

'Jared? What are you doing?' I hissed, but a pair of hands grasped me and pulled me to one side. Jared had stopped unbuttoning his shirt – stopping at the top button – and was now rolling up his sleeves.

'Stephen? What's going on?' My brother was still holding on to me as my husband had his episode on the stage.

My brother grinned at me. 'Just watch.'

'The karaoke will be starting very soon,' Keith Barry said, having taken control of the microphone again. 'But first, the groom would like to kick off the entertainment.'

What? I looked up at Stephen, who simply grinned down at me.

'My beautiful wife thinks the sweet buffet is her surprise,' Jared said into another microphone. 'And while it *was* a surprise, this is the real one. We've been working really hard on this, so please be kind.'

Then Jared was joined on stage by Erin, Quinn, Theo, Billy, Casey and Trina, who each had a microphone of their own.

'For one night only, ladies and gentlemen,' Keith Barry

said as the intro to S Club 7's 'Reach' began to play from the karaoke machine. 'It's Ruth's Club Seven!'

Suddenly, Erin began to sing Jo's part in the song. The others joined in the chorus, complete with synchronised dance moves. Then 'Reach' turned into the Spice Girls' 'Say You'll Be There', then Steps' 'Chain Reaction', B*Witched's 'C'est La Vie' and finally Kylie Minogue's 'Better The Devil You Know'. My husband and our friends had put together a medley of my favourite songs, and were performing them in front of everyone, complete with cheesy choreography. If that wasn't true love, I didn't know what was. The crowd got behind them, singing along and dancing. At the end, Ruth's Club 7 took a bow while the restaurant erupted in applause. I ran to Jared, throwing my arms around his sweaty shoulders.

'You're a nutter, do you know that?'

'I do know that. But if being a nutter shows you just how much I love you, I'm willing to make a fool of myself.'

'I love you, you great big fool.' I gave him a noisy kiss on the cheek. 'But now I feel bad. I haven't prepared anything for you.'

'Why don't you serenade me?' Jared suggested. 'Karaoke's about to start.'

FORTY-NINE

Trina

Ruth's Club 7 were halfway through their set when Trina spotted Aidan in the crowd. She hadn't expected to see him at Ruth's reception and seeing him grinning at her almost put her off her stride. While the others had been practising for weeks, Trina had been a late member of the troupe and so it wouldn't have taken much to push her off kilter with the routine. But luckily she kept on track and somehow kept up with the performance without falling on her face.

'What are you doing here?' Trina rushed over to Aidan as soon as the routine came to an end and the group had received a thunderous round of applause.

'Ruth invited me. You don't mind, do you? I could go if you want.' Aidan scratched the back of his neck, looking a little awkward. 'I don't mind. I just wanted to see you. It seems like we haven't spoken for ages.'

'I know. It's been difficult.' *To say the least. Who knew that life could become so complicated so quickly?*

'You've left Rory.'

'Yes.' Trina found that she couldn't quite look Aidan in the eye. Her cheeks burned with … what? Embarrassment? Bashfulness? She had to remind herself that this was Aidan standing in front of her. Her best friend. 'Did Ruth tell you?'

Aidan shook his head. 'I phoned the house. Some girl answered and told me.'

Some girl. Could have been Carrington – or Ginny. But it didn't matter. Trina's marriage to Rory was over. He was free to do whatever he pleased. He always had, anyway.

'Are you okay?' Aidan reached out towards Trina and she found her eyes filling with tears, which was ridiculous. Because she *was* okay, really. She wasn't happy that she'd chalked up a failed marriage or made a fool out of herself by marrying a man she wasn't truly, one hundred per cent in love with, but she'd survive with a little time and superficial wound-licking.

'Come here.' Aidan held out his arms and Trina fell into them. More than anything, Trina had missed her friendship with Aidan, but it was tainted now. Awkward. Could they go back to the way things were before?

Did either of them even want that any more?

'I'm sorry. I'm okay, really.' Trina pulled away and swiped at her cheeks to rid them of the rogue tears. She glanced around her, hoping nobody had witnessed her momentary crack.

'Do you want to get some fresh air for a few minutes?' Aidan asked.

Trina nodded. It would be easier to talk away from the restaurant full of people. Grabbing her jacket from the cupboard next to the kitchen, she and Aidan slipped out of the back door, through the little yard and out into the alley. They made their way along the passage until they reached the path at the end, neither saying a word until they reached a bus shelter, which seemed as good a place to stop as any other.

'I'm sorry I haven't been in touch.' Trina sat down on the bench, its cold metal biting through the thin material of her dress. 'I've had a lot on my mind. Rory. You. Us.'

'And have you decided anything? About us?' Aidan stared up the road, as though they were actually waiting for the bus, rather than at Trina.

'Not really.' Trina stared down at her hands, which were clasped on her lap, rather than at Aidan. 'It's all so complicated, isn't it?'

'Is it?' Aidan tore his eyes from the road but found he couldn't quite look at Trina's face. Instead he watched her hands.

'Of course it is. I married Rory, foolishly or otherwise. How can you ever forgive me for that?'

'I didn't fight for you. I should have fought for you. Can *you* forgive me?'

'I told you it was complicated.'

'Not the way I see it.' Aidan's eyes made it as far as Trina's shoulder. 'I love you, Trina. Always have.'

Trina gave a squeak of frustration. 'I love you too, but it isn't that simple. I'm married to Rory. I only left him a few days ago. I don't want to go rushing into another relationship and ruin everything all over again.' Trina knew that there would be no going back from that. If they went for it and it didn't work out, what then?

'Then let's not rush anything.' Aidan rose from the bench. 'We missed out on that first date – why don't we go on it now?'

'You want us to go on a date? *Now?*'

'I hear there's a party nearby.' Aidan held out his hand. 'Want to be my date?'

Trina looked at his hand. Could it really be as easy as that? What if it didn't work out, no matter how slowly they took things? What if their already bruised friendship was battered beyond repair?

But what if Trina missed out on the opportunity of

being happy with the man she loved?

'Yes.' Swallowing her fear, Trina clasped the hand and allowed Aidan to pull her to her feet. 'I would love to be your date.'

FIFTY

Ruth

The party was in full swing, with alcohol encouraging everyone to have a go at the karaoke. I'd only ever witnessed Keith Barry in action once before, but tacky seemed to be his thing, along with innuendo. He was wearing tight leather trousers and a shiny gold T-shirt with a hideously scooped neckline that revealed his mane of golden chest hair. He was in his element as my female guests took their turn to sing, salivating and thrusting and being a general sleaze. I was worried I'd made the wrong decision in booking the man, that the karaoke session was uncomfortable rather than fun. But Keith Barry got more than he bargained for when Mary took her turn.

'Hello, gorgeous.' Keith Barry slung his arm around my yoga pal and stooped so they were a similar height. 'Give us a kiss, foxy lady. I love an older woman.' Keith Barry winked at his audience, but the joke was about to be on him.

'Come here then, big boy.' Mary popped her dentures into the palm of one hand before grasping Keith's T-shirt with the other and pulling him towards her puckered lips.

'Oh my God!' Keith gasped for air when Mary finally released him, swiping a hand across his mouth. 'She slipped in the tongue and everything!'

'There's plenty more where that came from, my dear.' Mary popped her teeth back into her mouth and gave Keith a pat on the bottom. 'Now, am I singing or not?'

'You wanted your reception to be fun, and *that* was the funniest thing I've seen in a long time.' Erin was still clutching her stomach as Hot Chocolate's 'You Sexy Thing' began to play, with Mary dedicating her performance to Keith Barry.

'Even funnier than Theo trying to do an Irish jig to B*Witched?'

'Oh, now that you mention it ...' Erin and I giggled at the memory.

'What did Richard think of your performance?'

'He thought it was totally hot, obviously.'

'So he hasn't changed his mind about you moving in with him?'

Erin had told me her news while we'd reapplied our lippie in the loos earlier. She hadn't wanted to spill it during my wedding reception but, being her best friend, I knew she had some news – big and momentous – and I'd dragged it out of her, kicking and screaming. The news was wonderful and was the icing on an already very delicious cake.

'He'd better not have. We just told LuLu and Ralph and they're really excited.' Richard's children were currently attacking the sweet station. It was a good job Amanda wasn't present to witness the sugar-loading. 'LuLu wants to have a pyjama party on the night I move in. Do you think I should invite Amanda?'

I pulled a face. 'Maybe not. How do you think she'll take the news?'

Erin shrugged. 'Who knows? But Richard's going to tell

her when he drops the kids back tomorrow, so she'll have plenty of warning. He's going to make sure he points out that he's letting her know out of courtesy, not asking for permission.'

'Good on him.' It was about time Richard took control of his own life. Amanda's reign was over. 'Are you having a go?' I nodded towards the karaoke area, where Mary was gyrating at Keith Barry. He'd cowered in a corner but that didn't stop Mary.

'Absolutely. I've put mine and Richard's name down for a duet. We're singing "Don't Go Breaking My Heart". He doesn't know it yet, though.' Erin eyed the crowd. 'I'd better go and find him. Maybe he's got wind of my plans and he's hiding.' Narrowing her eyes, Erin set off in search of her unwitting karaoke buddy.

Mary was still enjoying being the centre of attention, jiggling her bosom in a horrified Keith Barry's face.

'Ruth, love.' Billy's stepmother, Pearl, tapped me on the arm. 'We're going to have to head off now. We've got a long drive back home.' Pearl pulled me into a lavender-scented hug. 'We're so happy for you. Your young man seems like a smashing fella.' Pearl released me, a smile playing at her lips. 'We always thought you'd end up with our Billy, you know.'

'Really?' I felt myself blushing, remembering the ill-judged one-night stand before I got together with Jared.

'Oh, yes. But I can see how much you love your Jared, and it looks like Billy has found himself a nice girl.'

'Yes, they're really well suited.' I was glad Billy had found Casey. It not only made Billy happy, but it also eased my guilt at breaking his heart.

'We haven't met her properly yet – you know what our Billy's like – but he's mentioned her a few times and Brian just caught them snogging like a couple of teenagers out in the yard.' Pearl giggled. 'Anyway, we'd better be off. Brian doesn't like driving when it's too dark. Congratulations again. I hope you'll have a lifetime of happiness together.'

'Thanks, Pearl.' I gave her another hug. 'I'll just go and get your coats.'

I weaved my way through the throng of guests, making my way to the walk-in cupboard next to the kitchen. I jumped back in shock when, amongst the coats, I discovered Theo. With my cousin Tori.

'Excuse me!' Tori extracted her tongue from Theo's mouth and glared at me. 'Ever heard of a little thing called privacy?'

Ever heard of a little thing called class? Obviously not, judging by the way Tori's skirt had ridden up to her hips. Lovely. Just lovely.

I was fuming with Theo, but I didn't have the time or head space to think about how I was going to break this to Quinn just yet. I *knew* Theo couldn't be trusted, but I hadn't expected to see the evidence quite so graphically – and on my wedding day, the pig.

'I'll just take these and leave you to it.' Grabbing Pearl and Brian's coats, I bolted from the cupboard, colliding with Casey in my haste. I almost knocked her to the ground and I reached out to steady her. 'I'm so sorry. I was in a rush. Are you okay?'

'I'm fine.' Casey barely acknowledged me as she scanned the restaurant. 'You haven't seen Theo, have you?'

I rolled my eyes. 'He's in there getting busy with my cousin.' I nodded towards the cupboard.

'He's what?' Stalking past me, Casey yanked open the cupboard door, yelping at the sight that greeted her. '*Theo!* What the hell?'

'Hello! A little privacy, please?' Tori yanked her skirt back into place, her face twisted at the inconvenience of it all. She attempted to stride out of the cupboard with her head held high, but Casey grasped her by the arm.

'Did you know we live together?'

Tori looked down at her arm, where it appeared Casey had a pretty tight grip. She unpeeled Casey's fingers one by one. 'Honey, I couldn't care less who you live with.'

'We do *not* live together, Case.' Theo emerged from the cupboard without having the decency to look sheepish. 'Not like that. We're housemates, nothing more.' He raked his fingers through his hair, leaving it in little peaks. 'I knew this would happen. Just because we've slept together a few times doesn't mean we're a couple.'

'Wait a minute.' I held up a hand. 'I thought you and Billy were together.' I looked at Casey, who screwed up her face. 'And I thought Theo was fooling around with Quinn.'

'I wish,' Theo laughed. 'Oof!' He doubled over as Casey elbowed him in the gut.

'No offence, Ruth, but Billy really isn't my type.'

'Then who was Billy snogging in the yard?' Sniffing the scent of gossip, I scuttled out to the little yard at the back of the restaurant. And there they were, entangled against the wall, exactly as Pearl had described. Now I really was confused.

'I thought you were seeing Theo?'

Quinn and Billy broke apart, eyes wide and lips pressed together (which they hadn't been a moment ago, believe me).

Quinn gave a little shrug. 'I may have told a teeny fib.' Her gaze dropped to the concrete flagstones of the yard.

'So you're not seeing Theo at all. You've been seeing Billy all this time?' It was such a relief, actually, despite the fibs. Theo would have discarded Quinn after a few tumbles beneath the sheets – you only had to look at Casey right at that very second to realise that – and Quinn wasn't the sort of girl who brushed herself off easily after a rejection.

'*That's* why you've been hanging around at Billy and Theo's all the time!' It all made sense. Perfect, beautiful sense.

'Sort of.' Quinn shrugged again. 'But it was mostly because we were rehearsing with Jared. When you started asking questions, I couldn't tell you the truth or it would have ruined your surprise. When you made the assumption that I'd fallen for Theo's charms, I let you think that.'

'You lied to me too.' I jabbed a finger towards Billy, who had a look of pure bliss on his face. It was quite nice to see, but I wasn't going to let him get away with telling me porkies that easily.

'I didn't actually lie,' Billy said. 'You made assumptions. *Again*. And I let you. I couldn't tell you that I liked Quinn, could I? She's way out of my league.'

'Apparently not,' I said as Quinn turned to Billy and snaked her arms around him.

'*Definitely* not.'

'But why didn't you tell me you liked Billy?' I asked Quinn. It would have been a lot simpler all round, and I would have been spared the icky thought of Quinn and Theo getting it on.

'Because … well, you know …'

I didn't, actually. That's why I was asking.

'You and Billy … I didn't know how you'd feel about me liking someone you'd … you know.'

I did know this time, but that subject was best left well alone. It was my wedding day, after all.

'Don't be daft! That's ancient history. We've all forgotten about that.' At least I hoped we had.

'So you're not angry?' Quinn, bless her, looked all wide-eyed and Bambi-like. She seriously thought I'd have a problem with it.

'Not in the slightest. I'm happy for you. For you both.'

I backed into the restaurant as they started kissing again. I wasn't quite ready to see that yet. Today had been a bit of a shock on all accounts. I needed a bit of a sit-down and something sweet. Perhaps I'd benefit from a stroll along to the sweet station …

'There you are! We've been looking everywhere for you.' Mum grasped my hand and started to tug me back into the throng before I'd even had the chance to sniff the cakes. 'It's time for your first dance.'

'But I have to give these to Pearl and Brian.' Their coats were still draped over my arm. I'd forgotten about them in all the drama. Poor Brian and Pearl.

'I'll do that.' Mum took the coats and gave me a push towards Jared, who was waiting alone in the middle of the dance floor.

'Ah, here she is. I was beginning to think she'd done a runner with the best man.' Keith Barry winked at Jared. 'Ladies and gentleman, please welcome the new Mr and Mrs Williams to the dance floor.'

I joined Jared, whispering my apologies. I had so much to tell him later: Erin and Richard deciding to move in together, plus the whole Theo/Casey/Billy/Quinn saga. I'd also clocked Trina and Aidan holding hands at the edge of the dance floor as Mum catapulted me towards Jared. The gossip was bubbling around inside me, ready to burst. But now was not the time. Jared took me into his arms, and our first dance song started. My head, already resting on Jared's shoulder, snapped up.

This was not our song.

'I changed it,' Jared whispered.

Jared was full of surprises today – everybody was, it seemed. We were supposed to be sharing our first dance to Etta James's 'At Last', a song we'd agonised over for hours. Our taste in music differed vastly, and 'At Last' had been our first lesson in compromise. Apparently it was important in a marriage.

Instead, the intro of the Spice Girls' '2 Become 1' filled the restaurant.

'I really do love you.'

'I really love you too.' Jared kissed the top of my head

and we began to sway to the music. Our loved ones surrounded us: Mum and Dad, Linda and Bob, our siblings and their children, our best friends. Even Aunty Pat, I suppose. They were all gathered to share this truly wonderful day with us and I couldn't have been happier.

I hope that you enjoyed reading A Beginner's Guide To Saying I Do. If you did, why not leave a review? I'd love to hear what you think and it helps other readers find books they'd enjoy too!

If you'd like to keep up to date with my new releases and book news, you can subscribe to my newsletter on my blog (jenniferjoycewrites.co.uk). I send out newsletters 4-5 times a year, with short stories, extra content, a subscriber-exclusive giveaway and more! Plus, you'll receive my ebook quick read, *Six Dates,* which is only available to subscribers, for FREE.

ACKNOWLEDGEMENTS

With thanks, as always, to my family for their support and encouragement. Andrew, I'm really sorry but there are STILL no chainsaws in my books. I will try harder.

Thank you to Rianne and Isobel, who don't seem to mind one bit when I disappear to my desk to tell my stories. I'm trying not to read too much into that. Also to Luna, who keeps me company when I work downstairs. She's a dog and won't be able to read this, but still…

Massive thanks to Jane Hammett for her editing skills. Thanks also to Ruth Durbridge.

Thank you to the SCWG for all their book nerdiness and writing advice, to Oldham Writing Group and the Savvys (with special thanks to the Manchester Chapter One group). Also to the book community on Twitter, Facebook and Instagram, who share their love of books daily. Special thanks to all the bloggers who have taken part in any of my blog tours and helped spread the word. Also thank you to everyone who has reviewed my books – reviews really do help! You're all ace.

Finally, the most humongous thanks to the readers. I still can't believe people are reading my stories. You've made this writer very, *very* happy.

Printed in Great Britain
by Amazon